W9-CAS-054

SWORDMAGE

Novels by Richard Baker

BLADES OF THE MOONSEA

Book I
Swordmage

Book II
Corsair

Book III
Avenger

THE LAST MYTHAL

Book I
Forsaken House

Book II
Farthest Reach

Book III
Final Gate

THE CITIES

The City of Ravens

R.A. SALVATORE'S WAR OF THE SPIDER QUEEN

Book III
Condemnation

RICHARD BAKER

SWORDMAGE

BLADES OF THE MOONSEA

BOOK I

Blades of the Moonsea
Book I
SWORDMAGE

Published by Wizards of the Coast, Inc. FORGOTTEN REALMS, WIZARDS OF THE COAST, and their respective logos are trademarks of Wizards of the Coast, Inc., in the U.S.A. and other countries.

Printed in the U.S.A.

Cover art by Raymond Swanland
First Printing: May 2008

9 8 7 6 5 4 3 2 1

ISBN: 978-0-7869-4788-1
620-21631720-001-EN

Library of Congress Cataloging-in-Publication Data

Baker, Richard (Lynn Richard)
Swordmage / Richard Baker.
p. cm. -- (Blades of the moonsea ; bk. 1)
ISBN 978-0-7869-4788-1
I. Title.
PS3602.A587S86 2008
813'.6--dc22

2008002708

U.S., CANADA,
ASIA, PACIFIC, & LATIN AMERICA
Wizards of the Coast, Inc.
P.O. Box 707
Renton, WA 98057-0707
+1-800-324-6496

EUROPEAN HEADQUARTERS
Hasbro UK Ltd
Caswell Way
Newport, Gwent NP9 0YH
GREAT BRITAIN
Save this address for your records.

Visit our web site at www.wizards.com

For Kim
Thanks for believing in me, honey.
You're the best part of me.

Prologue

18 Uktar, the Year of the Purloined Statue (1477 DR)

It was late autumn in Myth Drannor, a bright cold morning with the first snows of the year dusting the open spaces between the trees. The fall colors were fading fast, but the forest of Cormanthor still mantled the city in a glorious cape of red, gold, and orange. The sun was brilliant on the golden treetops overhead, and the sky was perfect and clear. In the shadows beneath the trees, Geran Hulmaster fought with all his strength and lore against the elf mage Rhovann Disarnnyl, dueling with blade and spell against spell and wand. Steel glittered and rang in the morning air as Geran parried bolts of crackling white force or deflected shining veils of madness in which Rhovann tried to ensnare him.

Geran wore the dove-gray coat and silver embroidery of the Coronal's Guard, but he was a human, tall and lean, with long black hair bound by a silver circlet. He wielded a fine backsword of elven steel, a graceful and strong weapon with a slight curve toward the point. It was longer and heavier than most such weapons, but in his hands the blade leaped and danced like a rapier. He kept his left hand free for spellcasting, fighting as elf swordmages did in the ancient bladesong tradition. Rhovann, on the other hand, was no swordsman; he had only his mahogany wand, and that was weapon enough for the elf mage.

Dueling was not permitted in Myth Drannor; this encounter was ostensibly an invitation to demonstrate skill through the lists in a tournament of the city's defenders. A small crowd of witnesses watched closely to ensure that the forms would be followed. Daried Selsherryn, the sun elf bladesinger who'd taught Geran his magic, stood by to serve as Geran's second. Daried watched with a disapproving frown, since he could tell already that the contest was long past a simple challenge of skill and was a duel in fact if not in name. Beside Daried stood Alliere, her face white with worry as she watched Geran and Rhovann fight. She was beautiful beyond comparison, a slender moon elf maiden not much older than Geran himself, with hair of midnight blue in which a slim diamond tiara sparkled like the stars in a dark sky. Geran was only a rootless human freebooter, a wanderer who had drifted into Myth Drannor and won himself a place in the coronal's service, but she had come to love him nonetheless, and in the golden light of this perfect morning, she was petrified with fear for him. But Rhovann—a proud and handsome moon elf of a high House—loved her too, and he had come to bitterly resent the affection she held for Geran. And so the human swordmage and the elf wizard fought with the passion of lions over some trivial insult one had given the other.

Rhovann hurled a mighty fire-blast from his wand, and the onlookers gasped in alarm. Geran warded himself with a countering spell, even though the violet flames singed his cloak and licked at his face and hands. The magical flames seared the frost and dead leaves beneath his feet into steam and smoke that fumed around the swordmage. Rather than retreat, Geran brought a spell of translocation to mind, fixed its symbols and syllogisms firmly in his thoughts, and snarled a single arcane word: *"Seiroch!"*

In the blink of an eye he stood close beside Rhovann, who'd lost sight of him for a crucial instant amid the steam and smoke. The moon elf whirled and started to raise his wand, but Geran was quicker. He brought his sword up in a disarming stroke that sent the wand spinning through the air and carried through to slash Rhovann across the side of his face. His enemy cried out and staggered back, falling to his knees.

Geran leaped after the elf and laid his sword point at Rhovann's breast. "Yield! You are defeated!" he shouted.

He held his blade still and steady despite the acrid stench of smoke in his nose and throat and the pain of his singed skin. Rhovann knelt in the thin snow, blood dripping from his handsome face. Brilliant hatred glittered in the wizard's eyes, and his teeth were bared in a feral snarl. The mahogany wand waited in the snow between the man and the elf.

"I will not yield, human dog," Rhovann hissed softly. Then he reached for the wand.

Without a moment's thought, Geran batted the wand away from Rhovann's hand, sending it spinning over the dead leaves and snow. The elf snarled in anger, and something dark and murderous erupted in Geran's heart. Every cold sneer, every veiled insult, every sarcastic remark Rhovann had ever uttered against him coalesced into a black wave that swept over Geran. It was as if his anger, his hate, and his loathing for his rival had delivered him into the clutches of something he was powerless to resist.

Rhovann lunged after the wand again, his fingers stretching for his weapon. Coldly, deliberately, Geran leaned in and struck, taking off Rhovann's hand at the wrist. Blood splattered the ice-crusted leaves. He heard cries of horror from those who looked on, and his adversary screamed in anger and fear.

Why did I do that? Geran wondered dully. He *knew* that maiming Rhovann in that way—cruelly, deliberately, when the duel had already been won—was a monstrous thing to do. He *knew* that Alliere and Daried and the other elves watching must be horrified by what he had done. Yet something spiteful beyond all understanding had driven him to it anyway. Once, when he was a boy of about nine or ten, his father had given him a fine toy lute inlaid with ivory, a gift carried back from a long journey to Deepingdale. Geran remembered how he had found himself twisting the neck from the drum, fascinated by the flex and strain of the fragile wood. And then, deliberately, knowing what would happen, he'd flexed it too far. He'd done it just to watch the toy break.

He looked down at Rhovann, huddled around his bleeding stump. The elf's hand lay on the ground quite near the wand, palm up, the pallid fingers twitching oddly. Geran raised his sword slowly, studying the crippled elf, and even though he felt dizzy and sick with horror, he aimed carefully at the elf's face. Without knowing *why*, he knew he intended to cut out an eye next, almost as if having already toppled into a shocking abyss, he meant to plumb its depths to the fullest, indulging this black compulsion until he sated it.

"Geran, *no!* It is enough!" shouted Daried. The graceful bladesinger ended the duel by leaping into the clearing and interposing himself. By the ancient rules, that spelled defeat for Geran, since Daried was after all his second and had intervened. But Geran sensed that the rules had been laid aside already. No one in the courtyard would argue that Rhovann had won the encounter, would they?

Geran felt his arm drawing back as if to drive his sword forward one more time, and then Daried seized him by the shoulders and wrestled him away. "It is *enough*, Geran!" Daried hissed into his face. "Have you lost your mind? That was cruelly done!"

Geran stared at his mentor, unable to find words. The black, murderous fury ebbed away as quickly as it had come over him, leaving him weak, empty. The sword fell from his fingers, and he shook his head, trying to clear his mind of the destructive impulse that had seized him. Why did I do that? he wondered. He despised Rhovann, true, but he should have been content with besting him, especially since the mage had instigated the whole thing. All he would have had to do is take a half-step and kick the wand out of reach again or perhaps set his blade across Rhovann's neck to demand surrender, and the coronal's judge standing by certainly would have ended the match.

"I had no intention to cripple him, Daried," he finally said.

The elf bladesinger sighed deeply. "Your intentions hardly matter at this point. You will be judged for this, Geran Hulmaster. And judged severely, I fear."

Several of Rhovann's friends were attending to the wounded mage or glaring at Geran with cold fury. Geran turned away slowly and rubbed his face with one shaking hand. When he looked up again, he found Alliere staring at him from the spot where she'd stood to watch the contest. She was as pale as the snow, her hands pressed to her mouth and her eyes wide with horror. The silk handkerchief she was to award the winner lay in the muddy snow at her feet. Their eyes met, and Alliere flinched away.

"What have I done?" Geran murmured. He took two steps toward her, reaching out. "Alliere, I didn't mean—I don't know—"

"Oh, Geran," she said softly. A small, sobbing gasp escaped her throat. "How could you do such a thing?" She backed away several steps and turned to hurry away, disappearing into the shadows under the trees. Geran took one step after her before he stopped where he stood. Alliere had looked on him with *fear*. What could he possibly say or do to explain himself to her?

Did I mean to wound Rhovann or myself when I struck that blow? he silently asked himself.

"Geran Hulmaster, come with me." The coronal's judge—a stern-faced moon elf in the colors of the royal court—approached Geran, one hand riding on the pommel of his sword. Two more Velar Guards waited nearby, equally stern. "You are summoned to appear before the coronal. She must decide this matter now."

The swordmage stared after Alliere, but she was gone.

One

11 Ches, the Year of the Ageless One (1479 DR)

The Moonsea crossing was wet and rough, three hard days of beating through whitecaps and spray in the cold, angry winds of early spring. By the time the battered coaster passed into the shelter of the Arches, every man on board was cold, tired, and soaked. Ships in the service of kings or great nobles accommodated their passengers in cabins and assigned stewards to wait on them, but the coaster was a plain Moonsea tradesman. It was a working ship that offered its passengers nothing more than a place to sleep on the deck. She finally tied up alongside the wharf at the foot of Plank Street shortly before sunset. Longshoremen swarmed aboard to begin unloading her cargo: sacks of flour, casks of wine, and countless other crates and bundles of goods from Vespin to the south. While the laborers began their work, the ship's only two passengers—one a dark-haired man of thirty or so, the other a well-dressed halfling—carried their own satchels down the gangplank to the creaking wharf.

"So this is Hulburg," the halfling said. He was of average height for his people, an inch or so over four feet, with a surprisingly sturdy frame under his damp green cloak. He wore daggers, several of them—two at the belt, one in the right boot, and a fourth strapped hilt-down in a large sheath between his shoulder blades—and a hard, suspicious look on his sharp-featured face. Cold water plastered his russet braids close to his scalp, and he began squeezing the water from each braid in turn. "I doubt I'll like it very much."

"My business here won't take long, Hamil," Geran answered. He towered over the halfling, of course, but in fact he was only a little taller than average. He had the rangy, lean build and the long, well-muscled arms of a born swordsman. Geran's hands were large and strong, well-calloused from many hours of practice. The sword he'd won in the Coronal's Guard, a long, elf-made blade with a hilt of mithral wire, rode in a scabbard he wore low on his left hip. His black hair was cut short above wide, thoughtful eyes of gray so it wouldn't obscure his vision in a fight, but left shoulder length and free otherwise. The swordsman had an unconscious habit of chewing his lip when deep in thought, as he was now. "We've already missed Jarad's funeral. Give me a few days to look after his affairs and see my family, and we'll be on our way."

"I guess we might as well wait for better weather before we cross back to the southern shore, anyway," Hamil said in resignation. He looked back out toward the Moonsea. Wild whitecaps marched and tumbled beyond the spectacular Arches, which divided the calmer waters of the harbor from the open sea. The slender stone ribs soared hundreds of feet into the air, leaping and plunging like the paths of a dozen skipping pebbles somehow frozen in pale green stone. The halfling studied them for a moment and added, "Those don't look like they belong here. Changeland?"

"The Arches? Yes, they're changeland. I'm told they erupted from the seabed in a single night in the Year of Blue Fire. Destroyed a quarter of the old city on the Easthead there, but they gave Hulburg the best harbor on the north shore of the Moonsea."

"Pretty, I suppose, but not much compared to the Claws of Starmantle." Hamil shrugged. Faerûn was littered with such wonders. Not two days ago they'd sailed beneath a forest-covered islet of stone adrift in the stormy skies forty miles out of Mulmaster. Towns and cities had long ago accommodated themselves to changelands as best they could. "So where are we going, Geran?"

The swordsman studied the town's waterfront, establishing his bearings. Hulburg was Geran's home, but he had left it behind him more than ten years ago, and this was only the second time he'd returned since. "Where, indeed," he murmured to himself. In his travels he'd seen dozens upon dozens of cities and towns. It surprised him how much Hulburg resembled the rest after such a long absence.

The town climbed and rambled over a low hill overlooking a sheltered bay between high, rocky headlands two miles apart—Keldon Head to the west and Easthead opposite. The sun was setting, and cookfires by the hundreds burned in stone hearths and outdoor kitchens, sending twisting spirals of smoke into the sky to be caught and carried off by the harsh spring winds. Hulburg was a young town built atop the ruins of a larger and older city. Brash new storehouses and sprawling merchant compounds crowded the harbor district, rambling along crooked, poorly paved streets that had grown like wild roots through the rubble and byways of the old city. Beyond the harbor and its walled tradeyards stood a town whose workshops and houses were made from stone taken from the nearby ruins or sometimes simply built atop the foundations of much older buildings. Most had upper stories framed in heavy timber and roofs covered in rough wooden shakes, since Hulburg had an ample supply of timber close at hand in the forested vales of the Galena Mountains; the steep headlands and hills surrounding the town were too windswept and rocky for trees of any size to find purchase.

Geran looked north along Plank Street and glimpsed the old gray keep of Griffonwatch glowering over the town. It was a mile from the harbor, perched atop a rocky spur of the eastern ridge. While it was not very well situated to guard the city against attacks by sea, that was not why Angar Hulmaster had raised his keep there. Griffonwatch faced north, inland, a defense against the savage orcs, ogres, and other monsters who dwelled in the desolate hills and moorlands of Thar. Many of the buildings and storefronts fronting the harbor or crowding along Plank Street were new to Geran, but the old castle, at least, had not changed.

I've missed this place, he found himself thinking. Twice now I've come back to bury someone, but never otherwise. Why is that?

"I'm soaked, and this wind is damned cold," Hamil observed. "Are we going to stand here much longer, Geran?"

"What?—Oh, of course." Geran looked up and down the busy Bay Street. It was more crowded than he remembered. Gangs of porters, shouting longshoremen, and merchants and their clerks hurried this way and that. Most seemed to be outlanders, men who wore the colors of foreign merchant companis or trading costers. "Forgive me, all of these merchant yards are new. The town's grown a lot in eight years."

"If you say so. It looks the back end of nowhere to me."

Geran snorted. "I certainly thought so when I was growing up here. I couldn't wait to leave the place." He pulled the hood of his cloak up over his head and allowed the peak to shadow his features. He didn't really expect that he would be easily recognized, but for the moment he didn't feel much like talking with anyone he might happen to meet. "Let's find something hot to eat before we do anything else. I've been seasick for three days, and I need something under my ribs."

The halfling glanced up at Geran and nodded in the direction of the old gray keep looming over the town. "Won't they feed you there?"

"They would." With Hulburg's cobblestones under his boots, Geran was beginning to remember why he had come home. Jarad Erstenwold was dead, murdered. Until he'd actually set foot in Hulburg, that news had been something to push off a few days. The difficulties of a four-hundred-mile journey from Tantras had served to occupy his thoughts for the last ten days, but having reached his destination, he could no longer turn away from the tidings that had brought him there. He sighed and ran his fingers through his damp hair. "Give me an hour by a good fire with a Sembian red in my cup. Then I'll be ready."

"As you wish." Hamil gave Geran a measuring look, but he said nothing else. Like any halfling, he seemed to burn food fast and rarely lacked an appetite. He wouldn't turn down a meal to settle his stomach.

The two quickly surveyed the collection of taverns and alehouses near the wharves, found the establishments there less than inviting, and turned up High Street and climbed into the commerce district. The large mercantile companies did their business in the walled tradeyards by the harbor, but along High Street, the town's shopkeepers, provisioners, and artisans had their places of business, along with the better taverns and inns of Hulburg. Geran passed two places he remembered well and settled on one he did not, a taphouse called the Sleeping Dragon. Clean fieldstone, dark timbers, and a brightly painted signboard marked it as new. Besides, it hadn't been there the last time Geran had been in Hulburg.

"This will do," he told Hamil and ducked into the front door.

The common room was crowded and loud. Most of the patrons seemed to be foreigners—Thentian and Melvauntian merchants in the doublets or quilted jerkins and square caps favored in those cities, Mulmasterites with their double baldrics and dueling swords low on their hips, and even a few sullen dwarf craftsmen in heavy fur and iron. A handful of Hulburgans were scattered through the crowd, notable because they tended to be much plainer in dress than the merchants and traders of other cities. Most people in Hulburg preferred a plain hooded cloak and a simple tunic and leggings to the less practical fashions of the bigger cities, since Hulburg was still something of a frontier town, and its people valued warmth and comfort over style. "Where did all these outlanders come from?" Geran wondered aloud. "The town's full of them."

"Doubtless most of the natives had the good sense to leave, as you did."

"Hmmph." Geran shook his head. Hulburg had been a sleepy little backwater ten years ago when he had set out to see Faerûn, but it seemed that was no longer the case. He realized that he'd seen more foreigners in the streets than native Hulburgans in their short walk up from the docks—men and women in the colors of merchant costers, guilds, and companies from all over the Moonsea. "I wasn't gone that long. It's only been ten years. Eight, really."

You spent too much time with the elves in Myth Drannor, Hamil answered him without speaking. He was a ghostwise halfling, and his people could make their thoughts heard when they wished. *I think they bewitched you, Geran. Ten years is a long time for humans or halflings alike. You've forgotten how the rest of us reckon the years.*

Geran frowned but made no reply. The two companions chose a table in a far corner of the room and worked their way through a serviceable supper of stew, black bread, and smoked fish. The Sleeping Dragon charged five silver pennies for their board, but at least they included a flagon of passable southern wine with the meal—though Geran doubted that it had ever been within a hundred miles of Sembia. He poured himself two cups and stopped, not wanting to dull himself before finishing the journey. There would be time for that later.

"You haven't said much about your friend Jarad," Hamil said after a time.

"Jarad? No, I suppose I haven't." Geran returned his attention to his small companion. "He was my closest friend when we were growing up. Once upon a time we were the young kings of this town. We hunted every hilltop and valley for ten miles around, we explored dozens of old ruins, we pilfered and begged and charmed our way through the streets, getting ourselves into more sorts of trouble than you can imagine. We taught ourselves swordplay and picked some fights that we shouldn't have, but somehow we always came through it. Mirya—that's Jarad's sister—and my cousin Kara followed after us as often as not. The four of us were inseparable." Geran smiled even though the memories made his heart ache. "Hulburg may not seem like much compared to Tantras or Mulmaster, but it was a good place to grow up."

"Jarad remained in Hulburg when you left?"

"He did. I was anxious to try myself against the world. I couldn't stand the idea of boxing myself up in this town, but Jarad didn't see things that way. So I went to study in Thentia, and then I traveled to Procampur to study from the swordmasters there and fell in with the Dragonshields, and I even visited Myth Drannor and lived among the elves for a time—as you well know. Jarad stayed here and became a captain of the Shieldsworn, the harmach's guards. More than once I tried to talk him into joining me in Tantras or Procampur, but he never had my restlessness. He used to tell me that he had too much to look after right here in Hulburg, but I think he simply liked it here better than anywhere else. He just didn't see a reason to leave." Geran drained his cup and set it down. "All right. I think it's time to call on my family."

They left a few coppers on the table and made their way outside. The sun had set, and the wind battered at shutters and doors with bitterly cold gusts. Signboards creaked and swayed. The few streetlamps in sight guttered and danced wildly, and people hurried from door to door clutching their cloaks tight around their bodies.

"Charming," Hamil said with a shiver. The halfling hailed from the warm lands of the south, and he'd never gotten used to the chill of more northerly lands. "I can't believe that people choose to live in places like this."

"Winter's worse," Geran answered. He turned right and set off along High Street, trying his best to ignore the cold. He was a native Hulburgan, after all, and he was not about to let Hamil see that it bothered him too. They came to the small square by the Assayer's House, a rambling old stone building where the harmach's officials oversaw the trade in gold dust and mining claims, and descended the stairs leading down to the Middle Bridge and Cinder Way. Once that part of town had been given over to several big smelters, but some sixty years ago Lendon Hulmaster had moved the stink and slag of the furnaces a mile to the east, downwind of the town.

Afterward a crowded district of workshops and poorly built rowhouses known as the Tailings had grown up in place of the smelters.

Geran remembered the Tailings as a sparsely inhabited and poor neighborhood, but it seemed it had taken a turn for the worse since he'd last been home. Outlanders crowded every dilapidated house or hovel—dirty and sullen men who gathered around firepits, staring at the two travelers as they passed. Who are these people? Geran wondered again. Miners with no claims to work? Laborers indentured to one of the guilds or merchant companies? Or just more of the rootless wanderers who seemed to collect like last year's leaves, blown here and there by the winds of ill fortune? The towns and cities of Faerûn were full of such men, especially in the years since the Spellplague.

Geran, Hamil said silently. The swordsman sensed his small companion's sudden alertness and slowed his steps. He followed Hamil's gaze and saw what the halfling saw—a gang of five men watching over the street. Three lounged on the sagging stoop of a dismal alehouse, and two gathered around a firepit on the opposite side of the street. They carried cudgels and knives, and each man wore a red-dyed leather gauntlet wrapped in chains on his left hand. *Crimson Chains. Slavers.*

"I see them," Geran answered. A slaving company from the city of Melvaunt, the Crimson Chain had a bad name throughout the Moonsea. He'd met them a few times in the Vast, but he never would have expected to find them in Hulburg. The harmachs had outlawed slaving long before he'd been born, and it was a law they kept rigorously. Geran's mouth tightened, but he kept walking. The Chainsmen might have some legitimate business in Hulburg, he told himself. And even if they didn't, it wasn't his place to object. The Shieldsworn would roust them out if they intended trouble.

"Not so fast, friends." One of the Chainsmen—a short, stocky man with a shaven head and a long, drooping mustache—stepped down from the alehouse stoop into their path. He grinned crookedly, but his eyes were hard and cold. "I don't think I've seen you around here before, hey? You've some dues to pay."

Geran scowled. He'd seen this sort of thing more than once, but never before in Hulburg. In any event, he was not inclined to pay off thugs anywhere as long as he had good steel on his hip. "Dues? What exactly do I owe dues for, and who's collecting?"

The bald Chainsman studied Geran with a shark's smile. "There are lots of bad sorts about, you know. I'm Roldo. My boys and I keep order in the Tailings. Your dues buy you safe passage, my friends. Everybody pays."

Hamil rolled his eyes. "And how much are your dues?" he asked.

"How much've you got?" another one of the slavers asked.

"More than I'd care to part with."

"Then hand over your purse, little man, and I'll see how much you can afford," the Chainsman Roldo said. He spat on the ground. "We're reasonable fellows, after all."

Geran studied the Chainsmen surrounding them. Five on the street and possibly more in the alehouse or another place nearby, and most looked like they knew how to use the cudgels at their belts. It would be easier to play their game and buy them off with a couple of silver pennies, but the thought of paying for safe passage in his own hometown did not sit well with him.

Besides, he told himself, they're probably not as reasonable as they say they are.

Deliberately, Geran let his duffel drop and shrugged his cloak over his shoulder, revealing the backsword at his hip. Harassing two nondescript passersby was one thing for a gang of ruffians, but a man carrying a blade might know how to use it. Hoping the Chainsmen might see things that way, he rested his hand on the pommel. "I think we'll look after ourselves," he said easily. "Now, if you don't mind . . . ?"

The slaver's face darkened, and his false humor fell away. He scowled and jerked his head, and the Chainsmen nearby pushed themselves to their feet and started to close in around Geran and Hamil.

"You don't understand, friends," Roldo rasped. "Half the ditchdiggers and dirtgrubbers in this town wear steel, hey. I ain't seen one yet who knows what to do with it. Everybody pays. And your dues are getting steeper."

Not so steep as you think, Geran reflected. He supposed he could simply walk off and see if the Chainsmen tried to stop him. Or he could wait for one of them to make a move. But he could see where this was going, and if he was right, well, there was no reason to wait for the slavers to start it, was there? He took a deep breath and looked down at Hamil.

The halfling glanced up. *Now?* he asked silently.

I'll take care of the alehouse if you deal with the other side of the street, Geran answered. *Try not to kill any of them if you can help it.*

Done, Hamil replied. Then, without another word, the halfling's hands flashed to his belt and came up with a pair of daggers. He threw both in the same motion, sinking each dagger into a Chainsman's knee. Before either ruffian could even cry out, Hamil had the big fighting knife from his shoulder harness in his hand, and he dashed into the stunned pair by the firepit without a sound. Apparently neither of the men there had really thought they might be set upon by someone no bigger than a ten-year-old child. To all appearances the halfling had simply gone berserk.

"What in the Nine Hells?" the leader of the gang growled. He went straight for his own knife, a good piece of fighting iron almost a foot and a half long. The two men on the wooden steps of the alehouse yanked their cudgels out and started to clatter down to the street—but Geran was faster.

By the time the leader had his hand on his knife hilt, Geran had already swept his sword from the scabbard. The elven steel was etched with a triple-rose design, and it was superbly balanced by a pommel in the shape of a steel rose. He'd earned it in the service of Coronal Ilsevele soon after arriving in Myth Drannor, and the sword suited Geran better than any other he'd ever taken in hand. He swept the point up and across the slaver's knife-hand in one smooth motion with the draw, laying open the man's forearm. Roldo cursed and reeled away holding his wounded hand, blood streaming through his fingers.

"Take 'em, lads!" he snarled.

The two men on the steps came at Geran in a quick rush. He retreated several steps, emptied his mind with the quick skill of long practice, and found the invocation he wanted. *"Cuillen mhariel,"* he whispered in Elvish, weaving a spell-shield with his words and his will. Ghostly streamers of pale silver-blue light gleamed around him, seemingly no more solid than wisps of fog. Then Geran stood his ground as the first man lunged out at his skull with the knobbed cudgel. The swordmage passed the heavy blow over his head with the flat of his blade, then slashed the fellow's left leg out from under him with a deep cut to the calf. The Chainsman went down hard with a grunt of shock.

The second man came at him an instant later. Geran spun away from the one blow, batted aside the other with a hand-jarring parry near his hilt, and smashed the rose-shaped pommel of his blade into the slaver's nose. Something crunched, and blood gushed as the fellow staggered back and sat down heavily in the street.

A sharp *thrumm!* whistled in the street. Geran caught a glimpse of a crossbow's bolt just before it struck him high on the right side of his chest—but his hasty spell-shield held. The bolt rebounded from a sharp, silvery flame flaring brightly in the shadows of the street and clattered away across the cobblestones. The Chainsman leader stood openmouthed, a small empty crossbow in his good hand.

"Damn it all, he's a wizard!" the first slaver by Geran snarled. The fellow scrambled awkwardly to his feet and quickly backed away, favoring his injured leg. Then he turned and fled into the night. The man with the broken nose followed, lurching blindly after him. On the other side of the street, the remaining two Chainsmen were limping away from Hamil as fast as they could, giving up the battle.

Geran ignored them. If they thought he was a wizard and wanted no more of him, he wouldn't say otherwise. He advanced on the slaver Roldo. The man was already drawing back the string of his crossbow for another try, but Geran put a stop to that by striking him hard across the side of the head with the flat of his blade. The blow split Roldo's shaven scalp and stretched him senseless on the wooden steps of the alehouse. "That was for taking a shot when I wasn't looking," the swordmage growled. He was tempted to give the slaver something more to remember him by, but he held his temper. At least half a dozen spectators were peering through the alehouse's windows and doors, and some might not be friendly.

Hamil sauntered up, sheathing his knives one by one as he studied the scene. "You let yours run off with hardly a mark on them."

"I'll set that straight if I see them again. Did you find all your knives?"

"I'm willing to loan them out for a time, but I want 'em back when all the dancing's done." The halfling stooped down to wipe off one last bloody knife on the tunic of the unconscious Chainsman at their feet. "So, is this the typical evening entertainment in Hulburg?"

"No," said Geran, "it's not."

He returned his sword to the sheath and looked up at the old gray towers of the castle overshadowing the town. Dim yellow lights burned in a handful of the keep's windows; other towers remained dark. Crimson Chain slavers seemed to think they owned the streets. What in the world had happened to Hulburg while he was away? How long had it been like this?

He picked his bag up from the ground and took a deep breath. "Come on, Hamil," he said. "I think it's time to find out just what's been going on around here."

Two

11 Ches, the Year of the Ageless One

The castle called Griffonwatch was not really a true castle. Most of its towers and halls were guarded by the steep bluffs of the castle's hilltop and did not require a thick wall for protection. Only on its lower northern face was Griffonwatch truly fortified, with a strong gatehouse and a tower-studded wall guarding access to the courtyards, barracks, and residences within. Geran had always thought of it as a great rambling, drafty, partially abandoned house that happened to be made out of stone, with the curious afterthought of one castlelike wall to guard the front gate.

"I have to congratulate the builders of the place," Hamil said. "They picked the highest, coldest, windiest spot in this whole miserable town for their masterpiece." The castle's causeway was completely exposed to the northwest wind once the visitors climbed above the roofline of the surrounding town, and the faded banners above the gatehouse flapped loudly in the stiff wind.

Griffonwatch's gates stood open. Hamil's step faltered as they entered the dark, tunnel-like passage through the gatehouse. "I never liked these things," the halfling muttered. He had an instinctive aversion to anything that felt like an ambush, and the front entrance of any well-made castle was designed to be a giant stone trap to its enemies. Menacing arrowslits overlooked the approach to the castle and the gate-passage proper. They stood dark and empty, but in times of war watchful archers would be posted there, ready to cut down attackers at the top of the causeway.

"Come on, Hamil," Geran said quietly. He clapped his friend on the shoulder. "It's out of the wind, anyway."

At the inner end of the gate, the castle's portcullis was lowered into place, blocking most of the passage. The heavy grate was fitted with a small swinging door. Two Shieldsworn guards waited there. They wore knee-length coats of mail under heavy woolen mantles and steel caps trimmed with a ring of fur for warmth. Both carried pikes—perfect for thrusting through the portcullis at enemies on the far side—and a pair of crossbows leaned against the wall nearby.

"Hold there," said the older of the men, a sergeant with a round, blunt face like the end of a hammer. "State your name and business."

Geran stepped out of the gate's shadow and reached up to draw back the hood of his cloak. "I'm Geran Hulmaster," he said. "And I'm here to call on the harmach and visit with whatever kinfolk of mine happen to be home this evening, Sergeant Kolton."

The sergeant's eyes opened wide. "Geran, as I live and breathe! It must be five years!" He fumbled with the small door in the portcullis and finally got it open. "Come in, sir, come in!"

Despite the sour mood that had settled over him after the encounter with the Crimson Chains, Geran smiled. He'd always liked Kolton, and he couldn't help but enjoy the man's surprise. "Eight years, Kolton. I haven't been home since my father died."

"Lord Bernov was a good man. Things around here might be different if he hadn't fallen." The sturdy soldier's face softened with memories, likely some old campaign or skirmish riding alongside Geran's father . . . and then Kolton's thoughts turned, and a sudden grimace stole over his features. He sighed and looked closely at Geran. "M'lord, I don't know how to tell you this—" he began.

Geran cut him off with a small motion of his hand. "I've heard about Jarad, if that's what you are about to tell me. My mother wrote me as soon as she heard." Geran's mother lived in a convent near Thentia now, but she still had many friends in Hulburg. She'd heard about Jarad only a few days after the Shieldsworn captain had been found dead on the Highfells. Her letter had reached Geran in Tantras half a month ago, and he'd left for Hulburg within the day.

"I'm sorry, sir," Kolton said. "I know he was a good friend o' yours. He was a good captain too. We miss him sorely."

They stood without speaking for a moment. The wind moaned across the stone battlements, and the castle's banners crackled sharply. Geran shivered in the cold, and he glanced down to Hamil. The halfling waited patiently, his cloak held tight around his body.

"Forgive me," Geran said. "Sergeant, this is my friend and comrade-in-arms, Hamil Alderheart of Tantras. He's a guest of the house."

"Of course, sir," Kolton said. "Leave your baggage here, gentlemen. I'll have it brought up to your rooms shortly."

"Thank you, Kolton." Geran set down his duffel and worked his shoulder a moment. "One more thing—Hamil and I ran across some trouble in the Tailings on our way here. A gang of Crimson Chains led by some fellow calling himself Roldo tried to extort a toll from us."

"We objected," said Hamil. "Hard words followed, and there may have been a minor stabbing or two."

"—and yes, we crossed steel. We didn't kill any of them, but I thought the Shieldsworn should know."

The sergeant grimaced. "You met Roldo, hey? I'm sorry to hear it, but I'll not shed a tear over any cuts or bruises you gave him. He and his thugs've been causing trouble in the Tailings for months now."

"Why haven't you rousted them out, then?"

"It's got to be murder or arson before we do, m'lord. We're down to a hundred and ninety Shieldsworn, and that ain't really enough to garrison Griffonwatch, man the post-towers, and keep a patrol or two out in the Highfells. We leave the keeping o' the law in the town to the Council Watch. The harmach's men only get involved when it's a matter of high justice."

Geran looked sharply at Kolton. He thought he'd heard the sergeant well enough, but there was very little that made sense to him. One hundred and ninety Shieldsworn? The harmach's guards should have been twice as strong. And he'd never heard of any Council Watch; that had to be something new. A town full of foreign merchants, gangs roaming the streets, and now this . . . it seemed that he had a lot of catching up to do, and suddenly Geran doubted he'd enjoy his education very much. A number of questions sprang to mind, but he settled for just one more: "Who or what is the Council Watch?"

"The lawkeepers who answer to the Merchant Council." Kolton's blunt face didn't move much, but his voice had a flat, hard tone. "They look after council matters and enforce low justice in the city proper, so that we Shieldsworn don't have to trouble ourselves with such business. Or so I'm told."

If they let the Crimson Chains walk the streets in the open, they can't be very good at their jobs, Hamil remarked to Geran. *Either they're hopelessly incompetent or they're paid not to notice such things. I know which side of that bet I'd cover.*

"Who do I talk to in order to set the watch on the Chainsmen?" Geran asked.

Kolton snorted. "Captain Zara, down at Council Hall. But you shouldn't expect much, m'lord. It seems to take a long time for Zara to be certain enough o' the facts to bring charges against someone, especially if that someone happens to be on a guild or House payroll. Maybe it would be different if you said something—you're kin to the harmach, after all."

"I'll bring it up with my uncle." Ten days of hard travel were catching up with him, and the whole sorry mess just left Geran tired, with the beginnings of a headache. He glanced up at the banners flying above the gatehouse. The highest was a blue banner with a white seven-pointed star; by the traditions of Griffonwatch, it flew only when the lord of Hulburg was actually present. "Is there any reason I can't see him now?"

"None at all," Kolton answered. He looked over to his companion. "Orndal, you've got the gate watch. Call Sarise from the guardroom to take my place, and send word to the chamberlain that Lord Geran's returned with a guest. Lord Geran, I'll show you to the harmach."

Geran nodded, and the Shieldsworn sergeant led him and Hamil across the courtyard to a wide set of stone steps climbing up between barracks, stables, armories, and storehouses of the Shieldsworn. In Geran's experience a third or more of the soldiers were posted in various watchtowers and patrols along Hulburg's northern marches at any given time, keeping watch for orc raids and spellwarped monsters out of the far north. Others would be on leave, staying with families down in the town or carousing in the taverns and alehouses. Either way, most of the barracks rooms were dark and empty.

Hamil studied it all with interest as they followed the guardsman. "I know that the harmach, Grigor, is your uncle," he said to Geran. "Who else lives here?"

"Grigor's daughter-in-law, Erna, and her children. Erna is the widow of my cousin Isolmar, Grigor's son. He was killed in a duel about four years ago. I suppose Natali and Kirr are the harmach's heirs now, but they're still quite young." They came to a second courtyard above the barracks and storehouses, where a large hall stood. Kolton trotted up the steps and opened the heavy wooden doors for them. The room beyond was a banquet hall and what served as the harmach's audience chamber. It was rather plain by the standards of the southern cities, and wind whistled through some unseen draft high up near the rafters. "My Aunt Terena lives here too," Geran continued. "She is Grigor's sister."

"And your father was Grigor's brother?"

"Yes. Terena has two children: my cousin Kara and Sergen, who is her stepson by her second marriage."

Hamil nodded. His people were very particular about relations. He sorted out family trees and remembered them with an uncanny ease—a useful advantage in the complicated dealings and rivalries of mercantile Tantras. Geran, on the other hand, had long since learned that he could never keep straight who was related to whom. He had to rely on notes in a journal. It was one more reason he appreciated Hamil as a business partner.

"Lady Kara rode out to the Raven Hill watchtower earlier today," Sergeant Kolton said. "She may not be back tonight. Sergen spends most of his time at his villa out on Easthead, but he's here now. This way, gentlemen."

They climbed a staircase at the end of the hall, where two more Shieldsworn waited. Kolton spoke briefly with them—Geran did not know either man well, but they recognized him and welcomed him home—and then the sergeant led them up another flight of stairs into the third portion of the castle. This was not a true bailey, but simply a small courtyard crowning the hill. The buildings here comprised the Hulmaster residence, and so visitors were not normally permitted to pass beyond the large hall and kitchens below without an invitation or escort. The courtyard was circled by a roofed gallery linking several small buildings—a chapel, a library, a small kitchen, and the Harmach's Tower itself, which was a good-sized stone keep sited on the highest point of the hilltop.

"One moment," Kolton said. He knocked on the library door and entered. Geran and Hamil waited for a short time in the courtyard until the sergeant reappeared. "The harmach'll see you now."

"Thank you, Kolton," Geran answered.

The stocky sergeant briefly inclined his head, which passed for a bow in Hulburg. "It's good to see you home, sir."

Drawing a deep breath, Geran let himself into the castle library. It was a small, cluttered space, really, but it did hold the largest collection of books for nearly fifty miles. It also served as the harmach's study; when Geran thought of his uncle, he imagined him in that very room. He remembered the smell from his childhood, the musty odor of damp paper and the sharper scent of pipesmoke. He and Hamil passed through the small foyer and stepped into the study proper.

"Uncle Grigor?" he said.

"Well, this is an unexpected surprise." Grigor Hulmaster sat behind a cluttered desk by a large window of leaded glass. He was a man of seventy-five years, tall and thin, stooped at the shoulder, with little hair remaining on his head except for a thin fringe that ran from the back of one ear to the back of the other. A knob-handled walking stick leaned against his chair, and his eyes were weak and watery. He pushed himself to his feet and peered at Geran. "Is that really you, Geran? How long has it been since you set foot in Griffonwatch?"

Geran came close and took his uncle's hand; a cold tremble weakened the harmach's grip. "Eight years last summer, Uncle."

"Not since your father's death, then. Your journeys in the south must have taken you to strange and far lands indeed. But, as they say, the traveler who walks the farthest yearns the most for home. I am glad to see you again, Geran." The older man beamed and turned his attention to Hamil. "And who is this lad?"

Lad? Hamil demanded silently of Geran. To his credit the halfling kept his outrage from his face.

"This is my friend and comrade Hamil Alderheart, Uncle Grigor. He is a halfling of the Chondalwood, lately of Tantras. He and I were both members of the Company of the Dragon Shield, and together we run the Red Sail Coster of Tantras. He claims to be thirty-two years of age."

"A halfling?" Grigor looked closer and shook his head. "I beg your pardon, good sir. I meant no disrespect. My eyesight is not as keen as it once was."

Hamil forced a smile and bowed graciously. "Think nothing of it," he grated.

The harmach does not look well, Geran thought. Grigor had never been a vigorous man, really. He was industrious and well read, but he had spent his life working with his head, not his hands, and he had never cared much for travel. As a young man a fall from a horse had left him with a badly broken hip that even the clerics' healing spells had never been able to repair completely. In cold, damp weather—something Hulburg had no shortage of at any time of the year—it pained the old man greatly.

Does he ever leave Griffonwatch anymore? Geran wondered. The steps must be difficult for him to manage.

"So, you must have heard about Jarad," Grigor said quietly. "Ill news carries swiftly and far, it seems."

"I heard about it in Tantras. I've come home to pay my respects."

"It's a terrible thing, Geran. Jarad was a good man, a good captain to the Shieldsworn, a valued advisor . . . and a friend, as well. I still can't believe that he is dead." The harmach sighed and passed his hand over his face.

"Can you tell me what happened? How did Jarad die?"

"No one but his murderers could say for certain. He was found out in the Highfells, near one of the old barrows. He was alone. I know Kara rode out to study the scene; she could probably tell you more."

"I'll ask her when I see her, then."

Grigor nodded. "Will you be staying long?"

"I don't know." Geran hadn't intended to, but standing in the old castle, listening to the cold hard wind, and breathing in the sights and sounds and smells of home, he found that old memories were pressing close around him. Strange how he had never let his footsteps turn toward Hulburg in the long months since that last day in Myth Drannor. What was I avoiding? he wondered. Perhaps he had allowed himself to become bewitched in Myth Drannor, as Hamil thought, but that was over. He had lost that long waking dream that was his life for four years in the city of the elves, ending it in one dark moment he still did not understand. His heart longed for autumn in Myth Drannor, for Alliere's musical laughter, but those things were not for him any longer. Geran closed his eyes to drive the image of her face from his mind, castigating himself in silence. It did his heart no good to dwell on her, but he seemed determined to anyway.

He must have frowned at himself. Grigor took his expression for disapproval and raised his hand. "I only meant that you're welcome to stay as long as you like," the old lord said. "There is always room for you here, Geran."

"Forgive me, it's been a long journey," Geran answered. He mustered a small smile for his uncle. "I have no business in Tantras that can't manage itself for a tenday or so. As long as I'm here, I might as well reacquaint myself with my kin."

"Good," said Grigor. "But Geran, please, be careful. The harmach's writ doesn't run so far as it used to in Hulburg. There are people in town who owe the Hulmasters no allegiance at all, much more so than when you were growing up. It was no accident when Isolmar was killed in that tavern quarrel, and I suspect that it was no accident that Jarad died alone out in the Highfells. When you set foot outside of Griffonwatch's walls, you must watch your back."

Hamil sketched a small bow. "That's why I'm here, Lord Grigor," he observed. "I have no use for a dead partner, so it's in my interest to keep an eye on him. Why else would I venture so far from civilization?"

Grigor smiled, but his tone was serious. "If you are a friend of the Hulmasters, Master Alderheart, you may need to watch your own back as well." He looked back up to Geran and indicated the study door. "Now, on to happier matters. Unless I am sorely mistaken, you have two young cousins who will be quite anxious to meet you. I expect they're in the great room, resisting their mother's efforts to put them to bed."

The old lord took a mantle from a hook by the door, pulled it around his shoulders, and with the help of his short walking stick made his way to the covered walkway and court outside. Geran and Hamil followed. The wind sighed and hissed among the eaves of the old castle's buildings, and the lanterns illuminating the way rocked in the breeze. Small yellow pools of light swayed and spun lazily beneath the wooden shakes.

"I've been meaning to have this enclosed," Grigor remarked. "It's a cold walk on a winter night."

Then he led them into the small tower fronting the high court—a simple square, low building of somewhat sturdier construction than the rest of the castle's upperworks. But as the harmach reached for the door, it opened from the inside, and a dark-eyed man with a pointed, black goatee and a crimson cape emerged, two armsmen at his shoulders.

"Ah, good evening, Uncle," the dark-eyed man said with a small nod.

"I was just—" Then his eyes fell on Geran and widened for an instant. He smiled, slowly and deliberately, and let out a small snort. "Well, I'll be damned. Look what the wind's blown up against our doorstep. Cousin Geran, you are the last thing I expected to see when I opened this door!"

"Sergen," Geran replied. "You look well." His stepcousin—if there was such a thing, he wondered—was in truth dressed quite well, with a red, gold-embroidered doublet, tall black boots of fine leather, and a gold-hilted rapier at his belt. In fact he looked more like a merchant prince of Sembia or the Vast than a son of northerly Hulburg. Geran remembered Sergen as a sullen, brooding young man, quick to find fault and take offense. But the man before him stood sharp-eyed and alert, brimming with self-confidence. "Ah, this is Hamil Alderheart, my friend and business partner. Hamil, this is my cousin Sergen Hulmaster."

The halfling inclined his head. "I'm pleased to meet you, sir."

"Likewise," Sergen replied, but his eyes quickly returned to Geran's. He stroked his pointed beard, and his brow furrowed. "I haven't seen you in years, Geran. So where have you been keeping yourself?"

"Tantras, mostly. Hamil and I are proprietors of the Red Sail Coster, dealing in the trade between Turmish and the Vast—timber, silverwork, wool, linen."

"Ah, of course. I've heard of it. But . . . why did I think that you were staying in Myth Drannor?"

Geran frowned. The question seemed innocuous, but he sensed a hidden stiletto in Sergen's voice. "I lived there for four years, but as it happened I left about a year ago."

Sergen's eyes widened. "Ah, that's right! I remember hearing something about that—a duel of some kind, love spurned, a rival suitor maimed, some sordid tale ending in your exile from the elf kingdom. Tell me, Geran, is any of that true?"

Geran stood in silence a long moment before he answered, "All of it."

Sardonic humor danced in Sergen's dark eyes. "Indeed! I would not have believed it if you hadn't said so." The rakish noble smiled to himself and reached out to clap a comradely hand on Geran's shoulder. "Well, I'm eager to hear your side of the story, Cousin. I am certain there were extenuating circumstances. Now, if you'll excuse me, I have a late dinner engagement this evening, and I must be going. Geran, you must promise me that you won't leave town without a good long visit." Sergen nodded to Harmach Grigor before he swept away across the bailey, his bodyguards in tow.

Grigor watched him leave. "A capable man, your cousin Sergen," he mused aloud. "Clever and ambitious. He has grand designs for Hulburg. If only half of what he means to attempt works out, we will be well on our way to becoming a great city again. But he has a cruel turn to his heart, I fear."

The dreams of a dragon, Hamil said silently. *We know his type well, don't we? Tantras, Calaunt, and Procampur are full of such men.*

But Hulburg isn't, Geran thought. Or at least, it never used to be.

The harmach shook himself and motioned to the door. "No reason to stand here in the cold," the old man said. "Come, Geran, you must see your young cousins Natali and Kirr. They've heard quite a few stories about the Hulmaster who's off seeing the wide world. You are something of a marvel to them, even if you don't know it."

The swordmage pulled his gaze away from his cousin's back. He had a feeling that he would see more of Sergen soon enough, whether he wanted to or not. Instead, he summoned a wry smile for his uncle. "I'm no marvel, but I suppose I have seen some marvelous things in my travels," he said. "I'll try not to disappoint them."

THREE

12 Ches, the Year of the Ageless One

Two hours before sunset, the orc-hold began to stir. Warriors rose from their pallets, stretching and yawning, heavy canines gleaming yellow in the dim light. Females stoked the cookfires, fed the livestock, and began their long round of drudgery and toil. The young scurried about underfoot, fetching water and firewood, emptying chamberpots, and tending to the scraggly goats, sheep, and fowl penned within the crudely built fortress. Orcs disliked the brightest hours of the day, and therefore the hold took its rest from shortly after sunrise to the late afternoon. Only the scouts, the sentries, and those young given the job of minding the herds in the fields nearby stayed awake through the bright hours of morning and midday.

The warchief Mhurren roused himself from his sleeping-furs and his women and pulled a short hauberk of heavy steel rings over his thick, well-muscled torso. He usually rose before most of his warriors, since he had a strong streak of human blood in him, and he found the daylight less bothersome than most of his tribe did. Among the Bloody Skulls, a warrior was judged by his strength, his fierceness, and his wits. Human ancestry was no blemish against a warrior—provided he was every bit as strong, enduring, and bloodthirsty as his full-blooded kin. Half-orcs who were weaker than their orc comrades didn't last long among the Bloody Skulls or any other orc tribe for that matter. But it was often true that a bit of human blood gave a warrior just the right mix of cunning, ambition, and self-discipline to go far indeed, as Mhurren had. He was master of a tribe that could muster two thousand spears, and the strongest chief in Thar.

Yevelda sat up when he threw off the furs. She was his favorite wife, a tigress with more human than orc in her, much like himself. Slender as a switch of willow by the standards of most of the tribe's women, she made up for her small size and clean features with catlike reflexes and pure, fierce intensity. With a knife in her hand, she was more deadly than many male warriors twice her weight. Even when he took her to the sleeping-furs, Mhurren never really let his guard down around her. She cuffed his two lesser wives, Sutha and Kansif, awake.

"Rise, you two," Yevelda said. "See to the kitchens and make sure our guests are looked after. They judge our husband by the table you set. Do not disappoint me."

The junior wives scrambled quickly out of the furs. Yevelda had shown more than once that she was quick to beat one, the other, or both if she had to repeat herself. Kansif was a young, full-blooded girl who was thoroughly cowed by the half-orc woman and desperate to please her. Sutha, on the other hand . . . Sutha was an older and far more cunning woman, the first of the three to have shared Mhurren's furs and a strong-willed priestess in her own right. She was a strong, fit mixed-blood who was not at all happy about having been supplanted by Yevelda as Mhurren's favorite. The chieftain guessed that Sutha was well along in several plots against Yevelda, but it wouldn't do to intervene. If the favorite couldn't keep the lesser wives in their place, then she wasn't fit to be the favorite, was she? As she left, Sutha brushed by him with a sly smile and let her hand trail over the thick mail of his broad chest, moving just quickly enough to deprive Yevelda of a reason to chastise her.

Mhurren grinned in appreciation as he watched his lesser wives dress themselves and hurry from his chambers. Then he moved over to the slitlike window and brushed the heavy curtain out of the way. The day was bright, and faint hints of green growth speckled the gray hills and moorlands surrounding Bloodskull Hold. Thar was a hard land, barely suitable for a few scrawny herds of livestock, but with the coming of spring the passes would soon open, and he'd be able to send hunting parties to the mountain vales and the open steppeland beyond. It would be good for his warriors to have something to do. Too many of his orcs were growing bored and restless after the long winter, and that usually spelled trouble.

He glanced to his left and scowled. The camp of the Vaasans was still there, perched in the shelter of a rocky tor a quarter-mile from the hold's walls. In the center of the humans' tents stood a small tower of iron, summoned up out of nothing at all by the Vaasan lord's magic. The humans had shown his tribe every respect, sending fine gifts ahead of their emissaries, and his scouts had counted an escort of almost two hundred spears for the lord they sent to speak to him—a sign of the man's importance. But the fact remained that if negotiations were to take an ugly turn, he was not sure that he could drive the Vaasan company away from his keep, not with the sort of magic the black-clad humans evidently commanded.

"What do they want with me?" he growled.

Yevelda stretched out atop the furs, deliberately not covering herself to remind him why she was his favorite. She answered him, even though he had not meant the question for her. "You will find out soon enough," she said in her throaty purr. "But if you must guess, then ask yourself this: What does the Vaasan lack?"

Mhurren grimaced in annoyance. Along with her straight, smooth limbs and dusky beauty, Yevelda's human blood blessed her with the same sort of fiery ambition and quick curiosity he himself possessed. She had a mind every bit as sharp as his own and seemed to feel that entitled her to help him rule over the Bloody Skulls. In truth, Yevelda might just be clever, strong, and ruthless enough to govern the tribe without him, but it was rare indeed for any woman, no matter how exceptional, to rule as queen over orc warriors. "He's here to bribe me to attack the Skullsmashers," he guessed. "The stupid ogres don't have enough sense to leave the Vaasans alone, so they send this man Terov to find my price for an alliance against King Guld and his band of dimwits."

"What price would you demand for your aid?"

"Gold, furs, wine, good steel . . . and some assurance that the Vaasans will actually fight. I'll be damned if I let my warriors get mashed to bloody pulp by the ogres while the Vaasans sit back and watch us kill each other."

Yevelda rolled over onto her belly and looked up at him. "It depends which warriors, doesn't it? I can think of a couple I wouldn't be sorry to lose."

Mhurren barked a short, harsh laugh. "True enough. The warriors grow restless, and it would be good to find someone to fight. My berserkers are ready to turn on each other. But I can't let the tribe think the Vaasans played me for a fool. That would look weak." He reached out and slapped her shapely flank. "I go to see what he thinks my price is."

He buckled on his weapon harness and padded out of his den. Six fierce warriors with the elaborate facial scarring of the Skull Guard waited for him. They grounded the butts of their spears against the stone and shouted, *"Kai! Kai!"* when Mhurren appeared.

Without another word they fell in around him and escorted him through the keep's tortuous passageways and cramped guardchambers, brutally striking and shouldering aside any who got in their way. Mhurren was as sure of their loyalty as he could be. He made sure that his personal guards freely plundered the rest of the tribe. Should anything ever happen to him, the warriors of the Skull Guard would not long survive his demise. And, just to be sure, years ago he'd had Sutha lay fearsome curses and compulsions on each Skull Guard with her priestess magic. But Sutha was likely not very pleased with him at the moment, not as long as Yevelda was first among his wives . . . he would be wise to have one of the battle-sorcerers or priests of Gruumsh test the spells that ensured his guards' loyalty. If, of course, he could find a spellcaster other than Sutha that he trusted.

No matter, he told himself. The game was to remain chief as long as he could, father a son strong enough to succeed him, and try not to kill the whelp—or let the whelp kill him—before he was ready. But that day was still many long years off.

The warchief marched into the keep's great hall, a long, low-ceilinged room with thick pillars holding up a simple masonry vault. Four heavy braziers full of red-glowing coals illuminated the room. The walls were bedecked with the trophies the tribe had taken over the years—the crudely preserved skulls of hundreds of enemies, steeped in a crimson dye so that they always looked as if they were fresh and gory. Dwarves, humans, goblins, orcs, ogres, gnolls, even a handful of giants, all were represented among the dangling bones. The tribe's priests knew the story of each one. Some were mighty enemies the Bloody Skulls had bested. Some were enemies known to have fallen beneath the axe or spear of a legendary Bloodskull chief or champion. But most expressed contempt, not respect. The skulls of women and children taken near places such as Glister or Hulburg or Thentia cluttered the walls, mocking enemies too weak to defend their families and homesteads from Bloodskull raids. Scores of orc warriors and their women slept in this room, and they were just beginning to stir when Mhurren and his guards made their appearance. *"Kai!* The warchief! The warchief!" shouted the Skull Guards as they kicked and prodded careless orcs out of the way.

Mhurren threw himself into the thronelike seat on its dais at the end of the hall, one hand resting on a short sword at his side. More than once he'd been attacked in that very seat, and he'd learned to keep steel close at hand. He surveyed the warriors in the hall for a moment and spotted one that would do. "Huwurth, take five spears and bring the Vaasan," he commanded. "Tell him that I summon him, and that I am ready to hear him out. Give him time to make himself ready, and let him bring two hands of bodyguards if he wants. If he wants more than that, tell him no. Come back if he refuses."

Huwurth, a young warleader, nodded. "I go, warchief," he said. Despite his youth he was quite clever and patient, a rare combination. He gathered five warriors from his band and led them from the hall. Huwurth was smart enough to ignore almost any offense the humans might give, as long as he was doing Mhurren's bidding. Others among the Bloodskull warleaders and berserkers simply couldn't have walked into that camp without finding some mortal quarrel with a human who met the eye too long, or looked away too quickly, or turned his back, or found some new way to invite a battle.

Mhurren composed himself to wait, brooding with his chin on his fist as he studied the warriors watching him. There was a small commotion off to his right, and the warpriest Tangar appeared with his group of acolytes. To become a priest of Gruumsh, He Who Watches, a priest had to pluck out an eye, so Tangar and his followers each wore a thick leather patch stitched to cheek and brow. Evidently the warpriest had hurried from his chambers, for his acolytes were still busy fitting his armor plate to him as he strode into the room. Doubtless Tangar could not abide the idea of Mhurren holding court without him present. "You send for the Vaasan?" the cleric demanded.

The warchief frowned. "I will hear him out, priest," he answered. He didn't like the idea of Gruumsh's priest hovering over his shoulder, but there was little he could do about it. He decided to occupy himself by tending to a chief's duties and looked to the nearest Skull Guard. "I will hold judgment," he said. "Does any warrior here have a quarrel to lay before me?"

A hale, scar-faced warrior came forward and dropped his spear on the floor. "I will speak," he growled. "I am Buurthar."

"I see you, Buurthar," Mhurren replied. "You have set down your spear. Speak."

Buurthar nodded and spoke briefly, explaining how another warrior's young sons had shirked their shepherding duties, resulting in the loss of two of his own sheep. "I say that Gaalsh must give me two of his sheep since his lazy sons were careless of mine. Gaalsh says that the missing sheep were likely taken by a red tiger, and so he owes me nothing. What is your judgment, Chief?"

Mhurren had to judge over quarrels just like this every day. If a strong chief didn't, one of the orcs in the quarrel would just kill the other, and the brothers or sons of the dead warrior would kill in return, and before long the hold would run red with the blood of the feuding orcs. Gaalsh, the other warrior, wasn't at Bloodskull Keep, so Mhurren decided against him. "Hear my word, all of you! Until someone finds some sign of this tiger, Gaalsh must give two of his sheep to Buurthar. Now, pick up your spear and go."

The veteran retrieved his spear, grinning in vindication. Mhurren doubted that any tiger had made off with the missing sheep, but he did not want to accuse a warrior who was not in front of him of stealing the other's livestock. He heard two more quarrels between his warriors. Then Huwurth and his followers returned to the great hall.

Before them strode a tall human in armor of ebon plate, his face hidden beneath a black helm that was fitted with gilded ram's horns curling from the sides. A single servant in a tunic and cloak of dark gray followed, a human woman who wore her reddish hair cut short in a warrior's manner. She had a light mask of black across her eyes, but her face was otherwise bare. Six Vaasan knights in fine black mail guarded them.

Mhurren motioned with his hand, and the orcs before his throne shuffled out of the way, making space for the humans to approach him. The Vaasan lord was confident enough; he strode through the ranks of orc warriors filling the room as if he couldn't care less that he'd just put fifty spears at his back should Mhurren decide to have him killed. The black knight halted a few feet before the throne and reached up to remove his helm. Beneath his helmet the man had pale skin, hair of iron gray, and a clean-shaven face. His eyes were a deep, bloody crimson.

"You are Warchief Mhurren?" the man asked in passable Orcish.

"I am Mhurren. Who are you, Vaasan, and what do you want with the Bloody Skulls?"

"I am Kardhel Terov, an fellthane of the Warlock Knights. And I am here to offer you power, Warchief—the power to make yourself the king of all Thar. Every tribe in this land will call you master and do as you bid them."

"We are already the strongest tribe in Thar!" Tangar the priest shouted angrily. "Who dares to make war against us? No one, human!"

Fanaticism was occasionally useful, Mhurren reflected. The cleric saved him the trouble of raising his own voice. He held up his hand to restrain the priest from speaking further, since he did not really want to provoke a fight with the Vaasans without at least finding out why they were here.

"Power? What power?" Mhurren sneered.

"I can deliver to you the Burning Daggers, the Skullsmashers, and the Red Claws," Terov said. "They will call you lord, pay you tribute, and march as you command. I can arm your warriors with a thousand hauberks of good steel mail. I can give you ten Warlock Knights to wield their battle magic in your service. And I have control over a number of strong monsters from the high mountains—manticores, giants, chimeras, even a young dragon or two. They will be yours to command. Tell me, Warchief Mhurren, what would you do with an army such as that?"

Mhurren laughed harshly. "Raze Glister, smash Hulburg and Phlan, lay Thentia and Melvaunt under tribute . . . and if you give us warships too, I suppose we might cross the Moonsea and burn Myth Drannor while we're at it! Why not?"

The Warlock Knight's mouth twisted in a cold smile. "I don't think we'll have to burn the elves out of their forest—yet. But as for the rest, so be it. The cities you named I will give to you to sack or enslave as you wish."

"They are not yours to give away, human."

"No, but they are yours to take, Chief of the Bloody Skulls. Glister you might manage without my help, perhaps Hulburg too, but the others are beyond your strength. I can change that. Are you interested? Or shall I go to Guld of the Skullsmashers or Kraashk of the Red Claws and make one of them king in your place?"

The warchief's laughter died in his throat. Mhurren leaned forward in his throne and scowled at the Vaasan. "You mock me, Vaasan," he said slowly. "Assuming you can do all that you say, why would you? What price do you demand?"

Kardhel Terov glanced at the crowded audience chamber and switched to the human tongue. *"I am told you understand Vaasan, but few of your warriors do,"* he said in that language. *"My price is an oath of fealty to the High Circle of Fellthanes, sworn on my iron ring."*

"You come into my keep and expect me to bend my knee to you?" Mhurren hissed in the human's language. He surged up from his seat and seized a spear from the nearest of his Skull Guards. With a fierce cry he hurled the weapon with all the strength of his rage right at the Vaasan's heart.

The heavy iron-shod spear flashed through the air, striking Terov in the center of his chest—and rebounded, shattered into kindling. The Warlock Knight staggered back a step and grunted from the sheer mass of the spear, but he was otherwise unhurt. Mhurren's sudden fury abandoned him. He knew his own strength. Thrown at ten paces, the spear should have transfixed the human and carried two feet or more through his back. But instead the weapon had snapped like a dry twig.

The surrounding orcs roared in anger and astonishment at the sorcery revealed in their midst. Some recoiled in fear, while others rushed forward to drown the Vaasans in a black tide of stabbing blades before any more magic could be used. But the black-veiled woman behind the Warlock Knight quickly slashed her hand across her body and hissed a few words in some sibilant language. A racing windblast of ebon flames appeared around the Vaasan party, howling and swirling as it walled the Bloody Skull warriors away from the humans. A warrior in the back of the room threw another spear, but it was caught by the sorceress's black flames and burned to ash in midair.

"Hold your warriors, Mhurren!" Terov shouted. "We are protected by powerful magic, and any who approach will be killed!"

Mhurren was sorely tempted to put the Vaasan's threat to the test, but somehow he found the last vestige of his patience. He could always order his warriors to fall on the humans later, but clearly Terov wanted to talk, and he'd been respectful enough of Mhurren's strength to protect himself with magic before entering the audience chamber.

The warchief motioned to the warriors filling the room and said, "Hold, warriors! We will see how long their spells last."

The Bloody Skulls gnashed their fangs and growled in frustration, but they obeyed, slowly edging away from the whirling black firestorm. A forest of spearpoints surrounded the small party of Vaasans, waiting for the black-veiled woman's spell to show any signs of weakening. Mhurren turned his attention back to Terov and said, "I do not know how long your woman's spells will last, but if you want to leave this room alive, convince me to spare you before they fail. Choose your next words with care, Vaasan!"

Terov held up his fist in reply. A heavy iron band carved with dire runes encircled his ring finger. *"Do you know what this is?"* he said in Vaasan.

"Your ring," Mhurren snarled. He'd heard stories of the Warlock Knights and their peculiar methods for ensuring obedience. It was said that an iron ring could not be removed once the wearer put it on of his own free will. *"What of it? Everyone knows that Warlock Knights all wear one."*

"It is a pact ring. I am bound by what I swear. And he who swears to me is bound too. If you take me for your liege, you will be accounted a lord of Vaasa, and I will give you a ring of your own so that you may bind others to their oaths. Yes, you will rule in the name of the Warlock Knights. You will send me warriors when I ask you to, and you will render to me the yearly tithes your oath demands. Those are the things a vassal lord owes his liege. But in turn I will be obliged to come when you call, to honor the laws and judgments you levy on your lands, and to respect the vassal oaths you extract from others. And perhaps most importantly, what you conquer in my name you will keep." Terov let his hand fall to his side and paused, measuring Mhurren's reaction. The half-orc chief glared at him but said nothing, so the Vaasan continued. *"Today I offer you Thar, but with the power I can give to you, the whole of the Moonsea North will be yours to govern as you see fit . . . with only a few small exceptions."*

"Hah! I thought so." Mhurren bared his fangs. *"All right, then. What 'small exceptions' do you have in mind?"*

The Warlock Knight shrugged. *"If I take some city or town under my protection, you may not sack it. I will levy suitable tribute against it and pay you your due, but once my word is given to someone else, I will not permit you to break it."*

Mhurren returned to his throne and sat down again. It would be easy to tell this Kardhel Terov no, or better yet, have his warriors draw and quarter the man for his impudence . . . if in fact they could overcome the powerful magic the Vaasans evidently wielded. On the other hand, if Terov made good on his offer, Mhurren would be the strongest chief for hundreds of miles around. Tribes such as the Skullsmashers or the Red Claws as his vassals instead of his enemies would give him enough power to dominate Thar and any city within a tenday's march. And the ability to demand unbreakable oaths from those around him would be useful indeed.

"What does the human offer us, Warchief?" the priest Tangar asked. "Does he insult us? I will gladly spill his blood on the altar of the Mighty One!"

Mhurren ignored him and spoke to Terov. "I claim the land from the Giant's Cairn to Sulasspryn and Glister to the sea as my kingdom," he said. It was a broad definition of Thar, broad indeed, but Terov nodded. "And before I agree to your terms, you will give me a sign of your sincerity: The arms and armor you mentioned, and the services of the Skullsmashers and the monsters at your command, so that I can raze the town of Glister. When Glister falls to the Bloody Skulls, then I will know that you speak truth, and you and I will swear oaths together."

Mhurren leaned back, satisfied with himself. If the Vaasan's promises failed to materialize, well, then, he wouldn't take Glister. And if Terov was as good as his word and Glister fell into Bloodskull hands, on that day Mhurren could decide whether he wanted to swear any oath or not. It had been a long time since any orc had been called the king of Thar, and if he brought about Glister's destruction, he would be the greatest of Thar's chiefs in centuries . . . maybe a king indeed.

"It is fair," Kardhel Terov allowed. *"But you will be obligated to me, King Mhurren, if I give you your arms and armor and Glister as well."* He bowed slightly and straightened. In Orcish he said, "I will arrange for the arms to be sent from Vaasa by the end of the tenday. And a Warlock Knight will

come in the next day or two to serve you. He will relay your commands to the giants and the other monsters who will answer your call."

Mhurren stood and descended the steps of the dais, approaching the human as closely as he dared with the sorcerous black flames flickering around the Vaasans. He stared closely into the man's face, trying to read something of his intentions. Kardhel Terov returned his gaze without blinking.

"As you say, then," the warchief said. *"But, tell me one more thing—why are you interested in Thar? What do you gain by making me your ally?"*

Kardhel Terov offered a small smile. *"Vaasa is a landlocked country,"* he answered. *"Impassable mountains surround our land on all sides save the southeast, and there the land of Damara stands astride our natural path of expansion. Most of my peers have their eyes fixed on the conquest of Damara, but I am more patient than they are. I believe Vaasa will grow more quickly by opening up trade with the lands of the west and filling our coffers with gold. The Moonsea is only forty miles from our southern plains. Should I secure a safe trading route across the mountains and moors of Thar to Hulburg or Thentia or Melvaunt, I would vastly enrich my land. To do that, I need a single strong chieftain in Thar who can guard Vaasan trade from any other chieftain or monster that might be tempted to interfere."*

"And I am the chieftain you have chosen for this . . . honor?"

"The Bloody Skulls are my first choice, but I will raise up another chief and another tribe if I have to. I am willing to pay that chieftain very well indeed for serving my purpose, but in turn I will demand loyalty." Terov's eyes were as cold as stone. *"Our oaths of fealty are inescapable, King Mhurren, both from lord to liege and liege to lord. You will help to make Vaasa rich, and in turn we will help you to build up a kingdom that will last for centuries, not a single lifetime."*

Mhurren thought for a long moment, his eyes narrowed. "Very well," he finally said, returning to Orcish so his warriors could understand him. "I do not trust you, Vaasan, but there may be something in what you promise me. I will weigh the truth of your words at the walls of Glister."

Four

12 Ches, the Year of the Ageless One

When the clocktower in the Assayer's House struck nine, Geran left Griffonwatch and descended the winding causeway to the town. Morning mists lingered in the lower streets, but the sunshine was bright and clear overhead. The fierce wind had finally died away, and the day promised to be mild and fair by the standards of the Moonsea spring. He'd left Hamil to look after himself for the morning. The halfling intended to spend the day looking into Red Sail business; Geran was content to leave it to Hamil for now, since he intended to put every street in the town under his boots at some point during the day. He wanted to see everything that was new or different or simply missing in Hulburg, and more importantly, he wanted to see everything that had stayed the same. He had exhausted his memories in the years he had been away, and he needed to collect the familiar sights and sounds and voices again.

Geran breathed deeply and threw his shoulders back as he walked, enjoying the cool, fresh air. He'd spent a good two hours of the previous evening reacquainting himself with his young cousins Natali and Kirr before their mother had ushered them off to bed—and not a moment too soon, because he was almost reeling from exhaustion by the time Erna put an end to their endless questioning. Natali was a slender girl of ten years who took after her father, Isolmar. She had the black, straight hair of the Hulmasters and a cat-quick sense of curiosity. Kirr was a rambunctious young fellow of seven whose reddish-gold hair favored his mother, Erna. Unlike his older sister, he seemed more inclined to measure his world by trying to break it one piece at a time. And, as Grigor had warned him, they wanted to know *everything* about every place he'd ever been and anything he'd ever done that might be considered adventurous, magical, or dangerous.

Isolmar would be proud of them both, Geran reflected. It was a heartbreak and a shame that they'd lost their father while so young, but that was hardly an uncommon thing in the Moonsea lands. Wars, monsters, feuds, and hard toil in hard lands orphaned many children and left most of those in much grimmer circumstances. At least Natali and Kirr had their mother and their father's kinfolk to look after them, as well as a castle full of men and women sworn to the Hulmasters' service. As far as he could tell, the servants and maids who worked in the castle loved the two young Hulmasters as if Natali and Kirr were their very own children.

He reached the bottom of the causeway, which was a small square called the Harmach's Foot. Mule-drawn wagons clattered over the cobblestones, a steady stream passing both north and south. Those heading north were bound for the mining and woodcutting camps beyond the Winterspear Vale with provisions of all kinds—salted meat, sacks of flour, casks of ale, wheels of cheese, blankets, tools, all the things that men living out in the field would need. Those heading south were coming into town from the valley farms. At that time of year, all they had were eggs, dairy goods, and meat to sell in the town's markets. It would be months before the summer crops came in.

He didn't recognize any of the drivers heading out to the work camps. If their accents and manner of dress were any guide, most were from other Moonsea cities. He saw more Mulmasterites and Melvauntians, and even a few Teshans. Geran shook his head, struck again by how crowded the town seemed. "Well, where to?" he asked himself.

He thought for a moment then struck out north along the Vale Road. Once he left the Harmach's Foot, the area between Griffonwatch and the Winterspear reverted to old, brush-covered rubble, with only a few buildings standing amid the remains of the old city. Most of the living town clustered close to the harbor, and the northern and western districts of Old Hulburg remained ruins except for the best sites, such as the Troll and Tankard, a taphouse on the edge of town.

When the Vale Road finally emerged from the ruins of Old Hulburg and headed north into the Winterspear farmlands, Geran turned west at the Burned Bridge. Centuries ago a fine and strong bridge had crossed the

Winterspear on five stone piers. In Lendon Hulmaster's time a simple trestle of wood had been laid across the remains of the ancient stone piers to link Griffonwatch more directly with Daggergard Tower, a small barracks and watchtower on the west bank of the river. Geran paused at the top of the bridge to lean on the rail and watch the water race by below. The snowmelt of spring was just beginning; in a few weeks the Winterspear would be ten feet higher, roaring with the voice of Thar's high snowfields and the distant glaciers of the Galenas.

He made his way from Daggergard along Keldon Way, heading south as he circled the town. Above him rose the strange stone forest the folk of Hulburg knew simply as the Spires. Soaring, club-shaped columns of pale green stone stood embedded in the flanks of the ridge marking the western edge of the town, in some cases bursting through the old foundations of the ancient ruins. The Spires were changeland too, just like the spectacular Arches that guarded the eastern side of Hulburg's harbor. Both were inexplicable legacies of the Spellplague that had swept Faerûn nearly a century ago. Odd landmarks such as the Spires or the Arches were commonplace in many lands—rock and root of alien Abeir, piercing Toril's flesh when the two worlds, long separated, had merged in a decade of unthinkable catastrophes following the Year of Blue Fire. Geran had heard that many such eruptions of Abeiran landscape in other lands were infested with all sorts of strange planar monstrosities or held undreamed-of marvels of living magic, but the Spires were simply tangled, fluted pillars of malachite, silent and inert. No alien perils or deadly magic were hidden within.

From the shadow of the Spires he descended quickly into the trading district at the foot of Keldon Head, where half a dozen tradeyards clustered near the wharves of the harbor. Here Geran slowed his pace and began to pay attention. The storehouse compound belonging to House Sokol of Phlan had stood in Hulburg for many years, but large new yards belonging to House Veruna of Mulmaster and the Double Moon Coster of Thentia were new. He turned eastward on Cart Street and found a striking new building, the Merchant Council's Hall, standing not far from the merchant yards. A pair of armed guards stood in front of it, men who wore cuirasses of iron and carried short pikes—the Council Watch, or so he guessed. He didn't like the idea of an armed company in

Hulburg other than the Shieldsworn, but the town seemed full of mercenaries and sellswords.

Geran threaded his way through heavier crowds along Cart Street. The triangle of tangled streets between the Harbor, Angar's Square, and the Low Bridge was the heart of Hulburg. Clerks hurried from place to place, carrying ledgers and quills. Porters threw barrels of ale or sacks of flour over the shoulders and carried them off. Children ran and shouted among the oxcarts and porters. "It seems that Hulburg isn't a backwater anymore," Geran muttered to himself. Was this what the harmach had meant when he mentioned Sergen's designs for the town?

He turned the corner to Plank Street, and his footsteps faltered. He hadn't even realized where he was allowing his feet to carry him, but now he was here, not more than ten feet from a familiar hammer-and-grain-sheaf emblem, hanging above a door. The signboard was old and battered, but he could still make out the faded lettering: ERSTENWOLD PROVISIONER.

The storefront was old and weatherworn too, but it was tidy. Barrels full of last fall's apples stood by the wooden steps. To his right, a large workyard and storehouse adjoined the store. The Erstenwolds had made a decent living for two generations by supplying foodstuffs, rope, canvas, woolen blankets, and iron tools to the ships that called on Hulburg and the miners and woodcutters who worked the hills to the north and east. Jarad's family could still look after themselves, and that was a small comfort at least.

He hesitated for a moment, studying the storefront while passersby made their way around him. What are you waiting for? he wondered. His mouth twisted with a grimace of irritation, and he deliberately set foot on the wooden steps leading to the door. Two quick strides, then he pushed it open and let himself inside.

The Erstenwold store consisted of a single long wooden counter that spanned the width of the room. Thick, smooth planks of hardwood gleamed underfoot, old and stained. Dim daylight filtered in through a row of thick glass-paned windows high on the opposite wall. Tack and harness filled the room with the rich smell of fresh leather, and rows of barrels, sacks, and crates lined the walls. A couple of customers—woodcutters in town to stock up on supplies, Geran guessed—negotiated with a clerk behind the counter.

It looks pretty much the same as ever, Geran decided. He knew the Erstenwolds' place of business almost as well as he knew his own rooms in Griffonwatch. Not terribly busy at the moment, but that was not unusual. If no ships or big supply trains were stocking up, a day could be surprisingly slow here.

"Can I help you, sir?" A dark-haired woman bustled into the room from a doorway behind the counter, brushing her hands against her apron. She was tall and slender, with strong, sharp features and wide-set eyes of a striking glacial blue. She wore her hair pulled back in a single stern braid, but a small spray of freckles danced across her cheekbones and the bridge of her nose in defiance of her unsmiling expression. When Geran didn't answer immediately, she gave a soft snort of annoyance and took a step closer. "Hey! I said, can I . . ." the shopkeeper began, then stopped. She looked again and shook her head as if to clear it of confusion. "It's you," she finally said.

"It's me," Geran said. "Hello, Mirya."

"Geran Hulmaster." Mirya Erstenwold crossed her arms, fixing him with her sharp, bright gaze. "What are you doing here?"

"I . . . I heard about Jarad. I had to come." He rested his hands on the well-worn wood of the counter and lowered his eyes. "Mirya, I'm sorry. I loved him like my own brother."

Mirya said nothing for a long moment. Then she sighed and smoothed her apron. "I know you did, Geran."

"Is there anything I can do?"

"No," she said. "We buried him last Fifthday, alongside my mother and father. It's done. You've no cause to worry on our account."

Geran winced. Once upon a time, Mirya wouldn't have used such a tone on him. Sometime in his seventeenth summer, he'd finally noticed that the sister of his best friend, a girl who had followed the two of them all over Hulburg and the wildlands nearby, was clever, strong, slender, and graceful as an elf princess . . . and that something in her eyes danced like sunlight on water when he was around her. She'd been his first love, and he'd been hers. But that carefree girl with the easy smile and the soft laugh was just a memory, just as much as the restless boy he'd once been.

"He didn't leave anyone behind, did he?" he asked. "I mean, I don't remember hearing that he'd ever married."

"Jarad was promised to Niamene Tresterfin. They meant to marry at Midsummer."

"Burkel Tresterfin's daughter?"

"Aye."

Geran remembered Niamene—a pretty little slip of a girl, perhaps five or six years younger than Jarad. The Tresterfin farm was a good piece of land in the Winterspear Vale, three or four miles north of town. She'd been a young teenager when Geran set out from Hulburg. But it seemed that she'd grown up while he'd been away. Strange how ten years changed such things, he mused.

"How is she?" he managed.

"Heartbroken, what do you think? She and her whole family too. Burkel and his wife liked Jarad a lot, and he liked them as well. It would've been a good match."

"I didn't know."

"No, you wouldn't have heard." Mirya glanced down the counter; the woodcutters were finishing their business with her clerk, who was busy writing out their order in a ledger. Satisfying herself that it was nothing she needed to worry about, she took a deep breath and looked back to him. "Where do you keep yourself now, anyway?"

"Tantras. A few years back I joined an adventuring band called the Company of the Dragon Shield. Tymora smiled on us, and we won a small fortune before we went our separate ways. My comrade Hamil and I bought owners' shares of a small trading company, the Red Sail Coster. We buy and sell cargoes in the Vast."

"I thought I'd heard that you were living in Myth Drannor."

His hand tickled, remembering the feel of brushing dry leaves of orange and gold from Alliere's midnight hair as she laughed and ducked away from him. Strange that his fingers recalled something his heart had no wish to, he mused. He looked down again to banish the memory from his mind. "I did for a time, but I've been in Tantras for more than a year now," he said. He paused and changed the subject. "Listen, Mirya, I know you said that there isn't much I can do, but. . . ."

She crossed her arms and fixed her gaze on him. "You don't need to worry about me, Geran Hulmaster. You've not been home in years, and you're sure to be on your way again soon. Spend an hour by Jarad's grave if you feel you should, visit with your family, take a ride in the Highfells if you still fancy the scenery. Then go back to whatever place you call home now. You've nothing more to do here."

Geran retreated a step. Mirya had good cause to be angry with him, after all. He'd broken her heart when he left Hulburg ten years past. He'd always meant to come back after seeing more of Faerûn, but after those first few years with the Dragonshields, he'd found himself enchanted in Myth Drannor, swept up in a dreamlike life that had made him feel like one of the Fair Folk himself, and the memories of his boyhood had seemed so faint and far away. He was still waking up from that strange dream.

"Mirya, I don't know what to say," he sighed. He couldn't think of anything more.

"Mother! Mother! I finished my letters. Can I go play kick-stones with Dori and Kynda?" Geran looked to the doorway leading back to the family quarters, where a young, dark-haired girl stood. She wore a long-sleeved dress of blue wool and was already pulling a brown hood over her shoulders, expecting to go outside. She gave a quick smile and dipped in a shallow curtsey when she noticed him looking at her. "Well, can I?" she repeated.

Mirya has a daughter? Geran blinked in surprise. Of course, Mirya was wearing her hair in a long braid. In Hulburg that was something married women did. When did that happen? he wondered. He knew he shouldn't have been surprised. What did he expect after ten years, after all?

Mirya's face softened for a moment. "Aye, go ahead, Selsha. But you be back here by noon. We're taking a big delivery from the brewhouse, and you're to help mind the store while I'm seeing to it."

"Thank you, Mother!" Selsha bolted back the way she had come. Her footsteps clattered in the hallway, and a door slammed shut.

"You have children?" Geran asked. "I never knew."

"Only Selsha," she replied. She stared after her daughter with the same mixture of love and just a hint of worry that mothers everywhere seem to have. "Selûne knows that she's enough. She's a wonder and a trial to me every day."

"How old is she?"

"Eight last month." Mirya glanced back at him. "She came about two years after you left Hulburg."

He nodded. In other words, Mirya was saying, she isn't yours. That would have been a few months after he'd returned home for his father's funeral, but Geran had stayed in Hulburg only a couple of days before leaving again. He hadn't seen Mirya then. "She's beautiful. Are you—I mean, who is—?"

"No, I'm not married. Her father's no one you know and no one that we'll ever see again." Darkness flickered across her face, and she looked away from him. "But we've got each other, and we make do."

There's more to it than that, Geran thought. Had she fallen in love with someone else after he'd left only to have her heart broken again? Or . . . well, there was not much point in speculating about it. Mirya had made it clear that it was none of his business. Strange, but the idea that she'd evidently moved on after he'd struck out on his own woke a small, bitter swell of resentment in him.

You have no right to feel that way, he told himself. You left her, after all. Was she supposed to remain chaste and forlorn until the day you decided to wander back into her life? And Alliere's ghost still haunted him every day.

"I should be going," he finally said. "I'd like . . . well, I'll stop in to say good-bye before I leave town."

She shrugged and started to say something, but then someone pushed the door open. Three men in mail shirts and tabards of green and white sauntered in. One ran his hand along the wooden counter as he paced toward Mirya, one closed the door behind him and leaned against it with arms folded, and the third wandered by the barrels and sacks stacked along the opposite wall. He studied Geran while feigning interest in the goods offered for sale.

"Well, now, Mistress Erstenwold," the first man said. "You seem to've neglected this month's council dues. We're here to offer a friendly reminder."

Mirya's face tightened. She stood her ground, not moving. "I've not paid any dues because I haven't joined the Merchant Council," she said. "Nor do I mean to, so you and your men can see yourselves out anytime you fancy."

"You certain about that, Mistress Erstenwold?" the first man asked. He was a big, round-faced fellow with the complexion of a ruddy ham. "These are dangerous times. It'll be difficult to do business without council protection." He nodded toward the man along the back wall, who drew a dagger from his belt and slashed open a sack of milled grain. It poured out onto the floor with a soft hissing sound.

"Enough," Geran said. He turned to face the men in green and white. "She asked you to leave, so leave."

"This isn't your problem," Mirya snarled under her breath.

"Mistress Erstenwold is right—this ain't your problem, stranger," the leader of the three said. He shifted his attention from Mirya to Geran and squared to face him. He rested one hand on the hilt of the long sword at his belt. "Why don't you shut your damned mouth and think of some other place you ought to be?"

Geran smiled coldly, but his eyes were hard. This was something else that he hadn't seen in Hulburg before. This makes twice in two days that I've faced foreigners wearing steel in my own hometown, he thought. "Whose colors are you wearing?" he asked the man.

The ruddy-faced man measured him for a moment before answering. "House Veruna. Lady Darsi's helping the Merchant Council to establish order in this miserable town. Everyone who wants to do business in Hulburg is going to join, one way or the other. Now, you're starting to annoy me, stranger. I'm telling you for the last time: Stand aside, and let me finish my conversation with Mistress Erstenwold here, or things won't go well for either you or her."

"Geran, you're not making things any better!" Mirya hissed.

He ignored her. "I'm not moving," Geran said.

Ignoring the dark looks the Veruna men shared with each other, Geran emptied his mind of distractions and concentrated on the secret arcane syllables he'd studied for so many months in the starlit glens of Myth Drannor. It was not enough to know the words; to invoke their magic, one also had to understand the strange associations of thought that gave the ancient words their power, then hurl the focused might of one's will at the combination of symbol and meaning. *"Theillalagh na drendir,"* he said aloud, clearly, his voice strong and confident in the ancient Elvish.

A faint veil of violet mist coalesced around him, growing stronger and brighter, shaping itself into hundreds of scale-like shards of diamond-bright force that rippled and cascaded from his shoulders to his knees. The elf swordmages knew the incantation as the Scales of the Dragon. It armored him as well as the finest dwarf-wrought plate.

"Did you hear that, Bann?" said the Veruna armsman by the back of the store. The man recoiled two steps. "It's elven witchery! He's a mage of some sort!"

"Steady, lads," the lead armsman, Bann—or so Geran guessed—said. His voice was steady, but his eyes narrowed, and he suppressed a small shiver. Slowly he drew his blade, a sturdy basket-hilted broadsword, careful to keep the point to the gleaming wooden floor. "Wizards are just men. They can bleed and die like anyone else."

"We'll see," Geran replied. *"Ilyeith sannoghan!"* He swept out his elven blade as he spoke the spell, and the subtly curved steel began to crackle with dancing sparks of yellow-white, almost as if he'd parried a bolt of lightning. In a voice as quiet as death he promised, "The next man who damages Erstenwold property will regret it for the rest of his life."

The Veruna armsmen exchanged glances and hesitated. None seemed willing to be the first to try Geran's steel, not while shimmering veils of magic shrouded him and brilliant sparks danced like fireflies along his blade. The armsman Bann met Geran's gaze with a fierce glare. "Fair is fair," he grated. "We told you our colors. So whose colors do you wear, wizard?"

"None but my own," Geran snarled. He shifted his feet, and raised his blade into a high guard.

"Stop it!" Mirya barked. "I'll not have this nonsense in my store! Take your quarrel to the street, all of you!"

No one moved. Mirya snorted in disgust, slid a few steps along the countertop, and pointed at Geran. "Oh, by all nine of the screaming hells. He wears no colors because he's Geran Hulmaster, kin of the harmach," she said to Bann and the other Veruna men. "Think on that before you strike!"

Geran scowled and moved away. "Stand aside, Mirya. I know what I'm doing. This'll be over with soon enough."

"The harmach's nephew?" the armsman by the door said. He frowned. "Bann, I'm not sure about this. Someone cut up the Chainsmen last night. I heard it was him. And what'll the townsfolk do if we hurt him?"

"If he chooses the quarrel, we've broken no laws," Bann said.

"Aye, but Lady Darsi'll have your heads if you lay a finger on him without her permission!" Mirya retorted.

That dart found its mark. The Veruna man winced, and uncertainty flickered across his face. He glared at Geran a moment longer, and then he contemptuously spun on his heel and slammed his sword back into the sheath. "You might be surprised, Mistress Erstenwold," he said to Mirya. He angrily jerked his head toward the door. "Come on, lads. We'll just come back sometime when Mistress Erstenwold isn't so busy."

The Veruna man strode out of the store, sparing Geran one more look before he bulled his way into the street. The other two blades followed him. Geran watched them pause and speak together for a moment out in the street before they turned and left together. He sighed and released the spells he'd been holding. With a simple flourish he returned his sword to the scabbard. "I suppose that's done for now," he said.

Mirya watched the Veruna armsmen leave, her face a tight mask of disapproval. "And when did you become a wizard?" she demanded.

Geran shrugged. "I know a few shields and evocations, but I'm no wizard. Sword magic is all the magic I can master."

Her eyes fell to the blade at Geran's hip, and she studied him more thoughtfully. "I've heard stories of elven swordmagic," Mirya finally said. "I thought the elves weren't in the way of sharing their magic with outsiders. Is the sword enchanted?"

"The lightning was a spell of mine, not the sword. But, since you ask—yes, the blade's enchanted. I earned it in the service of the coronal." He halted, unsure what else he could add. The people of Hulburg knew elves and elven ways only by what they heard from merchants of Hillsfar or Mulmaster, and the folk of those cities had good reason to fear the wrath of the elves. Consequently elves were likewise regarded as mythical and perilous in Hulburg too.

I'm going to have to be careful about saying too much about my time in Myth Drannor, he realized. He grimaced and moved on. "The Veruna men shouldn't trouble you for a while. I've dealt with their kind before."

"Well, that's helpful," Mirya said in a sarcastic voice. "And what do you think's going to happen when they come back after you've gone away again? I'll tell you, Geran Hulmaster: They'll hold me to account for your nonsense. That's what."

"If you have to, tell them that I interfered without your blessing," he said sharply. He'd expected at least a little gratitude for his trouble, after all. "It's true enough."

"It's not so simple, and you know it." Mirya clenched her fists in her apron. "You've been gone for ten years, and you're sure to be gone again before the month's out. I don't need you to pick a fight and then sail off, leaving it to me!"

Geran snorted. "If you beg forgiveness for standing up to a bully, you're asking him to rob you again. You should know that, Mirya."

"You've not been here, Geran, and you don't have half an idea of what's going on in this town!" Mirya snapped. "And it's not just my own neck that I'm worried for. What if those black-hearted scoundrels thought to teach me a lesson by hurting Selsha? Now how could I live with myself if I let her get hurt on account of my stubbornness? Or yours?"

"All right, then. I'll make sure that I don't involve you in my quarrels, Mirya. But I'll be damned if I'll stand still and watch some Mulmasterite thugs threaten my friends right in front of me. I promise you I'll make sure my fights are finished before I go." Geran shook his head and stormed away. He tried not to slam the door behind him, but he didn't quite succeed. Mirya shouted something after him, but he turned back toward Griffonwatch and set off without looking back.

Slavers in the Tailings, the Shieldsworn keeping no laws within the town's walls, and thugs dressed in the colors of foreign companies extorting native-born Hulburgans. Somewhere at the back of it all, Jarad Erstenwold had been murdered in the Highfells by tomb robbers. Geran fumed silently as he shouldered his way through the narrow streets. It seemed that looking after Jarad's affairs might take longer than he'd thought.

Five

13 Ches, the Year of the Ageless One

The day after the encounter at Erstenwold's, Geran rose early and spent half an hour practicing his weapon-forms in a little-used court on the castle's south face. When he finished, he returned to his chambers, splashed himself with cold water for a teeth-chattering bath, and dressed. Then, before leaving his rooms, he took a large book written in Elvish from his baggage. Geran spent an hour studying the words and symbols from the spellbook, pressing into his mind the arcane phrasings and signs he would need to unlock his magic quickly and surely should he need it. Given what he'd seen of the state of affairs in Hulburg so far, it seemed wise to be ready for anything.

With the swordmagic spells fixed in his mind, Geran took a few moments to renew the protective charms he usually maintained from day to day. He quickly rewove wardings of keen perception and deflection, defenses that just might save him from a dagger in the back or see him through an unexpected skirmish. His battle-shields were much more powerful, of course, but he couldn't maintain them for long; the wardings he could wear all day, like an invisible shirt of light mail. He returned his spellbook to the trunk at the foot of his bed and whispered a locking spell out of habit.

"All right," he said aloud. "Now for some breakfast."

He trotted down the stairs leading from his old bedchamber to the great room in the Harmach's Tower, where the family normally took their meals. Hamil was ahead of him, already finished with his own breakfast. The halfling was engaged in a game of dragon's-teeth with Geran's young cousin Kirr, who chortled with delight every time he found an opportunity to put one of his own markers on top of Hamil's. Somehow the halfling never failed to provide the young lad plenty of opportunities to take his pieces.

Hamil looked up at Geran with a doleful frown. "It seems I've fallen into the hands of a master strategist," he said. "I don't doubt that this young fellow will grow up to be the greatest general since Azoun of Cormyr. Neighboring lands should sue for peace now, while his terms remain generous."

"That's right!" Kirr declared. "Ha! You missed another one, Hamil!" He plunked a red tile down on top of one of Hamil's white ones.

"What—but how? You fiend! You have captured my last white!" the halfling spluttered in feigned outrage. The young boy cackled in reply, almost helpless with delight at his own cunning. His older sister, Natali, studied Hamil suspiciously while she arranged her own pieces for the next match, clearly aware that the halfling was throwing the game but wise enough not to say so right before she got a chance to play him.

Geran shook his head. In a hundred years he never would have guessed that Hamil had a weakness for children. He helped himself to a broad plate of honeycakes, bacon, and eggs from the breakfast service and sat down near the game to watch as he ate. "A word of advice, Kirr," he said between mouthfuls. "If Hamil loses again but suggests that maybe you should play for coin next time, say no."

The halfling snorted. "Even I am not that underhanded, Geran!"

"Do they play dragon's-teeth in Tantras, Geran?" Natali asked. She was quieter than her younger brother, but in two brief evenings Geran had already learned that she had a quick and lively sense of curiosity and never forgot a word she heard. Where Kirr was constantly in motion, fidgeting and standing and sitting and pushing tiles together when it wasn't his turn, Natali held herself as still as a falcon watching a mouse.

Geran nodded. "Yes, indeed. And people play dragon's-teeth in most other places I've visited too. In the Moonsea it's regarded as a children's game, but if you go down to Turmish or Airspur you'll see grown men playing all afternoon. They take tremendous pride in playing well, and sometimes they gamble bags of gold on games. The marks on the tiles are different, but the game's pretty much the same everywhere you go."

"Where do the marks on the tiles come from?"

He smiled at that, wondering why in the world she thought he might know. "I've heard that long ago they were runes in Dwarvish, but they've changed over the years. Dragon's-teeth is an old dwarven game. It's said that once upon a time dwarf merchants used the runes and tiles to strike bargains and keep accounts with each other."

The young girl studied the ivory tiles intently, her brow furrowed. "How could you make trades by playing dragon's-teeth?"

"I don't know, Natali. Maybe a dwarf could tell you."

He heard a light, quick step approaching and looked up to see a blonde woman in a mail shirt trotting up the steps. Geran swung his legs over the bench and stood. "Kara! It's good to see you!"

Kara Hulmaster smiled broadly when she caught sight of him and quickly crossed the room to throw her arms around him in a rib-cracking hug. "Geran! You're here!" she laughed. She was not much more than about five-and-a-half feet in height, but she had wide, strong shoulders and an acrobat's compact build, and when she squeezed, Geran had a hard time taking a good breath. "It's been years!"

"Too long, I know," he admitted. He returned her embrace and then stepped back to look at her. Her hair was paler than he remembered, bleached by long months spent outside beneath the sun every year, and laugh lines gathered at the corners of her eyes. Kara had the squarish face and fine, narrow nose of the Hulmasters, but her strikingly luminous eyes glowed an eerie azure with the spellscar she had inherited from her father. The serpentlike blue mark entwined her lower left arm and covered the back of her left hand, beautiful and sinister at the same time. Two or three generations past, someone in her father's line had come in contact with the virulent, unchecked Spellplague and had been changed by it. As far as Geran knew, Kara's father had never even known it himself—the Spellplague was capricious that way. Certainly Harmach Grigor never would have permitted his sister Terena to marry a man known to carry the defect of a spellscar. But no one had known the danger until Kara's spellscar had manifested early in her thirteenth year.

"I heard about Jarad," he told her. "I've come to pay my respects and look after anything that needs looking after."

"I should've known you'd come home," Kara said with a sigh. "I'm sorry,

Geran. I wish you were here for a happier reason." She glanced over to the table and noticed Hamil with Kirr and Natali. "Who's your friend?"

"My apologies. Kara, this is Hamil Alderheart. Hamil, this is my cousin, Kara Hulmaster."

Hamil slid off the bench, took Kara's hand, and kissed it lightly. "I'm pleased to make your acquaintance, Lady Kara," he said. If he was startled by her spellscar, he was careful not to show it. "Geran has told me a lot about you, but his reports simply don't do you justice. I am your servant."

Kara raised an eyebrow. "Why thank you, Master Alderheart."

Geran rolled his eyes. Hamil had never met a handsome woman he didn't try to charm, regardless of race or station. It was simply Hamil's nature. Geran had even known Hamil to court human women before, although the halfling preferred ladies not much more than five feet or so in height; Kara was really a little too tall for him. The swordmage cleared his throat and said, "Kara, I heard you were checking up on the border posts when we arrived. Is everything well?"

Kara shrugged. "It's been surprisingly quiet. I spent three days prowling around the watchtowers, and I didn't see or hear anything. Usually the tribes send out their scouts and hunters as soon as the snows melt. In any event, until the harmach names a new captain for the Shieldsworn, I'm standing in, so I wanted to take a good look for myself."

"I've been doing some of that too over the last couple days. The town isn't what I remember."

"A lot's changed in the last few years." Kara started to say more but thought better of it. Instead, she asked, "So what are you doing today?"

"I'm going to drive out to Keldon Head and visit Jarad's grave. I should've done it yesterday."

Kara gave him a small nod. "I'll ride with you, if you like. I can show you where it is."

"I'll be glad for your company," Geran told her. He quickly finished his breakfast and said his goodbyes to Natali and Kirr. Then he, Hamil, and Kara threw on cloaks and headed down to the stable.

They harnessed a pair of horses to an old two-wheeled buggy they found in the musty carriage house. Hamil scrambled onto the quarter-bench behind Geran and Kara, since it would have been a tight fit with all three of them in the single full seat. Kara took the reins and drove out under

Griffonwatch's gates into the bright morning. It was another cold and cloudless day, with a brisk westerly breeze raising whitecaps on the Moonsea. The *clip-clop* of hooves on stone and jingle of the harness preceded them as they rode down the causeway winding around Griffonwatch's crag.

Geran watched the town clatter past as Kara followed the same route he'd taken the previous day. The town seemed just as full as before. "What are all these people doing here?" he wondered aloud. "Is there a gold strike I haven't heard about? A war somewhere that people are fleeing from? It must be *something.*"

Kara glanced sharply at him. "Mostly it's the timber concessions," she said. "My stepbrother's idea. A few years ago he urged Harmach Grigor to rent logging rights in the Hulmaster forestland to foreign merchants. All the Moonsea cities are desperate for wood, especially since Myth Drannor put the woods of the Elven Court under its protection."

"We deal in timber sometimes down in the Vast," Hamil observed. "It doesn't hurt that Sembia's demand is driving up the prices everywhere." Geran looked back to Hamil, and the halfling shrugged. "While you were strolling around the town, I spent my day talking to the clerks and superintendents of the merchant yards. I was curious about whether the Red Sails ought to do some business up this way. Sembia is ten times as big as the whole Moonsea together and just as hungry for wood—shades or no shades. We should think about it."

"Which costers are here now?" Geran asked Kara.

"House Verunas of Mulmaster, the Double Moon Coster, House Jannarsk of Phlan, and a few others moved into town to handle the trade in timber," said Kara. "They shipped in poor laborers from the larger cities to cut timber, drive wagons, work in the yards and on the docks. And of course those laborers bring others with them, tailors and grocers, smiths and wainwrights, brewers and cooks. . . . In the last year or two the harmach's let out some mining concessions too, and the big merchant houses and costers are taking advantage of those as fast as they can."

"They seem to be doing well," Hamil observed. "The harmach must be making a fortune on his rents."

Kara shook her head. "Not as much as you might think. To pay off old debts the harmach borrowed heavily from the merchant guilds, and he had to rent out the concessions for a pittance by way of payment. The foreign merchants are keeping the better part of what they're cutting down in our forests and digging out of our ground. Except, of course, for the so-called 'licensing fees' Sergen and his Merchant Council capture from the whole business."

They came to the Burned Bridge and drove over the rickety wooden decking. It was covered by a dilapidated roof, and the hoofbeats echoed in the shadows of the bridge. Geran scratched at his jaw, thinking. He didn't like the idea of using Hulmaster land in such a way, especially if the harmach saw little return on the rights he rented out, but it wasn't really his place to say if it was a good idea or not. "What's Sergen's connection to the Merchant Council?"

"He's the keeper of duties—the harmach's representative on the council. Uncle Grigor put him in charge of releasing concessions, negotiating their prices, and administering the resulting trade."

So your cousin decides which properties will be up for bidding, who can purchase a concession, how much they'll pay the harmach, and how much they'll pay the council he presides over? Hamil observed silently. *If he were a corrupt man, that would be an awful temptation. I'm sure that isn't the case, though.*

Geran glanced back at his friend but didn't reply. He was not at all sure that Sergen wasn't corruptible. A younger, more vigorous harmach might have been vigilant enough to check any ignoble impulses someone in Sergen's position could fall prey to . . . but Grigor was not a young man anymore, and it seemed he relied on Sergen to look after his interests for him.

They drove on in silence for a time and began to climb again. The road wound through the mournful Spires on the town's western side, then followed the flanks of Keldon Head, the windswept promontory that sheltered Hulburg and its bay. The town's cemetery was atop the long, bare hill. A long time ago the ruins surrounding Hulburg had been plagued by undead, and so the townsfolk chose to bury their dead in the safe ground of the hilltop, well outside any lingering influences from the days before the town's refounding a hundred years ago. The cheerless stone markers and weathered mausoleums of the cemetery rose into view as the carriage neared the hilltop.

"Kara," Geran said quietly, "what can you tell me about Jarad's death? The harmach said that he was found alone in the Highfells, but that's all I know."

Kara briefly met his eyes, then sighed and returned her gaze to the road. "A shepherd found him by the door of a barrow mound up in the east Highfells, perhaps five or six miles from town. We've had a rash of crypt-breaking in the last few months—someone's been opening barrows and tombs, looking for funereal treasure, I suppose. You know how dangerous that can be in Hulburg, so Jarad began to search for those responsible. We think he finally managed to catch the tomb robbers in the act, but he was overpowered and killed."

"He took no one with him?" Hamil asked.

"No, he was alone. I don't know if he just chanced upon the tomb robbers, decided to set watch on a barrow he thought they might visit, or heard some rumor that led him to that spot."

The halfling nodded, thinking. Kara drove the carriage up to the cemetery gates and halted the team. She set the brake and hopped down; Geran and Hamil followed. "This way," she said.

The sunshine was bright on top of the hill, and the wind rustled and hissed through the long grasses. They followed Kara through rows of plain stone markers, some crumbling beneath decades of moss and weathering, others bright and new. She stopped by a raised stone bier surmounted by a heavy sepulcher of new white stone, its lid inscribed with Amaunator's sunburst emblem. Lettering chiseled carefully at the foot of the tomb read simply:

Jarad Erstenwold, Captain of the Shieldsworn.
His valor, compassion, and faithfulness
shall not be forgotten.

"Uncle Grigor paid for the monument," Kara said quietly. "He thought the world of Jarad. It's been hard for him."

Geran stood silent for a long moment. He reached out and rested his hand on the cold stone. It simply didn't seem possible that Jarad truly rested under that heavy slab. Behind him, Kara and Hamil exchanged looks and retreated a short distance, leaving him alone with his old friend. "Jarad," he whispered. He felt as if he should say something more, maybe give in to tears or try to find some shadow of a smile in a good memory, but there was nothing in his heart except a dull, cold ache. He let his fingers brush over the sun symbol atop the tomb, following the design aimlessly. I never knew he thought of himself as a follower of Amaunator, Geran reflected. Jarad was not a particularly religious man. Was it something the harmach had picked out for him? Or Mirya? Or the Tresterfins? He was engaged when he was killed, after all.

I wonder if I would have come home for his wedding, Geran thought dully. He hoped he would have. But ever since the terrible day when he'd left Myth Drannor, he'd avoided things that reminded him of who he used to be. Maybe he wouldn't have shown up after all.

"I'm sorry for that, Jarad," Geran said to the cold stone. "You deserved better from me. Everyone here did, I think." He heard the steady rhythm of hooves on stone and looked up. Someone else was driving up to the cemetery in a simple wagon. He put it out of his mind and let his hand fall from the stone.

"Ten years ago I would've followed the men who killed you to the ends of the world," he murmured softly. "I think you'd want me to look after things before I set out again. I'll see what I can do. And if I happen to run across the men you met out in the Highfells while I'm at it, well, so much the better."

Footsteps swished through the long grass. Geran looked up again. Mirya Erstenwold stood watching him, a small bunch of wildflowers in her hands. She dropped her gaze to the ground and said, "I'm sorry. I didn't mean to interrupt you."

"It's nothing." Geran noticed a small stone vase at the foot of the tomb, near where he stood. A small spray of wildflowers rested there, faded with the weather. He retreated a few steps and made room for her. "I'll leave."

"There's no need for that." She knelt by the foot of the tomb and began to remove the old flowers from the vase. "I met your friend Hamil. He seems a good man."

"You don't know him very well yet, then."

Mirya gave him a bleak smile. She replaced the old bouquet with the fresh one and took a moment to arrange the flowers. "I've come up here once a month since my mother passed," she said without looking at him. "It's a fair spot in the summertime. Sometimes I'll bring Selsha for a picnic."

"Did she know Jarad well?" Geran asked.

Mirya closed her eyes and nodded. "Aye. He supped with us once or twice a tenday and was always stopping by the warehouse. She cried for days when I told her that he was gone."

Geran's stern resolve cracked at the idea of a heartbroken little girl who'd never see someone she loved again and couldn't understand why he wasn't coming home. It ached like a cold knife in the center of his chest. He was a grown man, and he'd seen his share of death and misfortune, but the grief of a child was a damned hard thing to dwell on. He sank down against an old moss-covered tomb next to Jarad's with his hand over his eyes.

"Ah, Mirya, I'm so sorry," he breathed. "If I'd been here. . . ."

Mirya watched him in silence, and her stern expression softened. "Geran, what happened to Jarad was no fault of yours. Aye, things might've been different if you'd been here in Hulburg. But if you hadn't gone off to find your fortune in the south, who's to say that someone else wouldn't have died because you weren't there to stand by their side? Who in turn might have died because those people didn't live? And even if you'd come home to Hulburg before now, well, fate might have called you and Jarad to some ill end years ago. Why, if I hadn't—" Mirya stopped herself abruptly and sighed. She rose and brushed her hands against her skirts. "Anyway, there's no point to wishing on might-have-beens."

He looked down between his boots at the wiry grass, growing by a weathered stone marker so old that its inscription was only a set of illegible dimples in its surface. He knew that Mirya was right, and that there was no telling how things could have turned out if he'd made different choices . . . the duel against Rhovann in the glades of Myth Drannor, for example. He knew that he had no real cause to blame himself for failing Jarad. But it was the simplest and straightest course for his grief.

"I know you're right," he said. "I know it. But somehow I can't help but feel that this didn't have to happen." He kicked idly at the grass, pushed himself upright, and rubbed his hand across his eyes. "I'll be on my way."

She met his eyes briefly and found a small smile for him. "Take care of yourself, Geran Hulmaster."

Geran took a deep breath, turned, and made his way to the carriage where Kara and Hamil waited. They watched him pull himself up into the seat, adjusting his cloak to keep his sword arm free. "I'm ready to go," he said to Kara.

Kara nodded and said, "We can come back any time you want." She took the reins in hand.

"Geran, wait!" Mirya hurried up to the carriage, holding her skirts. She stopped and studied him, evidently considering what she wanted to say. Finally she spoke. "Listen, likely there's nothing at all to what I aim to tell you, but I thought you ought to know."

"What is it?" he asked.

"Several days past, I thought I saw something . . . Jarad had an elf-made dagger that he often wore. It was a handsome thing with a hilt of silver wire and a pommel in the shape of a sprig of holly. I think he got it from you."

Geran leaned forward in the seat. "Yes, he did. I sent him that blade shortly after I arrived in Myth Drannor. It was nothing, really, just an ordinary dagger of a coronal's guardsman, but I wanted to send him something elf-made, something to show that I'd visited the city of the elves. When we were boys we always talked about going there someday."

"It was nought to you, perhaps, but Jarad treasured it. He wore it at his belt always." Mirya's voice grew flat. "I think I saw that dagger on the hip of a hired sword by the name of Anfel Urdinger. He's in the pay of House Veruna. He and a few other Verunas were keeping watch on Erstenwold's from across the street. Like as not they were keeping count of my business to work out the Merchant Council's cut."

Hamil looked at Geran. "If it's a common design as you say, it may not be the same dagger. Or even if it is, it's possible that this man Urdinger simply got it from someone else—won it throwing dice, traded for it, stole it, who knows?"

"Aye, your friend may have the right of it," Mirya acknowledged. "But this I do know: Jarad wasn't afraid to interfere with Merchant Council business when he had a mind to, and interfering with Merchant Council business means interfering with Veruna business. If you mean to start asking questions, then you might start with asking whether House Veruna is interested in tomb-breaking out in the Highfells."

"Mirya, you should've told me about this," Kara said with a frown. "If there's any reason to suspect Urdinger, I need to know. Do you realize what you're suggesting? If you're right, House Veruna's armsmen ambushed and killed the captain of the Shieldsworn. That's a direct attack on the harmach."

"You were away up at the northern posts, Kara," Mirya replied. "Besides, what I saw's no proof of anything. Even if I've got the right of it, well, as Hamil said, Urdinger could claim that he came by that dagger in any number of ways. All I've got are my suspicions."

Geran met Mirya's eyes. "I take your suspicions seriously, Mirya. I'll remember what you've told me. And I'll keep my eyes open for this fellow Urdinger. He's got some questions to answer."

Kara shifted in her seat to look at both Geran and Mirya. Her armor rasped and jingled. "Geran, you've got to move with care," she said. "You can't just challenge this man in the street, regardless of Mirya's suspicions. The harmach's law applies to you as well as everyone in Hulburg—especially to you, since we can't afford to have anyone say the Hulmasters are above the law in this city. Besides, you might be playing into House Veruna's hands. Someone arranged for Isolmar to meet a professional duelist four years ago. Whoever arranged that for Harmach Grigor's own son wouldn't hesitate to arrange something similar for you."

"I hear you, Kara. I'll choose my steps carefully, never you fear." Geran leaned back in his seat and motioned at the road leading back down to the town below. "Now, before I go looking for this Veruna man, I want to take a look at the place where Jarad was found. Could you take me to the barrow?"

Kara nodded once and flicked the reins. The horses whickered and leaned into the traces, trotting on the mossy old cobblestones. As they turned out of the cemetery gate and began to descend, Geran glanced back up the hill at the lonely stone markers amid the long grass. Mirya stood there with the dead, faded wildflowers in her hands, watching him drive away until a bend in the road hid her from his view.

Six

13 Ches, the Year of the Ageless One

Noon was approaching when Sergen Hulmaster's chamberlain informed him that Lady Darsi's carriage was hurrying up the long drive leading to the broad porch of his villa. Sergen arose from his bath, allowed the bath attendants he'd chosen for the morning to dry him and drape a robe over his shoulders, and dismissed them with an absent wave. As the girls hurried away, he belted his robe, stepped into slippers warmed by the fire, and donned a plush lounging coat against the cold. Then he went to see to his guest.

Darsi Veruna waited in the house's great room, sipping from a goblet of mulled wine already provided by Sergen's servants. She wore a long green winter dress with a subtle trim of ermine fur at collar and cuff, with a matching fur-trimmed hat over her long, golden hair. "Ah, there you are, Sergen," she said in a rich, melodious voice. "Have I taken you from your morning's sport?"

Sergen made a small gesture of dismissal. "It's nothing, my dear. To tell the truth, I am rather bored with my attendants." He drifted over to the smorgasbord, which his servants set each day whether he intended to eat or not, and helped himself to a goblet of the warmed wine as well. A large, well-fed fire and bearhide rugs helped to keep the early spring cold at bay, but a warm goblet of wine was just the thing to chase away the last hint of a chill. He shook out his still-damp hair and said, "Tell me, what brings you to my humble home? How may I be of service to you, my lady?"

Darsi smiled at that and seated herself in a fine Turmishan couch by the fire. She removed her hat; her maidservant silently took it from her hand and withdrew again. Her hair was her best feature, a splendid cascade of molten gold that fell in soft waves to a handspan below the nape of her slender neck. Twenty years ago she had been a stunning beauty, a green-eyed enchantress with a heart-shaped face and perfect features. Men had killed to win the chance to woo her. She was still an exceptionally attractive woman, but the girlish softness had worn away from her features, and the barest hint of frown lines had crept into her face. "Well, my lord Hulmaster, it seems that your long-lost cousin Geran saw fit to stop my armsmen from collecting council dues from a small provisioner on Plank Street—Erstenwold's, in fact. And I've just received a note from your sister requesting an explanation for my armsmen's behavior."

Sergen grimaced. "I heard the same story. What will you tell my dear sister?"

"I'll tell her that armsmen in my employ are under strict instructions to follow all local laws, and that if in fact these three men conducted themselves as reported, then it was purely on their own initiative and for their own personal gain. Should their misconduct be proven, I will of course discharge them from my service immediately."

"Indeed." Sergen allowed himself a long, low chuckle. The situation was not amusing at all, really, but the audacity of Darsi Veruna's lies deserved some measure of approbation. Of course she'd known exactly what the three armsmen were up to, but Kara could never *prove* that she did. And without ironclad proof, well, the harmach and his agents simply lacked the political strength to accuse a powerful merchant company like House Veruna of unsavory conduct. Oh, Kara could lay out charges on behalf of their uncle, and in all likelihood she would be widely believed. But Darsi Veruna would simply hand over a scapegoat or three and House Veruna would carry on with its business. "I wonder what my stepsister will say to that?" he asked aloud.

"I doubt she'll be pleased," Darsi replied. Though her manner was cool and calm, Sergen knew her well enough to recognize the subtle sharpness of her tone as a sign of intense annoyance. "Perhaps I should curtail my efforts to enforce council edicts. If my men are discovered in the very act of extortion—or discovered in some of our less savory activities—even your feeble old uncle will have to do something."

Sergen's amusement vanished. "The council business is not that important, Darsi, but the search for the book must not be delayed. Need I remind you whom we are dealing with?"

"A reckless gamble, in my estimation. House Veruna is deeply invested in opening this rude little backwater of a town, Sergen. We've done well here, but we've spent a fortune to get to this point. If your uncle decides to slap my wrist, it could be extremely costly for my family."

"When I am harmach, any such costs you suffer will be repaid, dear Darsi." Now Sergen understood her true concern. The Verunas were nobles of Mulmaster, the powerful city-state across the Moonsea from Hulburg. Like several other important families of Mulmaster, their power was counted in the profitability of their trading ventures throughout the region. Setbacks Veruna experienced in Hulburg would reflect poorly on Darsi and damage her standing among her well-born but viciously competitive relations. It was time to remind her of the stakes of the game. "How much gold would pour into House Veruna's coffers if your rivals were suddenly subjected to a ruinous tariff? Or if you were given the opportunity to buy out the leases on their logging and mineral rights? A great prize is worth a modest risk, my dear; fortune favors the bold. Should my ploy work, you will make House Veruna the most powerful merchant company in the Moonsea by the end of the year."

"But first you must become harmach." Darsi Veruna folded her hands in her lap and regarded him with her catlike eyes for a long time, weighing his chances. Sergen met her gaze without flinching. Finally she inclined her head subtly, acknowledging his point. Veruna was the strongest coster in Hulburg, but it was only one of many in Mulmaster. It might cost her a small fortune to put Sergen on the throne, but it would give her a tremendous advantage over her rivals if she succeeded. "Speaking of which . . . tell me about your cousin Geran."

"A thickheaded fool who never had to work for anything in his life," Sergen said. He had no use for any of the so-called "true" Hulmasters, even though he'd claimed the Hulmaster name from the time he'd been twelve. "Don't worry about Geran. He left Hulburg ten years ago; he'll soon enough be on his way."

"Where has he been for all this time?" Darsi asked. "What's he been doing?"

"Supposedly, soon after he left to see the world, he fell in with a band of adventurers who called themselves the Company of the Dragon Shield. He won himself a small fortune by plundering some dismal dungeon in the Vast." Sergen swirled his wine in the goblet, stirring up the spices. He'd made inquiries over the last few years to find out more about where his so-called cousin had vanished to. "Seven years ago he bought an owner's share in the Red Sail Coster of Tantras and enjoyed some small success as a merchant speculating in various cargoes on the Sea of Fallen Stars."

"The Red Sails," Darsi murmured. "Yes, I know them. Go on."

"Geran's father, Bernov Hulmaster, was killed in a skirmish about eight and a half years ago. Geran came home for the funeral but stayed only a few days before returning to Tantras. His mother retired to an Ilmateran convent near Thentia soon after that. Then Geran simply vanished for several years, leaving the Red Sail Coster in the hands of his partners. No one knew where he'd gone, but a year ago last Uktar he resurfaced in Tantras. I learned that he'd been in Myth Drannor, where he'd won the favor of the coronal. There were rumors that he was suddenly exiled. I heard stories of a feud with a rival, a duel fought for the favor of an elf princess, even whispers of some black curse hanging over him that forced the coronal to send him away." Sergen smiled darkly. "I still don't have the whole tale, but it seems clear that Geran left Myth Drannor under a cloud. You should have seen his face when I asked him about it."

"My armsmen told me that he used magic when he confronted them in Erstenwold's shop," Darsi said, gazing thoughtfully down at her goblet. "They said he carried a blade of elven steel. And I've heard that he used the same sort of swordmagic against the Crimson Chains he and his little halfling friend cut apart in the Tailings. Is that something he learned in Myth Drannor?"

Sergen shrugged. "I suspect the reports are exaggerated, since I've never known him to demonstrate any such ability. I doubt that Geran would have the aptitude or discipline to learn magic, but I suppose he might have found an enchanted sword during his travels."

"So what does his return signify for you?" Darsi asked.

"Most likely nothing. I expect that Geran will tire of Hulburg and go back to Tantras, Myth Drannor, or anywhere else but here soon enough. There is little to hold him here. He'll be gone within a tenday."

"Most likely," Darsi agreed in a pleasant voice. "But what if he decides to stay? What happens if you find yourself sharing your family responsibilities with another capable Hulmaster who's not a spellscarred bitch? Is there any chance that Grigor might decide that Geran would make a better regent for his grandson, Kirr, than you? Or, for that matter, a better harmach?" Her eyes glittered cruelly as she delivered the barb.

"Unthinkable!" Sergen snapped. "I've stayed in this miserable, sodden dungheap of a town for years, looking after all the business Grigor was too stupid or inattentive to look after for himself. Without me the family would be penniless and Hulburg would still be a wretched little backwater."

"Geran is of the Hulmaster blood, and you are not."

"You need not remind me." Sergen paced away from the fire, glaring at the row of bright windows that faced out over the town. He'd come to Hulburg as a boy of twelve, when his father, Kamoth—a merchant and adventurer from Hillsfar—married the harmach's widowed sister, Terena. The marriage had not gone well. Kamoth was caught plotting against the harmach and fled Hulburg to escape death or imprisonment. Sergen had been left among his stepfamily, an unwanted interloper in Griffonwatch. No one had ever accused him openly of disloyalty, but he'd heard the whispers and felt the suspicious stares throughout his adolescence. He'd resolved years ago to succeed where Kamoth had failed, but to do that he'd had to embrace the name of the family that had ruined his father. He was long since ready to shed those pretenses and take what was rightfully his.

"Would it be useful if Geran met with some misfortune?" Darsi asked.

Sergen shook his head. "Too obvious," he said. "Everyone remembers all too well how Isolmar Hulmaster met his end, and now that Jarad Erstenwold has been removed . . . how would it look if someone else close to the harmach died under mysterious circumstances? Even if I had nothing to do with it, suspicion would naturally fall on my shoulders."

Darsi rose from the couch and drifted over to where Sergen stood, resting a hand on his shoulder. "It may become unavoidable, if Geran continues to stumble into affairs that are none of his business."

Sergen glanced over his shoulder at her. "Perhaps we should set a spy on him to watch his movements."

"Hmmm, I believe I have just the spy." Darsi slipped her hands around

Sergen's chest and pressed herself close behind him. "I will summon Umbryl and set her on your cousin's trail. And, should Geran prove troublesome, he will never see her claws before she strikes."

"Make certain that your pet knows that she is not to kill Geran unless you order her to," Sergen answered. He turned to face Darsi and slid his hands around her waist. He leaned forward and nuzzled her neck, kissing the base of her throat. "Mmmm. Are you certain that you came here to talk about my cousin? Or did you have some other purpose in mind?"

Darsi let her hands slide inside his robes and caressed him. "I interrupted your bath. The least I can do is to help you finish it."

Seven

13 Ches, the Year of the Ageless One

Since it was still early when Geran, Kara, and Hamil returned to Griffonwatch, they sent to the kitchens for a small sack of food to take with them. They returned the buggy to its house and the horse team to the livery, since no roads led up into the Highfells, and the few tracks that did wind up into the hills and moors were far too difficult for a wagon or carriage. Instead they chose horses from the Shieldsworn stables and saddled their mounts. Kara kept a horse of her own in Griffonwatch, a big roan mare named Dancer that she'd trained for years. Geran chose a strong bay gelding, and for Hamil they found a small, sure-footed mare. Halflings generally found ponies better suited to them than horses, but Hamil had spent enough time around the larger animals to handle them easily enough despite his small stature.

An hour before noon they set off again. This time, instead of turning at the Burned Bridge, they followed the Vale Road north from Hulburg, keeping on the right bank of the Winterspear. The river was shallow and swift, rushing over a stony bed in a broad, braided stream that narrowed quickly as they headed inland. Farms clustered close by the southern end of the valley amid stands of birch and ash, but as they continued northward the farms grew fewer and farther between.

About three miles from Griffonwatch, the road passed through an old ditch-and-berm of earth, now grassy and overgrown. "Lendon's Dike," Geran told Hamil. "My grandfather raised it more than fifty years ago, back when orc raids in the Winterspear Vale were common." He pointed toward the far side of the vale. "Lake Hul lies under the western hills there, so the earthworks run less than two miles."

Hamil studied the old fortifications. "Seem to have had little use of late."

Geran nodded. "Orcs haven't come into the Winterspear Vale in numbers since my father was a young man. The Highfells make for good walls."

A short distance beyond the old dike, Kara turned eastward along a cart track that ran past the long fieldstone cowsheds and hay cribs of an old dairy farm. The track petered out into a footpath and began to climb steeply up the side of the valley. Trees and brush thinned out quickly as they gained height, and soon they were picking their way through the steep meadows and mossy rock outcroppings of the hilltop. From their vantage they could see the broad path of the Winterspear all the way to Hulburg's distant rooftops. Then they crossed over the crest, and they were in the Highfells proper. To the north a long line of low gray downs stretched off until they simply melted into the distance; eastward the rolling downs marched for miles until they began to climb up to meet the wooded ramparts of the Galena Mountains, perhaps twenty miles distant.

Raw, blustery wind whistled through the grass and heather, pushing the brush first one way and then the other. The sky was blue and cloudless, marked only by a distant earthmote drifting aimlessly against the wind. Hamil surveyed the view. "This is the so-called Great Gray Land of Thar? There doesn't seem to be much to see."

"Here, near the Moonsea, the moorlands break up into the steep glens and valleys that we call the Highfells," Kara answered him. The wind blew her hair into her face, but she shook it off, paying no attention to the raw cold. "But if you ride a few more miles north or west of here, yes, you'd be in Thar."

"How far does it run?" the halfling asked.

"From here west to the Dragonspine Mountains and the Ride beyond, close to two hundred miles." Kara turned and pointed off to their right, where the mountains fenced the horizon. "To the mountains, not more than another twenty miles or so. Vaasa's about seventy miles east of us, on the other side of the Galenas."

Hamil waved his hand at the downs ahead. "And to the north?"

"For the most part, more of the same until you reach Glister, a hundred and fifty miles away," Geran said. "There's a shifting stretch of dangerous Spellplague-riddled changeland in the middle of the moor, and a couple of days' ride past Glister there is a much wider stretch of changeland that runs for hundreds and hundreds of miles. All sorts of plaguechanged monsters roam those lands, and sometimes they come down into Thar. No one I know of has ever found out what might be north of *that,* but sooner or later I imagine you would run into the Great Glacier and snows that never melt."

"And no one lives up here?"

"None but orcs and ogres, and their tribes generally keep to the northerly parts of the moorland," Geran answered. "Shepherds and goatherds graze their flocks up here in the summertime, but other than that, the land's not good for much. The soil's thin and poor and doesn't drain well. You'll want to be careful of your mount—this isn't good ground, and there are a thousand places where a horse can snap its ankle."

The halfling silently absorbed the view for a moment. Geran could guess what he was thinking; the idea of so much land that was so wide, so open, and yet so desolate was likely foreign to his experience. Hamil had grown up in the warm forests south of the Sea of Shining Stars; the Moonsea's northern shores must have seemed like the very end of the world to him. For his own part, Geran found the cold, clean air and long views bracing. It was a hard land, to be sure, but it was a simple land. The complexities and confusion of life held less of a grip on his spirit here.

He glanced over to Kara. Since her thirteenth summer, the summer when her spellscar had manifested itself, she'd found a refuge up in those barren and lonely places. Geran and Jarad used to come to the Highfells to savor the independence and freedom the wild country offered. But Kara had taken to spending as much time as she could in the wild land around Hulburg simply because there was no one there to shy away from the deformity of her spellscar. He'd long since learned that Kara's spellscar was not dangerous, but all too many people around Hulburg—or any place, really—regarded the spellscarred with fear and suspicion. It didn't surprise him to see that Kara had continued to seek solitude in the high country in the years that he'd been away from Hulburg.

They continued on, riding more east than north, keeping a cautious pace. No trees grew in the Highfells, of course, but in small hollows or sheltered spots, thick low gorse grew, and sometimes they found small shelters of fieldstone and turf in these places—lodges used by herdsmen in the warmer months. From time to time they came across sudden steep-sided streambeds, narrow and deep, or passed by old cairns and low, rounded barrow mounds. And on one occasion they rode along the rim of a sharp, steep-sided bowl of changeland easily two hundred feet deep, its sides made of glistening blue stone grooved with strange whorls. Geran remembered the place well; one summer afternoon in his fifteenth year, he and Jarad had explored the sinkhole by roping themselves down to its floor, only to find that its lower reaches were honeycombed by crevices where repulsive, silver-winged eel-like creatures laired. They'd had to climb back up with smoking torches clutched in their hands to keep the nasty things from chewing them to pieces.

Another half-hour brought them to the edge of a barrow field, a wide expanse of small burial mounds. The southern borders of Thar were strewn with the ancient tombs left behind by people long since lost to history. Hundreds of the mounds lay within a day's ride of Hulburg. Sometimes dozens stood together within a few hundred yards of each other, and sometimes a single barrow stood all by itself, a dismal and lonely sentinel on the open downs. Geran had never learned why that was so.

Kara stood up in her stirrups, taking a moment to gain her bearings as she studied the barrow field. This one was well ordered; the barrows stood in low rows, serried ranks of weary soldiers standing watch against the cold north wind. She looked left, then right, and nodded to herself. "We're here," she said. "This way."

They followed behind Kara as she rode up to one of the larger barrows. Long ago someone had excavated its door, revealing a low, black opening in the hillside. The whole thing was better than a hundred feet across and almost twenty feet high, which suggested to Geran that someone important had been buried in the mound; most barrows were quite a bit smaller. Kara slid out of her saddle, patted Dancer's muzzle, and made her way slowly into the open space before the barrow's black doorway, her head down and her eyes on the ground. Geran and Hamil dismounted as well and waited for a moment as the ranger studied the moss-covered rocks and wiry grass of the hollow.

"Here," she said over her shoulder. "This is where Jarad was found."

Geran felt a cold shiver in his heart, but he forced his feet into motion. He came up beside Kara, looking at the ground where she pointed. He couldn't see much, but that didn't surprise him; Kara had always been much better at reading tracks than he. Hamil joined them a moment later, squatting to run his fingers lightly over the ground.

"The Shieldsworn sent for me as soon as they learned Jarad had been found," Kara said quietly. "I had a good look at the scene later that day. You can't see much, since it's been almost a month now, and we've had a lot of rain since. But you can still make out the impression in the heather, there, and just a bit of rust from his mail. He'd been here for about two days before he was found."

Geran took a deep breath and straightened up to look around the hollow. "What do you make of it, Kara?"

"Jarad rode up from the south side of the barrow and hitched his horse back behind those boulders there." She pointed at a jumble of gray stone and gorse a couple of bowshots from the door, more or less back in the same direction from which they had just approached. "He approached the barrow on foot, circled the area briefly, and chose a spot where he could lie low and watch the door—over there, in the gorse. There's a depression that would make for good cover. I'll show you."

She led them away from the barrow door about forty yards, angling away to the side, until they stood by a tuft of wiry brush. "He waited here for a short time, perhaps an hour or so. Then a party of five riders approached the barrow from the south and dismounted right in front of the door there—four men and a woman. A fight followed; I think Jarad wounded two men before he was cut down, right where his body was found. No one moved him."

"You're certain of all that?" Hamil asked.

"I told you, I had a good look at the scene."

Geran smiled humorlessly. "What Kara isn't saying, Hamil, is that she's the best tracker between Melvaunt and Vaasa. I'll say it for her. You can consider everything she just said ironclad fact. Though I wouldn't be surprised if she's read a few more pieces of the puzzle she hasn't shared yet, because she can't quite put them together."

"All I have left are guesses," Kara said. "For example, I can't tell you why he rode to this particular barrow and waited here. Nor can I tell you if the riders were the people he was waiting for."

"He might have guessed which barrow the crypt-breakers were likely to try next," Hamil suggested. "Or, more likely, someone told him. He came to this barrow because he expected someone to be here."

"I think you're right, Hamil." Kara gave the halfling a long look. "But that begs the question of whether Jarad's source was sincere or lied to him in order to lure him to a place where he could be ambushed. Either way, it doesn't explain why Jarad broke cover. From this spot he could easily have seen he was outnumbered. With five riders to deal with, Jarad should've stayed in his hiding place. You can see for yourself; if I get down under this brush, you can't see me from in front of the barrow. You would have to be right on top of me to know I was here."

Geran closed his eyes. He found himself imagining the encounter . . . the black doorway in the low, rounded hillside, nervous horses tethered on a line, a sky of sullen, gray-black rain, cold wind making the long grasses ripple and hiss. Jarad lying flat beneath the gorse, cold and wet, a big, strong man with a long braid of straw-colored hair, scowling fiercely at himself as he debated whether to go for help or deal with matters himself. Was it a sudden furious skirmish in the dell when he gave his location away? Or had he challenged the intruders, demanding their surrender? And who were the killers? A band of adventurers passing through, a reckless gang from town, or men sworn to some guild or merchant company? "Jarad was always confident of his sword arm," Geran finally said. "Maybe he was afraid the tomb robbers would elude him again if he rode away to gather more men. Or maybe he thought he could spy them out, mark their faces, and apprehend them later in town."

Or maybe he didn't think the riders were enemies, Hamil said silently to Geran. To Kara, the halfling spoke aloud. "Kara, earlier this morning you said that crypt-breaking was especially dangerous in Hulburg. Why is that?"

"Aesperus, the King in Copper," Kara answered. "He was a fearsome necromancer who ruled over this part of the Moonsea hundreds of years ago. He survives as an undead lich who commands the dead of the barrowfields. Too many things that should lie dead and buried under stone rise and walk the Highfells once their tombs are breached."

"It's one of the few laws the harmachs enforce without mercy," Geran added. "No one is to open a tomb anywhere within land claimed by Hulburg. And it's considered high treason to collect anything of value buried in a barrow."

"Sensible enough, I suppose." Hamil glanced at the barrow and the moorland surrounding the old mound. He shook his head. "A damned lonely place to die."

They stood in silence for a moment, quietly surveyeing the scene. It was the middle of the afternoon; Geran guessed that they'd need to turn for home in an hour or so if they hoped to reach Hulburg before dark. If there was anything to find here, he couldn't imagine what it might be. Kara had been over the ground more than twenty days ago, and if she hadn't found anything more then, he certainly wouldn't now. The wind shifted again and streamed the long grass atop the barrow to the other side, revealing a silver-green underside to the stalks. He shivered, and then his eye fell on the cramped, dark doorway leading into the barrow.

"Kara," he said, "did anyone enter or leave the barrow?"

The ranger nodded. "Yes, the riders did, after they'd killed Jarad. But there isn't much inside, just a short passageway ending at a fieldstone wall. If they were tomb-breakers, they didn't do much to the place before giving up."

"Let's have a look anyway," Geran suggested.

He led the way to the low, overgrown opening. It was half-sunken into the side of the barrow, more like a storm cellar than an actual door. A cold, stale smell clung to the passage. He felt in his belt pouch for a copper coin and whispered the words of a simple light spell—one of the more elementary spells he happened to know. The coin began to shine with a bright yellow radiance, driving the darkness back into the hill. Holding the coin before him, Geran ducked under the heavy stone lintel, his right hand on his sword hilt. Hamil followed close behind him, and Kara hovered in the doorway, a tight frown on her face.

As she'd said, the passage ran straight for a short distance, took a sharp right turn, and ended in a rough wall of stones piled high across the narrow corridor. Geran studied it for a moment, thinking. Something was odd here, he was sure of it. Many barrows were sealed by similar walls across the entranceway; the people who'd interred their chiefs and heroes in such places simply walled them up when the burial rites were over, and then buried the passage they'd used to carry the dead man and his belongings into the burial chamber. He knelt and felt at the floor by the base of the wall. Rock chips and discarded stones littered the ground atop a thin layer of damp dirt.

"Hamil, have a look at this," Geran said. "I think this wall's been taken down and put up again."

The halfling leaned close, studying the loosely piled fieldstone. "You're right. All the dirt and mold from between the stones is knocked out."

Kara leaned over his shoulder. "Yes, I noticed that before. It didn't make sense to me. Why would tomb-breakers put the wall back behind them?"

"Why, indeed," Geran murmured. Because they wanted to keep people out? Or had they wanted to seal something inside? He found a deep, dirt-filled crevice between stones in the wall beside him and wedged the illuminated coin into it to free his hands. "All right, be ready. I'm going to move a few stones and have a look at what's on the other side."

"Geran, that might be dangerous," Kara warned. "You know the harmach's law."

"I know it. But someone knocked this wall down and rebuilt it not too long ago, so it's hardly like we're the first people to open this barrow." Geran found a loose stone near the top and began to pry it out. "Besides, if someone wanted to keep something dangerous inside, I doubt they would have taken the time to pile up rocks here. They'd have run for their horses and ridden off across the Highfells. I think that this wall was piled up here to keep us out, possibly by the men who killed Jarad. I want to know why."

Kara gave him an unhappy look, but she came forward and helped him pry stones away from the wall. Hamil stayed back out of the way, moving the rocks they dislodged back down the passage to keep the way clear. In a few minutes Geran managed to open a sizable hole near the top of the wall. A cold breath of air with the distinct smell of stale meat sighed through the opening.

"I can smell something dead in there," Kara said, grimacing. "Maybe we shouldn't take out any more stones."

Geran paused and listened carefully. It felt cold and the air was tainted . . . but he could not feel anything unnatural waiting in the darkness beyond. He and Hamil had plenty of experience with old crypts and tombs, including some that were haunted by the restless dead. He thought he knew the feel of such creatures close at hand. But to reassure himself, he retrieved his shining coin from the crack where he'd wedged it and held it close to the opening they'd made to peer through to the other side. He couldn't see much yet, just the hint of more passage beyond. "Just a few more," he decided.

"If a wight lunges out and claws off your face, it won't be my fault," Kara muttered. But she returned to the work, worrying free another stone.

Geran did the same, and then he was able to put his shoulder to the remaining mass and shove over most of what was left with a terrible crash and a great cloud of dust and dirt. Coughing, he backed up to let the dust settle.

In the dim yellow light of the spell, they found that the passage ran a bit farther to a burial chamber. Once it might have hidden the funereal wealth of an important chieftain, but it was clear that it had been emptied long ago—likely by the same men who'd originally excavated the mound's doorway, Geran figured. The grave itself was a simple depression in the loose flagstone floor, covered by a chipped slab of roughly cut stone. The three companions spread out through the chamber, silently taking in the scene.

I don't like this, Geran, Hamil whispered in his mind. *You say that the dead in this land don't rest well. We shouldn't be here.*

Something isn't right here, Geran answered him. He'd been in a few barrows long ago, mostly ones long since opened and home to nothing but mice and dust. The harmach's prohibition did not apply to tombs that someone else had already opened, after all. But something in this burial mound was out of place . . . the air was cold, and the smell of death lingered more strongly there. Why does it still smell that way? he wondered. It was hundreds of years old.

"Someone has been in here recently," Kara said. She knelt, her fingers spread over the rough stones of the floor. Black earth and mold filled the crevices between the stones. "The same men who were outside when Jarad was here. I can tell by the bootprints. And there's a lot of old blood here."

The tomb slab, Geran realized. He moved over and crouched beside the heavy stone that covered the grave. "So some old party of tomb-breakers dug out the barrow and removed everything from this chamber," he mused aloud, "but either they didn't take anything from the body under this slab, or they put the slab back when they were finished. Neither seems very likely to me."

Kara glanced over from where she knelt, and she frowned. "No, it's not," she agreed. She moved beside him and looked for herself. "This slab was dragged over and set here not long ago."

"I thought so," Geran answered. He glanced up at Kara and Hamil. "Be ready in case I'm wrong." Then he shifted to get his fingers under the edge of the slab, tested its weight briefly, and breathed, *"Sanhaer astelie!"* Magical strength flooded into his limbs, and with one great heave he rose from his crouch, lifting with the power of his long legs, and threw the heavy slab away from the dank hole beneath. A sickening stench of foul air rose around him.

"Damnation!" Hamil hissed. Only a handful of despoiled bones remained of whatever chieftain had been buried there. But atop the ancient skeleton lay two additional bodies—the corpses of a young woman in a tattered dress of red wool and a short, broad-shouldered man in a shirt of mail. The woman's skin was darkened and tight, and her sightless eyes stared up at the ceiling. Her throat had been cut. The soldier's coat was dyed red from a wound just under his ribs that had left a long scarlet trail down his coat.

The smell was strong and unpleasant, and Geran quickly backed away, covering his mouth and nose. Kara and Hamil did likewise. "Two of Jarad's killers, I suppose," he managed from under his hand.

Kara held her hand over her nose. "I think she's the woman who was with the riders. Her shoes match the marks I found outside. I was wondering why someone up in the Highfells would wear shoes better suited for a dance hall. As for the warrior, he could very well be one of the men injured in the fight in front of the barrow door. Perhaps Jarad managed to mortally wound one of his attackers before they cut him down."

"Do you know the woman?" Geran asked.

Kara shook her head. "No, she could be anybody." She knelt and looked closely at the body. "She's dressed like a townswoman. And her wrists are tied behind her back."

"What of the armsman, Kara?" Hamil asked.

"Look at the mail," Geran answered for her. "It's barred horizontally, Mulman-style." That meant little in and of itself, but it was an unusual style. None of the armorers in Melvaunt or Thentia made their armor in that fashion; it was favored in the city of Mulmaster. He realized that he'd noticed mercenaries wearing Mulman-style mail recently and simply hadn't thought much of it at the time. Thousands of armsmen wore Mulman armor, after all.

The ranger looked at the man's body. "No coin or jewelry that I can see. They didn't bother to strip the armor, but his weapons are gone. An old scar across his cheek . . ." She frowned suddenly and straightened up. "Damn. I think I've seen this man before. It's a little hard to tell in this condition, but that scar, I know I've seen it."

Geran glanced at Hamil then back to Kara. He waited in silence, allowing her to search her memory without interruption. After a moment, she gave a soft snort and nodded. "He's a House Veruna man. I've seen him around town, usually in the company of other Veruna armsmen. Most of them are Mulmasterites and wear mail coats just like this. He left his colors at home, naturally. There's nothing here to positively identify him as House Veruna."

"So, they dragged the dead or dying armsman in here and left his body in the barrow grave. But why was the woman killed?" Geran wondered aloud. "I doubt that she was part of the ambush, since she's hardly dressed for a fight."

"She outlived her usefulness," Hamil said darkly. "The Veruna men brought her here as a prisoner, maybe for the purpose of luring your friend Jarad to this spot. Once they'd killed him, she was nothing more than an inconvenient witness. Her bad fortune, I suppose."

"We only know of one Veruna who was here, and he's in the ground at our feet," Kara answered. "We don't know for sure that the others were Veruna men too."

Geran made a sour face. "I have a strong suspicion about that, especially after what Mirya told me about Jarad's missing dagger."

Kara grimaced, but she didn't debate Geran's point. Instead she stared at the two bodies, her azure eyes gleaming in the dim light. "What I don't understand is why they left Jarad outside," she said. "If they went to the trouble of burying two bodies in here, why not three? Why leave Jarad out in the open to be found? If they'd simply dragged his body in here too, we might still be looking for him."

"That's simple," Hamil said. "They wanted his body found. The killers wanted to send a message, something more pointed than an unsolved disappearance. But why bury these two here, where they might be found?

It would've been better to carry these bodies away and bury them somewhere else."

"It would have been awkward if they'd met somebody else out on the Highfells while carrying the bodies with them?" Geran guessed. "They were lazy? Or perhaps they thought that the harmach's law would keep anyone from looking too closely at the barrow?" He shook his head. "It could be anything. All right, let's have some fresh air while we figure this out."

They withdrew from the barrow chamber and made their way back out from the entrance, climbing into the bright afternoon sunlight. The wind was cool and deliciously fresh after the stale dead murk of the barrow. Geran took several quick strides out into the hollow around the mound, straightening and stretching, before he realized that someone was standing by their horses, watching him. "Hamil!" he hissed.

The halfling stopped close behind him, and Kara halted too. They stared at the man who was watching them. He wasn't human, that much was apparent. His skin had a ruddy brick hue, and two sharp, black horns jutted from his forehead. He dressed in a long coat of bright scarlet embroidered with gold thread over a ruffled white shirt, and his black silk breeches were bloused into low boots of fine leather.

"You should be more careful," the horned man said in a rasping voice. "There are dangerous men abroad these days. They might have been lying in wait for you."

Geran set one hand on the hilt of his sword and slowly moved away from his friends. "Well, it seems that we were fortunate to encounter you instead of them."

"I didn't say I'm not a dangerous man too," the stranger replied. He carried a short, rune-carved staff in the crook of his left arm, but kept it at his side. He nodded at the barrow behind them. "Did you find anything in there? Anything like a book?"

"A book? No, only corpses," said Hamil with a scowl. He shifted behind Kara to hide his knife hand from view.

The horned man snorted impatiently. "Well, of course. Barrows are full of them."

Geran narrowed his eyes. He could make out some of the sigils on the horned man's staff, and he didn't like what he saw. Unless he misjudged the horned man badly, they were dealing with a formidable sorcerer of some sort. Symbols of fire and lightning glinted among the runes.

"Who are you?" Geran challenged. "What are you doing here?"

The sorcerer's nostrils flared. "Who I am is no business but my own. As for what I'm doing here, well, I'm looking for something. But if this barrow's empty, then it would seem I am in the wrong place. I will trouble you no more." With an eye over his shoulder, he turned away and started back down the thready trail.

"Not so fast!" Kara called after him. She hurried after him. "In the name of the harmach, stand where you are! I will have some answers from you!"

The sorcerer glanced back in irritation. "I think not," he said, and he struck his staff to the ground. *"Arkhu zanastar!"* he cried, and then he leaped up into the air. His scarlet coat rippled behind him as he soared off into the sky.

Kara swore and dashed over to where Dancer neighed and pranced nervously, reaching for the bow cased by the saddle. But by the time she retrieved the weapon, the horned sorcerer was only a distant speck in the sky, speeding away over the moorland until he topped a low rise and vanished from view. "Damn," she snarled. "If that . . . *person* . . . was not involved in this somehow, then I'm an orc. What was he, anyway? Some manner of devil?"

Hamil shook his head. "No, a tiefling. They come from the distant east. They've got some infernal blood in their veins, but they're not really devils."

"On the other hand, that fellow was clearly a sorcerer of no small skill," Geran added. "I think you ought to be glad that you didn't have your bow closer to hand. If you'd shot at him, he might have taken offense."

"I don't care who or what he is, I won't stand by and let him spite the harmach's laws," Kara retorted. She returned her bow to its case, still looking after the vanished sorcerer. Her brilliant eyes glowed with anger, and she turned away to collect herself. After a moment she shook herself and looked at Geran. "We should at least take the bodies back to Hulburg for a decent burial. I don't like the idea of leaving the woman out here for Aesperus, and I intend to ask Darsi Veruna how one of her men ended up dead at the scene of Jarad's murder. She still hasn't given me a good answer about the business at Erstenwold's, anyway."

"We might as well get started then, since the afternoon is getting on," Geran answered. They'd have to wrap the bodies well to keep the horses calm, double up on one of the mounts, and they wouldn't make very good speed returning to town. "I'd just as soon not be out on the moors after dark."

"What's our next move, then?" Hamil asked Geran.

"I'm not sure," he admitted. "But I think I'll follow Mirya's advice and try to figure out why Veruna's mercenaries are suddenly interested in barrows."

Eight

14 Ches, the Year of the Ageless One

Sometime in the cold hours before dawn, snow began to fall around Hulburg. When Geran awoke and looked out his window, the higher hilltops were covered with a dusting of white, and fat, wet flakes were sticking along the castle's turrets and rooftops. He performed his morning exercises in a fitful flurry that stopped and started several times as he practiced his forms. Spring snow was not at all unusual for the northern shores of the Moonsea, but it rarely lasted long.

The cold air spurred him fully awake and chased the last dregs of sleepiness from his mind. It had been a long ride back to Hulburg from the barrow the previous evening and a longer night of explanations, as Kara insisted on setting down their recollections of the discovery inside the mound before allowing Geran and Hamil to retire for the evening. She'd also been careful to set down their descriptions of the sinister sorcerer they'd encountered too. Geran had no idea if anything would come of either account. He sincerely doubted that anyone at House Veruna would admit that the dead man was in the barrow on company business, and as for the sorcerer, he doubted whether the Shieldsworn could arrest and hold such a creature against his will. It seemed unlikely that he had anything to do with Jarad's murder or the deaths of the Veruna armsman and the townswoman, simply because Geran couldn't imagine why the fellow would return to the scene or ask them whether they'd found a book. He finally gave up with a shrug. Strange folk roamed the Highfells at times; either they'd see him again, or they wouldn't, and there was little point looking for him.

Geran bathed quickly, dressed himself, and headed down to find himself some breakfast in the family great room, turning events over in his mind. By the time he'd finished his breakfast—and games of dragon's-teeth with the younger Hulmasters—Geran had decided on his next course of action. He clapped Hamil on the shoulder and said, "I think I'd like to seek gainful employment for the day. If you're done with allowing Kirr to instruct you in grand strategy, why don't you come with me?"

"Gainful employment?" Hamil raised an eyebrow. "Very well, then."

"But I was winning, Geran!" Kirr groaned.

"Nonsense!" Hamil replied. "You were but one tile away from falling into my insidious trap. You'll see when we resume this contest."

The halfling bowed to his diminutive opponent and followed Geran down through a servant's stair into the depths of the castle kitchens. In a few moments the two travelers came to the laundry room, where a couple of servant girls worked at a big tub of warm water, washing the castle's linens.

"Oh, so it's the wash, then," the halfling said glumly. "All right, I suppose I have to earn my room and board somehow."

"Some honest work would do you good," Geran answered him. He spoke briefly to the young women working at the tubs, and they directed him to a large storeroom nearby. Battered old trunks packed with old clothing filled the room. Geran removed his sword belt and began to rummage through the trunks. The swordmage found a threadbare old tunic and a nondescript cloak of plain gray and held them up for a look.

"Ah, this should do," he said.

"For mucking out the stables?" asked the halfling.

"Not a bad idea, but that's not what I had in mind. I was thinking that we might look for some work as teamsters, and House Veruna might be a good place to look. I'd rather not be recognized. Here, try these."

Geran and Hamil soon enough patched together mismatched working garb to reasonably disguise themselves as common laborers. They stopped by the Shieldsworn armory, and Geran replaced his elven blade with a plain short sword of the sort that a poor driver might carry for defense against bandits; Hamil found a well-worn crossbow. Then they visited the stables and harnessed a simple buckboard wagon and a pair of mules and drove down from Griffonwatch into town, joining the stream of cart traffic and wagons rumbling along the Vale Road in the wet snow.

They stayed east of the river down to the Lower Bridge, crossed over to Bay Street, and drove along the wharves past the tradeyards of various merchant costers—the Double Moon, House Sokol, House Marstel. Then they came to the Veruna compound and drove through its gates into the bustling yards beyond. Like most other trading companies in Hulburg, Veruna owned several storehouses that were enclosed together by a sturdy wall. Barracks, offices, stables, a smithy, and the stone-and-timber houses of Veruna officials clustered together within the Veruna holding, a town within the town.

It seems ordinary enough, Hamil said silently. *This could be the Red Sail yard in Tantras. What are we looking for?*

The mercenaries, Geran answered. He looked around, sizing up the place. A handful of armsmen in the green-and-white tabards of the House watched over the business in the yard; they seemed bored and disinterested. *I expect that most of the Veruna operations here are perfectly legitimate, so I'm not worried about what's in the storehouses or where it's going. I'm more interested in the sellswords. Mark them well—I want to find this man Urdinger, and I want to see if any of them are riding off into the Highfells to go poke around in barrows when they don't think anyone is watching.*

The halfling nodded. "That might take days," he warned. *And it'll look a little suspicious if we just sit here all day eavesdropping on the guards.*

"I know," Geran replied. He spied the big Veruna armsman Bann, the fellow he'd confronted in Mirya Erstenwold's store, and he carefully shifted to lower his hood over his face and keep his eyes away from the man. The mercenary led half a dozen more Veruna men past the wagon without giving Geran so much as a second glance and headed out into Bay Street intent on his own business.

You recognize those men? Hamil asked.

I saw one of them at Mirya's. Come on, we might as well ask about work. It'll give us a good chance to spy out the place, and we should fit right in.

Fortunately, a fair number of the wagon drivers in the town were halflings; it was a little unusual for a human and halfling to work together, but not strange enough to be conspicuous, or so Geran hoped. Besides, he'd observed in the last few days that most of the wagons heading out of town carried at least two men. It always helped to have an extra hand along to carry a crossbow and keep an eye out for trouble.

He swung himself down from the wagon and headed toward the nearest Veruna clerk he saw. The fellow was a tall, stoop-shouldered man with thinning hair and a heavy green cloak to ward off the wet snow.

"Well met," Geran said gruffly. "I've got a wagon and team for hire. Got any work for me?"

"Just a moment." The Veruna clerk carried a small ledger and consulted it with a frown of annoyance. "I'll need a load of stores taken up to a camp in the foothills soon. It pays five silvers, and you'll get fodder and stabling for your team and a hot meal for yourself."

"Good enough. Where am I going?"

"You'll be with some other wagons. The other drivers know the way. Stay with them, and you'll be fine." The clerk looked up at Geran. "I haven't seen you before. New in town?"

Geran shrugged. "I heard there's work and good coin here."

"We need all the drivers we can get." The clerk pointed at a storehouse across the compound. "Take your wagon over there, and tell Koger—he's the short fellow in the brown hood—that you've been hired for the Troll Hill train. You're expected to lend a hand with the loading and unloading."

Geran gave him a resigned nod and returned to the wagon. "We're hired," he told Hamil. "Keep your eyes and ears open, and we'll see what we can learn."

The halfling grimaced. "I hope they're paying us well, at least."

The two comrades spent most of the next five days hiring their wagon to House Veruna and driving provisions of all sorts out to the House's mining camps and lumber yards in the hills east of town. Geran and Hamil turned in a more or less honest day's work for their wages and made a point of trying to haggle a little more coin from the clerks, since Geran didn't want to attract attention for working too little or too much for the pay. As he'd hoped, the work gave him an excellent opportunity to examine for himself the extent of Veruna's holdings and watch their sellswords at close range. The mercenaries paid little attention to the teamsters who were constantly coming and going from the tradeyard, and Geran and Hamil found plenty of opportunities to ask questions of their fellow drivers and listen in on the hired swords without raising too much suspicion.

Geran soon learned much more about the merchant coster and their mercenaries. A noble family from Mulmaster owned the house; the Hulburg holdings were in the hands of Lady Darsi Veruna, who resided in a small manor on the slopes of the town's eastern headland, rarely visiting the merchant yards. Geran and Hamil could think of no legitimate reason to drive a wagonload up to her residence and did not actually lay eyes on her, but they did learn that she was constantly attended by several ladies-in-waiting, manservants, and guards. A cadre of master merchants who answered to Lady Darsi oversaw the Veruna business in Hulburg's lands; the head of the Hulburg yard was a stout, black-bearded man named Tharman Kurz, whose demanding nature and foul temper created no small amount of misery for the clerks. Master Tharman was nominally in charge, but the large contingent of sellswords who guarded the Veruna holdings did not answer to the Veruna master merchants. Small groups and bands of mercenaries in green and white came and went from the Hulburg yards and the other Veruna holdings constantly, sometimes escorting wagonloads of provisions bound for the camps, or timber, fur, and precious metals bound back to the merchant yards, but sometimes heading off on patrols or errands of their own.

On the evening of the last day, just as they finished manhandling a load of hardwood planks into the Hulburg storehouse, half a dozen Veruna mercenaries rode into the merchant yard. At their head rode a lean, hawk-faced man who wore his red hair shaved down to angry orange stubble over his scalp. He wore enameled black half-plate armor under his Veruna surcoat, and he had a gold crest atop his helmet, which hung from the saddlehorn. The red-haired man rode up to the master merchant's residence, swung down from the saddle, and handed the reins to a valet, while the rest of his men dismounted. Geran watched the sellsword over his mule team, idly patting the neck of the nearer animal. The mercenary stretched briefly and rolled his head from side to side, working out the kinks of a long trip in the saddle.

"Who is that?" Hamil asked quietly from the wagon's bench. The halfling was careful not to look directly at the mercenaries.

"I don't know," Geran answered. He glanced to his left, where one of the Veruna teamsters they'd driven with was unhitching his own team, and called over. "Say, Barthold—who's the captain over there?"

The other driver looked over. "Him? That's Urdinger. He's in charge of the armsmen. You'll want to be careful around him, he's got a short temper.

I heard that he beat another driver senseless when the fellow spilled a load into a ravine out near Troll Hill. Why d'you want to know?"

Geran was too far away to see whether the Veruna captain was wearing an elven dagger at his belt. He peered closer, trying to get a better look, and realized that he was staring at the Veruna captain with far too much interest. He quickly looked back to the other driver and forced a lopsided grimace onto his face. "I think I heard the same story out by Sterritt Lake. I was just wondering if that was the man."

Urdinger went inside the master merchant's house, and the rest of the guards dispersed. Geran and Hamil finished their work, collected their silvers from the paymaster, and drove slowly out of the Veruna yard. The swordmage scowled, caught up in thought. He'd marked Urdinger well enough to recognize the man when he saw him again, but that begged the question of what to do next. None of the Veruna men seemed to have noticed his spying so far, but if he confronted the captain of their mercenaries it would be difficult to conceal his identity, to say the least. He could try to figure out where Urdinger preferred to drink and eavesdrop on the fellow or perhaps try to confront him away from the rest of the armsmen . . . but if the Veruna captain simply denied any involvement in the tomb-breakings or the murder of Jarad Erstenwold, it would be difficult to compel him to speak the truth.

Assume that Urdinger is involved in both, Geran decided. What did the Verunas want with the barrows, anyway? Was it simply a matter of mercenaries looking for some easy riches that could be had from plundering the tombs of the forgotten dead, ignoring the danger that might attend? Or was it something that Urdinger had ordered his men to do for some reason of his own?

"Well, what now?" Hamil asked, interrupting Geran's musings. "A good night's sleep so that we can get an early start on tomorrow's provisioning? If we get to the tradeyard at sunrise, I believe we could get in two round-trips before dark and double our daily pittance."

"I think we're done playing at mule drivers."

"I thought I'd never hear you say that. Well, good. What do you propose next? Lie in wait for this fellow Urdinger and ambush him? Trail the Veruna blades and see where they go when they leave the camps?"

"Some of them are likely patrolling the wildlands near the camps, watching for monsters or marauders," Geran answered. He clicked his tongue at the mules and lightly flicked the reins to urge them onto the Lower Bridge. "There's little point in following them. And even if we were confident that we were following the right group of armsmen at the right time to catch them in some mischief, well, it's damned difficult to trail mounted men out on the Highfells without being spotted yourself. No, I think we're going to have to lay a trap for them."

"We could start a rumor that someone else opened a barrow and found something," Hamil said, thinking aloud. "With sufficient riches in the tale, they'd have to investigate. We could set watch over the barrow in our story and wait for them."

"Not a bad idea, but half of Hulburg might show up on our doorstep." Geran smiled grimly at the notion. Few native Hulburgans would open a tomb in defiance of the harmach's law, but the town was full of poor and desperate outlanders these days. And no laws pertained to looting burial mounds that were already standing open. "We might waylay dozens of men before the ones we're looking for show up. We'd have to stack them up like cordwood behind the mound so that we didn't scare away the rest."

Hamil laughed and shook his head. "I see your point. Never mind."

"We'll talk with my uncle tomorrow," Geran decided. "He'll know which barrows have been broken into. Maybe we can discern some pattern to it all if we see more of the burial mounds the Veruna men have visited."

To finish out their ruse, Geran and Hamil picked up a few barrels of salted meat and sacks of flour and drove back to the castle. Drivers delivered provisions to the garrison often enough that one more wagon wouldn't seem unusual. No one seemed to pay any special attention to them, so they left the the wagon with the Shieldsworn stables and returned to their rooms for much-needed baths, changes of clothing, and a good night's sleep in warm beds.

In the morning, Geran rose, exercised, and dressed, then met Hamil in the great room. After breakfast, they made their way across the small court in front of Harmach's Tower to the library. A steady, cold drizzle was falling, a mix of rain and sleet. As before, they found a pair of Shieldsworn standing watch by the harmach's door. A small handful of clerks and chamberlains hurried in and out, carrying out the business of the castle. Geran and Hamil waited only a moment before they were shown in to see his uncle.

Grigor Hulmaster sat at his writing desk, studying a stack of parchment as they entered. "Ah, Geran! Master Hamil!" the old lord said warmly. "You have certainly made yourselves scarce lately. I understand that you had quite an adventure with Kara a few days ago, and I've been waiting for a chance to ask you about it."

"I doubt I can add much to what Kara must have told you already," Geran observed. He took the seat his uncle indicated. "I wanted to see for myself the place where Jarad was killed, so we rode up to the Highfells to have a look."

He went on to describe their exploration of the barrow to the best of his ability, including the discovery of the two bodies and the encounter with the strange sorcerer. Grigor listened attentively without interrupting; the harmach might not have been a young man, but he had a keen memory and never forgot the details of a story. Geran knew that his uncle would get around to his own questions eventually, after he'd had ample time to weigh all the accounts.

When Geran finished, Grigor leaned back in his leather chair. "Weren't you worried about breaking into the barrow? You know that's dangerous."

Geran met his uncle's gaze evenly. "Someone had moved those stones recently, and I wanted to know why. Kara didn't want to disturb the burial mound, but I thought there wasn't much risk."

"As it turned out, you were right. It's not in Kara's nature to trust her intuition, but I'm glad that you trusted yours." Grigor sighed heavily. "I knew that Darsi Veruna and the rest of the Merchant Council had reasons to want Jarad Erstenwold out of the way, but I had no reason to think that Veruna mercenaries might be involved with the tomb-plundering that Jarad was investigating."

"Speaking of which, I'd like to know exactly which barrows have been broken into, and when," Geran said. "Jarad must have discerned some pattern to it. He had a reason for choosing that barrow to keep watch over."

"You believe the Verunas aren't finished plundering the barrows?" the harmach asked.

"We've spent the last few days watching the Veruna sellswords," Hamil said. "Small bands of Darsi Veruna's armsmen are constantly coming and going from the camps and yards. By our rough count, we'd guess that as many as a third of the Veruna men—thirty to forty mercenaries, all told, mostly in bands of five or six at a time—are engaged in some activity that takes them away from Veruna mines, sawmills, and wagon trains." The halfling glanced at Geran and back to the harmach. "We doubt they're all out patrolling the wilds at the same time."

The harmach sat in silence for a long moment, gazing out the leaded glass windows of the library. Finally he said, "Assuming your suspicions are well founded, Master Hamil, what business is it of yours? You are not sworn to my service—nor is Geran. There is no reason to make Hulburg's troubles your troubles too."

"As I told you before, my lord Harmach, I'm here to look after my partner." Hamil nodded at Geran. "A few years back, when Geran and I were both members of the Company of the Dragon Shield, Geran saved my life at terrible risk to his own. I'm obligated to him for that, if nothing else. But beyond that, Geran is my friend, and his fights are my fights too." The halfling paused. "Besides, it seems that many of the foreigners in this town know your men all too well. We might be able to get answers your Shieldsworn couldn't."

"In that, you may be correct, Master Hamil." Grigor shifted his watery gaze to Geran. "But, Geran, it doesn't explain why you've chosen to make this your fight. I've never blamed you for your decision to seek your fortune elsewhere. You have no debt to repay me or Hulburg."

"I've nothing in Tantras that I need to hurry back to, and I think I'll be staying a little while." Geran kept his eyes locked on the harmach's. "I find that I'm not satisfied with the questions that are left unanswered, Uncle. And I don't like what I've seen so far of this Mulman merchant coaster that Sergen has apparently sold Hulburg to. This whole business doesn't sit well with me."

"Nor with me," the harmach answered, with surprising firmness in his voice. "Very well, then—I have the reports of tomb-breaking close at hand." He pulled open a drawer in the desk, then checked another. "Ah, here they are."

The old lord glanced through the papers and handed them to Geran. Most were in Jarad's handwriting, simple and terse summaries of each break-in he'd discovered.

"There were five instances that we know about before Jarad's encounter," Grigor said. "Of course, there may be more we haven't discovered yet.

There are literally hundreds of barrows scattered from Thentia to the ruins of Sulasspryn, and most are so far from traveled paths and grazing land that no one would ever know if they'd been broken into."

Geran looked at them quickly and handed them to Hamil. He'd read them more thoroughly later. But first, he wanted to see where the robbery attempts had taken place. He glanced at the crowded bookshelves in the harmach's study. "Do you still have Wolther's map, Uncle?"

"Of course," Grigor answered. He pushed himself to his feet with a slight wheeze and shuffled over to a rack where dozens of large leather cases lay gathering dust. He ran his frail fingers over each, muttering quietly to himself, then he settled on one case and tapped it once before removing it and bringing it back to the desk. "This is the one."

Geran waited while Grigor carefully opened the case and pulled out the large, yellowed parchment map. He spread it out over the top of his desk; Geran and Hamil stood and gathered around to see it better. The map showed the hills and valleys around Hulburg in exquisite detail, dotted with lakes and bogs and crisscrossed by small streams and old footpaths. Small triangular marks speckled the lands surrounding the Winterspear Vale. "My father hired the mapmaker Wolther to make a survey of the Hulmaster lands," Grigor explained to Hamil. "It would be more than fifty years ago now, but no one's ever taken a better measure of the lands around Hulburg."

"What are the triangles?" the halfling asked.

"Marker cairns," Geran answered. "You've seen a few already—the whitewashed stones out on the Highfells. You'll see that Jarad's letters begin by mentioning the cairn nearest to each of the broken barrows. Read them off to me, Hamil."

The halfling looked back down at Jarad's letters. "The first is, let me see, 'Twelve north-northeast, eight hundred yards southeast, right of small rise.' You can make sense of that?"

"The marker cairn is twelve miles north-northeast of Griffonwatch. From the marker, the barrow is eight hundred yards to the southeast." Geran found the marker symbol on the old map and carefully marked it with a pin. Hamil read off the rest, and Geran marked each. When he finished, no immediate pattern seemed obvious. Some of the barrows were east of the Winterspear Vale, some were west, and none were particularly close to each other.

"That doesn't help very much," Geran said.

"What did you expect to see?" the harmach asked.

Geran sighed. "I don't know," he admitted. "I was hoping that something might seem obvious once we'd looked at all of the locations together." He looked at Hamil. "How do you feel about sleeping under the stars tonight?"

The halfling grimaced. "It seems likely to rain all day, in case you hadn't noticed."

"If we leave soon, I imagine we could visit all these sites by midday tomorrow, so it's only one night out in the Highfells. And there are plenty of herdsmen's shelters and huts up there, so we'll probably have a roof over our heads."

"I think we'd be better off watching the Verunas," Hamil said sourly. "I propose that we spy out the taverns their armsmen frequent and eavesdrop on them for a few evenings. We'll have to make ourselves comfortable, eat well, spend coin generously, and feign revelry, but I am willing to make those sacrifices. That seems to offer better prospects than riding around to look at abandoned barrows."

"We'll try your suggestion next if the barrows have nothing to say to us." Geran glanced at his uncle. "Can we borrow paper and ink? I'd like to copy down the locations."

"Of course." Grigor found Geran a small journal, and the swordmage carefully copied Jarad's notes about the barrows that had been found open. He thought he knew at least two of the mounds already, just from Jarad's descriptions, but distance and direction could be deceptive on the Highfells. Geran did not want to spend hours riding around in circles looking for a marker or a barrow because he hadn't bothered to write anything down.

When he finished, he tucked the small book into his vest pocket. "Thank you, Uncle," he said. "We'll be on our way. I expect we'll return tomorrow."

The harmach took his hand. "Be on your guard, Geran. I will see you soon."

Nine

19 Ches, the Year of the Ageless One

Orange pillars of smoke filled the night sky above the mining town of Glister. It was not much of a town by human standards, of course, little more than a permanent camp and trademeet in the foothills bordering Thar. Few women or children lived there; it was a place where hard and desperate men came to work and wring gold from the ground, gold that they could then carry back to the so-called civilized lands and use to buy better lives. That did not diminish Warchief Mhurren's pleasure at Glister's pillage. His nostrils flared wide as he tasted the hot reek—wood, grain, straw, and wool burning in the ruin of the town, and the sweet smell of burning flesh too. That was livestock, of course; the townsfolk had abandoned the town to the Bloody Skulls and their allies. A few screams echoing through the muddy, smoke-filled streets suggested that not all of the town's inhabitants had fled in time, but that sport wouldn't keep Mhurren's warriors entertained for long.

"A good beginning," Sutha said to him. She stood behind him, dressed in chain mail with the symbol of Luthic, the Cave Mother, hanging on a chain around her neck. The Skull Guards surrounded them both, watching for any danger. Mhurren had reluctantly left Yevelda at Bloodskull Keep. He couldn't have left the two of them alone while he went off to war, or he was sure that he would have returned home to find one or both of them dead. And Sutha's priestess-magic was unquestionably useful on the battlefield. "The weaklings fled at the mere sight of us!"

Mhurren shook his head. "They were wise to give up the palisade and the town. We outnumber the humans and filthy dwarves ten to one. We would have slaughtered them all in an hour."

He pointed to the unconquered stronghold at the top of the steep-sided hill on which the town stood. It was a crude stone fort known as the Anvil. Little more than a thick fieldstone wall enclosing the hilltop, it had a strongly defended gate and a single squat tower. "That is where they will stand and fight. Other tribes before us have plundered the town, but none have taken the Anvil. Glister is not destroyed until it falls." He grinned at the challenge of it and shook his spear. "Come on, Bloodskulls! I want to hear for myself the bleating of the sheep in their little stone pen."

He led the way beneath the open gate of the palisade and up through the town's rough, muddy streets. Glister stood on a rocky prominence in the center of a steep-sided valley in the shadow of the Galena Mountains. The buildings were thick-walled bunkhouses and storehouses of fieldstone and turf, with a few ramshackle wooden buildings scattered here and there. Those accounted for most of the fires, since the stone-and-turf buildings did not burn well at all—one more measure of defense in a town whose location was decided by defense instead of comfort. Mhurren doubted whether there was much worth looting in the parts of the town that had been abandoned to the Bloody Skull horde, but for the moment he was content to let his warriors and their allies have their fun. Soon enough there would be real work at hand.

He heard heavy footsteps and snarling curses approaching from a side street and suppressed a growl of annoyance. The one-eyed priest Tangar stormed up to him, his fangs bared in fury. "We are betrayed!" the servant of Gruumsh roared. "Where are the old, the weak, the women, the children? They have escaped us! The Vaasan warned them of our attack!"

Mhurren scowled, careful not to allow his canines to show. As much as the priest irritated him, he couldn't risk an open break with Tangar and his followers. "I did not think to surprise them, Tangar," he answered with more patience than he felt. "We have many spears. Of course the rock-diggers and goat-herders heard of our march. But do not fear—they did not run far." The scouts told Mhurren that a number of the Glister-folk had fled along the trails leading south to Melvaunt and Hulburg, but Mhurren's new Red Claw allies were watching those paths. Those humans who hoped to carry their families or their gold to safety would be easy prey for the wolf riders. He pointed up at the fortress with his spear. "Most of the Glister-folk hide behind the walls of the Anvil with their gold and their women. No, they did not run far at all."

He came to a broken storehouse at the upper end of the town, not more than eighty yards or so from the Anvil's gatehouse. From there he had a good view of the challenge ahead. A narrow path led up to the sturdy iron-riveted timber gates. The walls of the stronghold were not very tall—twenty feet or so, it seemed—but, other than the path leading to the gatehouse, it was a steep scramble up a bare and open slope to reach the foot of the walls, and Mhurren could see the dark shapes of bowmen and spearmen hiding behind the crenellations, waiting to repel an assault. No doubt the Glister-folk had food and water enough to withstand a siege of a month or more. The humans and dwarves who lived in this remote place had waited out more than one orc or ogre tribe, hiding behind their walls until the besieging forces grew hungry, or bored, or turned against each other.

Mhurren did not intend to repeat the mistakes of chieftains before him. There would be no siege against the Anvil. Instead, he meant to storm the stronghold before dawn.

"Bring the Vaasan here," he told his Skull Guards. One of the warriors dipped his spear and jogged off into the smoke and darkness. A few minutes later, he returned with the Warlock Knight Terov. The human wore his battle armor of black plate with the ram's head helm, but he seemed to handle the weight of the steel well. Several Vaasan knights accompanied their lord—likely to protect him from any sudden misunderstandings with his Bloody Skull allies.

The human glanced up at the walls, measuring the likelihood of an arrow from the ramparts, and then turned his back on the defenders contemptuously. "Well done, Warchief Mhurren," he said. "You have boxed the badger in its den. Will you smoke him out, or do you have something else in mind?"

"We have not yet tested our new Vaasan mail," Mhurren answered. He had kept his own armor, which included heavy plates worked in the form of snarling demon faces over the mail he routinely wore, simply because he didn't want his warriors to think he'd become too close to the Vaasans. But eight hundred of his best spearmen had traded their leather jerkins and crude scale shirts for the strong Vaasan hauberks, helms, and greaves. Since the Glister-folk had not defended their palisade or town, Mhurren hadn't yet had the opportunity to see how it stood up in battle—but he knew good steel, and Terov hadn't stinted on his promise. "I will take the Anvil before sunrise."

Terov nodded. "Your warriors came here for a fight, and they haven't had one yet. Better to give them one before they decide they're content with burning the town."

"You understand us well," Mhurren answered grudgingly.

"How can I help?"

Mhurren pointed at the gatehouse. "First, I want them blinded. Use your magic to conjure a fog or smoke before the gate, so that Guld and his ogres can get close without being feathered with arrows. Then, when I signal, I want your manticores and wyverns to rake the defenders from the walltop to the north, there."

The Warlock Knight nodded. "What of the giants?"

"With my Bloody Skulls. Guld might force the gate, but the north wall is the attack that will carry."

"As you say, then. I will conjure you a fog. Send your orders to our monster handlers, and they will see to it that the flyers do as you command." Terov glanced once more at the battlements and strode away with his guards in tow.

Mhurren growled in approval and turned away from the stronghold. "Messengers!" he called. Young warriors not quite grown enough to stand shield-to-shield in the tribe's muster leaped to their feet, ready for their duties. Mhurren quickly gave his commands, made each messenger repeat his orders twice, and sent them on their way—most to Bloody Skull warbands, two to Guld the ogre, two to Kraashk of the Red Claws, others to the Vaasans' monsters. Then he settled down to wait. He would do nothing until he received word back that his orders had been delivered.

One by one, his messengers returned. In the town below he began to hear the sounds of movement amid the roaring and crackle of the flames, the heavy tramp of armored feet, and the shouts of harsh voices. Sharp whipcracks echoed through the darkness as leaders and priests beat and bludgeoned overeager pillagers away from the meager prizes they had already found and brought them back into battle order.

"Dawn approaches," Sutha said. Mhurren glanced eastward. Pearly gray streaks were beginning to lighten the sky. Sunrise was not more than an hour away.

"No matter." He looked over to his drummers and said, "Beat the first signal."

The drummers seized their mallets and struck a long, slow roll on their massive instruments. Each wardrum was a good five feet across, its voice so deep and powerful that it could carry for miles in the right conditions. In Glister's narrow vale the high stone cliffs surrounding the town caught the heavy *thoom-thooooom* beats and threw them back until it seemed the whole town quivered in response. Then Mhurren slashed his hand, and the drummers fell silent.

From somewhere off to his right, he heard a human voice calling out some sort of invocation. A single torch came hurling out from the shadows of the buildings in that direction, clattering to the ground a short distance in front of the gatehouse. For a moment the torch simply guttered there on the ground, and Mhurren's brow furrowed as he wondered if that paltry gesture was all that Terov could provide in the way of magic. But then the torch began to smoke, to smoke heavily, and in the space of a few heartbeats it began to produce immense, thick, yellow-gray billows that heaped up over the spot where it lay, quickly hiding it. Two more torches arced through the night and landed on the hillside by the foot of the wall and began to smoke as well. In moments the whole wall facing Mhurren was obscured by the growing cloud. Cries of consternation rose from the dwarves and humans defending the wall.

"Now for Guld's part," Mhurren said. "The second signal, now!"

Again the drummers began their ominous beat and scores of great, bellowing roars erupted in response. The Skullsmasher ogres rushed out into the open from where they had waited, swarming up the path to the gatehouse. Each ogre stood almost ten feet tall, with long, powerful arms and short, crooked legs. Many carried huge hide shields larger than a full-grown man or orc, and these led the way for their fellows. None of the Skullsmashers wore much armor, trusting instead to their size and thick hides to protect them from arrows and spears. In the middle of the ogre assault, a dozen of the hulking beasts carried a crude ram—a tree trunk thirty feet long. They vanished into the smoke, and a moment later the first great thudding *boom!* echoed from the Anvil's gate. Stray arrows hissed out of the smoke, some finding ogre flesh, others simply disappearing into the night.

"Get ready," Mhurren told his Skull Guards. Then he shouted to his drummers, "The third signal, *now!*"

The wardrums shifted from their slow, heavy beat to a fast, frantic double-time as a second drummer joined in at each, striking furiously. Mhurren leaped out and began to run toward the wall, his guards following him. From the dark streets north of the Anvil, hundreds of Bloody Skull orcs poured out in a black river, slipping and scrambling as they swarmed up the steep hillside toward the fortress wall. Five hill giants strode ponderously alongside the orcs. If Mhurren had timed it right, the ogre assault on the gate had drawn off many of the defenders, while on the south side of the Anvil—where its tower stood—the Red Claws showered the ramparts with arrows, giving a demonstration of their own and leaving the walls in front of the Blood Skulls with a perilously thin garrison. Those who remained raised more shouts of alarm and began to loose arrows as fast as they could at the oncoming horde, and the orcs answered with a wild sea of battle cries, shouts, and screams of murderous rage.

A wild arrow whistled out of the darkness; Mhurren caught it on his shield and kept going. Nearby, one of his Skull Guards suddenly screeched and dropped kicking to the ground, shot through the eye by a lucky or skilled archer. The defenders began to drop heavy stones from the battlements; even if they found no orc directly underneath, the stones bounced and rolled down the steep hillside with enough force to snap the legs or crush the ribs of those warriors who didn't see them coming.

The warchief reached the relative safety of the wall footing, holding his shield over his head. "The grapples!" he shouted. "Hurry up, you dogs!"

The steep hillside made scaling ladders almost useless against the Anvil's walls, so the Bloodskulls carried grappling hooks and knotted ropes instead. Dozens sailed up and over the walls. The hill giants—some fairly well pincushioned by arrows by then and furious on account of it—carried much heavier hooks affixed to chains that no mere sword blow would sever. They hurled their own hooks, and in moments dozens of orcs were swarming up the ropes and chains, pushing their way up with feet against the stone wall. The first few warriors to begin their ascent were cut down by arrows or crushed by stones dropped from above, and Mhurren swore viciously to himself. It was a good plan, but it could still go awry if . . .

" 'Ware the manticores!" a panicked human voice shouted from over his head.

The warchief risked a look from under his shield, just in time to see three of the great bat-winged monsters swoop down out of the darkness overhead. Each snapped its wings out to full extent and arrested its flight for an instant as its long, barbed tail whipped beneath its body, unleashing a hail of metallic spikes as deadly as crossbow quarrels. A few hasty arrows shot back at the flying monsters as they flapped away, then a pair of wyverns streaked over the battlements low and fast, snapping with their powerful jaws and knocking men down with their thickly muscled tails. One unlucky human was caught by a claw and carried away screaming into the night sky. Mhurren grinned at the sight and threw away his shield to grasp the grapple line closest to him and begin his own ascent. The whole time the flying monsters were harrying the defenders, the Bloody Skulls continued to climb.

"Up the ropes, Bloody Skulls! Don't give them a chance to recover!" he shouted and pulled himself upward. A handful of defenders returned to the walltop and dropped more stones on the orcs milling at the foot of the wall. The grapple line next to his was suddenly severed, dropping several warriors back down to the ground—not a lethal distance, but more of a fall than Mhurren would care to experience. Then two of the manticores swooped by again and loosed another fusillade of their tail spikes. Iron clanged and clattered against stone or sank into flesh with an awful sound.

To his surprise, Mhurren reached the top and clambered over unmolested. He quickly moved away from the rope to make room for the Skull Guards following him and drew a short fighting-axe from his belt, since he'd had to leave his shield and spear on the ground below. Dozens of Bloody Skulls were already on the battlements, with more swarming up over the edge every moment.

"We have them," Mhurren snarled.

"Die, orc!" a dwarf shouted near him and sprang forward to bury his axe in Mhurren's neck with a powerful two-handed swing.

The warchief leaped inside the dwarf's axe swing and rammed the spike of his own fighting-axe into the dwarf's face. Bone crunched, and blood spurted. The dwarf howled and reeled back, but Mhurren followed and butchered him with a hail of short, furious strikes, hacking the dwarf again and again. He roared in triumph and let the blood-madness take him, throwing himself headlong into the first knot of struggling warriors he saw. He struck with axe, with mailed fist, with kicks and punches, and even one frenzied bite when a luckless human was pushed into him. He sent the poor wretch screaming away from him, missing an ear that Mhurren spat out on the ground.

He looked around for another foe, but no more warriors stood against him. Mhurren roared in frustration, then slowly shook himself out of his rage. There was no one left to fight because the Bloody Skulls had taken the wall. His warriors were streaming into the Anvil's crowded bailey, where the Glister-folk shrieked and ran and wept in terror. Across the way, Guld's ogres had broken through the gate and were already at work on the small keep—whose rooftop had been left undefended, because the wyverns had alighted there to feast. "It's done," he said aloud. "By Gruumsh's black spear, the Anvil is ours!"

Mhurren descended into the courtyard. Blood ran down his arm and dripped from his fingertips. Somewhere in the melee he'd taken a stab in the meat of his left arm, though he couldn't remember being wounded. That was the nature of the battle-madness. Well, it would serve to increase his already considerable standing with his warriors. They would not forget that he had left some of his blood on the Anvil's walls, just as they had.

"You have your victory, Warchief. Glister is yours." Warlock Knight Terov approached, picking his way through the dead and wounded. The Vaasan's face remained hidden beneath his horned helm, but Mhurren could feel the man's confidence. "Are you satisfied with our bargain?"

"You have done all you said you would," the chief answered. "But I think now that I could have taken Glister with the Bloody Skulls alone. It was weak."

"Possibly," Terov conceded. "But how many more of your warriors would have died taking this stronghold, I wonder? No ogres to break down the gate, no manticores to scour the walltops, no Vaasan magic to blind the defenders at the crucial moment? I think you might have found it too costly for your taste . . . especially if the Red Claws were still your rivals and perhaps jealous of your success."

"Enough," Mhurren said. "I know what you have done for me, Terov."

"So, I ask again: Are you satisfied with our bargain?"

The warchief looked at the carnage of the taken fort, and smiled coldly. "I think I have a taste for more. We could be at Hulburg's doorstep in a tenday, and that is a town worth pillaging."

The Warlock Knight nodded. "And you may—if they refuse you tribute. But I have use for Hulburg, so if the harmach accedes to your demands, you will not destroy it."

Mhurren scowled. "And if I refuse you?"

"You and your Bloody Skulls may go your way, but I think you will find that the Skullsmashers and the Red Claws no longer answer to you. Nor will the giants, the manticores, or the wyverns. I doubt that you have the strength to overwhelm Hulburg without the aid I can provide."

Mhurren did not like the idea of submitting to the human, but Terov did not lie. Like it or not, he needed the Vaasan's aid if he hoped to continue his conquests. "You have whetted my warriors' appetites for plunder, Terov. Now that they have tasted a victory such as this once, they will demand another."

The Warlock Knight remained motionless. "As I told you, Mhurren, I have need of Hulburg unless it refuses to yield. But I have no use for Thentia. I cannot promise that you will be able to march against Thentia this year, but if the orcs help me to master Hulburg, I will deliver you Thentia soon enough. Now, I ask for the final time: Are you satisfied with our bargain?"

The chief of the Bloody Skulls glanced to the east. The sun was coming up. Already his warriors were choosing new trophies for the great hall in Bloodskull Keep. More were almost within his grasp. He squeezed his left fist and watched the blood drops spatter on the ground.

"All right, Terov," he finally said. "I am satisfied. I will swear your oath."

Ten

21 Ches, the Year of the Ageless One

Geran decided to head for the farthest barrow first, then work his way back toward Hulburg. After provisioning themselves from the castle kitchens and choosing new mounts from the Shieldsworn stables—a strong black charger for Geran and a big, shaggy Teshan pony for Hamil—they rode again. This time they rode better than eight miles up the valley before climbing into the highlands west of the vale. After a short rest and a cold lunch of dried sausage and sharp cheese, they ventured up into the moorlands proper, and the Winterspear Vale fell away behind them.

During their previous ride into the Highfells with Kara, they'd traveled north and east from Hulburg, heading toward the Galena foothills. This time, they were heading west and north, more or less straight into the open, rolling upland of Thar. These lands were drier and less boggy than the eastern Highfells. Rain sweeping in from the west usually passed over the barren hills on this side of the Winterspear Vale as a wet, windy mist that didn't really turn to rain until it met the mounting rampart of the Galena Mountains. Barren sheets of rock began to appear underfoot, gray and damp, and the ground cover grew sparse and wiry. Geran pointed out two of the old marker cairns to Hamil as they rode past. The whitewash of the old stones was weathered almost completely away.

Three miles from the place where they'd climbed out of the Winterspear Vale, they came to a serrated fault of fluted rosy stone that marched across the land like a crooked, titanic step ten feet tall and miles long—a ribbon of changeland dividing the moor. The trail led to a spot where the natural rise and fall of the ground brought them within two feet of the top of the winding pink wall; Geran and Hamil dismounted to lead their horses carefully to the top. The alien stone ran for miles like a sloping causeway or road, but it was not more than fifty feet in width. Carefully they picked their way across and back down to the natural moorland on the far side, their sodden cloaks flapping in the strong, steady wind.

"I find that my determination to follow you all over these dismal moors is rapidly waning, Geran," Hamil called against the steady, mournful moaning of the wind as they remounted. "At this point I frankly don't care what the Verunas want with old barrows."

"It's not much farther now," Geran answered him. "Four or five miles, and then you'll have an opportunity to get out of the rain and the wind."

"By clambering around in some musty, dank, foul-smelling barrow, likely filled with hungry wights or soul-stealing ghosts." The halfling shivered. "What in the world do you think to find out here?"

"If I knew, I wouldn't have to go look." The swordmage allowed himself a small smile at his friend's complaining. Hamil was riding at his back and couldn't see it anyway. Geran twisted around in his saddle to address his companion, but something else caught at his eye. Atop the rose-colored rampart of changeland receding behind them, he glimpsed a dark shape, something large and catlike that bounded quickly over the alien stone before leaping down out of sight.

"Behind us!" he hissed to Hamil, reining in his horse. He pulled his mount around to the right and turned the animal in place to get a better view of their backtrail.

"What?" Hamil quickly glanced over his shoulder and then shifted his eyes back to the front and swept the area around them for close threats before following Geran's gaze back the way they had come. He reached down and freed his shortbow from the holster by his knee. "What did you see?"

"I don't know," Geran said quietly. Nothing but tatters of mist lay behind them now. He stared for a long time, allowing himself to look past the landscape without really focusing on anything, letting the scene sink slowly into his eye—to no avail. Whatever he had glimpsed, it was no longer in sight. But he thought that he could just barely *feel* something on the moor with them. "It looked like a big cat of some kind, perhaps a red tiger or a rock leopard. But it was black, and I thought it looked longer in the leg than a tiger or leopard."

"Are they common out in the Highfells?"

"No, they're not," Geran admitted. "Red tigers favor woodland, and the leopards hunt in the high valleys and passes. I've seen a tiger or two closer to the foothills, but not around here. This isn't their kind of ground."

They waited and watched for ten minutes more, anxiously searching the moorland around them. Nothing more appeared. Finally Geran sighed and rubbed his eyes. "Maybe I was seeing things."

"I don't believe that for an instant."

"Nor do I. Well, let's continue. If something's caught our scent, we'll just have to keep our eyes open and hope that it loses interest soon." Geran shook his head. When he closed his eyes to go to sleep tonight, he knew he'd be thinking about a quick catlike shadow slinking over the moors toward him. If they didn't find a shelter or hut with a stout door, they might have to think about keeping watch.

They rode on another hour more without catching any more glimpses of dark shadows on their trail, and then they found the marker cairn Geran was looking for. It stood near the edge of another old barrowfield; a score of low, grass-covered mounds stood scattered at odd intervals for hundreds of yards around. The swordmage consulted the notes he'd taken in the harmach's study, carefully marked the direction from the cairn, and rode slowly toward the north. They passed several old, crumbling mounds and found the one that had been broken into, exactly where Jarad's notes had reported it.

It was a relatively large and intact mound, round and dome-shaped, with a steep stairwell in its center descending straight down between large plinths of stone. Muddy heaps of damp earth and loose rock surrounded the stairwell, attesting to its recent excavation. The two travelers dismounted and rigged a picket line for their horses, and Geran decided to take down the saddlebags from his mount.

Hamil noticed and frowned. "Are we planning on staying here long?"

"I don't know what I saw back by the stone wall," said Geran, "but if something scares off our horses, I'd just as soon have my bedroll and my dinner with me instead of bolting off across Thar."

"Point taken," the halfling replied. He followed Geran's example. The two travelers left their saddlebags by the stairs leading down into the barrow and descended into the gloom, feeling their way down the narrow stone steps.

"Aumie," Geran said softly, conjuring a simple globe of light to illuminate their way. The steps led them to a small antechamber, muddy and damp after lying open to the weather for months. The air was dank and stale, but the swordmage ducked down under the low arch and pressed forward, one hand on his sword hilt. Since the barrow had been plundered already, it seemed unlikely that any watchful undead waited there—but he didn't intend to be caught off his guard just in case he was wrong.

The barrow proved to consist of three cramped chambers joined by low doorways. Little in the way of funereal wealth had been buried with its occupant, who rested beneath a heavy sarcophagus of stone under the dusty symbol of Lathander, the ancient deity of the dawn. He was still widely worshiped under the name of Amaunator, though Geran had always preferred Tymora and Tempus—deities of luck and battle who looked favorably on adventurers. He moved closer to the stone crypt and glanced inside. The moldering bones of some long-dead person of importance stared sightlessly back up at him, still wrapped in the rotting remnants of a shroud.

"The tomb-breakers didn't take much," Hamil observed. He stood on tiptoe to peer down at the old skeleton. "Look, there's still a couple of rings on the fingers. Why did they leave those?"

"They're only copper. No precious stones."

"Yes, but if you go to all the trouble of excavating the stairs, why leave a penny behind?"

"There could be a curse on the treasure. Or perhaps there's a ghost or something else equally unpleasant around," said Geran.

Hamil frowned and quickly backed away a step. Geran decided to examine the floor more closely, just to make certain that he wasn't missing anything. He tapped on the old flagstones underfoot, listening for any hint of crypts hidden beneath this one, but the ground sounded solid enough. He turned his attention to the walls and determined that there simply wasn't anything more to the barrow. An old inscription was carved into the wall above the head of the sarcophagus. He moved closer and brushed his hand over the runes.

"Is that Dwarvish?" Hamil asked.

"The runes are Dethek, but it's not Dwarvish, it's old Tesharan. They were the first humans to settle the lands north of the Moonsea. They used the dwarf alphabet." Geran studied the markings carefully. "I think it says, 'Here sleeps Evanderan, High'—councilor? Prince? I don't know that word—'to Thentur, Keeper of the' . . . something . . . 'servant of Lathander.' Then there's some sort of prayer to Lathander. That seems to be all."

"Well, Evanderan is a cryptic fellow, and I don't feel that he has been very forthcoming with his secrets," Hamil said. "What else are we looking for, Geran?"

The swordmage shook his head. "I don't think there's much more to see here. Let's head for the next barrow. It should be about three or four miles to the northeast."

They climbed back up from Evanderan's barrow, found that nothing had troubled their mounts while they were inside the mound, and saddled up again. They rode to the next barrow and found it more or less similar to the first—a round, dome-shaped structure with a steep stairwell cut into the roof. This one stood alone by a small hillock, with no other mounds nearby. Again, they carefully picketed their mounts and descended into the mound.

After an hour of exploring the second barrow's cramped passageways and musty chambers, they found nothing more than they had in Evanderan's tomb. As before, Geran and Hamil carefully searched for secret passages, but the barrow was unremarkable. The Highfells were littered with examples of similarly plain burial mounds.

Geran climbed back out. The rain had finally let up, but the sky was still sullen and overcast. Two very ordinary barrows, neither with any appreciable wealth for the would-be thieves to remove . . . and neither haunted by fearsome specters or hateful wights. He supposed that most of the unopened barrows on the Highfells were likewise uninteresting; legends of barrow gold and barrow wights were probably greatly exaggerated. "Maybe we'll find something more interesting at the next barrow," he muttered to himself.

When they'd gone a little more than a mile, they passed a small herdsman's hut in a sheltered declivity. Geran reined in, looking the place over. The afternoon was growing late, and the ominous shadow he had seen earlier still weighed on his mind. "Let's make camp here," he suggested to Hamil. "We don't have much daylight left, and I'd rather have a roof over my head than sleep out in the open tonight."

The halfling eyed the small structure distastefully. It was made of stones piled crudely in the rough outline of walls, chinked with old mud, and roofed with squares of turf. "If you say so," he said.

They picketed the horses near the hut, built a fire from a small bundle of wood they'd brought along, and cooked up a simple supper as the sun was setting. Then Geran carefully drew warding sigils and spells around the hut. He'd learned a few such things in Myth Drannor, and while he was not very confident in his efforts, he figured that it certainly couldn't hurt anything to try. With that attended to, the two travelers secured the hut's door and stretched out their bedrolls on the bare wooden frames inside the shelter.

The night passed quietly, though Geran found himself starting at every gust of wind or unexplained sound in the darkness. Once or twice the horses outside caught a scent they didn't like and whickered uncomfortably, but nothing drove them off or tried to eat them. In the morning their mounts were still there, whole and unharmed. Geran cooked some bacon over the coals, and they broke camp. The morning was misty and wet, but the wind was not blowing, and Geran had some hope that the overcast might burn off during the day.

"More barrows today?" Hamil asked, yawning.

"Three, I hope." Geran stretched, then slowly turned in a circle to study the barrow's surroundings and get his bearings toward the next tomb-breaking. Then he frowned.

"What? What is it?" Hamil asked.

"The first barrow was on the edge of a whole field of burial mounds," Geran said. "There must've been a couple of dozen within a mile or less of the one that was opened. But there were no other barrows around the second mound. It was alone."

"Is that unusual?"

"No, I suppose not. There are plenty of barrows in the Highfells that don't have other barrows nearby. Only . . . why ride an hour to find another barrow to open, when there were many others close at hand? Why skip those mounds and go on to the second one?"

"They opened that one first and then moved on to the field we visited first?" Hamil guessed. "Perhaps they meant to open more of the barrows in the big field."

Geran pulled out his pocket-journal and checked the notes he'd taken in his uncle's study. "Possibly, but the first barrow was found opened before the second one. The tomb-breakers started with one barrow in the big field, then went to a different one several miles away."

"You know, the Mulmasterites might just be looting random crypts. It could be pure happenstance that they chose either one. For all we know they might be throwing dice to see which mound they open."

Geran looked down at his friend. "Do you really think so?"

Hamil sighed. "No, not really. Let's go back to the first barrow and have another look around. There must be a reason why they chose it out of a field of dozens."

"I admire your conscientious attitude."

"I've decided to charge you for my services. I expect to be paid by the hour; take all the time you like."

Geran laughed and clapped a hand on Hamil's shoulder. "In that case, you'll be disappointed to learn that the third barrow I intend to visit is back in that general direction. Evanderan's tomb isn't too far out of our way." Then the two travelers saddled their mounts again and spent the morning making their way back toward the first barrow they'd seen.

As they approached, Geran paid more attention to the other barrows around Evanderan's mound. Some were very old, little more than crude heaps of fieldstone and turf that had long since fallen in on themselves. Others were long, rectangular mounds that looked almost as if someone had long ago buried a barbarian chieftain's hall in its entirety—the barrow where Jarad had been ambushed was one of those. They returned to the Lathanderian's burial mound and dismounted, gazing around the landscape. The morning was growing late, but the skies showed signs of clearing—a bright wall of yellow sky showed to the west, marking the trailing edge of the rainclouds. "Clear and cold when the clouds pass, I think," Geran observed.

Hamil didn't reply immediately. He was studying the closest of the barrows, staring at it intently. "Geran," he said, "is there any significance to the different styles of the mounds? That one over there is a big rectangular affair, but the next one past it is a tumbled-down heap of fieldstones like a giant cairn. Did different people raise them?"

"I don't know." Geran scratched at his chin. It was plain as day now that Hamil had pointed it out, but he'd never really given it a moment's thought before. "It seems likely. Some are clearly much more weathered than others. I'd guess they might be centuries older. For that matter, they might not be human at all. Some of these might hold dwarves, or orcs, or even ogres."

"This is the same type of barrow as the second one we saw yesterday. Look, they're both round, not too large, finished with dressed stone, and they both have entrance stairways near the middle of the mound." Hamil glanced up at him. "The Veruna men might be looking for barrows of that type."

Geran nodded. "For that matter, this was the tomb of a Lathanderian, and there was Lathander's symbol on the sarcophagus in the second barrow, too." He pulled out the pocket-journal and checked his notes on the remaining barrows, then measured the weather with a quick glance at the sky. "The next barrow on the list is another five miles or so. If we hurry, we can visit it and still have a little time to move on to the next one before dark."

They headed south, angling indirectly back toward Hulburg across the open, trackless moorland to save time. For the moment, no more mysterious black shadows dogged their trail; perhaps whatever it was had given up the chase, if in fact it had ever been pursuing them. Around noon they halted to make a quick lunch from the provisions they still had on hand. The cloud cover had drifted far to the east, and the wind was beginning to pick up. It might have been wiser to rest their mounts a little more, but curiosity gripped Geran. He wanted to see what the third barrow would tell them.

Another hour of riding brought them to the third barrow on the list. This one sat in a small hollow, not far from a tumble of old stones that once might have been a circle of menhirs. The instant Geran caught sight of the old burial mound, he grimaced and reined in his mount. Beside him, Hamil did the same. They exchanged glances, then slowly rode closer.

It was a circular mound, small, with sides of roughly dressed stone. Someone had excavated the old stairwell in the middle of the mound, leaving heaps of damp black earth and small stones to mark their digging. "Well, well," Geran murmured. "Perhaps you were right, Hamil."

"Best go inside and make sure," the halfling replied. As before, they picketed their mounts then scrambled up on top of the low mound. Geran summoned his light spell again, and they descended into the mound. This one showed more signs of damage; several old doorways had been sealed with fieldstone and mortar by the mound's builders, and the rubble of freshly broken rock showed that the intruders had knocked them apart with prybars and sledges.

They found the sarcophagus lying open, the bones it contained scattered haphazardly in the burial chamber. The stone lid of the crypt was lying to one side, broken into three pieces . . . but the sunrise emblem of Lathander was still intact on the largest piece. More of the Dethek runes graced the broken stone; Geran knelt beside it and ran his fingers over the engraved letters. "It says, 'Sister Kestina Ellin,' " he read aloud. " 'Born Thentur, Year of the Keening Gale; died Thar, Year of Slaughter. She fell in battle against the Burning Fist horde.'"

"That makes three," Hamil said quietly. "Your Mulmasterites are searching for a specific barrow. It's the tomb of a Lathanderian. Do you want to check the fourth and fifth to be sure?"

"They're on the way back home, so no reason not to," Geran said. "But at this point, I'm inclined to agree, Hamil. I certainly wouldn't wager against you." He rocked back on his heels and looked around, frowning in thought. "This tomb seems to have been plundered more aggressively than the last two," he observed. "There's a lot more damage here."

"Perhaps there was treasure worth carrying away. Or maybe we're looking at the work of two different gangs—one's more careful, and the other more concerned with speed than with safety." Hamil peeked into the room's antechambers and shook his head. "Not much left in here now, that's for certain."

"It's not a good idea to carry off barrow treasure anyway. I wouldn't want to explain to Kara or my uncle how your pockets came to be stuffed with gold. They might not expect much of me, but I'm sure they expect at least that much."

"Well, the Veruna men seem inclined to flout the harmach's law. What about barrow gold they've already removed? If we take it from them, we can hardly be expected to put it back!"

"First we'd need to find the men who broke into this barrow. And I remind you, they might not be House Veruna." Geran nodded at the stairs leading back out of the barrow. "Come on, Hamil. I'd like to see one more barrow to be sure of things."

Eleven

23 Ches, the Year of the Ageless One

The fourth barrow was only about two miles farther on, but it proved difficult to find. Geran and Hamil crisscrossed a low, fencelike ridge of old weathered tors pocked with crudely built fieldstone cairns for almost two hours before they finally found the right burial mound. Geran couldn't imagine how anyone had noticed that it had been broken into, since it was well off any track or footpath he could find. In any event, it was another round, dome-shaped one, as they'd come to expect.

"Care to wager whether it's a priest of Lathander in there?" Hamil asked. Geran just shook his head in reply.

Inside, they found that even less of the interior had survived intact than the third mound they'd visited. Geran couldn't be certain that it was a Lathanderian's tomb at all, but the construction of the place was similar enough to the other mounds that it seemed to him that someone looking for tombs of a particular appearance might have included it just to be thorough. After sifting through the debris for an hour, they gave up and climbed back into the thickening dusk. A handsbreadth of ruddy orange remained on the western horizon, and the wind was picking up again, keen and shrill.

"You should've taken the bet," said Hamil.

"If I had, you'd still be inside looking for proof that you'd won," Geran said. "As it was, that's the last of our daylight." He shivered; the night promised to be bitterly cold, and he hadn't seen any suitable shelters in quite some time. They could sleep in the barrow, which would be covered from the weather and reasonably defensible, but he didn't see much that would fuel a fire nearby. Nor did he especially care to sleep in a burial mound. They hadn't seen any restless spirits yet, but the back of Geran's neck prickled at the thought of closing his eyes in the dank stone tomb. If that didn't invite a haunting of some sort, he didn't know what would.

Hamil glanced around the rocky hollow where the barrow stood, and he frowned. "I think I can hear something on the wind, Geran," the halfling said quietly. "We need to be careful tonight."

"I feel it too." Geran turned in a circle, scanning the moorland around them. "Most of the time the Highfells aren't that bad when the sun goes down, but every now and then you get a night when dark things stir . . . this feels like it might be one."

"Stay here, or find another spot to bed down?"

"I don't want to stay here, but I can't promise anything better." The swordmage ran a hand through his hair and sighed.

"If this is a Lathanderian tomb, chances are good it's warded against undead."

"It could be—" Geran stopped and glanced toward the south. Hamil had given him an idea. "Wait, I think I know where we can spend the night. And we might find someone who can tell us something about Lathanderian tombs too. There's an old abbey five or six miles from here. It's mostly in ruins, but some monks still live there."

"Six miles? That's going to be a long, cold ride," Hamil said dubiously. "Can you find your way there in the dark?"

"I'm not Kara, but I'll do my best." Geran leaped down from the mound and gathered up his saddlebags. "If nothing else, we might find a better place to camp along the way."

They'd left their horses saddled, since they hadn't expected to spend much time at the fourth barrow. The two companions quickly gathered their belongings, tightened the saddle straps, and mounted. Geran took a moment to mark his heading as best he could, then set off at a good trot, posting with his mount's easy gait. It would be a hard ride, but if he didn't get lost—or if the horse didn't step in a hole in the dark—it would not be much more than an hour. He glanced back at Hamil, but the halfling's big pony seemed to keep up well enough.

They jogged over the moors as the sunset faded to a dull red crescent limning the horizon to their right, and stars began to emerge from the retreating overcast. The wind grew stronger, hissing through the long grasses and moaning over the bare gray stone. Geran's hands soon ached with cold, and he shivered inside his cloak. When they'd gone two miles or so, it had grown dark enough that he began to seriously worry about one of the horses missing a step, so he cast another light spell and set the dim blue globe bobbing a few feet in front of him.

"Anything within a mile of us will see that light, Geran!" Hamil called.

"I know, but I don't want to risk the horses in the dark. It'll be a long walk if one of them breaks a leg." The horizon was no longer visible, and Geran couldn't make out his landmarks any longer. He picked a dim star that he hoped was in the right direction and urged his horse onward. The jogging pace was beginning to wear on him, making his thighs and back ache.

Some subtle note in the wind changed, and the steady moaning took on a new tone. Cold, distant voices seemed to mutter and whisper in the wind, and Geran's heart skipped a beat. "Barrow-spirits," he said softly. Ghosts, wraiths, some sort of dreadful phantoms—whatever they were, they meant no good to the living. He and Hamil needed to get off the moor, or they'd soon find out exactly what was abroad on the night wind.

Do you hear them? Hamil called silently.

Geran simply nodded in response. He felt something drawing closer and glanced quickly to either side. Nothing was there—but when he looked again at the path in front of him, a spectral figure seemed to hover in the air a short distance before him. It was the image of an ancient warrior, dressed in the simple mail hauberk and nasaled helm a warrior of five centuries past might have worn. His braided beard was gray and tattered, and his blank eyes shone with a pale green light.

"Thy doom is upon thee, mortal," the ghost whispered. "Thou shalt sleep under cold stars this night, and never again the sun shall find thee."

Geran's horse tossed its head in panic, and icy dread seemed to rob the swordmage of his will. He stared at the apparition for a long, terrible moment. Then he tugged at the reins and turned his horse away from the dour spirit. He kicked his heels to the animal's flanks, and with a shrill whinny of terror the black charger bolted off into the night. Geran leaned down low over its neck and let the animal run; he heard the hoofbeats of Hamil's mount falling behind him. Finally he slowed the horse's pace, and Hamil soon caught up.

"Don't stop now!" the halfling said. "I think it's following us!"

Geran kicked his mount back to speed and led Hamil over the moors. Whatever track they were following was long behind them, and he did not want to try to find it again. They came to a steep-sided gully that cut across their path, and Geran swore. He had to detour one way or the other around it. His sense of direction told him to veer left, but in that direction the terrain generally became more rugged as the land descended toward the Winterspear Vale. To the right they had a better chance of finding a place to cross, but he was afraid that would set them even farther off course. The swordmage grimaced and decided to head right first. They rode westward for several hundred yards, and the gully shallowed enough to cross. When they scrambled back up the other side, Geran caught a glimpse of a dim yellow light far across the moor.

"Thank Tymora," he breathed aloud. "I think that's the abbey."

"Good," Hamil replied through chattering teeth.

The travelers picked up their pace, following the distant light. For a long time it seemed to recede before them, never growing brighter, but finally they began to make up the ground, and a sprawling heap of broken towers and grass-grown stone appeared atop a short, steep-sided hill. Faint light showed from a few shuttered windows and a lantern swinging in the wind. They crossed an old stone-flagged causeway and scrambled up onto the road, and Geran breathed a sigh of relief as they stretched out into an easy canter and hurried the last few hundred yards.

They rode up to the weatherbeaten door in the crumbling wall and dismounted. Geran found a pull-rope by the door and tugged on it. From somewhere inside he heard the flat clang of a small bell. Nothing happened for a while, and he rang the bell again. Then he heard the rasp of wood on wood, and a small port in the door opened. The eyes of an aged man gazed out at him.

"Yes?" the fellow asked. "Who are you, and what do you want at this hour when no honest folk are abroad?"

"I'm Geran Hulmaster; this is my companion Hamil Alderheart. I ask shelter for the night. And I'd like to speak with the Initiate Mother."

The monk's eyebrows rose. "Geran Hulmaster? What in the world are you doing out here tonight, lad? It's the dark of the moon. Don't you know who walks the Highfells on nights such as this?"

"I'd rather not find out. Can we come in?"

"Yes, yes, just a moment." The port closed. Then a heavier timber slid somewhere out of sight, and the abbey gate opened. The old monk appeared in the doorway a lantern in his hand. "Come on, then. Hurry, lads, it's not safe to linger outside the walls tonight."

Geran and Hamil led their horses into the doorway, and found themselves standing in an old courtyard. The monk pushed the heavy door closed and slid the bar back in place before turning to face them again. "Welcome to Rosestone," he said with a wry smile. "I know the abbey has seen better days, but you're safe enough inside these walls. I'm Brother Erron. Here, let's stable your mounts and get you something to eat."

"Thank you, Brother Erron," Geran murmured. He glanced around at the crumbling towers and the broken pavement of the courtyard, then followed the old monk to a stable that evidently had not seen a horse in quite some time. Still, it was better than spending the night outside. He could no longer hear the chill voices in the wind, which led him to guess that old priestly wardings likely kept the restless dead far from Rosestone Abbey.

After stabling their animals, Geran and Hamil followed Erron to the abbey's refectory. A handful of other monks waited there, and they provided the two comrades with a plain dinner of cured ham, boiled potatoes, black bread, and sharp white cheese, washed down with a tankard of hot cider.

"All right, Geran," Hamil admitted. "This is better than huddling in some barrow out in those dreary hills, waiting for ghosts to come for us. But we were lucky to find the abbey when we did. There was a whole company of ghosts following us for that last mile."

"You didn't say anything about that," Geran said.

The halfling shrugged. "I wanted you to keep your eyes on what was ahead of us. I was keeping watch behind."

When they'd finished with their supper, Brother Erron appeared by the table and bowed. "Gentlemen, if you please, the Initiate Mother would like a word with you. Will you follow me?"

The two companions pushed themselves away from the table, rose, and followed the aged monk. He led them through a maze of passageways that took them through the main chapel—a tall room whose eastern wall was graced with a great window of stained glass depicting a glorious sunrise in panels of red, rose, and gold—and then a dark scriptorium filled with wooden writing desks and scroll racks. For all of the abbey's weathering and the poor condition of its outer walls and towers, the interior seemed to be in good shape. On the far side of the scriptorium, Erron led them to a sturdy wooden door in a deep stone arch and knocked twice.

"Initiate Mother?" he called. "I have brought Geran and his companion."

"Enter," a muffled voice called.

Erron opened the door and led them into a small study or office, sparsely furnished. A stocky woman in yellow robes with iron-gray hair and a nut-brown complexion waited for them by the fire. She had a stern, lined face that would have been quite severe if not for her warm brown eyes, well creased by crow's feet.

"Ah, Geran Hulmaster," she said in a rich, melodious voice. "I have not laid eyes on you in ten years or more. And this must be Master Alderheart. I confess I am more than a little surprised to find you on my doorstep on such a bitter evening."

"Mother Mara," Geran said with a smile. He'd always liked her. From time to time he and Jarad had passed by the abbey in their youthful ramblings, and the monks of Amaunator had always been happy to set places at their table for two hungry young hunters. He crossed the room to bow and take her offered hand, raising it to his lips. "I'm glad that Brother Erron let us in. It would've been a long, cold night otherwise."

"We are honored to be of service," she replied. "Please, sit. I've heard that you were back in Hulburg, but I would love to know what business brought you out on the Highfells this evening."

Geran looked around and found a plain wooden chair. He seated himself, while Hamil scrambled up into a matching one nearby, and the Initiate Mother took a seat across from them. "We're looking for tomb robbers," he answered. "My uncle told me that Jarad Erstenwold was found near a broken barrow, and that he'd been chasing after some gang of robbers who were opening burial mounds when he was killed. I decided to look into it for myself, and Hamil here offered to help me. We spent the day visiting tombs that had been broken into recently, but I suppose we stayed out later than we should have."

The abbess nodded. "Yes, I know about the tomb-breakings, but I hadn't heard that they were connected with Jarad's murder. Have you learned anything new?"

"Maybe," Geran said. "We've got reason to believe that one of the merchant houses in Hulburg is involved. And we might have learned something important this evening: All of the barrows that were broken into were burial mounds of priests of Lathander."

The abbess sat up straighter and locked her eyes on Geran's. "That I did not know. Go on."

"The tombs we've seen look to be about the same age. Going by the inscriptions we can make out, I'd guess they date back about four or five centuries to the time of Thentur," Geran continued. "Do you have any idea why the tomb-breakers would choose those barrows and ignore any others? What could they be looking for?"

The priestess frowned and looked down at her hands, thinking for a long time. Finally she shook her head. "I can't imagine what they expect to find, Geran," she said. "As you know, Amaunator was called Lathander in those days, so these are the tombs of the fathers of our faith you are speaking of. But to the best of my knowledge none of my antecedents were buried with any great treasure. I expect that the barrows of old Tesharan chieftains or ogre kings would be much more attractive to those who seek to plunder the wealth of the dead."

Geran scowled and sat back. If Mara didn't know why those tombs might be important, he didn't know who would. Maybe he could find something in the harmach's library that could shed some light on the mystery. . . .

"Initiate Mother," Hamil said slowly, "do you think they might be looking for a book?" He glanced over to Geran and shrugged. "The sorcerer was looking for one, after all. Maybe they're after the same thing."

"A book?" The priestess's brow furrowed in concentration, and then surprise flickered across her face. "A book! Yes, it is indeed possible, Master Hamil. They might be looking for the *Infiernadex* of Aesperus."

Hamil glanced at Geran and back to Mara. "The what of what?" he asked.

"The *Infiernadex.* A book of spells or rites that once belonged to Aesperus. By all accounts it was filled with dire and dangerous invocations. It lies in the tomb of a priest of Lathander."

The halfling grimaced. "Geran, Aesperus is the lich you and Kara were talking about a few days ago, right?"

Geran nodded. "He's called the King in Copper—why, I couldn't tell you. He came to power in the city of Thentia several centuries ago and brought much of the Moonsea North under his dominion, including Hulburg. His realm was known as Thentur, and the old stories say that he used necromancy to cling to power for many years. Eventually the people rose up against his tyranny and overthrew him. Hulburg and the other towns and cities under Thentur's dominion became free, and Aesperus fled. Many years later he turned up again as a powerful lich, haunting some place under the Highfells known as the Vault of the Dead. It's said that he's the master of all the undead of Thar." He looked back to the Initiate Mother. "But I've never heard any story about a book of his that might've ended up in a Lathanderian tomb."

"You know only part of the story, Geran," Mara answered. "Few remember it now, but the chief agents of Aesperus's defeat in Thentur were the priests of Lathander, led by the High Morninglady Terlannis. She and her priests rallied the people of Thentia and Hulburg against the tyrant. The war to defeat Aesperus took years, but Terlannis and her forces slowly pushed the king and his loyalists to the eastern frontiers of the realm, where Aesperus held out in a strong fortress called the Wailing Tower. After a long siege, the Lathanderians successfully stormed the Wailing Tower, broke Aesperus's army, and razed their stronghold. They found no sign of the king, but they seized many of his weapons and treasures—including the *Infiernadex.* Aesperus eluded Terlannis, but he escaped with little more than the robes on his back."

"How do you know all this?" Geran asked.

"I have read the accounts of the rebellion Terlannis herself set down after her victory. She was quite thorough in describing the wizard-king's treasures and the dispositions she made with them. Some things she destroyed, some she felt safe in giving away, and other things she thought best to conceal and protect." Mara folded her hands in her lap and met his gaze calmly. "The *Infiernadex* is the only book mentioned by name in her accounts. She feared that the book might survive any attempt to destroy it and perhaps reassemble itself in some distant land, so she directed it to be safely interred for all time, guarded by powerful wards.

"In fact, when her death approached, Terlannis instructed her followers to entomb the book with her, so that Lathander's blessings would keep the *Infiernadex* hidden from evil hands forever. The book lies in her crypt."

"So, if the tomb-breakers are indeed looking for this magical tome, then they're not simply looking for Lathanderian tombs," Hamil said. "They're looking for the tomb of Terlannis." The halfling scratched at his chin, collecting his thoughts for a moment before looking back up to Geran. "How many Lathanderians are buried on the Highfells? Do we have any idea how many burial mounds the Verunas have to search?"

Geran started to shrug helplessly, but the Initiate Mother answered for him. "Somewhere around eighty-five or so, Master Hamil."

Hamil winced. "So many?"

"Some are priests, and others are laymen who gave noteworthy service to Lathander during their lives. We have good records of which mounds are sacred to Amaunator, since we naturally honor those who followed the Sun Lord in his earlier incarnation as the Dawn Lord."

"Well, it's a start at least," Geran pointed out to Hamil. "We think we know who's opening barrows, and we think we know what they're looking for. The vast majority of the burial mounds around Hulburg are no longer of interest to us. We can concentrate on the Lathanderian mounds, and maybe we can determine which are likely to be visited next." He returned his attention to the abbess. "Do your records mention any distinguishing features of Terlannis's tomb? Markers, inscriptions . . . anything?"

"They do not, but I doubt that you will need them," the Initiate Mother said. "You see, I know where High Morninglady Terlannis is buried."

Twelve

24 Ches, the Year of the Ageless One

The Harmach's Hall seemed draftier and more drab than Kara Hulmaster remembered it. The rare occasions when the harmach took his seat in the high, open-raftered hall were most often feasts or banquets, held after sundown when the great chandeliers blazed with the warm light of hundreds of candles and the floor was crowded with merry, well-dressed people. In the gray light of a dull, overcast day, it simply struck her as dusty and unused, like an old barn left to fall down in a forgotten field. By the dreary daylight the old banners hanging from the rafters looked threadbare and worn, and the thirty or so people in the great room seemed out of place.

"Is the harmach coming?" Kara asked Sergeant Kolton, who stood beside her on the small mezzanine above the banquet hall and below the doors leading to the upper bailey. Six Shieldsworn guarded the upper doors of the chamber, commanding a good view of the spacious chamber below. Another half dozen of the harmach's guards stood watch by the great doors leading to the lower bailey. All the Shieldsworn were armed and armored for a fight; they wore long coats of mail and carried crossbows or halberds and long swords. They weren't the only soldiers in the room. More armsmen in the colors of various merchant costers or guilds stood watch by their council members assembling around the table in the center of the hall.

"I think he'll be here momentarily, Lady Kara," the round-faced soldier said. He glanced to the gilded doors—now old and peeling—that led from the banquet hall to the interior courts and passageways of the castle. Then he looked back down at the hall below and shook his head. "Doesn't seem proper to me, though. He shouldn't be at anyone's beck and call."

"It would be worse if he didn't greet his guests," Kara said. She sighed and descended the stairs that led down to the hall's floor. In the middle of the room, immediately before the harmach's carved wooden throne on its old dais, Griffonwatch's servants had set up a horseshoe-shaped table facing toward the hall's doors. Nine chairs were spaced around the table for the Harmach's Council, and behind the council's table, the castle staff had arranged plain wooden benches for the councilors' retinues, such as they were. She took her seat at the foot of the right-hand arm of the horseshoe, automatically arranging the skirts of her own mail over the chair and turning her sword parallel to the ground so the hilt wouldn't poke her under her ribs. She made sure to sit a good two feet back from the edge of the table. If she needed to get to her feet and draw her blade fast, she didn't want the council table in her way.

"Ah, Lady Kara. Perhaps you can tell us what this is all about?" Kara glanced to her left, where Lord Maroth Marstel had his seat at the table. The Marstels were descended from a high-placed captain of the old Red Plumes of Hillsfar, a lord who had taken up residence in Hulburg after the Red Plumes had been driven out of their city, and he'd established a wealthy estate with the plundered loot and sworn armsmen he'd taken with him. Maroth Marstel was a tall, red-faced man of middle years who affected a much higher station than his family's checkered past likely warranted. "This is most irregular. Our bylaws insist on three days' notice of a meeting of the council."

"That's a custom, not a law," Kara replied. She had always found Marstel a leering boor, but as a Hulmaster and advisor to the harmach she was expected to sit at the table alongside buffoons such as the head of House Marstel, whether she wanted to or not. She set aside her irritation at his insipid manner and said, "It's not for me to say why you have been summoned, Lord Maroth, but you'll see soon enough."

She took her eyes from his and glanced at the other members of the Harmach's Council. They did not meet often; most attended to their own particular duties in administering the small realm of Hulburg and rarely needed to confer with the others. Directly across from her was Wulreth Keltor, the Keeper of Keys—a careworn, petulant old man who administered the sorely depleted treasury and the public works of the city. Beside him sat the wizard Ebain Ravenscar, the town's Master Mage. He was a young, dark-bearded Mulmasterite who was in theory the most competent wizard residing in Hulburg. The Master Mage was supposed to be responsible for ensuring that practitioners of magic observed some basic precautions while within the city, and he was entitled to the ear of the harmach. In practice Ravenscar gave his official duties little attention, and Kara strongly suspected that the wizard was well paid to be so inattentive.

Next came the chair reserved for the captain of the Shieldsworn. Jarad Erstenwold's seat sat empty, and Kara didn't know when it might be filled again. The sight of the vacant chair gave her a pang in her chest; she missed Jarad's crooked smile and plain-spoken ways every day. At the head of the table sat Lady Darsi Veruna, head of the Merchant Council, stunning in a dress of deep blue with an ermine stole over her shoulders; Theron Nimstar, the town's High Magistrate; and then her stepbrother, Sergen, the Keeper of Duties and the harmach's deputy on the council. Finally, on the other side of Lord Marstel, the old, white-haired dwarf Dunstormad Goldhead brooded in his own seat. He was the town's lord assayer, but in practice Sergen's oversight of the Hulmaster lands left him with little to do except indulge his passion for drink.

"It seems we're all here," Kara murmured to herself. She couldn't remember the last time she'd seen all of the council at a meeting, let alone one called on such short notice.

The ranger heard a rustle of motion behind her and looked up to the stairs at the back of the hall. Harmach Grigor made his way stiffly down the steps with the aid of his heavy cane. He wore a long burgundy coat over a ruffled white shirt, with a matching hat and gold medallion of office around his neck. Two Shieldsworn guards flanked him, ostensibly to guard him from an unexpected attack, but more likely watching for a stumble on the old steps. Everyone in the hall rose to their feet and waited until Grigor took his seat on the dais overlooking the council's table. He leaned his cane against one arm of the great seat and said, "Please, continue. Sergen, summon the messengers when you are ready."

Sergen looked up and down the table, reassuring himself that all the council members were indeed present, and then motioned to Sergeant Kolton. "Bring them in, sergeant. Be on your guard."

Shieldsworn guards at the lower entrance to the great hall pulled open the doors. There was an uncertain swirl of motion as they stepped aside and more guards entered. Then the orcs pushed their way into the hall—five of them, all draped in heavy hauberks of mail. One was older than the others, a hulking gray-haired brute with only one tusk. The others were younger warriors, fierce and proud. They glared at the humans around them, their hands gripping tightly the hafts and hilts of weapons they wore on their crude harnesses. Each warrior had a simple red emblem painted across the mail of his chest—a jawless red skull. The gray-haired one even had a red-painted skull hanging from a short chain at his hip. "I am Morag One-Tusk, Morag the Slayer, Morag the Old," he roared at the great hall. "I speak for King Mhurren, the Scourge of Glister. Who here is chief?"

Bloody Skulls, Kara thought. She hid her consternation behind narrowed eyes. She knew something about the tribes of Thar, having hunted—and been hunted by—quite a few of them over the years. The Bloody Skulls were about the strongest and most numerous of Thar's orcs, but fortunately they had rarely troubled Hulburg, since the territory of several smaller tribes lay between Bloodskull Keep and the Winterspear vale—the Red Claws goblins, the Bonecrusher ogres, and a few other smaller bands as well. The fact that the Bloody Skulls thought that Hulburg was a concern of theirs was a bad sign. Something must have happened to turn the alliances and enmities of the Thar tribes in a new direction, and Kara suspected that she would not like it at all.

"I am Grigor Hulmaster," the harmach said. He kept his voice even. "I am the harmach—the chief—of Hulburg. You stand before the council of Hulburg, Morag. You told my soldiers that you had a message for the leaders of Hulburg. We are here to listen to your words. Come forward and speak."

Morag and the other four advanced, looking around the room with poorly disguised contempt. They marched to the foot of the council table, heads high, sneering at any who met their gaze. The old orc looked at the councilors in their seats, snorting in derision when the Keeper of Keys averted his gaze, growling when he caught sight of the dwarf Goldhead, and finally pausing when his eyes reached Kara. "You, I know of," he muttered. "The Blue Serpent, mighty hunter. You do not look so fearsome to me."

Kara's spellscar seemed to writhe and itch under the skin of her left forearm, but she made no move to cover the serpent-shaped mark. *"I have heard of Morag the Slayer,"* she answered in Orcish. Years ago he had led a bold raid that sacked a caravan on the Coastal Way west of Thentia. He was an important Bloodskull chief. She met the old warrior's eyes, and she bared her teeth in what passed among orcs as a gesture indicating both respect and a fierce willingness to face challenge without quailing.

Morag grunted in approval and showed his own fangs before he strode boldly to the center of the horseshoe-shaped table. He stood motionless and silent for a moment, his eyes fixed on Harmach Grigor, paying no attention to the mailed swordsmen who surrounded the dais or the council members who waited on him. Then he threw out his chest and spoke.

"You are weak," the gray-haired orc snarled at the harmach. "Your town counts thirty score spears, but King Mhurren counts six times that number. Once, many years ago, all the lands north of the Moonsea belonged to the King of Thar. Then came the humans of the south and the *burkhushk* dwarves—" that was a word in Orcish Kara was frankly glad no one else in the room understood— "from out of their mountains to dig Thar's gold, to cut Thar's stone, to hunt in Thar's hills, and drink Thar's water. Yet never once did you bargain with Thar's rightful masters for these things. You came and you took. You slew our sons where you found them and then hid behind your walls of stone to deny us just revenge.

"King Mhurren will stand this no more. You must pay for the things you have taken from our lands, or we will take our lands back and drive you into the sea."

The Hulburgans stirred and muttered at that. Some of the fainter-hearted paled or looked uncertainly to the faces of those around them, hoping they had not heard the Bloody Skull messenger correctly. Most of the Shieldsworn tightened their grips on their weapons until knuckles whitened, lips pressed together and eyes cold.

Sergen Hulmaster stood, leaning on the table with his hands, and looked the old orc in the eye. "You come here to issue threats? We will not be cowed by vain orc boasts in the Harmach's Hall!"

"I do not make threats," Morag scoffed. "I speak truths, pinkskin. We are strong; you are weak. Give us what is ours or we will take it from you—and more. If you do not hear the iron in my words, then you are deaf." He grasped the red-painted skull hanging by his hip, ripped it free of its chain, and tossed it onto the table in front of Sergen. Bone cracked, and chips fell to the floor. "Ask the Overmaster of Glister if the Bloody Skulls make threats. There he sits on your table, speaking truth to you. Do you hear him?"

Sergen's handsome face darkened, and he straightened up. But before he could say anything, Grigor spoke. "I hear you, Morag. Mhurren of Bloodskull Keep demands tribute. What does he think I will give him?"

"Five wagons of gold. Two hundred cattle and one thousand sheep or goats. Two hundred casks of wine or ale. Two hundred coats of mail, two hundred steel swords, five hundred steel axeheads or knife blades." Morag grinned in challenge. "And you will present one hundred slaves between ten and thirty years of age. Twenty at least must be women suitable to be taken as wives. All this you will do at Highsun each year, or Mhurren will lower his spear against you, and all that you have he will take."

The room erupted with protests. Wulreth Keltor, the Keeper of Keys, simply stared at Morag with his jaw slack and his face stricken. No doubt he was staggered by the enormity of the orc's demands.

Beside Kara, Lord Marstel pushed himself to his feet and barked, "We will not give you a copper piece, let alone condemn our women to rape and drudgery in some filthy cave, you ill-bred louts!"

Hearing that, Kara leaped up herself to defend the empty-headed lord against the mortal insult he had just issued to Morag—but fortunately others were shouting too. The lord assayer shouted, "That would ruin us! The demand is outrageous!"

And one of the Veruna mercenaries behind Lady Darsi actually drew his blade and shook it as he snarled, "Kill them! Kill them for their insolence, and perhaps Mhurren will learn to send messengers with better manners next time!"

"And perhaps Mhurren will learn that he should kill those we send to speak to him!" Kara snapped. "You fool. The day may come when we need to talk with the chieftains in Thar, and if we kill their messengers, how will they treat ours?"

"Enough," Harmach Grigor said. The shouting went on around the table, and the harmach slowly got to his feet and struck his cane to the floor with a resounding *crack!* "Enough!" he shouted, and this time he managed to quiet the hall. "No messenger before me will be killed because I do not like his words. Put down your swords, those of you who drew your weapons. You will not violate the ancient rules of parley in my hall." Morag grinned again at that, but the harmach turned and pointed at him next. "And you, Morag, be glad that you speak under a flag of truce. You will not be killed for what you say, but if you insult me in my own hall, you will be driven from my door with nothing but your bare hands to take back to your master."

The old chief's grin faded to a sour frown. "If you dishonor me, human, you dishonor my king."

"If I decide that your king means to march against me no matter what I do, then I see no reason why I should concern myself with his honor," Grigor retorted.

"As you say, then," Morag growled. "So what is your answer, Chief of Hulburg? Will you render tribute or will you choose war?"

The harmach leaned on his cane and studied the orc for a time. Then he sighed. "I must weigh your words, Morag. I will give you my answer soon. Now go."

The gray-haired chief snorted. "King Mhurren said that humans can decide nothing without endless talk. He told me to grant you three days. If you do not give me an answer by sunset of the third day, I will tell Mhurren that you have chosen war. I go to wait at my camp." He turned slowly, contemptuously turning his back on the harmach and striding back to the door. His escort of warriors followed, snarling at anyone who came too close.

In a few moments the Bloody Skull emissary was gone, and the Shieldsworn pushed the heavy doors of the hall closed with a resounding *boom.*

Harmach Grigor gazed after the orc messengers. Then he sighed and sagged back down into his seat. Quietly he said, "Well, you've all heard Mhurren's demand. What say you?"

"The Bloody Skulls are blustering," Maroth Marstel said at once. "They have never threatened us in the past. Their keep is more than a hundred miles from here. I say that they hope to extort a kingly ransom from us by simply baring their filthy fangs and snarling. Well, I for one am not impressed!"

Ravenscar, the master mage, cleared his throat and looked to Kara. "Lady Kara, you know the tribes of Thar as well as any. Is Morag telling the truth about Bloody Skull numbers?"

"He could be. I would guess that they could muster about two thousand warriors from their various strongholds, but if they managed to subjugate some of the nearby tribes and add their numbers to their own . . . yes, it could be close to four thousand. But they wouldn't all get along with each other."

"What of his words about Glister?" the mage asked. "Have the Bloody Skulls sacked it?"

"They may have," Kara answered. "Yesterday a man from Glister came into town with his wife and children. They fled Glister seven days ago because they'd seen orc scouts and marauders in great numbers, and they had word that orcs were marching against the town. What might have befallen Glister after they fled, I can't say. But I'll have scouts on fast horses sent out within the hour to see."

The High Magistrate, Theron Nimstar, leaned forward to look at Kara. He was a stout man with a heavy beard of rusty gray, thoughtful and deliberate in his words. "Assume that Morag is telling the truth. Can the Shieldsworn defend Hulburg against so large a horde?"

"No, my lord." Kara saw the sharp shock in the man's face and let it sink in for a moment. "We could defend Griffonwatch and Daggergard Tower and shelter hundreds of townsfolk within their walls. I feel confident that we could withstand a siege of months. But the town itself would belong to the Bloody Skulls, and most of our people would have to flee, since we wouldn't have space for them within our castles."

"What if you added the armsmen belonging to the Merchant Council to the Shieldsworn?" the old magistrate asked. "Would that help?"

"Certainly," Kara replied. "I think Morag included those when he said that we could muster six hundred, because that's three times the number of Shieldsworn in the harmach's service. But we'd still have to meet them in the open field to keep them away from the town, and I can't promise you that we'd win such a battle—if Morag was truthful about the Bloody Skulls' numbers."

The mage Ravenscar looked around the table. "If we decide not to fight, can we actually meet the tribute demand?"

"The tribute he demands is beyond the Tower's purse," Keeper Wulreth said in a quavering voice. "One time, perhaps, we could gather the gold, livestock, and arms. But it would ruin us, and it would be years before we could manage another such ransom."

"And what is the cost to the Tower of sending one hundred people into thralldom?" Kara asked sharply. "Whose daughters do you intend to provide as 'wives' to the Bloody Skulls?"

"The Bloody Skulls likely don't care where their slaves come from," Sergen said thoughtfully. "No Hulburgan need become an orc's thrall when there are slave markets in other cities that could meet our need."

"Which would also be a substantial expense," Lord Assayer Goldhead grunted. "It would cost thousands of gold crowns to purchase so many slaves in Melvaunt or Mulmaster."

"How is it better to condemn some other unfortunate souls to drudgery and death in the Bloody Skulls' hands?" Kara demanded. "At one stroke you'd have us become the most vile slave merchants in the Moonsea!"

"I will have no more talk of this," Harmach Grigor said firmly. "My father decreed that no slave would be taken or sold in Hulburg, and I will not be the harmach to reverse his law. We will buy no slaves to send to the orcs."

"Then you must fight, or you must send one hundred of your own to become thralls," Darsi Veruna coolly observed. "I suppose you might try to negotiate with Mhurren and see if he can be persuaded to accept a lesser tribute. But I suspect that he is not inclined to bargain with you, Lord Grigor."

Silence fell over the great hall. The harmach looked down at his lap, his brow furrowed in thought. Finally he shook his head and slowly stood. "We all must think on this more," he said. "Keeper Wulreth, prepare an exact accounting to see if we could possibly meet the demand. Kara, send out your riders. I want to know if Glister has been sacked—and if it has, there may be refugees abroad in Thar who are trying to find their way to safety in our lands. And I want to know where the Bloody Skull horde is, and its true numbers."

"Yes, Harmach Grigor," Kara answered. "I'll see to it now." She rose with a jingling of mail, bowed to her uncle, and headed for the door. As she left, she heard the arguing begin again.

Thirteen

24 Ches, the Year of the Ageless One

Geran and Hamil rode out from Rosestone Abbey two hours after sunrise. The morning was dank and gray, but the bitter cold of the previous night had passed in the dark hours before dawn. It was wet and windy on the Highfells, but there was no sign of the grim specters that had dogged their heels the night before.

They rode for most of the morning in silence, heading westward from the abbey. The city of Thentia stood a little less than fifty miles off in that direction, and the two travelers soon found their way onto a rough, lightly traveled trail between Hulburg and Thentia that meandered past Rosestone. Most traffic between the two cities went by sea or followed the so-called Ruined Way closer to the coast, which was relatively level and wide enough for cart traffic. Geran had come by the abbey's path once or twice as a young man, but he'd never followed it all the way to Thentia.

A few miles from the abbey, the trail started to climb along the bare shoulders of brown, sere hills, some of the highest prominences to be found in the Highfells. Geran began to watch the trailside more carefully for the landmark the Initiate Mother had told him about, and soon he found it—the old stone foundations of a long-vanished watchtower.

"We turn here," he told Hamil.

The halfling glanced at the old ruins. "Who put a tower here?" he wondered.

"Mother Mara said that this old path used to be an important road of old Thentur. I suppose it fell into disuse when war wrecked the kingdom and

Hulburg—the old city, that is—was destroyed." Geran turned his mount uphill and left the path, picking his way toward the bare stony hilltop. "It shouldn't be far now."

There was a very faint track above the old trail. It wound higher up the hillside. Geran supposed that the view over the moorlands would have been spectacular on a clear day, but as the weather was overcast, the hilltop was shrouded in blowing mist. They crossed over a shallow saddle, and there on the south-facing slope of the hill stood a large, solitary burial mound.

"I think this is it," Geran said. He reined in before the mound and swung himself down from the saddle. Like the other barrows they had visited in the last couple of days, it was a circular mound covered with turf. A waist-high wall of crumbling fieldstone edged the mound, so that the whole thing looked a little like a large, windowless storehouse half-sunk into the dry grass of the hillside. He scrambled up onto its turf roof and climbed to the peak; it was perhaps twenty-five yards in diameter, a little larger than some of the others they had seen, but not by much. Near the top Geran found a shallow set of stone steps that descended four or five feet and ended in a mortared wall beneath a large keystone—a keystone engraved with an ancient sunrise design. "It's got Lathander's mark on it," he called to Hamil.

"It seems to be the right age and construction," the halfling answered. He shaded his eyes and scanned the hillside around them for a long moment, looking for any sign that they were not alone, and then shrugged and slid down from his Teshan pony. "Is it open?"

"No, we'll have to dig."

"What about the harmach's law?"

"If I've got good reason for what I'm doing, my uncle will understand," Geran answered. He didn't like the idea of being the first to open a barrow, but if Mara was right and this was the tomb of Terlannis, then it was likely warded against the minions of Aesperus or any other undead spirits that might otherwise have taken up residence inside. He simply hoped that he truly had a good reason.

The Verunas already know that they're looking for a tomb under Lathander's mark, he told himself. It was only a matter of time until they discovered this one. He could try to disguise it—perhaps destroying or altering the sunrise mark on the keystone, for instance—but the mercenaries might be using some kind of divination magic to find the tombs they meant to search, and Geran couldn't be certain that any steps he took to disguise the mound would fool them.

"Of course, this tomb might be better warded than anything I could come up with, and if the book's here, then it might be best to leave it where it lies," Geran murmured to himself. "But I won't know that it's safe until I see for myself. If it's well protected, I can leave it here and do what I can to disguise the mound. If it's not, then I have to hope that the Verunas never stumble across this place, or I've got to remove it if I want to keep it away from the Verunas . . . as well as that tiefling we met."

Do you have a better hiding spot in mind? Hamil said silently. The halfling might not have been close enough to hear Geran muttering to himself, but apparently he'd been close enough to catch Geran's thoughts with his mind.

"Keep it in the vaults of Griffonwatch? Or give it to the Initiate Mother and let her look after it since it belonged to a priestess of Lathander?" Geran trotted back down to the mound's edge and hopped down. "For that matter, I could do worse than to hide it under a rock in some lonely hollow out here in the Highfells. If we actually find it, I'm sure I'll think of something."

They picketed the horses at the base of the mound and carried their saddlebags and provisions back to the stairwell at the top. Then Geran took a heavy pry bar down the filled-in stairway and set to work on the old mortar and stone under the sunrise symbol. There was not room for more than one to work at a time, but Hamil helped carry up the stones Geran dislodged. The halfling was careful to spread out the rubble instead of leaving it in a pile that might be seen from a distance.

After half an hour of vigorous work, Geran broke through the mortared wall to a space beyond. Cold, stale air sighed out of the opening. He quickly backed away to avoid breathing in the barrow-air. Old, foul air could kill the unwary, so he decided to let the barrow breathe while he and Hamil sat a short distance away and ate a cold lunch. At one point Geran stood to stretch, and he thought he glimpsed a shadow slinking beneath the bare stone of the hilltop, a shadow where one shouldn't have been. But when he stared up at the spot, he saw nothing unusual.

"Is our friend back?" Hamil asked.

"I'm not sure. I didn't get a very good look—it could have been anything." Geran glanced over to the picket line, but the horses placidly grazed, plainly unconcerned. "The horses don't seem nervous."

"I'm not reassured."

"Nor am I." Geran rested a little longer before he returned to the stairwell and attacked the wall again, working to make a hole big enough to wriggle through. Despite the chill mist that blew over the Highfells, Geran was soon streaming with sweat, but he shed his cloak and kept at it until he had an opening he could squeeze through.

"You should knock out a few more stones," Hamil observed. "You might get a small pony through there, but I don't think you could fit a draft horse yet."

"Feel free to have a go at it," Geran said with a snort.

"It's not my fault that my people have a sensible stature, while all you Big Folk take up three times as much room as a normal person and manage to get half as much done. I could've been in that barrow half an hour ago."

"Well, then, why didn't you go on ahead?"

"I didn't want to get lonely," Hamil answered.

Geran shook his head and turned away. He decided to examine his shields and wards before going any farther; the barrows they'd seen before had been opened by others, but this one hadn't felt fresh air in hundreds of years. They'd seen no evidence of traps or guardians in the other Lathanderian tombs, but that didn't mean the tomb of Terlannis would be safe. Closing his eyes, he stilled his thoughts and focused his awareness into a single bright point. The Elvish swordmage spells rolled easily from his heart and will as he renewed the spells he routinely wore. To these he added another defense and whispered the words to summon the pale aura of the silversteel veil. Finally, for good measure, he drew his elfmade sword and passed his palm over the eldritch steel. *"Reith arroch, reith ne sylle,"* he chanted softly. A thin white radiance began to shine in the blade.

Hamil looked up from where he stood, stringing his bow. "I don't recognize that one."

"It's a spell of sharpness, but it's especially baleful to ghosts and other such spirits." Sword in hand, Geran descended the narrow stairwell again and peered once more through the dark opening he'd made below. A small, dusty passage led deeper into the mound, but he saw nothing else. Carefully he set one foot on the far side and ducked under the sill, working his way inside. In the shadows, the pale radiance of his sword began to shine more brightly, driving back the darkness. Geran advanced a few steps down the passage, and Hamil followed a moment later, an arrow laid across his small horn bow. The air was cold and stale.

The passage led to an antechamber, where two dark doorways beckoned. A niche in the wall between the low doorways held a small statue of an angel, made from some porous white stone that was splotched green and black with mildew. Geran ventured right first and descended two steps into a larger, barrel-vaulted chamber. Here stood two full-sized statues of armored warriors, one on each side of a heavy frieze in bronze that was set into the far wall. A faint yellow light spell still glimmered in a small, tarnished lantern suspended from the ceiling. The swordmage studied the chamber from the doorway for a long moment and nodded. "I think it's a memorial," he told Hamil. "The crypt must be in the other room."

"What does it say?" Hamil asked.

Geran moved closer to the frieze. It showed a battle scene; a lady in armor riding a great charger led soldiers over a drawbridge against the gates of a dark castle. Mailed skeletons stood in serried ranks against the lady and her soldiers, but she was raising high a rod with a sunburst device for its head. Rays sprang from the rod, striking the dark castle's gates, which seemed to go up in fire at their touch, while skeletons in the way withered away like autumn leaves. Dethek runes nearly filled in with dust and debris were cut into the smoothly dressed stone beneath. Geran knelt and brushed his hand over the old runes until he could make them out.

"Old Tesharan again," he murmured. "I think it says something like, 'The downfall of the Wailing Tower . . . the—glory? fire?—of Lathander burns the' . . . something 'warriors' . . . 'Aesperus is cast down in defeat . . . High' . . . something . . . 'Terlannis in her hour of victory, may Lathander's . . . blessing? . . . follow after her forever.' "

"So this is Terlannis's crypt." Hamil padded closer and studied the frieze himself before pointing to the far corner of the work. "Look, I bet that's Aesperus there. He doesn't seem very happy."

Geran followed Hamil's finger. Flanked by knights in black armor, a skeletal king in regal robes fled from the destruction of the gates, going down into some sort of tunnel or doorway that disappeared from view.

"It shows events pretty much as Mother Mara explained them. Terlannis destroyed the tower, and Aesperus fled into some dungeon or retreat below his fortress. Let's have a look around and see if the book is hidden somewhere in this room."

They carefully tapped, poked, and prodded at the frieze, the warrior statues, even the walls and the floors as thoroughly as they could, but they found no secret compartments or hidden doors. Giving up for the moment, Geran returned to the antechamber and tried the other doorway. This led down several steps into another barrel-vaulted room, dominated by a great stone crypt. Its lid was carved in the image of a stern woman in plate armor lying in repose, her hands holding a great sunburst emblem over her heart. The walls and floor were finished with smooth, polished stone, but the chamber was otherwise bare.

"Terlannis, I presume," Hamil said.

"So it would seem." Geran could make out her name cut in runes at the foot of the sarcophagus. He looked at the big stone structure and frowned. Was the book actually entombed with her remains? Digging out the stairwell to gain access to the chamber in the mound was one thing, but he found that he didn't want to be the one to actually damage the crypt. It was possible that they might be able to drive anchoring pitons into the ceiling over the crypt and rig some sort of block and tackle . . . but he would still have to disturb the ancient priestess's bones, and somehow he felt that Amaunator—Lathander—would not look kindly on that. "I hate the idea of breaking into the sarcophagus."

"Afraid of curses? Guardian spirits?"

"Among other things, yes." Geran looked around and sighed. "Let's check everything else before we try the tomb itself."

They carefully examined every corner of the room, feeling along the walls and tapping the flagstones with the pommels of their daggers. After a long, careful search, nothing seemed out of the ordinary. Not really expecting much, Geran finally took a few minutes to speak a simple elven finding charm. He'd learned a thing or two about finding well-hidden things in Myth Drannor; he'd seen more than one elf-made door that simply couldn't be found by someone who didn't already know it was there. Doubtless the tomb was warded against such minor magic, but he figured it was worth a try. He whispered the words in Elvish . . . and he felt a slight tug, a gleaming in the corner of his eye, from the antechamber outside the tomb. "I think I've got something, Hamil," he said, and he hurried back out to the room outside Terlannis's crypt. He turned in a small circle, trying to sharpen the glimmer of perception he'd felt, and then his eye fell on the small statue of the angel in its niche.

"There," he breathed. He bent close to examine the small statue in its niche and thought he could make out a paper-thin seam in the joining of its arm to its shoulder. "Hamil, have a look at this."

The halfling moved up close beside him and peered at the angel statue. Geran had learned to respect Hamil's skill with subtle traps, hidden triggers, and concealed mechanisms during their time with the Dragon Shields; the halfling had made it his business to know as much as he could about such devices, prowling the curio shops and antique collections of every city in the Vast to collect clever puzzles, charms, locks, and even toys in order to study the workings of each. Hamil's house in Tantras was littered with those devices he prized enough to display for visitors . . . and guarded by more subtle and dangerous ones to make sure that no uninvited visitors would find it safe to linger there.

Hamil studied the statue for a long time, then examined the niche all around it carefully. Finally, he drew out from a pouch at his belt a small paper tube full of silvery powder, which he blew out over the statue. It sparkled oddly in the shadows as it settled. "No hidden rune-traps or symbols," he said. "I think it's a simple lever. Likely it opens a hidden panel or doorway."

Geran glanced around the antechamber. "It's very well hidden, then. We both had a good look here."

"Should I pull it?"

"I really don't want to try the sarcophagus before we've exhausted all other options. Give it a try."

"Stand back," Hamil warned.

The halfling slid to one side of the niche, pressed himself up against the wall, and gently pulled the angel's arm toward him. The seam between arm and body widened. Then Hamil rotated the arm back—it did not move that way far at all—reversed his motion, and twisted it forward. It moved a good quarter-turn and clicked, and the whole statue rose a quarter of an inch; the halfling rotated the angel on its base until he heard another faint click, and he raised the arm again until it locked back in place.

Metal and stone groaned somewhere under the feet, chains clanked slowly, and suddenly the floor of the antechamber began to sink. Geran quickly stepped back into the doorway leading to Terlannis's crypt, while Hamil moved to the door opposite. A section of floor about ten feet across sank until it was a good eight feet lower than it had been, revealing a door of brightly polished bronze, untarnished despite the age of the mound. Hamil looked across the space to Geran. "I guess it was an elevator," he said. "The sounds you heard were the counterweights. Clever. I didn't expect the floor to move."

Geran stooped down to grip the stone sill, swung himself over the edge, and dropped easily to the floor. He crossed over to give Hamil a hand down, since it was a long drop for the halfling, and the two companions turned their attention to the polished bronze door. It was inscribed with a great sunburst, ringed by a strange, flowing script.

"What does it say?" Hamil asked him.

"I don't have the faintest idea. I think the script might be Celestial, but I can't read a word of it." The swordmage frowned and whispered another spell of perception—this one to reveal the presence of magic. The beautiful lettering shone with a fiery gold radiance in his eyes, and he felt the old, undiminished strength of ancient wards. "It's divine magic of some kind. Some sort of spell of concealment? I can't be sure."

"Well, that would stand to reason. If the Lathanderians buried something here to keep it away from Aesperus, they would have used magic to deflect his efforts to scry its location." The halfling blew a little more of his silver powder over the door, and again it sparkled as it drifted down to the flagstones. "No symbols or runes here, either, but it's locked. Do we open it?"

"Yes. If we can find this place, so can Veruna's soldiers."

"All right, then." Hamil worked for a moment on the lock and pushed the door open. Cold, dry air sighed out of the room beyond—a large, low-ceilinged hall, its roof supported by dozens of pillars. A great bronze statue of a leonine creature dominated the center of the chamber, lying with its paws outstretched on the floor and its head held high. Its face was human in shape, surrounded by a great mane. Behind the statue stood a stone chest, covered in fine carvings. Ancient sconces holding slender golden staves lined the chamber walls; as Geran and Hamil moved into the room, flickering flames guttered into life around the golden staves, giving the room a rich yellow glow.

"Well, the servants of Lathander hid a crypt below a crypt," the halfling observed. "I admit, I didn't expect work of such skill here."

"The chest," Geran said. He looked carefully at the room and did not see anything to alarm him, so he started to circle around the statue to the left.

He was only five paces from the door when the lion opened its eyes and looked at him.

The statue shuddered once, and old metal squealed against old metal as it slowly began to clamber to its feet. Geran stepped quickly back, moving away from the thing, but a bright golden fire sprang up in its eyes, and it opened its mouth to speak. In a voice that sounded like the clashing of cymbals, it roared in Old Tesharan, *"Speak now the Three Secret Names and state thy purpose here, or I must destroy thee!"*

A guardian construct! Hamil said in alarm. He retreated too, backing away in a different direction. *Geran, what in the Nine Hells did it say?*

Geran felt a pillar at his back and stopped retreating. The bronze lion was not alive, of course—it was an enchanted statue, long ago imbued with the power to animate and attack any strangers who made it into the vault chamber. It might lack the speed and ferocity of a real sphinx or lammasu or whatever it was supposed to be, but it would be a formidable war machine nonetheless, tireless and implacable. *We're supposed to know a password!* he replied to Hamil.

"Answer now, interloper, or thy doom is assured!" the statue roared again.

The bronze monster was easily the size of a large horse, its clawed feet the size of dinner plates. We need time to think, Geran decided. We might be able to puzzle out the password, but not quickly. "Back out!" he said.

He turned to race for the doorway, only to spy something above the door's lintel—a baleful golden rune inscribed on a heavy keystone, facing in toward the lion. They'd walked right under it when they entered the chamber, which was likely what had triggered the magic to animate the statue and give it a voice. But two other runic marks were cut into the stone on each side of the glowing golden one, and when Geran's eye fell on them they kindled to life as lines of sullen crimson fire. "Wait, no!" he shouted. "Stay away from the door. There are symbols over it!"

Hamil was closer to the door than he was; when the symbols awoke, he gave a strangled cry and fell to one knee, already within the influence of the magical trap. Somehow he managed two staggering steps away from the door, but now the statue turned with a scraping of bronze and fixed its burning golden eyes on him.

"Defiler! Infidel!" the statue's voice proclaimed. It advanced on Hamil, who still reeled from his brush with the Lathanderian runes.

"Damn!" Geran swore. They had a fight here, whether they wanted it or not. He quickly cast his dragon-scale spell, even though he was not sure how much it would help against a foe of such strength. *"Theillalagh na drendir!"* he whispered, and around him the cascading scales of glowing violet light shimmered into existence.

The swordmage darted forward to distract the thing from Hamil and lunged out with his blade at the statue's eye. Elven steel clanged shrilly against ancient bronze; the impact jarred his hand, and Geran almost dropped his sword. The thing was *hot,* radiating heat-shimmers. The leonine monster turned on him with startling quickness for something so big and inflexible, and raked at him with its huge paw. Geran leaped back out of the way, and the statue followed, bulling its way straight at him. He saw that his thrust had dug a deep gouge just under the blank molten eye, creasing the bronze without penetrating it. He ducked behind one of the pillars in the chamber, trying to keep it between the statue and himself.

How do you destroy something made of metal? he thought furiously. He'd encountered animated statues and magical constructs before in his years with the Dragon Shields, and he well remembered that they were difficult to defeat. Some had vital mechanisms that could be ruined by a very well-aimed sword blow, but this one had been brought to life by powerful magic; as far as he could tell, it was a cast statue of bronze, hollow inside, with no vital mechanisms to destroy. The bronze itself was not even articulated; the magic of the ancient ritual that animated the thing gave the cast metal the suppleness and flexibility of living flesh.

While he tried to figure out how to deal with the thing, the statue moved around the pillar to get at him, and Geran circled away from it. It reversed its course and tried the other direction, and once again Geran moved with it. Then the bronze sphinx simply hurled itself straight at him, shouldering its way past the pillar. Stone cracked and splintered under its weight; dust sifted down from the ceiling. Geran grunted in surprise and danced back before taking his sword in a two-handed grip. He threw all his strength into a mighty cut across the statue's face, and this time the elven steel actually parted the bronze in a shallow cut; molten red-gold fire seeped from the wound. A drop splattered the top of his boot and set the leather to smoking. Then the statue caught him with one mighty paw. Geran's dragon-scale spell held, mostly—the deadly claws did not tear through his flesh, only scoring him lightly. But the spell did not guard against the crushing impact of the blow. He was batted away like a mouse flipped head-over-paws by a cat, and he skidded to the ground a dozen feet away.

The bronze sphinx bounded after him, but just as it raised its paw to crush his skull, a pair of arrows thudded into its golden flank. "Come on, you lump of lead!" Hamil shouted. "Chase after me for a bit!"

The halfling had rallied from his brush with the symbol spell and crouched behind a pillar on the far side of the room, firing arrows as fast as he could draw his bow. They did not penetrate far into the bronze hide, but the range was short enough for the halfling to drive the steel points half an inch into the old bronze. More molten metal began to leak from the pinprick wounds, and the statue whirled away from Geran to pursue the halfling.

Geran groaned and rolled over to all fours, slowly pushing himself to his feet. His whole left side ached from where the sphinx's bronze paw had caught him. He found his sword lying nearby and stood again. On the other side of the chamber, the statue snapped and clawed at Hamil, who dodged from pillar to pillar, just trying to stay out of its way.

"We need a better plan, Geran!" Hamil shouted to him.

The swordmage glanced left, right, and all around as he cast about for some position or advantage over the powerful bronze sphinx. Then his eye fell on the first pillar he'd used for cover against the construct. Its head was visibly out of vertical, and deep cracks spiderwebbed its surface. A desperate idea sprang into his mind, and he quickly measured the vaulting of the ceiling with his eye.

"Stay near the wall!" he called to Hamil. "I'll get its attention again!"

"You're welcome to it," Hamil answered.

Geran ignored him and charged the statue's hindquarters, taking a strong cut at its hamstring—or at least where its hamstring would be, if it were a living creature. He creased the bronze enough to spill a little more of its molten metal and drew back quickly, even as the monster whirled to face him again.

"Come on!" he shouted. "After me!"

The construct hurtled after him, and Geran darted back several steps. At the last moment he ducked behind the damaged pillar . . . and the statue lunged after him in response, striking the column almost dead-on. The pillar toppled with an awful roar of shattering stone, and the ceiling over it sagged and collapsed.

"Seiroch!" Geran shouted—a spell of transposition, magic that simply teleported him from one place to another close by in the space of an instant. He flickered out from under the collapse, reappearing on the other side of the room beneath the vaulting by the wall—the strongest part of the ceiling, or so he hoped. The warm yellow light filling the chamber dimmed and failed as billowing clouds of dust and debris choked the chamber. More of the ceiling gave way, and a cascade of rock and earth poured down into the middle of the room . . . but finally the collapse slowed, and an eerie silence settled over the room.

Hamil coughed once on the dust and looked up at Geran. "What would you have done if the whole ceiling had come down?" he demanded.

"I was hoping that it wouldn't." Geran eyed the heap of debris filling the center of the chamber. He could see one great bronze paw amid the wreckage, but it was hollow, empty; there was no molten fire within. Wearily he sheathed his sword—the magical steel was unmarked from its encounter with the old bronze—and picked his way over to the stone chest against the far wall. It was carved with images of angels armed for war, carrying swords and shields. Another trap would seem redundant, but he could not be certain. "Hamil?"

The halfling joined him by the chest and quickly examined it with his silver powder and a careful visual inspection. "I think it's safe to open."

Geran nodded and lifted the lid, which was cleverly counterweighted so that it operated easily despite its weight. Inside, wrapped in cloth that had long since disintegrated to dusty scraps, lay a large tome bound in black leather. He reached in and lifted out the book, brushing the remnants of the wrapping away. Lettering embossed on the cover in the old Dethek runes read: *The Infiernadex, being a Compilation of Spells & Arcane Lore set down by the Hand of Aesperus, King of Thentur.* He was sorely tempted to flip it open to a random page, simply to see what sort of things Aesperus might have deemed worthy of compiling, but that was not a good idea. Reading from magical books could be quite dangerous or cause unintended consequences of all sorts. For the moment, it would be enough to secure the thing and spirit it away to some place where the sellswords in Veruna's service couldn't find it. Instead, he wrapped the book in a spare cloak and slipped it into his pack. "Now, we'll have to find a new hiding place House Veruna's men won't suspect," he said.

"First, we'll have to find a way out of this chamber. I'm not eager to venture too close to those symbols again," said Hamil. The halfling gestured at the doorway, where the symbols burned dully. The large one in the center was dark—its magic had likely ended when the animated statue was destroyed. But the other two remained active. "I suppose we could try to dig our way out. If my sense of direction is right, we're under the memorial chamber."

Geran looked up at the gaping hole in the ceiling and turned to the symbols gleaming over the door. "I'm afraid it would be too easy to bring the chamber above us down around our ears if we picked the wrong place to dig, but I know a spell or two that might get us past the symbols. It might take a little while, but it will be a lot easier than digging."

"Done," Hamil said. He sat down on the dais by the stone chest and waved toward the opposite door. "Have at it. Let me know if there's anything I can do to help."

"There isn't." Geran studied the markings over the door for a long moment, then sat down gingerly to examine his own spellbook, looking for something that might work. The ceiling overhead creaked ominously, and more dust drifted down. No, tunneling out was not an option. He meant to walk out of the room by the door through which he had entered . . . or did he? He looked up at the doorway, measuring the distance with his eye. "Yes, that would work," he muttered. "But I'll have to study new spells first. Hamil, make yourself comfortable. I have to rest a while before I can get us out of here."

Fourteen

25 Ches, the Year of the Ageless One

After Geran and Hamil ate a cold lunch from the rations they had on hand, Geran laid out his bedroll and stretched out on the cold stone floor. He was not especially sleepy, but if he could lie quietly and let his mind rest for a time, he would be able to ready himself for studying his spells. He knew from experience that he couldn't fix a spell in his mind when he was tired or distracted. The long ride over the moors, the excavation of the stairwell, the exploration of the vaults, and finally the battle against the sphinx-statue had worn him too much to try his spellbooks with any hope of success. The words were simple to commit to memory, of course, but each spell also required a carefully built structure of symbology, philosophy, even a certain attitude or particular mode of thinking that would imbue the words he spoke with real and significant power. He needed only a few minutes' meditation to restore the expended power to many of his minor spells, but his longer incantations were far more strenuous and took much longer to replenish.

Geran dozed for a long time, then rose, ate and drank a little more, and began to study his books. He didn't use some of these spells very often, so he studied them carefully to make certain that he would be able to speak them correctly. Six hours after he'd entered the vault of the *Infiernadex,* he was ready to make his exit. He replaced his spellbook in his pack and stood, wincing when his bruised ribs protested. "All right, Hamil. Ready to leave?"

The halfling jumped to his feet. "I've been ready for hours. Can you erase the symbols?"

"No, we're going to go around them. I don't have quite the right spell to do it directly, but I can manage it with three. But I'll need a little light, first." Geran dug a copper coin out of his pocket, whispered a light spell, and tossed it through the doorway to the darkened antechamber outside. With relief he noted that the floor remained depressed to the level of the buried vault. If the floor had raised itself back to the original level, his task would have been much harder. Geran moved closer to the doorway, remaining a short distance outside the influence of the symbols. He concentrated, focused his will, and said, *"Seiroch!"*

An instant of darkness, and then he was standing on the floor of the antechamber, looking back through the doorway at Hamil. He waited a moment to see if any new traps had been activated, but nothing happened.

"Well, it appears that you've seen to your own escape," Hamil remarked. "Shall I just wait here, then?"

"I'm not finished," Geran said. He took a deep breath, stilled his mind, and unlocked the unfamiliar structures of a spell he rarely used. *"Sierollanie dir mellar!"*

A faint violet light sprang up around Hamil, who looked startled, and a similar one appeared around the swordmage. Then once again he felt the brief instant of lightless cold, and he was standing back in the chamber of the *Infiernadex,* while Hamil was outside in the antechamber.

The halfling looked around, and laughed. "My circumstances have improved, but you are right back where you started, Geran! Is this one of those fox-goose-and-grain problems? If you're stumped, I may be able to help, you know."

"I'm still not finished. Give me a few moments." Geran sat down to compose himself and rest, closing his eyes and using the elven methods that Daried had taught him in Myth Drannor. A few minutes later, he was ready. He stood up, checked his location, and repeated his spell of transport: *"Seiroch!"*

One more instant of dizzying darkness, and he stood beside Hamil in the antechamber. "I don't know any spells that would let both of us teleport together," he explained. "So I had to settle for the spell that would switch our places. The minor teleport only takes me a few minutes to ready."

Hamil gave him a small bow. "You are a more accomplished wizard than I remembered, Geran. Did you learn that in Myth Drannor?"

"If I were a true wizard I could've simply conjured us both out of the vault and saved us the ride back to Hulburg for that matter. But yes, that's a spell I learned in Myth Drannor, along with a few others." Geran made a stirrup of his hands to help Hamil back up to the passageway above. Then he leaped up, caught the edge, and scrambled up with a hand from the halfling. He looked back down at the door to the secret vault. "We should put the floor back. The Verunas might miss the vault, and they won't realize that we've been here already."

"Done," said Hamil. He leaped corner-to-corner over the pit and worked his way around to the statue with its niche. In a moment he rotated it back into place. The antechamber floor rose back into place with a heavy scraping of stone on stone and the clanking of hidden chains. "I hope our mounts haven't run off or been eaten by something. I don't care for a long walk back to the abbey."

"Nor do I." Geran led the way back to the wall they'd opened at the foot of the stairwell and ducked through it again. It was dark outside, but he'd expected that. They'd opened the mound in the early afternoon, and they'd been inside for many hours. He climbed back up into the night—cold, damp, windy, and mist-blown, as so many nights on the Highfells were. He looked around to see whether their horses were still present. The animals stamped and neighed nervously where they'd been picketed, the saddles and tack piled up where they'd left it. Geran slipped down the side of the mound and headed toward the animals, wondering if perhaps they'd caught more of the strange shadow's scent.

Hamil followed after him. "Do we try to make it back to the abbey tonight?"

Geran started to answer, but paused. He thought he heard something, a faint creaking, perhaps the jingle of mail. He slid his sword out of its sheath and peered into the darkness. They'd had the light spell to see by in the barrow, but he hadn't stopped to let his eyes adjust to the night. Now he realized that he couldn't see very well at all, whereas someone who might have been waiting outside would be quite used to the darkness.

"Hamil, someone's here," he said softly. *"Cuillen mhariel!"*

The faint sheen of the silversteel veil flickered around him. He felt Hamil close behind him and heard the rasp of steel on leather as the halfling swept out his own daggers. "We walked right into it," the halfling muttered.

Silently, men in mail stood from where they'd been lying in the heather. They were empty black shadows in the moonless night, but then several of the men unshuttered lanterns and shone them at the two companions. In the sudden circle of light, Geran saw that they were surrounded by close to a score of armsmen in the green and white surcoats of House Veruna. Several aimed bows at Geran.

"Well, here they are, lads," one of the shadowy figures rasped. He came closer, and Geran recognized the lean, hawkish features and ebon half-plate armor of Anfel Urdinger, captain of House Veruna. "I think you've got something I want, Geran Hulmaster. Lay down your sword at your feet, and throw your pack over here. Your small friend too, and you can tell him that he'd better keep his hands where we can see them."

Of all the luck! Hamil said silently. *They finally find the barrow they're looking for on the day we visit!*

To Bane with luck, someone must have told them where we were, Geran answered his friend. This barrow was simply too far from the others that had been opened; it was too much of a coincidence to believe that Urdinger and his men had happened across it. Mostly to give himself a moment to think, he called back to Urdinger, "If we surrender our arms, what guarantees do you give us?"

"I don't see that I need to give you any at all, but I suppose I'll let you ride away with no more trouble," Urdinger answered. "The book's my only concern. Do you have it?"

They can't let us live, Geran, Hamil said. *If we give up our blades, they'll take what they want and kill us anyway. Best to make a break back for the barrow and hope we don't get shot down before we get there.*

I know it, Geran replied to his friend.

Against three or four men—perhaps five—he might have tried to fight his way clear, even with the disadvantage of being caught by surprise. But there were simply too many mercenaries around them. A retreat to Terlannis's barrow was the best of their poor options; in the cramped passage at the foot of the stairs, their opponents' numbers would mean nothing, and they might achieve a standoff of sorts. Geran edged back a couple of steps, weighing their odds of reaching the barrow entrance, but then he sensed stealthy movement behind him.

He turned to look. There, not twenty feet away, the night mists swirled and coalesced into a great black panther who padded out of the fog. Its yellow eyes glittered with malice . . . and perhaps a glint of intelligence. In any event, it was between the two comrades and the dubious safety of the barrow entrance.

"I see you've met Umbryl," Urdinger said with a nasty laugh. "I'd stand still, if I were you. Now, if you don't do what I say and drop your damned elf-sword to the ground, I'm going to let the panther have you."

That explains much, Geran decided. The panther trailed them, and it must have gone to summon the Verunas when they entered the barrow. The swordmage took one more look around and grimaced. "You can have the book, then," he said. He let his rucksack slip from his shoulder, knelt, and rummaged through it for the *Infiernadex,* one eye on the spectral panther. In a moment he stood back up with the ancient tome in his left hand, the sword in his right. He felt Hamil shift uncomfortably, all too aware that the necromancer's book was their only bargaining chip, but the halfling said nothing. He whispered to the halfling, "Watch yourself."

Make your move, Hamil answered.

Geran lowered his voice and muttered a spell: *"Arvan sannoghan,"* he hissed, and all at once bright blue-white flames sprang into existence all along his sword. He raised it over the heavy tome he held in his other hand and shouted, "Not a single move, or I will destroy the book!"

The Veruna swordsmen surged forward in anger, but a single sharp command from Urdinger stopped them in their tracks. "Hold!" the Veruna captain shouted at his men. Geran risked a glance behind him and saw the spectral panther crouch and hiss, but it did not spring at them. Urdinger's good humor—such as it was—fell away, and the mercenary glared at Geran. "You fool," he spat. "If you harm that book, there'll be no reason to let you leave this place!"

"I can't see a reason why you'd let us go, whether you get your hands on the book or not," Geran retorted. "If you intend to kill me no matter what, I might as well burn this musty old collection of hexes just to spite you before I die."

"I can have my bowmen shoot you down right now."

"Are you that certain of their aim? Miss by just a little, and I'll burn the *Infiernadex* to ash with my last breath." Geran paused, measuring the effect of his words on the Veruna captain, and added, "I'll trade the book for our lives. But you won't have both, I can promise you that."

The mercenary captain scowled. "All right, then. Make a suggestion."

Hamil glanced up at Geran, then back to the Veruna men surrounding them. "Yes, make a suggestion, Geran," he said.

"Give us two horses," Geran said to Urdinger. "Then draw back outside of bowshot. I'll leave the book here, and we'll ride off."

"What's to keep you from riding off with the book once we draw back? Or destroying it once we're too far away to interfere, for that matter?"

"What's to keep you from pursuing us once you've got the book?" Geran answered. "The only way this works is for both of us to do what we say we're going to do and believe that the other fellow means it. As for destroying the *Infiernadex*, well, I have it in my power to do that right now, so what would change?"

Urdinger frowned and turned away to mutter something to the mercenaries next to him. But he never said whatever he intended to say next, for abruptly the wind died, the night grew bitterly cold, and white hoarfrost appeared on the heather. Geran's breath steamed before him, and even the flickering blue flames of the fiery aura on his sword dimmed and wavered. The Veruna men shifted nervously and looked around, and the two companions did likewise.

The chill voices are back, Hamil said. *Something is coming.*

"I feel it too," Geran said. "What else can go wrong?" He glanced back at Umbryl, but the spectral panther had disappeared. He swore under his breath and tried to watch in all directions at once. That's what I get for asking, he told himself. Now I have to wonder if the damned panther is sneaking up behind me.

Suddenly a column of dark, cold flames erupted from the ground not far from where Geran and Hamil stood, and a figure of nightmare stepped forth. It was a skeleton, dressed in the old, tattered remnants of regal robes. A heavy golden band served as its crown, and it carried a tall, twisted staff of dead gray wood in its bony talons. Geran heard metal rasping on metal as the thing emerged from the black flames. The skeleton's bones were riveted together by bands of rune-inscribed copper, green and dull with age. Its eyes were burning points of phosphorescent emerald fire, keen and malevolent.

The swordmage's heart froze in his chest at the mere sight of the thing, and he took a step back without even realizing it—an unseen mantle of dread and despair seemed to flow before the apparition, as if its mere presence cast some grievous shadow on the souls of the living. Several of the Veruna men actually fell and buried their faces against the ground, unable to endure its presence at all. Part of Geran's mind noted that the apparition's appearance had provided the best distraction they were likely to get if they were to attempt a break for the barrow, but he was unable to wrench his eyes away from the dreadful king.

The grim figure fixed its burning green eyes on Geran. It was all that he could do to stand without quailing in front of it. Then it spoke: "Five centuries have I waited for that book to be brought out of the Lathanderian wards. I will not permit you to damage it now, young fool."

Geran was frozen in the icy grip of the skeleton's gaze. "You are Aesperus," he said in a weak voice. He'd heard enough tales whispered by firelight in Griffonwatch when he was young to recognize the dreadful lich who had stalked the Highfells for centuries—a mighty wizard dead for hundreds of years, yet preserved by dark and potent necromancy. Geran had always wondered why he was called the King in Copper; now he knew. The lich's bones were fairly held together by it.

"King Aesperus to you," the lich hissed. He glared at Geran, and his eyes flamed brighter with the intensity of his scrutiny. "Hmmm. You are a Hulmaster; I know the smell of your blood. Isolmar is dead now, so you must be Bernov's son Geran. Of you I have heard little."

Geran said nothing for a long moment; it was terribly hard to form a thought, let alone speak, while Aesperus held his gaze. Finally he managed to say, "I'll barter the *Infiernadex* for our lives, King Aesperus."

The lich laughed coldly. "What care I for your lives?" he said. He stretched out his clawlike hand and made a small gesture, and the *Infiernadex* was wrenched out of Geran's grasp by some unseen force, savagely strong. The book soared to the lich's hand, and Aesperus twisted what remained of his face into a horrible smile. "Good-bye, Geran Hulmaster. I expect that you and I will speak again soon, when you have been laid under stone as your forefathers were."

Aesperus turned away from Geran, and the swordmage felt strength and volition returning to his limbs. The lich looked at Anfel Urdinger, who averted his eyes and stared at the ground between his feet. "Tell your mistress that I hold her part of our bargain accomplished. Disturb no more barrows, Captain. You have no more reason to plunder my realm." Then Aesperus took an old amulet of verdigris-covered copper from his rotting robes, and put it in Urdinger's hand. "He who wears this toaken may call on my minions, and they will answer and do his bidding. Now I have upheld my own part, too."

"Yes, mighty king," Urdinger mumbled. He took the copper amulet and slipped it into a pouch at his belt. "I'll tell Lady Darsi what you have said."

"Tell her this too: Do not use my gift in the bright hours of day, and do not try to send my minions far from the amulet. She should choose the time and place carefully, for my servants will answer but grudgingly." Tucking the tome under his bony arm, the lich strode off into the night. On the third stride he simply melted into a black mist that dissipated as the wind quickly arose again. The white hoarfrost covering the heather vanished as well, and Geran took a deep breath.

They were still surrounded by a score of Veruna guardsmen. And he no longer had the book to bargain with.

Urdinger looked back up and shook himself. Then he fixed his eyes on Geran with a wide, predatory smile. "It seems that you've lost your bargaining chip, Lord Geran. Your previous offer was the *Infiernadex* in exchange for your life. Have you got anything else to add at this time?"

This does not look good, Hamil observed. *Try for the barrow?*

Agreed, Geran answered. *Follow me when I move.* Then he quickly called out a spell: *"Theillalagh na drendir!"*

The violet ripples of his dragon-scale spell shimmered brightly around him, and Geran hurled himself into motion. He darted off to his right, heading for the nearest bowman he could see. Arrows thrummed and hissed as they flew at him, but he'd judged his moment well; most of the Veruna men had lowered their weapons when the lich had made his appearance, so they hastily raised and drew while he was already in motion. One arrow was deflected by his silversteel veil, another struck his dragon-scale spell and rebounded as if it had hit thick plate armor, several more hissed by him, but one well-aimed arrow found its way through his spell-shields and buried its broad head in his left arm.

Geran cried out and staggered but managed to recover his stride. The man in front of him leveled his bow right at Geran's face—but Geran was upon him, and he slashed his burning sword across the man's weapon, cutting the bow in two and sending the Veruna archer to the ground with a long, seared cut across his face, neck, and chest. The man shrieked and thrashed.

"Get them!" Urdinger roared. "They can't get away!"

Two men in mail tried to cut off Geran, but he was faster than they were. A quick passing parry, and he was by them. He heard Hamil's bowstring sing and a strangled cry from behind him, but he didn't slow down. He rounded halfway around the barrow, scrambled up onto the sloping top, and ducked into the steep stone stairwell just ahead of more arrows and several of the Veruna swordsmen. Hamil skidded down the steps behind him, and Geran dove headlong through the hole he'd made in the wall at the bottom of the steps. Hamil followed after him. The halfling rolled easily to his knees, spun, and fired a couple of arrows back up the stairwell.

"I don't believe that worked," Hamil muttered. "Are you all right, Geran?"

"Almost," Geran answered. His arm burned fiercely, it seemed that he'd knocked his shins against the stones in the stairwell, and his ribs still hurt from the fight against the bronze sphinx earlier. But he seemed more or less intact. The arrow in his arm was not as deep as he had feared—his spell-shields had likely slowed it some before it struck. He gritted his teeth and carefully worked it out. Blood streamed down his arm and dripped on the cold flagstones. "How about you? Are you hurt?"

"Me? No, they were all shooting at you. You're a much bigger target, and your sword's on fire. I could have slunk off into the fog, and they never would've noticed." Hamil peered back up the stairwell and risked another quick shot. Another man cried out and cursed viciously.

"Watch it, you fools!" Urdinger shouted from somewhere out of sight. The Veruna mercenaries shouted at each other for a brief chaotic moment, then the captain's voice carried over the others. "Shut your damned mouths! Keep it quiet!"

Well, now the darkness favors us, Hamil said silently. *It's pitch black down here, and anybody who sets foot on the stairs is silhouetted against the sky. So what next?*

"I'm still working on that," Geran whispered. They could stay barricaded inside the barrow entrance for quite some time—the stairs would allow only one man at a time to approach, and it would be almost impossible for the Veruna archers to shoot past their own man on the stairs. What would he do in Urdinger's place? The mercenary captain could simply fill in the stairwell and leave, but he couldn't be sure that Geran and Hamil wouldn't dig themselves out after he left. So maybe he'd just set watch over the top of the stairs and let them die of thirst or starvation. "Or maybe a shield or mantlet of some kind," Geran mused. "Carry it in front to block our arrows, move down, and get to the wall. But then you'd still have to get through the hole."

They could smoke us out, Hamil offered. *Use a mantlet to get down here and then throw some burning brands through the hole, drive us back from the gap. And . . . don't forget that panther they have. As far as we know it could simply appear behind us and catch us looking up the stairs.*

Geran glanced over his shoulder at the black passageway behind them. "That's a reassuring thought," he muttered. He peered up the stairwell as far as he dared. Urdinger was certain to be turning over the same possibilities in his own head. Likely he had an option or two that Geran hadn't even considered yet, such as hiring a wizard to blast open the barrow or summon some demon who could simply rip them apart, swords and arrows be damned.

They heard a sharp exchange of voices atop the barrow, but it wasn't very clear. Geran thought he heard Urdinger say something that ended with, ". . . it's none of your affair!" The other voice responded, too far downwind to make out clearly. Geran glanced down at Hamil. "Something's going on up there," he said. "Are they arguing—?"

Before he finished his question, a brilliant flash of light seared the darkness outside their bolthole, followed by the low rumbling *whoosh* of fire. Mercenaries suddenly shouted in panic, and Urdinger shouted, "Archers! Bring him down *now!*"

The night blazed again with a brilliant yellow flash, a sharp *crack,* and a deafening peal of thunder that jarred a pinch of dirt loose from the passage ceiling. An acrid smell drifted down to where Geran and Hamil crouched, and the Veruna mercenaries cried out in dismay. An instant later, more fire belched across the night sky.

"What in the Nine Hells is this?" Geran said.

"They're trying to lure us out?" the halfling guessed.

"Somehow I doubt it." Geran stared up at the mouth of the stairwell. He could hear men shouting and running, the distant ring of steel, the panicked whinnying of horses. They could wait it out and see what happened next . . . or they could move while the Verunas were distracted. In an instant, Geran made up his mind. He clambered back out of the hole in the wall, crouching low in the stairway, and carefully climbed the steps, expecting another arrow at any moment.

You've lost your mind! Hamil said, but he climbed out as well.

Another thunderbolt pealed across the hilltop, and in the single brief flash of light Geran saw something completely unexpected. The Veruna mercenaries ran this way and that, hugging boulders and tufts of high grass for cover as they confronted a single man—the horned sorcerer that Kara, Hamil, and he had met up with at the barrow where Jarad had fallen. He stood in midair fifteen feet above the ground, surrounded by a storm of fire, his coat of scarlet and gold billowing in the wind. One of the Verunas shot at him with a crossbow, but the sorcerer batted away the bolt with a gesture and turned a fearsome glare at the fellow who had shot. The crossbowman staggered back, his clothes smoking, and then he burst into flame. Screaming horribly, he flailed away into the night fog.

Two of the Veruna armsmen still crouched nearby, distracted by the battle raging a short distance away. Then one glanced down and caught a glimpse of Geran by the light of a blast of fire. "The others!" he shouted. "They're making a break—" Then a short arrow took him in the face and sent him staggering backward.

"Shhhh," Hamil said. "That's a good fellow."

Geran quickly bounded up the steps as the armsman waiting there scrambled to his feet and launched himself down. They met on the top stair; the man parried Geran's thrust at his midsection and replied with a vicious cut at Geran's head that the swordmage simply ducked under before surging up and scoring with a long passing cut to the neck as he shouldered the man out of the way. The Veruna man spun half around and fell where he stood.

From the foot of the barrow, a man Geran hadn't noticed before raised a wand and pointed at the sorcerer in scarlet and gold. A trio of shrieking blue missiles screamed out of the wand, weaved their way through the sorcerer's fiery aura, and hammered home against his side. The horned man cried out and staggered in midair, clamping a hand to his injury. The Veruna mageling shouted in triumph and aimed another burst at him. Geran had no idea whether the horned man—the tiefling, that's what his kind was called—was an enemy or not, but for the moment the mercenaries of House Veruna were a common foe, so he raced down the side of the mound and hurled himself at the unsuspecting Veruna mage. The fellow sensed danger and started to turn just in time to see the swordstroke that decapitated him. Hamil followed a step behind him, now with knives in his hands since he'd shot all his arrows. "Are you sure this is our fight, Geran?" he called.

"I'm making it ours," Geran answered. He found himself engaged with another Veruna swordsman and fought a furious duel for several long moments, Mulman broadsword against elf-wrought backsword, blades flashing in the darkness and firelight. Hamil skirmished against another swordsman who moved in to attack Geran's back while Geran was battling the first, and managed to slash the man across the knee badly enough to put him on the ground—at which point the halfling swarmed over him and finished him with a dagger through the visor of his helm.

For his own part Geran almost stepped onto his opponent's swordpoint but saw through the feint at the last moment. He beat his adversary's point up into the air, and ran him through beneath the arm. The swordmage quickly spun clear, searching for another foe, but no more Veruna men remained on their feet nearby. He caught a glimpse of Urdinger and half a dozen men galloping away into the darkness, pursued by flaming bolts the tiefling hurled after them. Then the battlefield fell silent except for the low, smoldering crackle of grassfires kindled by the sorcerer's fire. The tiefling snarled something after the fleeing mercenaries and allowed himself to drift back to earth. Then he caught sight of Geran and Hamil.

"Hold!" Geran called. "We've got no quarrel with you."

"That remains to be seen," the tiefling answered. He held his curved metal rod at the ready, but he did not move to attack. "The book!" he demanded. "Where is it?"

Geran studied the tiefling for a long moment before answering. The man was obviously a very capable sorcerer, but Geran knew that his spell-shields would stand up better to blasts of flame and bolts of lightning than the mundane mail the Veruna men wore. He took his time answering in order to make sure that the sorcerer would understand that he did not answer out of fear. "If you're speaking of the *Infiernadex,* then the lich Aesperus has it," he said. "The Veruna men followed us to this barrow, and I think Aesperus followed them. He took the book from me and departed not more than half an hour ago."

"You should take up the matter of the book with him," Hamil offered.

The tiefling's face darkened, and he turned away, snarling something in a language that Geran didn't know. He kicked at the ground and slashed his weapon through the air in frustration. "You led them right to this place! Aesperus never could have removed the book from the Lathanderian's barrow by himself. You have delivered his prize to him, you fools!"

"The Verunas were searching barrows all over the Highfells," Hamil retorted angrily. "Sooner or later, they would have found the right one. Don't blame us because you didn't find it before we did. For that matter, I'd like to know how you found us here too."

"I followed the Verunas. I was going to let them remove the book then take it from them." He glared at Hamil. "Your meddling has cost me six months of labor. You halfwits have no idea what you've done!"

Geran decided to let the sorcerer's sharp words pass for the moment. "This is the second time I've met you on the doorstep of a barrow," he said. "I am Geran Hulmaster, of the harmach's family, and we have laws against disturbing burial mounds in these lands. Who are you? And what do you want with Aesperus's book?"

The tiefling calmed himself with a visible effort, and looked back to Geran and Hamil. "I am Sarth Khul Riizar," he answered. "My interest in the *Infiernadex* is my own affair. But if Aesperus has found it at last, I doubt that I will ever be able to lay my hands on it. He is a foe beyond my strength."

"We're in your debt, Sarth Khul Riizar," said Geran. "Your arrival distracted the Veruna men from the task of figuring out how they were going to kill us."

"Such was not my intent," the sorcerer said bitterly. "Still, I suppose you made yourself useful in the fight, and you have my thanks for that." He frowned at the two companions again, then shook his head and muttered a spell under his breath. With a single bound he leaped into the sky and shot off eastward over the fells. In a moment he was completely out of their sight.

"Did you hear that? We made ourselves useful," Hamil said. He sighed and looked around. A cold drizzle began to fall. "Ah, wouldn't you know it? Our horses ran off with theirs."

"Rosestone is three or four hours off by foot," Geran said. He sheathed his sword and took a deep breath. "If we start now, I think we can be there before sunup."

Fifteen

26 Ches, the Year of the Ageless One

Council Hall was one of the largest and most striking buildings in Hulburg. Its lower walls were made of thick, strong stone every bit as sturdy as a watchtower's, and its upper stories were well-fitted hardwood, with beam-ends carved into leaping dolphins and vigilant hounds—images of commerce and good fortune. Sergen Hulmaster glanced up as his coach rolled under the expensive carvings overhead; there was a gold dragon's head over the front door that he liked best of all. In the fading afternoon light it took on a striking orange gleam.

"We're here, Lord Hulmaster," his driver said. The coachman reined in the team, and Sergen's footman hopped down to hold open the door for him. Two Council Watch guards who rode on the coach's running boards climbed down and arranged themselves on either side, ready to fall in and escort him. The watchmen looked competent and crisp in black tabards over breastplates of browned iron. They might not have been a match for the professional sellswords Veruna and the other companies employed, or even the harmach's Shieldsworn, but Sergen intended to remedy that soon enough. Besides, an armed escort was one of the trappings of privilege, and he insisted on it.

"Very well," Sergen said. "Wait for me here. I don't intend to remain inside for long." He smiled to himself as he stepped down to the cobblestones in front of the fine stone stairs leading up to the hall's doors. He did every time he caught sight of the grand edifice, since it was really *his* building, a symbol of his personal power and importance in Hulburg. Oh, the Merchant Council was ostensibly an association of equals, with each merchant of consequence in the city commanding one seat on the council, and he merely presided over it without a vote in its deliberations. But Sergen was Keeper of Duties, which gave him all the power he needed to buy or sell votes as he liked, while the support of House Veruna—and its immense wealth—made him master of the council in fact as well as name. For years now he had dictated to lesser members the positions they should adopt and the measures they should support or ruined them by giving Veruna opportunities to plunder their interests. It hadn't taken the smaller companies long to learn the cost of not doing what he wanted.

Sergen climbed up the steps and strode into the building, paying the guards posted by the door no mind as they grounded the butts of their halberds for him. The council chamber itself was to his right, but he walked past it and up a grand wooden staircase in the foyer. His chambers were on the second floor, a large suite that included working rooms for his staff, a library, a sitting room, servant's spaces, and even a modest bedchamber if he decided that he didn't care to return to his grand house in the hills after an evening in Hulburg. Few of the council clerks or attendants were in the building since the working day had ended an hour ago, but those who crossed his path were careful to stop and bow with murmured greetings of "Good evening, Lord Hulmaster," or "By your leave, Lord Keeper."

Sergen's guards preceded him into the Keeper's chambers. He swept in on their heels, doffed his expensive fur mantle, and handed it to his valet. "Is Ironthane here?" he asked.

"Aye, Lord Hulmaster," one of the guards answered. "He waits in the captain's room."

"Show him upstairs immediately, then," Sergen answered. "I am attending the theater tonight, and I don't want to be late." The guard withdrew and hurried off. Sergen sat behind his desk and quickly studied the documents and orders his minions had left for him to review before signing. He found nothing of any real importance at a quick glance, but before he could begin a more serious examination, he heard footsteps in the hall, followed by a knock at the door. "Enter," he replied.

"Captain Kendurkkel Ironthane, my lord," the guard said. He moved aside to make room for a wide-shouldered, black-bearded dwarf in heavy mail-and-plate, who wore a vast bearskin mantle over his armored shoulders and a wide gold chain to secure the fur. The dwarf had a long-stemmed clay pipe cupped in one hand and rested his other hand on the handle of a vicious-looking throwing axe that hung at his left hip. He was tall for his kind, just an inch or two under five feet, and was extraordinarily burly with shoulders that seemed a yard wide. He looked Sergen up and down and puffed once on his pipe.

"Welcome, Captain," Sergen said. He looked at the other guards and attendants in the room and dismissed them with a gesture. Then he stood up and bowed slightly. "I am Sergen Hulmaster, Keeper of Duties in Hulburg."

"I've no' been long in Hulburg, but I've been here long enough t' learn who you be," the dwarf said. "You're master o' the town, as near's I can tell. So what d'you want with me Icehammers?"

"Have a seat, Captain." Sergen waited for the dwarf to make himself comfortable then went on. "I believe I have need of your mercenaries. I wish to engage your company as a special auxiliary to the Council Watch. You'll report to me, and me alone. Are you interested?"

The dwarf shrugged. "It depends where you mean t' send me lads, an' who you expect us t' fight, Laird Hulmaster."

"You'd remain in or near Hulmaster for now—within an hour's march, I would imagine. As for fighting, well, I doubt you'll see any pitched battles. The Bloody Skull orcs are demanding tribute from the harmach, but I intend for that to be little concern of yours. I want to use your company to help establish and keep order in town and perhaps assist me in suppressing enemies of the Merchant Council."

"An' who be those enemies?"

"Whomever I tell you to consider an enemy, Captain." Sergen leaned forward on his desk and steepled his fingers in front of him. "Lawless gangs in the Tailings. Outlaw bands on the Highfells. Merchant companies that refuse to abide by the fair rules this council enacts. Perhaps . . . others."

Ironthane smoked for a moment, his dark eyes unreadable. "How long will you be wanting the Icehammers at your beck and call, Laird Hulmaster?"

"Until I feel that good order has been established in Hulburg, Captain."

"So y'want me to take an open-ended contract with no specific enemy in mind, other'n whatever poor bastards y'tell me to handle for you?" The dwarf tapped his pipe against the arm of his chair to settle the embers to his satisfaction. "In that case, I expect t'be retained month-t'month.

Meet our price, an' I'll keep me lads ready for you as long as you're to keep payin' me."

Sergen leaned back and frowned. He sensed that it might be better to be direct with Ironthane. Dwarves had a reputation for bluntness, after all. "I was hoping you would find something like that a reasonable arrangement. I foresee trouble in the next few months. Abrupt and decisive action may be called for. My Council Watch is a constabulary, not an army, but that's exactly what I may need soon."

"You want your own army, then." Ironthane smiled humorlessly. "Well, Laird Hulmaster, it will no' be cheap. Me Icehammers'll cost you two thousan' gold crowns up front and another thousan' crowns per month, plus decent quartering and provisions. If you can't provide quarters or rations, it'll be another six hundred per month. I expect t'be paid the first o' the month each month. If you pay me no', you're in breach of our contract, and we'll walk out on you. That coin buys you our services as guards, roustabouts, an' a standing force in case y'need two hundred well-armed veterans at short notice. If you want us t' undertake a major action—say, anything where me lads face more'n twenty enemies under arms at the same time—well, we'll have t'negotiate a special bonus." Kendurkkel Ironthane grinned to himself. "We're no' patriots, we're no' fanatics, and we won't give you a moment's loyalty that you don't pay for, Laird Hulmaster. But we observe our contracts an' fight damned hard when we've struck terms. You won't find a tougher company than the Icehammers anywhere north o' the Moonsea, and no' all that many south o' it neither."

Sergen winced at the cost. "You'll be looking after your own accommodations and provisions. I'm willing to go as high as twelve hundred per month. And we'll need to come to a better understanding of what you mean by a special bonus and just what triggers it."

"I'm willing t' split the difference," the dwarf said. "Fourteen hundred per month?"

Sergen considered for a moment, then nodded. "Done." He stood up and offered his hand; Ironthane took it, and they clasped palms. "Pick out a good site for a barracks within half a mile of town, and tell your men to keep this quiet until I tell you otherwise."

"Two hundred men, close t' hand, no particular duties yet, an' keep it quiet," the dwarf repeated. He puffed on his pipe, eyeing the human lord with interest. "If I didn't know better, I'd think you intended a coup, m'laird."

"Let's just say that I believe in the value of being prepared." Sergen stood and inclined his head to Ironthane. The less said about his actual intentions, the better; he really did not know how much he could trust the mercenary captain yet. "You'll receive two thousand gold crowns first thing tomorrow. We'll speak more then. Now, if you'll excuse me, Captain, I'm meeting someone at the theater. My men will show you out."

"Enjoy the play, Laird Hulmaster."

Sergen smiled sourly. "It's supposed to be wretched beyond description," he replied.

He left Ironthane in the company of the council guards and made his way back downstairs to his waiting coach. The driver clucked to the team, and the coach clattered off over the rough cobblestones. Sergen patiently endured the jolting and jostling from side to side that was the price of a carriage ride in Hulburg's rough streets. He was a man of means, after all, and it wasn't seemly to walk the four or five blocks to the playhouse. In a few minutes his coachmen drove up to the Crown and Shield, one of only two dedicated theaters in Hulburg. Sergen allowed his valet to open the door for him and then swept through the small foyer with its bowing theater attendants. He allowed them to show him to House Veruna's private box and took his seat. The show had already started, a bawdy farce called *The Bride of Secomber.*

"You're late," Darsi Veruna said as he sat down.

"A small matter of business I needed to attend to. Forgive me."

"Has your uncle decided what he'll do with the Bloodskull tribute demand?"

"The arguments continue," Sergen replied. The private box was a good place to speak freely. With the musicians below, the actors giving their lines, and the laughter—or groans—from the rest of the audience, there was not much chance of being overheard. "My uncle doesn't want a war, but he can't stomach the idea of giving in to the orcs' demands, especially the demand for slaves. His position is difficult."

"What will he do, then?"

Sergen frowned. "Kara advises him to stall. She believes that the longer things can be drawn out, the more likely it is that this King Mhurren will have his attention drawn away from Hulburg by some other event—an unexpected feud within his tribe or perhaps an attack by some other enemy."

Lady Darsi looked away from the performance and met his eyes. "Stall? How? Morag was quite insistent on a yes or no answer. How could the harmach stall?"

"Send the emissaries back with an impressive array of gifts and the message that Hulburg *might* pay if the tribute demand were just a little more reasonable, and sufficient time allowed for the harmach to levy the necessary goods and coin from Hulburg's people and the merchant companies in the city."

"He intends to make *us* help him pay off this orc brigand?" Darsi demanded.

"Well, my dear lady, you and your House are theoretically at just as much risk as the harmach and his people. My uncle believes that you're obligated to contribute something to the effort."

"That is unacceptable," Darsi snorted. She returned her attention to the play, and Sergen leaned back to watch as well while he continued to think on matters. He had an idea about what might be done next . . . but he wished to mull it over for a time, and so he paid some small attention to the action on the stage as his mind worked. Early in the second act, the final pieces worked their way into place, and he smiled in satisfaction despite the truly execrable quality of the shoddy little production playing out before him.

The sorry affair rambled on for another hour and a half before it mercifully staggered to an end. A poor script, a bumbling score, and actors who seemed to think that the height of their craft was to shout their lines at the audience made for a memorable night at the theater, Sergen decided. The best humor of the evening had come from watching for the next unexpected gaffe or badly delivered line. And, to be honest, he felt a distinct sense of relief when the curtain finally dropped at the end of the show. In that much, at least, watching *The Bride of Secomber* was not unlike repeatedly striking one's head against a wall: It felt good when it ended.

"I believe I might go down to the proprietor and beat him until he returns my eight silver talents," he said aloud. "The coin's a pittance, of course, but as a matter of principle, I won't stand for robbery."

"What did you expect in Hulburg?" Darsi Veruna asked. She ignored the half-hearted applause rippling through the audience as the cast members came forward to take their bows. "In Mulmaster, the audience might wait around for the opportunity to stab one or two of those actors when they leave the theater."

"An enlightened and cultured city," Sergen remarked. He looked over to Darsi, who made a small face at him. "I've been thinking. I believe the Bloody Skull threat offers just the opportunity we've been looking for. In fact, the worse it appears, the better for us. To that effect, I have a small request for you, my lady."

Darsi motioned with her hand. "Go on, my lord."

"Would you place your pet Umbryl at my disposal later this evening?"

"Possibly. What do you want her to do?"

"Take a direct hand—or claw, I suppose—in negotiations with the Bloody Skull emissaries. I've determined that the harmach is about to send their heads back to Mhurren with some suitably insulting reply to the orc king's demands. Of course, my uncle doesn't know that's what he intends to do. I must see to it for him." Sergen leaned closer, since the lights were brightening and the audience was beginning to file out. "As far as my uncle and the rest of the idiots on his privy council will know, the orcs will simply disappear. They'll guess that Morag and the others ran out of patience and left early."

"But you'll have the orcs killed?"

"I will have the orcs killed and make sure that it's clear to everyone here that they broke camp and left. I need Umbryl to carry their heads in a bag back to Bloodskull Keep and drop it at Mhurren's feet. That should bring the Bloody Skull horde to Hulburg's doorstep in a matter of days." Sergen smiled.

"Correct me if I'm wrong," Darsi said, "but if the Bloody Skulls are as strong as they claim to be, won't that result in the sack of the city and the loss of a tremendous amount of House Veruna property? As well as no small risk to our own lives?"

"It might, except that we now have a powerful ally who can repel the orc horde whenever he likes: Aesperus. The King in Copper owes us a great boon, and fearsome though he may be, he's a man—so to speak—of his word."

Darsi stood and motioned for her ladies and attendants. One hurried forward to drape an expensive stole around her lovely shoulders, while the men-at-arms—resplendent in light shirts of gleaming mail with surcoats of green and white—began to clear the rest of the departing crowd from her path. She lowered her voice and leaned close to murmur in his ear. "Speaking of Aesperus, my men report that he took the trinket he wanted right out of your cousin's hands. Geran will soon report to the harmach that the lich has the book and that armsmen of House Veruna gave it to him."

The ambitious lord scowled. "It would've been better if your men had killed him in the Highfells, so that he wouldn't carry tales back to my uncle."

Darsi ran her nails softly across Sergen's chin. "I think I am glad that I'm no kin of yours, my dear. Do you really hate them all so much?"

Sergen's expression darkened even more. "The Hulmasters wronged my father grievously, Darsi. Whatever befalls any of them is nothing compared to the humiliation they heaped upon him. They *will* make amends for their perfidy. I've sworn to it." He paused for a moment, collecting himself, and then found the sardonic smile he habitually affected. "In any event . . . yes, you're right, Kara will no doubt demand an explanation from you within an hour of Geran's return. An attempt on the life of a Hulmaster, even a rootless vagabond like Geran, will no doubt fill her with righteous wrath. You'll have to make a show of surrendering those responsible."

They made their way out of the private box and strolled slowly down the carpeted stairs to the foyer. Veruna men kept the rest of the crowd at a comfortable distance, earning a few resentful glances that Darsi ignored. "My men are loyal and well paid, but I doubt that they'll confess to an attack against the Harmach's own nephew simply because it's convenient for me if they do."

"Oh, don't worry about that," Sergen answered. "Your men are protected by the laws of concession. I can argue that it's an affair for the Council Watch, not the Shieldsworn, and I'll make sure that my dear stepsister remembers that. Of course, I'll have to thoroughly investigate the entire matter . . . *very* thoroughly. By the time I'm forced to move, it should all be moot."

He accompanied Darsi outside to where the Veruna men had already drawn up her coach, and joined her inside when she graciously invited him to. He dismissed his own driver and coach, and they drove away from the Crown and Shield through the cold fog blanketing the streets.

After a long silence, Darsi spoke again. "I think you may be too confident of your cleverness, Sergen," she said. "Your wayward cousin has exposed House Veruna's efforts to scour the Highfells for Aesperus's book. And he must certainly suspect our involvement in Jarad Erstenwold's death. The harmach may not be a decisive man, but this isn't something he will let lie. Geran is dangerous to us. We need to find a way to neutralize him."

"Leave him alone. He'll soon grow bored," Sergen replied. Darsi shot him a dubious look, and after a moment he sighed and met her eyes. "Or he might not. Very well, what do you propose?"

"We can't move directly against him," Darsi said, idly examining the exquisite rings that graced her hands. "It would lend far too much credence to any accusations he makes against my House." She thought for a moment, looking out the coach window at the glowing halos the streetlights carved from the drifting mist. "Ideally, we would find a way to encourage Geran to neutralize himself, something that might encourage him to abandon Hulburg again or discredit him in the eyes of the harmach. Perhaps he can be lured into drawing steel against us. If we're seen to be simply defending ourselves from an unwarranted attack, well, that would be acceptable."

Sergen nodded in agreement. Darsi Veruna was so beautiful, so sophisticated in her decadence, that he sometimes overlooked the sharpness of her mind. She was right, of course, but how to encourage Geran to foil himself? He closed his eyes, summoning to mind everything he knew of his stepcousin . . . and something occurred to him. "Ah, I think I've got it," he said. "The key to Geran is Mirya Erstenwold. If I know him at all, you'll find that he will go to great lengths to protect her, great lengths indeed." He smiled coldly. "Why, with the proper motivation, he might even do something rash."

SIXTEEN

27 Ches, the Year of the Ageless One

As it turned out, Geran and Hamil did not reach Rosestone until almost noon, hungry and exhausted. The monks were happy to provide them with a good meal and allowed the two travelers to rest in their hostel. By the time Geran and Hamil rested and told the story of the tomb of Terlannis and the appearance of Aesperus to the Initiate Mother, the afternoon was waning, so Geran reluctantly decided to spend the night at Rosestone. It was noon of the second day after their fight at the barrow when the two companions trudged wearily up the causeway of Griffonwatch and climbed to the Harmach's Tower, footsore and fairly well soaked from a long morning's walk in the warm spring showers that had settled over Hulburg during the previous night.

"Look! Look! Hamil and Geran are back!" Kirr and Natali were at their lessons in the family's great room but cast aside their primers and crowded close to the weary travelers, shouting a dozen questions at once. "Where have you been? You've been gone for days! Did you fight any monsters? Did you find any gold?"

Geran looked down in surprise at the top of Natali's head as she threw her arms around his waist and hugged him. He shrugged his rucksack off his shoulder and patted her back with his other arm. Strange how quickly children decide you're family, he mused. They've known us only for a tenday, but I can't remember the last time someone was so happy just to see me walk in a door. Maybe it was still the novelty of someone new under the same roof. "One question at a time, you two," he said. "We've been out on the Highfells, riding all over the moors. And yes, we met some fearsome monsters, and no, we didn't find any gold, and then our horses ran off so we had to walk all the way home."

"Did you see the orc army?" Kirr asked. "Do you think there's going to be a battle?"

"Orc army? What orc army?" Geran asked.

"Bloody Skull orcs came to Griffonwatch while you were gone," Natali explained breathlessly. "We weren't supposed to watch, but we did. We crept into the Great Hall and listened to them talk to Grandfather and all the other important people like Kara and Sergen and the rest. They seemed very angry, and they threatened Grandfather. They said that if he didn't give them five wagons full of gold they'd burn Hulburg." She looked up at Geran, a trace of uncertainty in her eyes. "Do you think the orcs will really come here?"

"I doubt it, Natali," Geran said. "The orcs of Thar haven't mounted a serious attack against Hulburg since before I was born. We'll have to watch out for raiding parties, though." The Bloody Skulls? he wondered. They'd never troubled Hulburg before.

It seems that a lot has happened in five days, Hamil said silently to Geran. *I wonder what all this is about?* For Kirr, he smiled and set his hands on his hips. "We didn't see any orcs, General Kirr. But we did see a big black ghost-panther that hunted us for days, and we barely escaped from bloodthirsty ghosts who chased us through fog and shadow. We defeated a sphinx made out of bronze, and finally we met the King in Copper himself and lived to tell the tale. So what do you think of that?"

Kirr's mouth dropped open in astonishment. He stared up at Hamil and simply said, "Ohhhhh."

"Better not say too much more, Hamil," Geran said. "Erna will give us an earful if we fill them with stories that keep them up all night."

"Tell us! Tell us!" Natali said. "We won't tell Ma."

Geran shook his head. "Maybe later, but only if your mother says I can. Now, I need to put on some dry clothes."

He left the young Hulmasters downstairs and went up to his room to change, taking his battered rucksack with him. He took a few moments to wash his face and towel off, found a clean change of clothes in the trunk at the foot of his bed, and trotted back down the stairs to the great room, settling his baldric and scabbard over a much drier tunic. But at the foot of the steps he found Kara waiting for him, her face taut with worry.

"The Shieldsworn told me you'd returned," she said. "I'm glad you're here, Geran. A lot's happened in the last day or two. The harmach wants to speak with you right away."

"I need to speak with him too," Geran said. "I have quite a story to tell you, and I'm not sure what it all means."

"Where have you been for the last few days?"

"Up on the Highfells, but that's part of the story. You'll hear it soon enough if you have half an hour to spare." He heard a light step on the stairs and glanced up; Hamil was coming down as well, having availed himself of the chance to change into dry clothes too. "Hamil, will you join us? My uncle wants to speak with me, and it might be helpful to have two accounts of the last few days."

"Of course," the halfling replied. He nodded to Kara. "A pleasure to see you again, my lady."

"And you, Hamil," Kara replied. She offered him a fleeting smile and inclined her head. "This way; the harmach's hearing counsel in the trophy room."

Geran and Hamil followed her as she led them down a flight of stairs into what would have been the foundations of the Harmach's Tower. However, since the tower sat atop Griffonwatch's steep crag, its basement formed another floor just beneath the buildings of the upper courtyard. A long row of windows facing south looked over rain-slick balconies and ramparts toward the Moonsea, a dark gray line beyond the rooftops of the town. The castle had several such hidden floors, some carved out of the living rock in the heart of the hill. Geran fondly remembered exploring all of them with Kara and their cousin Isolmar when all three were children not much bigger than Natali or Kirr. At the end of a long hall stood tall double doors of dark, gleaming wood. There were no Shieldsworn guards in sight; they were well within the Hulmaster family quarters, and the harmach's men usually watched the doors and halls that led into this part of the castle instead of standing guard within the family residence.

Kara paused by the doors, knocked twice, and let herself in. The room beyond was a large chamber with heavy wooden beams overhead, a long table of fine cherry wood, and a handful of dusty bookshelves and mounted trophies along the walls—a red tiger pelt, a suit of plate armor, a dusty wyvern's head, and the two-handed greataxe of a frost giant, a weapon fully ten feet long. The chamber was really a smaller, more secure banquet room than the great hall that divided the lower castle from its upper parts, one that just happened to be decorated with a handful of trophies taken by Grigor's father in his youth.

"Uncle, I've brought Geran," she said.

"Have you? Good." Harmach Grigor sat in a large, high-backed chair at the head of the table. To his left sat the old keeper of keys, Wulreth Keltor, and beside him High Magistrate Theron Nimstar. Across the table Sergen Hulmaster paced absently. The harmach looked up from his advisors and motioned to Kara. "Come in, come in," the old lord said. "I am afraid we have much to discuss, and little time."

"First things first." Sergen turned to face his stepsister, his hands clasped behind his back. He wore an elegant black tabard embroidered with a golden dragon design, and his habitual smirk was nowhere to be seen. "Did you find any sign of the orc delegation?"

"No, none yet," Kara answered. "I haven't had the chance to examine the site personally, but my scouts tell me that their camp is empty and there's no sign of Morag and the others. I can only guess that, for whatever reason, they decided to leave."

"But that makes no sense," Theron Nimstar protested. "They gave us until sunset tomorrow to give our answer. Why leave before they have heard it?

"Perhaps they expected the harmach to refuse outright and were merely playing at offering a chance to buy peace," Sergen said. "They might have already settled on war, in which case the whole point of the delegation was simply to take our measure."

"That seems unlikely," Kara answered. "Orcs are direct—far blunter than we would be. For good or ill, they rarely say anything they don't mean. They wouldn't feign a demand for tribute."

"I've heard that this Mhurren has human blood," Sergen answered. "Perhaps he's got some human guile in him, too."

Kara frowned but held her tongue. Geran took the opportunity to step forward. "Forgive me, but Hamil and I have been riding all over the Highfells for days, and we returned only an hour ago. When did the Bloodskulls show up? What do they want?"

"They came to the Raven Hill watchtower under a flag of truce three days ago and demanded to be taken to the harmach," Kara answered him.

"The Shieldsworn escorted them to Hulburg, and the Harmach's Council heard them out the day before yesterday. They issued a demand for tribute and gave us three days to choose whether to pay or fight." Kara glanced to the Harmach and then back to Geran. "The orcs were camped in the ruins of the old Windy Ridge post, waiting for our answer. But they seem to have left."

"Perhaps their nerve failed them, and they feared they would be killed for throwing such an insult in our teeth," Wulreth Keltor said aloud.

Kara shook her head. "That's not likely, either. I can't offer a good explanation for why they left, but I'm certain of this: If the Bloody Skulls didn't wait for our answer, then they've chosen war, and we must prepare ourselves."

No one spoke for a long moment. Then Harmach Grigor sighed and looked over to the two officials. "Theron, Wulreth, I suppose there is no more point in debating whether we should pay or negotiate. If the orcs have chosen war, then that is that. Wulreth, find some coin to finish the repairs to Daggergard's gate. I want that work finished as soon as possible. Raid other works if you must. For that matter, we may need to hire mercenaries to fill out our ranks—I'll take every copper you can find me."

The keeper of keys made a sour face, but he nodded. "I will do everything I can, Lord Harmach." He stood and bowed to the harmach; Theron did likewise. Then the two officials left the room, hurrying off to attend to their appointed tasks.

Geran waited for them to leave then cleared his throat. "Uncle Grigor, I think the Bloody Skulls aren't the only problem at hand. I need to tell you what I've learned in the last tenday about Jarad's murder, House Veruna, and the King in Copper."

"Aesperus?" Kara shot a surprised look at Geran. "What in the world does he have to do with us?"

Sergen snorted. "He's a useful bogeyman for scaring ill-behaved children, nothing more."

The swordmage ignored his stepcousin's derision. "I'm not sure, Kara, but Aesperus has something to do with House Veruna, and they in turn had much to do with Jarad's murder."

Both Grigor and Kara glanced at Sergen, who simply rolled his eyes, folded his arms, and leaned against a bookshelf. The harmach looked back to Geran. "You'd better tell us the whole story," he said.

"All right." Geran paused a moment to collect his thoughts then began. "As you know, I wanted to look into Jarad's death. About ten days ago Kara took Hamil and me up to the barrow where Jarad was killed. We noticed that the barrow had been resealed recently, so we broke in to see what might have drawn the tomb robbers—and presumably Jarad—to that place."

"You broke the harmach's law against entering a barrow?" Sergen asked sharply.

"Someone else already had," Hamil answered for Geran.

"I judged it worth investigating," Geran continued. "Inside we discovered two fresh bodies hidden beneath the burial stone—a young woman and a man that Kara identified as an armsman of House Veruna."

"He was buried in his Veruna colors?" Sergen said.

"No, but I recognized him," Kara replied. She glanced at Geran. "I asked some questions around town after we returned. The dead armsman was Zormun Kelfarel—a Mulmasterite sellsword in the service of House Veruna. And yes, Sergen, I realize that his employers might've had no idea what he was up to, so don't bother to say it."

"Your discretion is admirable, dear Kara."

"I also found out more about the tiefling we met outside the barrow, by the way," Kara continued. "His name is Sarth, and he came to Hulburg about four months ago. Several of the merchant costers tried to hire him on, including House Veruna. All of the merchants look for competent spell-casters to strengthen their private armies."

"We ran into him again—but I'll get to that in a moment," Geran said. He paced absently around the table, organizing his thoughts. "Since we had good reason to be suspicious of House Veruna, I decided to take a closer look at their activities. Hamil and I disguised ourselves and went to work in the Veruna tradeyard for a few days, watching Veruna's sellswords closely. Did you know they have well over a hundred men under arms in and around Hulburg? In any event, I got to know many of the Veruna men by sight, including their captain, a man named Urdinger. Hamil and I found that the Veruna sellswords were keeping themselves quite busy, constantly coming and going from their timber camps and mines all around the area."

"Which is hardly suspicious," Sergen pointed out. "All of the merchant companies patrol the wildlands around their camps to protect their investments. And I'll also point out that what you were doing was in breach of the concession laws. The harmach and his agents aren't allowed to interfere in legitimate business of the merchant costers."

Hamil grimaced. "Interfere? We gave them an honest day's work. They've never had a better team or wagon."

"This will go faster if you don't interrupt me, Sergen," Geran said. He was rapidly remembering why he'd never liked his stepcousin very much. "After watching the Veruna mercenaries for a few days, I decided to try a different tactic. I set out to look into the tomb-breakings Jarad was investigating. Uncle Grigor gave me the reports Jarad had compiled, and Hamil and I set out to visit each scene. We rode up to the Highfells and examined the barrows. First of all, we noticed that the barrows were not looted indiscriminately—whoever was breaking into the barrows was looking for something specific and leaving other valuables behind. And we noticed something else—each barrow was about the same age. Each was the burial mound of a servant of Lathander, and each dated from the time of old Thentur.

"Once we figured that out, I decided to seek some expert assistance. We went to Rosestone Abbey—a harrowing ride, since the dead walked on the Highfells that night—and spoke with the Initiate Mother. I asked her what tomb robbers might be looking for in the barrow of a Lathanderian from the days of Thentur, and she had an answer for me: a book called the *Infiernadex* that once belonged to Aesperus himself."

"The tiefling was looking for a book," Kara said.

"The same one," Geran confirmed. "Anyway, Mother Mara told me that it was hidden in the barrow of a high priestess named Terlannis, and she told me where to find it. I decided to remove the book to keep it out of the hands of the men who were looking for it.

"Two days ago, we broke into the barrow of Terlannis. We discovered a secret vault hidden under the burial chamber and found the *Infiernadex.* But when we emerged from the barrow, we discovered that we'd been tracked. A company of Veruna armsmen was waiting for us."

"And I suppose *these* men were wearing their House colors?" Sergen demanded.

"In fact, they were!" Hamil snapped. "And Captain Anfel Urdinger himself ordered Geran to surrender the book at swordpoint."

Sergen began to reply, but Harmach Grigor held up his hand. "A moment, Sergen. Finish your tale, Geran. What happened then?"

"I threatened to destroy the *Infiernadex*, because I couldn't see why they would let us go to carry tales back to Hulburg if I surrendered the tome. But Aesperus appeared—the King in Copper himself. He seized the tome before I could even think of protecting it from him. Then, once he had it, he told Urdinger that he held Veruna's part of the bargain accomplished, and that he would soon make good on his part."

Hamil interrupted. "He also said that Urdinger and his men were to despoil no more barrows. I certainly took that to mean that the Veruna men had broken into a number of barrows looking for Aesperus's book."

"Aesperus teleported away after that," Geran continued. "Hamil and I ran back into the barrow we'd just left, hoping to fight off the Verunas. We'd likely be there still, except that the tiefling Sarth arrived and attacked the Verunas. He distracted Urdinger and his men enough for Hamil and me to fight our way back out. The Verunas retreated, and the tiefling—Sarth Khul Riizar is his full name, Kara—flew off into the night, after some sharp words to Hamil and me for allowing Aesperus to reclaim his old book.

"After that, Hamil and I retraced our steps to Rosestone, rested there a night, and set out at first light this morning for Hulburg." Geran paused, thinking over what he'd just said, and leaned on the dark cherrywood table to meet his uncle's eyes. "What it all means, I can't say. But now I know that House Veruna men were the ones breaking into the tombs on the Highfells, I know that Veruna men killed Jarad Erstenwold, I know they struck some sort of bargain with the King in Copper, and I *know* Veruna men were ready to kill Hamil and me to keep us from telling you what we saw."

The harmach frowned and rubbed his hand over his eyes. "That is a black tale you bring to us, Geran. I know that Darsi Veruna is no friend to me, but treachery and murder such as this. . . ."

Sergen began to chuckle, then laughed deeply and richly. "Surely you don't believe all this, Uncle? It's a wild exaggeration at best, and more likely an outright fabrication!" He pushed himself upright from the bookshelf he had been leaning against and looked at Geran. "Aesperus himself took the book from your hands, and you were rescued by a mysterious devil-spawned sorcerer who then flew off into the night? Ah, goodness! I had no idea you were capable of such ridiculous invention, Geran! Why, *The Bride of Secomber* couldn't best that tale! Are you sure you're not a playwright?"

Geran stood up straight and glared at Sergen. "Every word I've spoken here today is true. Don't call me a liar again."

"Why should we believe you?" Sergen asked. His easy smile fell from his face, and his dark eyes glittered like serpent scales. "You haven't seen a reason to spend ten days in this house in the last ten years—the house of your father and your father's father. You're a feckless wanderer, Geran, chasing after childish dreams of glory and fame. I don't doubt that a man such as you might invent any sort of fantastic tale to justify a few more hours of adoration from those too foolish to look past your wild claims and ask for some small shred of proof."

"Enough, both of you," Harmach Grigor said. "We have—"

"Now that's odd," Geran retorted to Sergen. "You haven't seen fit to spend a single day in your father's house in all that time. Where is he now, I wonder? Selling children into slavery? Robbing and murdering his way through the world as a common highwayman? Or perhaps groveling in front of some demon's bloody altar? As I see things, Sergen, you've claimed my family's name and sold off my family's property for your own riches. Maybe we should've run you off all those years ago when that traitorous, blackhearted father of yours fled for his miserable life!"

"That is enough!" the harmach snapped.

"You'll regret those words," Sergen hissed. He took a step toward Geran, his hand dropping to the hilt of his rapier.

For his own part, Geran rounded the table and took three strides toward his stepcousin. He'd be damned if he would let Sergen call him a liar. "What are you hiding?" he growled. "Why are you trying to protect House Veruna? Did they buy your loyalty, such as it is? Perhaps you hope to succeed where your father failed? "

"Geran, I will have no more of this!" Grigor roared. He stood and struck his cane against the floor. "Sergen may not be of Hulmaster blood, but my sister raised him as her own son, and I will not hear another word about his father's deeds!"

Geran hesitated. In all of his life he had never heard the harmach raise his voice so. Sergen fell silent too, but still glared at Geran. Kara stepped between the two and then looked to the harmach. "Uncle Grigor, we all know that Sergen is . . . close . . . to Darsi Veruna. Geran's charges against the Verunas are serious and must be answered, but Sergen's not likely to demand explanations from House Veruna."

Sergen turned a black look on his stepsister but mastered himself with a visible effort. "I don't deny that I am courting Lady Darsi. Nor do I deny that we've had a profitable association—all of us. House Veruna accounts for almost half of the concession fees collected on Hulmaster land. But that doesn't make Geran's wild accusations true, Uncle. I have in fact already heard a different account of what transpired on the Highfells. I didn't want to mention it for fear of shaming a kinsman I haven't seen in a long time, but it seems clear that I must speak of it now." Sergen frowned and shook his head. "I don't know how to say this, but . . . Captain Urdinger reported to Lady Darsi that he and his men were performing a routine patrol when they stumbled across a pair of bandits looting a tomb in search of nothing more exotic than barrow-gold. When they challenged the looters, they discovered Geran and his small accomplice there, who attacked them rather than allowing themselves to be taken into custody. They murdered several Veruna armsmen and fled into the mists." He looked at Geran and added, "So where have you hidden the gold you've looted? How many more barrows do you intend to pillage before you flee Hulburg and go off to plunder some other land?"

"You lying serpent . . ." Geran snarled in fury.

Easy, Geran, Hamil told him. The halfling set his hands on his hips and looked up at Sergen. "So, Lord Sergen, are Geran and I responsible for the barrows that were plundered *before we even arrived in town?* If we didn't do it, then who did?"

Kara narrowed her azure eyes and folded her arms over her breastplate. "For that matter, Sergen, why didn't you report this dire tale as soon as you heard it?"

"Frankly, I thought Geran had already fled Hulburg again," Sergen answered. "He hasn't been seen here in days, after all, and I hoped to spare the family any story of his misdeeds. You all seem to think well of him, after all." He glanced down at Hamil and shrugged. "As far as who opened barrows before you arrived, well, we have only your word that you returned to Hulburg when you claim you did. How do we know you haven't been here for months, searching out barrows to loot? For that matter, how do we know that *you* weren't the very tomb robbers Jarad Erstenwold died trying to arrest?"

"Now that's ridiculous!" Kara snapped. "Perhaps you'd like to suggest that Geran is responsible for the Spellplague and the Time of Troubles too, while you're at it?"

The harmach sighed. "Sergen, I don't find your accusations against Geran very credible. Your anger is speaking for you."

"They are not *my* accusations, Uncle. I'm only reporting what's been told to me. Regardless of what you find credible, there are a dozen Veruna blades who can swear to their account of what happened on the Highfells two nights ago." Sergen drew himself up and measured Geran sternly. "Geran may have inveigled you with his self-aggrandizing tales, but I think the Merchant Council will be less easily swayed by old affection."

"I *will* lay Geran's charges against House Veruna before the Merchant Council, Sergen," the harmach warned. "And I expect them to be investigated thoroughly and impartially. If you are not capable of doing that, I'll appoint a new keeper of duties to oversee the Council Watch and see to it."

"So you take Geran at his word?" Sergen pointed at Geran and snarled, "While *he's* been off playing at adventure in foreign lands, *I've* stayed here and built Hulburg from a forgettable little backwater into a prosperous town! What's he ever done for this city or this family? This drafty old castle would be crumbling around your ears if not for the coin *I* brought in. I refuse to let his wild stories antagonize a trading partner as valuable as Mulmaster!" He glared defiantly around the room and then abruptly shouldered his way past Geran and stormed out the door, slamming it shut behind him.

Geran drew a deep breath and ran his fingers through his hair; the harmach sat down slowly and leaned his cane against his chair. No one else said anything for a long moment, and then Hamil cleared his throat and said, "Forgive me if I'm speaking out of place, but why charge Urdinger and the Veruna men through the Merchant Council? Why not send the Shieldsworn to arrest them?"

"My hands are bound by the laws of concession, Master Hamil," the harmach answered. "Matters of justice pertaining to the merchant costers are dealt with by the Merchant Council. My Shieldsworn aren't permitted to set foot in the conceded territory, nor are they allowed to arrest foreigners employed by a merchant company holding a concession. We must lay our charges before the Merchant Council and allow the council to arrest, try, and sentence their own."

"And do you trust Sergen to charge and try House Veruna's armsmen?" Geran asked.

Grigor glanced out the leaded window at the warm rain pattering down over the town. "Sergen has shown that his loyalty lies with our family on many occasions, Geran," he said quietly. "I've always believed that trusting someone can make that person worthy of trust, and Sergen long ago made up for the harm his father intended against us. But it might be true that he's become too entangled with the merchants he deals with."

"He's protecting Jarad's murderer, Uncle Grigor."

"Which he may not have known he was doing until you reported what you'd found in the Highfells," the harmach pointed out. He shifted his gaze back to Geran and met his eyes. "I'll give him a few days to show me that he can set aside his dislike for you and act on the information you've brought to light, and if he doesn't, then yes, I will replace him. Now—tell me everything about Aesperus and this book. I want to know what the King in Copper has to do with this whole affair."

Seventeen

27 Ches, the Year of the Ageless One

Later in the afternoon, Geran decided it was time to visit Mirya Erstenwold again. She'd insisted that there was nothing that he had to do about Jarad's murder on her account, but that didn't mean she didn't deserve some answers. After all, when they'd met at Jarad's graveside, she'd seemed to understand that he needed to settle Jarad's business for the peace of his own heart, if not hers. By sharing her suspicions about House Veruna, she'd given him her blessing to follow his own path through grief. Geran was slowly resigning himself to the idea that he might not ever find out which of the Veruna armsmen had actually waylaid his friend in that wild and lonely place, but he could certainly tell Mirya what the Veruna men had been seeking and how Jarad had come to get in their way. Besides, Mirya *needed* to know what he'd learned about Veruna's involvement. The men who'd murdered her brother might be the same men who now threatened her family's livelihood with their extortion and intimidation.

Wrapped deeply in his thoughts, Geran slipped out of the castle an hour before sunset, leaving Hamil to entertain Natali and Kirr. He set out from Griffonwatch on foot, dressed in a nondescript gray cloak, only one more man among the hundreds in the streets who hurried about on their own business. The rain had diminished to a cool, steady mist that beaded his cloak without really soaking the dense wool, and faint tatters of cloudwrack drifted over the town only a few hundred feet overhead. He took Cinder Street through the Tailings—by daylight the neighborhood was simply run down and poor, not dangerous—crossed the Winterspear at the Middle

Bridge, and climbed the steps up to the square by the Assaying House and High Street.

As he threaded his way through the sodden streets, Geran brooded over the question of how to hold House Veruna to account even if the harmach couldn't. When he considered events coldly and carefully, he decided that it didn't matter all that much which of the armsmen had been involved. The Veruna men were mercenaries, paid to do what they did without asking questions, and the ultimate responsibility for Jarad Erstenwold's murder rested with the man or woman who had ordered the mercenaries to kill him. It seemed likely that Anfel Urdinger might be that man—after all, Mirya had seen him wearing Jarad's elf-made dagger. And the encounter at the barrow of Terlannis suggested that Urdinger was the sort of captain who was inclined to personally see to important missions. The only real question in Geran's mind was whether Urdinger had conceived the plans to loot the barrows, deal with Aesperus, and assassinate Jarad Erstenwold himself, or simply followed the orders of Lady Darsi or some other high-ranking member of House Veruna.

Geran reached the intersection with Plank Street and turned the corner to Erstenwold's. The first sign of trouble was the two mercenaries in tabards of green and white standing outside the door of Mirya's store with insolent smirks. Passersby gave them a wide berth, staying well clear of the doorway. The next sign was the sound of breaking glass and coarse laughter from inside.

Geran's step faltered. "Ah, damn it all," he muttered. "Geran, you fool!" The Veruna men were back, vandalizing the place to teach Mirya a lesson for letting him stand up for her. But whether it was a message for him or a message for her, he wasn't going to stand by and let Darsi Veruna's mercenaries hurt Mirya or drive her out of business. *I think I've had about enough of Darsi Veruna's hired blades*, he decided. He paused in the shadow of a doorway and quickly spoke a couple of his swordmage spells. Then he crossed the street, heading for the steps where the mercenaries waited.

"Find another store, friend," one of the men said coldly. "This one's closed."

"That's not for you to say," Geran replied, and he whipped his cloak free of his shoulders, dropping it into the muddy street without breaking stride.

His right hand rode on his sword hilt. "Now get out of my sight, because Torm knows I've had all I can stand of your stink in my town."

"Damn it, Terth! That's *him*!" the second man said to the first. "That's Geran Hulmaster!"

"I don't care if he's the king of Cormyr," the first armsman said. He set his hand on the hilt of his own sword and grinned in challenge at Geran. "I don't mean to step aside for him."

"Sanhaer astelie!" Geran snarled.

He lunged forward and caught the first Veruna man with his bare hands by the belt buckle and the collar. With the burst of magical strength the spell gave him, he simply plucked the man right off the top step, holding him above his head. He wheeled and took three strides with the Veruna bladesman waving and kicking helplessly in midair before he rammed the man headfirst into a big barrel full of rainwater that stood by the corner of the store. The man's feet kicked and scissored in the air, but it was a big barrel, and it was full; it rocked but didn't tip.

"Stay there as long as you like!" Geran snapped.

He heard the rasp of steel against wood and leather behind him and turned to face the second Veruna man hurrying down the porch. Geran swept his elven backsword from its sheath, flinging water from his wet sleeves, and bounded forward to meet the man. The mercenary aimed a high cut at Geran's head, but Geran batted the blade over his head and then laid the man's swordarm open from elbow to wrist. The mercenary's sword clattered across the cobblestones, and the man hissed a curse as he jerked his arm back. With the last glimmer of his strength spell, Geran seized him by his good arm with one hand, spun in a half-circle, and propelled the wounded man headlong into the side of the building. The Veruna man hit hard and went down in a jingle of mail, splattering blood from his wounded arm all over the whitewashed timber.

Without even pausing to think about it, Geran leaped up the steps into the Erstenwold storefront. Two more Veruna men were inside. One—the mercenary sergeant Bann, whom Geran had seen in the store the last time he visited—had dragged Mirya out from behind her counter and stood holding her with his hand knotted in her dark hair. The other man was systematically breaking every jar of goods on the shelves behind the counter.

"Let go of her," Geran said coldly.

Bann looked up in surprise as Geran stormed in, but the big mercenary recovered quickly. "You know, I've been waiting for this," he remarked. He dragged Mirya out of his way and shoved her violently to the floor, then slowly drew his own blade. "I wonder if you're man enough to meet me steel to steel, or do you need to lean on your damned elven witchery?"

"Mirya, get out of the way," Geran said. He waited a moment for her to pick herself up from the floor. Her chin was already beginning to bruise, but her eyes blazed with an icy fury, and she threw her shoulders back and walked proudly to the doorway leading back toward the rest of her storehouse.

"He's strong, but he's slow, Geran," she said. "Try not to kill him in my shop if you can help it."

"Done," Geran said. He glided forward, point low and guard high, and stamped his lead foot down as he started with a series of short slashes at the mercenary's legs. Bann parried the first and the second, then just missed the third and earned a quick cut above the knee. He swore and beat Geran's point up into the air, then put his size and power into a whistling backhand cut that Geran caught with a sliding block and stepped away from. Steel rang shrilly on steel as the two men traded cuts and parries.

"You ain't that good without your magic, are you?" Bann grunted. But a trickle of sweat beaded at the man's brow, and his breath grew heavier.

"I'm not in any particular hurry," Geran replied. He let his momentum circle him around and attacked the lead leg again as Bann turned to follow him. This time he buried three inches of his point in the meat of Bann's thigh just under his mail, and the Veruna bladesman grunted and hobbled back, beating Geran's point away again. "I've got hours to slowly cut you to pieces."

"Cyric take me if you do!" Bann swore, and he suddenly lunged forward, bulling straight for Geran to catch the blades breast-to-breast. The bigger man grinned and pressed down, shoving the swordmage back three paces across the old, smooth floorboards. Geran's boots slid without giving him purchase, and he started to stumble—but he caught his back foot against one of the posts in the center of the room, bent both knees a bit, and shoved back and up with all his strength. He might not have been as big as the Veruna man, but he was quick and strong, and he knocked Bann's sword up over his head.

Before the mercenary could recover, Geran simply slugged him hard in the mouth with the heavy hilt of his sword. He felt teeth shatter, and the Veruna man spun away from the blow, blood splattering from his mashed lips. Geran cut his back leg out from under him, and Bann went to the floor heavily, at which point Geran kicked his sword away and struck him senseless with another kick.

"I was a pretty good swordsman *before* I went to Myth Drannor, you ox-brained fool," he said to the unconscious Veruna man. Then he glanced around for the other, the one behind the counter.

The last mercenary glared at him and started to edge his way around the counter, moving to get clear. His hand settled on his sword hilt as he moved to put the open door at his back.

"You—get out of here now, or I'll feather you right in the eye, eh?" Mirya spoke in a voice that was deadly and certain.

Geran glanced around. Mirya had quietly slipped back behind the counter to retrieve a small but efficient-looking crossbow, which she'd leveled at the other Veruna man. Evidently the fellow had been so caught up in watching his sergeant fight that he'd forgotten to keep an eye on her.

The man spat once on the floor and backed up a step. "You'll be sorry for this," he said.

"Drag that thickheaded fool with you when you go," Geran said, nodding at Bann. The last Veruna man scowled, but he grasped the big sergeant under his arms and dragged him to the door.

Mirya kept her crossbow trained on him until he backed out of the door then slowly lowered it. She shuddered and set the weapon down on the countertop. "May demons carry off those brigands and all their kin, straight to the bottom of the blasted Abyss. What have I got that's worth their trouble?"

Geran motioned for her to wait. "Just a moment," he told her. He turned his back on Mirya and stepped out onto the porch, sword still in hand; a small crowd of townsfolk stood and stared at him. The last Veruna man had Bann upright, aided by the mercenary with the wounded arm. The two of them shot murderous glances back at the swordmage as they retreated back down the street. Geran glanced over to the corner. The water-barrel lay on its side, and there was no sign of the man he'd dropped into it. The swordmage looked at the nearest person, an old dwarf in a crumpled hat. "The other one ran off?" he asked.

"Aye, m'lord," the dwarf grunted. He smiled crookedly at Geran. "Half-drownded he was, but he tipped himself over an' crawled out."

"My thanks," Geran replied. He wouldn't have wanted to drown the Veruna man, which is why he came out to make sure the sellsword had actually escaped from the barrel . . . but coming within an inch of drowning the fellow did not bother him at all.

He drew an oilcloth from a small pouch by his scabbard and wiped down the fine steel blade as he stepped back inside. With a graceful flourish he sheathed the sword and faced Mirya in the wreckage of her business. She stood with her arms hugged close to her body, watching him with an absent frown creasing her brow.

"Are you hurt, Mirya?" he asked quietly.

She reached up to touch her jaw and shook her head. "I've taken no hurt. But if you hadn't come along when you did, I've a feeling it was going to get a lot worse."

"I wish I could promise you that they won't trouble you anymore, but I can't." Geran stooped down to right a small keg of nails that had been kicked over on its side. "I think you need to hire a couple of good men to guard your place. Or close up shop for a tenday or two, keep to yourself, and stay safe until things settle down."

"I know it." Mirya went to the door, closed it, and threw the bolt. Then she turned to study the damage to the shelves and wares and took a deep breath. "What a mess they've made of the place. It'll take me all the night to clean this up."

"Mirya, I'm sorry that I brought this on you. I thought that I could solve your problems for you with a few hard words and a show of steel. That's what I know how to do. I suppose I felt that I owed it to Jarad . . . and you. But I shouldn't have stepped into the middle of your troubles without asking."

Mirya didn't reply for a time. She reached up to brush her disarranged hair out of her eyes. Her braid had come lose during the struggle. "Thank Ilmater that Selsha's back at the house with my mother," she finally said. "If she'd been here . . . I haven't the heart to even think about it." She sighed and found a seat on a heap of grain-filled sacks. "Whether you were here or no, the Merchant Council would still trouble me, Geran Hulmaster. They aim to drive all the smaller merchants out of town to make more room for Veruna and Marstel and the other important companies. They've already arranged the harmach's laws to suit them, and that's not enough, so they mean to ruin the rest of us. Maybe you've got the right of it, and it's your stubbornness as brought those brigands back to my shop today. But I'm beginning to think that your way of things might be exactly the change that's needed in this town."

"I'm only one man," Geran answered. He shook his head. He never would have imagined that things could turn so ugly in Hulburg in just a few years, but if Mirya said it was so, he believed her. He found an overturned barrel, rolled it up on its end, and seated himself on it. "Listen, Mirya, I came to see you for a different reason . . . there's something I need to tell you. I've found out a few things about Jarad's death. And you should know that House Veruna is at the bottom of it."

She glanced sharply at him and nodded once. Clearly, Mirya was not surprised to hear that. "Were the barrow robbers Veruna men?"

"Yes, they were—and you haven't heard a quarter of the story yet." He began the tale of how he'd spent the last tenday with his visit to the barrow where Jarad Erstenwold had been killed, the days he and Hamil had spent spying out House Veruna's enterprises, and the decision to retrace Jarad's steps and visit the other barrows. He recounted the visit to Rosestone and his decision to find the barrow of Terlannis before the Verunas could pillage it, and told her about what he and Hamil had found there and the ambush waiting outside when they emerged.

Mirya listened intently, her keen eyes never leaving Geran's face. When Geran described how Aesperus had made an appearance, her eyes widened and she leaned forward. "The King in Copper himself," she breathed. "Everybody's told tales of that one for years, and all this time I've believed they were nought but stories."

"He knew me for a Hulmaster, but other than that, I was almost beneath his notice," Geran said. "He was only interested in the book. He left after he took it from me, but not before he told Urdinger that Veruna had met their end of the bargain."

"Bargain? What bargain?"

"I didn't find out. Hamil and I made a break for it after Aesperus left. Our chances didn't look good, but the sorcerer we met at the first barrow showed up again and started slinging spells. We were able to fight off the Verunas in the confusion. Anfel and his men rode off, but we lost our horses and had to walk back. We didn't get back to Hulburg until early this afternoon," Geran finished. "I came to see you as soon as I could leave Griffonwatch."

"So the Veruna mercenaries opened the barrows to find this book for Aesperus," Mirya murmured, more to herself than to Geran. "Jarad stood in their way, and for that they killed him. Stealing barrow-gold I might've guessed, but searching for Aesperus's spellbook? That's a dark and strange tale, and there's no doubt of it." She remained silent for a long moment, looking down at her lap. Then she shook herself and raised her face to Geran again. "So what does the harmach mean to do about it?"

"I'm not sure. As you know, the Verunas can hide behind the laws of concession. My uncle can't lightly set those aside, no matter how much he might want to." Geran scowled. "I think that he feels that he's got to give Sergen and his Council Watch a chance to show where their loyalties lie. Of course, when I told my tale in front of Sergen and the harmach, Sergen was quick to speak in Veruna's defense. He went so far as to suggest that my friend Hamil and I were the barrow-robbers and were casting accusations at House Veruna to cover our own crimes."

Mirya's mouth twisted in a small, bitter smile. "He did not!"

"He did. Even my uncle—who's tried hard to believe the best about Sergen for fifteen years—had a hard time with that."

"Did Sergen have aught to do with the whole scheme?"

"I couldn't say. He might have been protecting Veruna as a matter of simple self-interest. It seems that he's prospered greatly with the rise in House Veruna's fortunes, and that might be reason enough for Sergen to side against me." Geran smiled humorlessly. "Then again, Sergen's hated me since we were children. I'm sure that had something to do with it too. We had hard words for each other in front of my uncle. Sergen won't forget them. Nor will I."

Mirya started to say something else, but a sharp rap at the window beside the bolted door interrupted her. Geran glanced around behind him;

the old dwarf from across the street was peering inside. The dwarf met his eyes through the wavy glass and gave a sharp jerk of his head before ducking away.

"Now what was that about?" Mirya said.

"Trouble. I think the Verunas are coming back." Geran stood. He could leave and try to avoid further trouble, but they might take it out on Mirya. The best thing might be to meet them in the street, distance himself from Erstenwold's, and try to keep the mercenaries' attention on him.

He closed his eyes and concentrated, unlocking a spell in his mind, and breathed the words for his silversteel veil. "I'll meet them outside."

Mirya didn't protest. She simply met his eyes and nodded slowly. "I'll ask the neighbors to send for help," she said and hurried out the back of the store.

Geran moved to the door, unshot the bolt, and stepped out onto the porch. He glanced down the street; three men in green-and-white tabards pushed through the passersby. He descended from the store's covered porch to the cobblestones and strode out into the middle of Plank Street to await them. Two of them were men he hadn't seen before . . . but the third was Anfel Urdinger, wearing his armor of black plate under his Veruna tabard. The captain's face was set in an angry scowl. The three Veruna mercenaries came to a halt seven paces away from him, and the people moving about on the street nearby fell silent to listen and watch.

"You've made a serious mistake," Urdinger grated. "Trying to beat me to my prize up on the Highfells was one thing. The book was there for the taking, after all. But now you're interfering in our business. My House paid well for our place in this wretched little town. If you think a few brave words and some elf-magic are going to make me surrender it, you're dead wrong, Hulmaster."

"It seems to me that your House's place in this town consists of robbing Hulburg blind, threatening unarmed women, and dealing with the harmach's enemies," Geran retorted. "I'd suggest that you ought to change your ways, but somehow I doubt that would make much of an impression. So I suppose I'll have to frame my point in terms you can understand: Every time a Veruna man hurts a Hulburgan or damages his property, I'll make certain that he soon regrets it."

"Fool," the mercenary captain spat. "When you draw steel against a man in our colors, you draw steel against all of us. When we're done with you, you'll never hold a sword again."

The other two mercenaries started to circle slowly around Geran. The swordmage shifted his stance a step but kept his eyes on Urdinger. The mercenary captain shrugged his cape over his shoulder, clearing his sword hilt, and then Geran saw something familiar: On the mercenary captain's right hip rode an elven dagger with a pommel shaped like a sprig of holly.

Geran stopped and stood his ground, narrowing his eyes. "Where did you get that dagger, Urdinger?" he asked in a cold voice.

The mercenary glanced down at his hip with a frown, then he looked back up with a short rasp of cruel laughter. "What, this? I suppose I found it out on the Highfells. Why do you care?"

"I gave that dagger to Jarad Erstenwold three years ago." Geran drew his sword in one easy motion, leveling the point at the Veruna captain. "I name you murderer, thief, and tomb-robber, Anfel Urdinger. And I name you a craven coward as well, since you seem to be unable to challenge a son of Hulburg without a three-to-one advantage in numbers."

The Mulmasterite's coarse amusement died in his throat, and an angry flush reddened his face. Geran had chosen his barb well; in Mulmaster, words such as Geran's were words to kill over. With two of his own armsmen and a handful of Hulburgan bystanders close at hand, Urdinger could not let it pass. "No man calls me a coward and lives," the mercenary hissed.

One of the Veruna armsmen spoke. "Captain Urdinger, he's baiting you—"

"Shut your mouth!" Urdinger snarled. "And stand aside, both of you. This lies between me and him." He drew his own blade, a well-made long sword engraved with the image of a serpentine dragon. The captain quickly moved the blade through several quick passes, slicing the air as he settled the sword in his grip, and then he advanced on Geran. "I'll have satisfaction for your insults, my lord. You'd have been wiser to keep your accusations to yourself."

With a sudden martial shout, the Mulmasterite sprang at Geran and attacked. He slashed high, recovered from Geran's parry with a jab at the swordmage's face, and then lunged quickly at Geran's belt-buckle while Geran was still leaning back. Geran barely knocked Urdinger's point aside. The mercenary was a fine swordsman, noticeably quicker and more skilled than Bann, and for a few moments Geran was hard pressed to keep up a defense, let alone riposte. Another vicious thrust at his mid-section he only deflected, and the Mulmasterite's point stopped only when the silversteel veil turned it away from piercing Geran under his right-side ribs.

"Elf witchery," the Veruna man snarled. "And you accuse me of cowardice!"

"You wear steel plate," Geran answered. "My spells are my armor."

Urdinger attacked again, trying out Geran's measure more deliberately, seeking an opening. Geran fell back, choosing to use his footwork more as he studied Urdinger in return. The Veruna man was a master of the Mulman style—hard strikes, hard parries, an emphasis on attack over defense. It was fairly common in the Moonsea lands. The cobblestones scuffed under his boots as he circled Urdinger, and the shrill ring of steel against steel filled the narrow street. Geran's own style was much less formal. He'd spent his early years largely teaching himself, learning to fit his bladework to his own strengths instead of the other way around. He'd come by his formal schooling much later, in Myth Drannor, learning from elf blademasters who had studied their art for centuries.

A small scowl of frustration began to work its way across Urdinger's face. He'd thrown himself into a sudden, fierce assault, but Geran had survived it, and in the space of three heartbeats, the initiative in the duel passed from the mercenary to the swordmage. Geran shifted from parries and ripostes to more deliberate and dangerous attacks, throwing Urdinger on the defensive. Steel flickered and darted in the fading daylight, and the two duelists exchanged places several times in a row as Geran's passing attacks carried him to Urdinger's right flank, and the Mulmasterite quickly reciprocated.

"Stand still, damn you!" the Mulmasterite growled.

Geran saw his chance. He feinted with his feet, bluffing at another passing attack, and Urdinger anticipated the move and gave way too soon. With the quickness of a striking serpent, Geran circled his point under the Mulmasterite's parry and then up and around in a looping cut that found the juncture of helm and shoulder. The last four inches of Geran's point slashed through Urdinger's neck, flicking scarlet drops across the street, and then Geran gave back a couple of steps.

Urdinger grunted and recovered his guard, ignoring the blood coursing from his collar and bubbling between his bared teeth. He fixed his eyes on Geran and returned to the attack for two, then three swings, each growing wilder, and then he stumbled to all fours. His sword clattered to the cobblestones, and his eyes widened in shock.

"Not . . . like . . . this . . ." he rasped.

Geran lowered his point and gazed coldly at the Veruna captain. "I met you steel to steel, Urdinger," he said. "You might be a murderer and a thief, but I must say it: You're not a coward."

The Veruna captain pitched forward to the street and fell still, blood pooling beneath him. Geran knelt and pulled the elf-dagger in its sheath from Urdinger's sword belt. "This was Jarad's," he said to no one in particular, and then he straightened and looked around. The townsfolk stood watching him, not saying a word. The remaining two Veruna men stared at their fallen captain with astonishment. Geran ignored them. He shook the blood from his sword and sheathed it.

"Word's on its way to Griffonwatch, Geran," Mirya said. She stood on the steps of Erstenwold's, her face set in a worried frown. She wouldn't miss Anfel Urdinger, of course, but Mirya had sense enough to see that this wasn't the end of the affair. "The Shieldsworn ought to be here soon enough. Are you wounded?"

He realized that his side hurt, and glanced down. A small round spot of blood stained his tunic on the right side of his torso, where Urdinger's blade had pinked him. He was lucky. If his spells hadn't held ,that could have been a mortal thrust. Not all of Veruna's blades are as slow or clumsy as Bann, he told himself. Urdinger might have beaten him on a different day, and there were likely other Verunas who could as well. "No, I'm fine," he rasped.

"What do you aim to do now?" she asked.

Geran remembered standing on frosted grass beneath the last leaves of autumn under the towers of Myth Drannor, watching the blood drip from his elven steel. He could still taste the rich, wet scent of the fallen leaves. He remembered looking up from his maimed enemy and meeting Alliere's stricken gaze, the cold sick shock that marked her perfect face, and the look of her turning away from him.

He raised his eyes to Mirya's face. She didn't flinch away from him; she was made of sterner stuff. But there'd be trouble from his duel with Veruna's captain, and they both knew it. It was inevitable. Geran shrugged. "I'll wait for the Shieldsworn," he said.

Eighteen

28 Ches, the Year of the Ageless One

Five severed heads stared sightlessly at Mhurren, arranged in a gore-spattered line across the steps of Bloodskull Keep. The half-orc chieftain sat next to the head of Morag, fuming with a black fury as wild and deadly as anything that had ever come over him on the field of battle. Two Bloodskull warriors lay dead by his own hand not ten feet behind him, killed because they had somehow failed to notice the appearance of the gruesome tokens on Mhurren's very doorstep. When he thought about it rationally, he had to admit that it was a feat of no little stealth and daring to deliver such a message to the Bloody Skulls. But at the moment, Mhurren was strongly disinclined to think about anything rationally. He wanted to kill and kill again, to find someone to serve as the object of his wrath and beat the life out of him with his bare hands, to bludgeon and hammer until bone broke and flesh pulped under his naked fists. And until he knew that he could master his rage sufficiently to keep himself from falling on his own warriors or tribesfolk, he simply sat motionless on the steps and stared out at the cold, cloudwracked dusk dying out over the barren hills of Thar.

It was the sheer insult of the thing that truly enraged him. Not only did the Hulburgans refuse to accord him the least measure of respect, they *dared* him to come try their strength. To kill the messengers was not entirely unexpected; it was always a possibility, one reason why Morag had asked to go and speak for the Bloody Skulls. It was a fine way to demonstrate a fitting indifference to death. Granted, it was a little unusual for humans—normally so fearful and cautious—to provide such a clear and unmistakable answer to Mhurren's demands, instead of hours of empty, wandering words. But to send the severed heads back and so scornfully display them on the steps of *his own keep* showed such contempt for Mhurren that at first he'd wondered if perhaps the Red Claws or the Skullsmashers had captured Morag and his band and killed them to declare their rebellion against his rule.

The message Mhurren's warriors had found with the heads answered any such suspicions. It was written on a piece of parchment, rolled in a small leather tube, and jammed into Morag's mouth. The Red Claws would have carved their words into the dead faces of his warriors. The Skullsmashers couldn't have managed any words at all. Mhurren looked down at the scrap of parchment in his hand and scowled. He could read well enough, having learned the skill from a human thrall who'd survived a few seasons in bondage. The harmach's response was simple and to the point:

I will not pay a single copper piece to a beast-man brigand. Any orc I catch within thirty miles of Hulburg will be treated exactly as these were.

—Harmach Grigor Hulmaster

Mhurren crumpled the parchment and slowly stood. He took a deep breath and decided that he was the master of his anger. Then he turned around to face the Skull Guards who watched him silently, the warriors who stood at their posts by the gate—two newly summoned to the task, of course—and Sutha and Yevelda, who also waited for him to speak.

"Send for the keepers of the skulls," Mhurren said. "Morag was a mighty warrior and a wise subchief. His skull should rest in honor. Let the skulls of the others be treated honorably. They were good warriors all, and it was no fault of theirs that the humans acted with such treachery."

"I will see to it," Sutha said. She was intelligent enough not to ask about the two guards Mhurren had killed. Whether they had really earned their deaths through a lack of vigilance, Mhurren could not say. But he had said it and killed them for it, so now he must act as if it were the judgment of Gruumsh himself. Sutha understood that without being told. The two gate guards would be discarded with the keep's rubbish, to be gnawed upon by whatever scavenger came along.

Mhurren's eye fell on one of the orcs who had been summoned to replace the previous guards. "Buurthar, come here," he commanded. "You are a skillful tracker. Tell me, how could someone bring five heads to our doorstep without being caught at it?"

The warrior nodded and came down the steps. He squatted by the first of the heads, frowning as he studied the nearby ground, and slowly moved along the whole line. Then he dabbed his fingertips in one of the blood-spatters and held them to his nose, inhaling deeply before opening his mouth to rub a small smear over his thick tongue. Having fixed the scent in his nostrils, he circled the area, following the unseen trail. Not all orcs had noses as keen as Buurthar's, and Mhurren could never have managed it—a weakness of his human blood. After a short time the tracker returned to the castle steps, still frowning. "I have read the ground, Warchief, but the tale it tells makes no sense to me."

"Then tell me what you can, Buurthar. I will not be angry with you."

"I hear you, Warchief." Buurthar moved around to a confused series of splatters near the last head in line, the one on the lowest step, and pointed with the tip of his spear. "Here all five heads were dumped together on the ground. Emptied out of a sack, I think. The creature who set the heads where you see them carried them one at a time from this spot. It was a big cat, like a red tiger—look, here you see where it stepped in blood and left a paw print. But it was not a red tiger. I know their sign and scent well."

"An *animal* carried the heads in a bag and dumped them here?"

Buurthar shook his head and motioned for Mhurren to follow him. "This is the part that makes no sense to me," he said. He led the chief and the others about fifty yards from the keep, into the barren, rock-strewn ground a little way off the cart track leading to the gatehouse, and pointed again to the ground. "The blood-scent, the cat-scent, the paw prints . . . they all stop here, right at this spot. If the creature had carried these heads any farther, I would smell it. It is as if the creature simply appeared right here. It is not natural."

"Nor is it natural for a tiger, or something like it, to carry heads in a bag and line them up neatly when it finds the right spot," Mhurren muttered. "You can go, Buurthar. I cannot ask you to track ghosts."

The warrior struck his spear to his hide shield and trotted back to his post.

"The harmach had some sorcerer with a spell of shapechanging deliver

Morag's head to us," Sutha said quietly. "Or he had one of his infidel priests summon some sort of invisible cat-demon to perform this task. It is not hard to explain."

"Explaining it is not the problem," Yevelda corrected her. "There were two messages sent here, my chief. The first is the one you saw on the steps of the keep. The second is that the harmach commands magic or magical allies to deliver it. If he could arrange for some monster to appear fifty yards outside your walls, he could arrange for that monster to appear *inside* your walls. Or perhaps in your bedchamber, to murder you in your sleep."

"I understand it, Yevelda," Mhurren said.

He turned on his heel and stalked back toward the keep, his mind filled with thought. Before Glister, he already would have had his warriors mustering for the march to Hulburg. But if he began his march, and Kardhel Terov told him to cease, then Mhurren would appear fatally weakened in the eyes of the Bloody Skulls. He would have to make sure that the Vaasan lord would make no effort to restrain him before he told his subchiefs and war-leaders to send their spears south. The notion of *asking* for permission to make war against Hulburg and avenge the mortal insult given to the Bloody Skulls made him seethe with anger, but that was the price he had paid for Vaasa's aid. If he hadn't agreed to do as the Warlock Knight bade, Mhurren had no doubt that Terov would have elevated some other chief of Thar to dominance, and the Bloody Skulls would now be another tribe's weaker allies. If he could not run free, well, then he would make sure that no other wolf sat closer to the master's table than he did.

Mhurren passed through the gate and turned aside into the stairs that led up to the keep's eastern tower. These chambers had been given over to the Vaasan warlocks who remained with him to provide his army with its newly found battle magic. Human guards in fine black mail bowed to Mhurren when he approached. "I am not to be disturbed," he told them.

"Yes, Warlord," the guards answered. They grounded their halberds to the floor.

At the topmost floor of the tower, Mhurren came to a door, struck it twice in deference to the human custom, and entered. "Avrun!" he said in Vaasan. "I need your speaking magic."

A fair-haired Vaasan sat behind a small desk, poring through a thick tome. He looked up at Mhurren, slowly stood, and offered a shallow bow behind a cool smile. "Of course, Warlord. I presume this is in reference to the return of your envoys from Hulburg?"

"I want you to tell Terov that the Hulburgans killed my messengers. I march against Hulburg tomorrow at sunset with all my strength. I mean to raze Hulburg, kill all its men, and take its women and children for thralls. The harmach will rue this day before long, I promise you."

The Vaasan wizard nodded. "Give me ten minutes to prepare the magic, Warlord."

Mhurren waved his hand in assent, and the human quickly and efficiently began to make ready his ritual. From shelves along the wall he took a variety of arcane implements—tall candlesticks of wrought iron topped with fat yellow candles, jars filled with strange liquids, a skull made of some reddish crystal. He arranged the candlesticks in a five-pointed star, lit the tapers with a magic word, and sprinkled drops from the jars around the candlesticks. He sat down cross-legged on the floor in the center of the candles and used another minor spell to suspend the crystal skull in the air over his shoulder. Finally Avrun opened his heavy tome and read a long passage of some sinister gibberish while Mhurren paced anxiously outside the circle.

The wizard finished with his chants and made a small gesture to the floating skull. The rosy crystal began to glow with a ruddy light. "Kardhel Terov," he intoned. "This is Avrun, speaking for Mhurren. Hulburg slew his envoys and sent back their heads. Mhurren marches tomorrow night to attack and raze Hulburg."

Mhurren shuddered at the crawling sense of sorcery filling the small room. For a long moment nothing more happened, and the orc chief wondered if the spell had somehow failed. But then Avrun grunted and straightened, and the crystal skull began to speak. "I am Terov," it said. "March on Hulburg, crush their defenses, but spare the town until I arrive. I need it. You will be well satisfied with the ransom they pay."

"Ransom is fine, but Harmach Grigor must die for the insult he gave me!" Mhurren snapped. "I warn you, Terov, it will have to be a rich prize indeed if I find Hulburg helpless before my horde!"

The candles around the Vaasan mage abruptly guttered out, and the small crystal skull sank down in the air. Avrun reached up and deftly caught it in his hand and shook himself slightly before climbing to his feet. "I am sorry, Warlord, but the magic of the sending ritual only allows me to send a single message and receive a single answer. Fellthane Terov did not hear the last thing you said. It would take me some time to make ready another one."

Mhurren growled and waved his hand. "No matter. I heard all that I needed to hear. The rest can wait for now."

"Shall I have my Warlock Knights make ready to march?" Avrun asked.

"If you have been told to remain close to me, then you will," Mhurren answered him. "I go to Hulburg to put my steel at the harmach's throat. And then we will see what ransom he can pay that will satisfy me."

Nineteen

28 Ches, the Year of the Ageless One

Early on the morning after the duel with Urdinger, Harmach Grigor surprised Geran with a sharp rap at his chamber door. Geran had just finished his morning exercises and was preparing to refresh his arcane wards and spells, but he set aside his tome and stood when the old lord limped into the room, leaning on his cane. Grigor glanced at the spellbook. "You're more of a student now than you once were," he observed. "You had little interest in arcane matters when you were a younger man, but I see that you've learned much in the years you've been away from home."

"I didn't know it myself until I went to Myth Drannor," Geran answered. "I learned Elvish there and studied under an elf bladesinger named Daried Selsherryn. My swordplay caught his eye, but he saw that I also had a talent for magic that I'd never suspected." He closed his spellbook. "What can I do for you, Uncle Grigor?"

"I hope you will forgive the interruption, but Sergen came to see me shortly after sunrise this morning. He presented a demand from House Veruna and the Merchant Council for your immediate arrest on charges of murder."

Geran snorted in disgust. "The forms might not have been strictly observed, but it was a duel, not a murder," he said. He'd told Grigor, Kara, and Hamil about his encounter with the Veruna captain the previous evening, expecting that his uncle and his cousin would be appalled by his rashness. To his surprise, Grigor simply heard out his account of events and then asked him to remain at Griffonwatch until the consequences of the duel sorted themselves out. The fact that the harmach was standing in his room seemed to suggest that those were already upon him. "I fought Urdinger fairly—he struck first, by the way—and the other Veruna men stayed out of it. There were many witnesses."

"Oh, I believe you, Geran. I told Sergen as much. He argued that until the circumstances of the duel had been verified by the council's inquest, you should be remanded to the Council Watch and held. I said that I'd arrange for a fair and independent inquiry, but that you'd remain at liberty until it was concluded—not that I expected any fair inquest to incriminate you if the accounts I'd heard were accurate." The harmach paced over to the window-seat in Geran's room and leaned against the padded bench. "At that point Sergen insisted that you'd proven yourself a murderous scofflaw several times over, and that you were singlehandedly ruining our family fortunes by ignoring Veruna's rights and protections under the laws of concession."

"Ruining our fortunes or his?" Geran muttered darkly. He looked over to his uncle. "What did you say?"

"I told him that his generous interpretation of the laws of concession did not take precedence over the harmach's interpretation of the rest of the harmach's laws, and that as far as I knew, I was still Harmach of Hulburg. I'm afraid Sergen left after that."

"I'm not surprised. The Verunas missed their chance at me on the Highfells and then again yesterday, so they sent Sergen to persuade you to arrest me for them." Geran remembered Veruna's mercenaries wrecking Mirya's store, and his mouth tightened. It was bad enough that foreigners had such contempt for the harmach that they believed they could simply lay the town under tribute and plunder it in the guise of trade laws. But his step-cousin was clearly doing everything in his power to ensure their success. The question was, why? Sergen must have been bought completely—or smitten, perhaps—by Darsi Veruna, since he was so faithfully working in her interests . . . but something about that struck Geran as not quite right. Sergen had always been keenly aware of his own self-interest, even as a boy. It wasn't like him to faithfully work at anything he didn't want for himself. Which meant that Sergen wasn't seeing to Veruna's interests by keeping his Merchant Council out of the way of the foreign costers. He was likely seeing to his own. Perhaps the Verunas were working for Sergen instead of the other way around. "That must be it," Geran murmured aloud.

"Some new thought has struck you, I see." Grigor set his hands atop the head of his cane. "What is it, Geran?"

"I think Sergen means to supplant you, Uncle. He doesn't work for House Veruna—they work for him. Everything he's done to increase the power of the Merchant Council, he's done to add to his own base of power. You must move against him before he moves against you."

"Geran, even if you're right, I cannot easily remove him," Grigor said wearily. "What happens if I attempt to oust Sergen, and he still retains control of the Merchant Council? I must tell you frankly that I don't know if my Shieldsworn could overcome the council's combined forces. Even if my Shieldsworn succeeded in disarming the foreign companies, we'd face the complete ruin of Hulburg's commerce, because you can be sure that the merchants will put a stop to all trade in or out until they are once again content with the state of affairs. Unless, of course, the Bloody Skulls prove as dangerous as Kara fears, in which case we all might be swept into the sea because we were too busy fighting each other to defend our borders against Warlord Mhurren's horde."

Geran stood in silence for a long moment. He hadn't really appreciated the difficult course his uncle was trying to chart. Do nothing and allow the foreign interests to devour Hulburg a small bite at a time . . . or resist and risk catastrophe? In that light it was not unreasonable to seek some accommodation with the foreigners, an understanding about just what belonged to them and what remained the harmach's. "Would it be better if I left Hulburg?" he finally said. "It seems that I've brought troubles to your doorstep that you hardly need. If I went back to Tantras, Sergen would no longer have the pretext of my so-called scofflaw deeds to challenge your authority."

"You didn't cause our troubles, Geran. They were here before you returned, waiting for you to find them." The harmach glanced out the window; the day promised more warm spring rain, somewhat out of season even for the end of the month of Ches. "I think you've opened my eyes to the dangers that I've been trying to grope my way through for some time now. I am not happy to see these things as they are, but only a fool would hope to remain in ignorance instead of facing an ugly truth." The old lord laughed softly and without humor. "On the other hand, I'm pleased that at least one of the men who murdered Jarad Erstenwold has met with justice, and I'm pleased that you took a stand against extortion in any guise. Darsi Veruna was long overdue for just the sort of check you've given her thugs; they've bullied honest Hulburgans for too long. But now I fear for your life. The Verunas will certainly seek a way to retaliate against you, so that they will not appear weak to their rivals and competitors."

"I won't hide in Griffonwatch," Geran answered him. "House Veruna struck their bargain with the King in Copper for a reason, and I still mean to find out why. And I don't believe for a moment that Sergen will leave Mirya Erstenwold alone, not as long as I'm here." He shrugged. "What's happened so far is only the first pass of steel in a long fight."

"I can't have you pursue a vendetta against House Veruna, Geran," the harmach said sternly. "Like it or not, the laws of concession apply to you as much as any Hulburgan. You can defend life or property, as you did against the Verunas wrecking the Erstenwold store, but they must offer you a cause to intervene. After all, any free man is obligated to protect others who are threatened with harm. But, whatever you do, stay out of Veruna's compounds or tradeyards. If you fall into their power in one of the concessions, I won't be able to protect you."

Geran grimaced, but he nodded. Trade concessions were much the same all over the lands of the Inner Sea; in effect, the property owned by House Veruna was a little piece of Mulmaster in the middle of Hulburg's dock district, just as the Red Sail's storehouses in Impiltur were protected by the laws of Tantras. But something else in the harmach's words had given him the glimmers of an idea. . . . "I understand, Uncle Grigor," he replied. "I'll watch where I step."

"Good lad," said Grigor. He stood up slowly, gripped Geran's shoulder, and limped out of the room.

Geran sat down at the small writing desk and gazed out the window for a time, organizing his thoughts. Then he returned to his magical studies and finished weaving his wards and protections. He threw his good wool cloak over his shoulders, buckled on his sword belt, and went in search of Hamil.

It took longer than he expected. Hamil was nowhere in the Harmach's Tower or the upper bailey. Geran finally resorted to asking the servants and guards and found the halfling in the castle's sallet, a large, wooden-floored practice room near the lower gatehouse. Hamil was engaged in a furious, hard-fought bout against Kara, so Geran waited and watched. He'd known for years that Hamil was one of the fastest blades he'd ever seen and an expert acrobat as well, but he remembered Kara as exceptionally quick footed and agile. Both fought with buckler and rapier—equally unfamiliar to each, really, since Hamil preferred knives, and Kara usually carried a long sword. She was twenty inches taller and had a considerable advantage in reach and strength; when Hamil managed to get inside her guard, his smaller stature turned to his advantage. While Geran watched, Kara raced across the floor and spun past Hamil, her practice sword flicking out in a lightning-quick passing cut, but Hamil batted the stroke high with his buckler and lunged at her hip. Kara was not there; she was already moving away, opening the range to restore the advantage of her reach.

Hamil pressed closer and quickly somersaulted up under Kara's blade, but the ranger stood her ground, twisting away from his point, and brought her own rapier straight down from overhead in an inverted thrust that touched Hamil at the back of the neck. Geran smiled to himself; she'd met Hamil's unorthodox attack with a similarly unorthodox riposte. The halfling's roll would have worked better with a shorter blade; it simply took Hamil too long to ready his attack with the rapier, though Geran did not doubt that he would have spitted most ordinary swordsmen; Kara was almost as quick as he was. "Not bad," Hamil admitted. He straightened up and gave her a small bow of respect.

"Likewise, Master Hamil," Kara said with a smile. She stepped back and saluted with her rapier. "I'm afraid I must attend to my duties. If I don't leave soon, I won't be able to get back by tomorrow."

"Riding up to the watchtowers again?" Geran asked.

"I want to have another look around Raven Hill. If the Bloody Skulls mount a raid against us, I think it'll come from that quarter." Kara looked at Geran's cloak and tunic and frowned. "You're not leaving the castle, are you?"

"I won't find many more answers here, Kara."

"The Verunas will be looking for a chance to challenge you, Geran. You'd be wiser not to play their game."

Geran shrugged and picked up another practice sword from a rack close at hand. He executed several quick blocks. "The Mulmasterites begin to open barrows—Jarad fails to stop them. We learn that Urdinger is seeking something in an ancient priest's barrow—Hamil and I fail to keep the *Infiernadex* out of their hands. Sergen's Merchant Council threatens Hulburg's small traders—so I try to drive off Veruna thugs who are trying to intimidate and bully Mirya Erstenwold." The practice sword whistled through the air as he spoke; then Geran shifted from parries to a sudden, fierce thrust at his unseen foe. "Everyone who finds himself in opposition to House Veruna does nothing but parry. I think it's time for a riposte."

Kara frowned unhappily. "Geran, what do you intend?"

He turned and looked over to Kara. "Is Durnan Osting still a captain of the Spearmeet?"

"Durnan? Yes, I suppose so."

Hamil looked up at Geran. "What's the Spearmeet?"

"My apologies, Hamil. It's the militia of Hulburg. In the years after the Spellplague, Harmach Angar decreed that all landowning households must arm a spearman and drill together regularly. Most of the old families of the town pass down a mail byrnie, a steel cap, a good hide shield, and some weapons. Some of the townsfolk—especially those who live up in the Winterspear—used to take it quite seriously."

"Only a few of the musters still gather now," Kara said. She looked at Geran and folded her arms over her mail shirt. "There hasn't been much need for the Spearmeet in recent years. What do you want with them?"

"The Spearmeet is made up of old native families like the Erstenwolds," said Geran. "They're the people who have the most loyalty to the harmach, and they've got little reason to be happy with foreign merchants taking over the town. I think it might be a useful lesson for the Merchant Council if a thousand Hulburgans decided to put on their family mail and shake the rust off their old spears. Besides, if the orcs of Thar are coming, it might be a good idea anyway."

"They're not professional soldiers, Geran. I doubt that the Verunas or Sokols or any of the others would be much impressed. But still, you may be right about the Bloody Skulls." Kara brushed some of the perspiration from her face and then nodded. "I'll speak to the harmach about calling out the Spearmeet simply to count heads and see who turns out. It couldn't hurt."

"Thank you, Kara," Geran said. He looked over to Hamil and asked, "How do you feel about a visit to a taphouse?"

"I regard the prospect with pleasure, as always," Hamil answered. "But isn't it a little early?"

"Not if you want to speak to the master of the house before his establishment is full of customers demanding service." Geran waited while Hamil stripped off his practice jerkin, pulled his fine ruffled shirt over his torso, and threw on his cloak. Then they took their leave of Kara and left the sallet. The taphouse Geran had in mind was close by Griffonwatch, so he and Hamil strolled down the castle's causeway on foot through the light rain.

In the square of the Harmach's Foot, Geran turned right and followed the Vale Road to the north, away from the town proper. Wagons and carts creaked by alongside them, a steady parade of provisions heading out to the mining camps, and farmers headed in the other direction, bringing food into town for sale. A couple of hundred yards brought the two companions to the Troll and Tankard, on the northern edge of the town. It was a big, sprawling building, its lower floor made of heavy fieldstone, its upper story timber. The taphouse stood astride the ancient walls of Hulburg. Even though they had been destroyed centuries ago, a low mound of broken masonry ran from the building's foundation to the riverbank. "Here we are," Geran said. He led Hamil to the sturdy front door and let himself inside.

The interior of the taphouse was as drafty and drab as the inside of a barn. The air was thick with the smell of brewing beer, and dozens of small kegs were stacked up along the walls. Little daylight filtered in through the small, dirty windows high overhead. "Charming," Hamil muttered. "I can see why you favor the place, Geran."

A beefy, brown-bearded man with a swaying belly under his apron appeared from the back room, carrying a heavy keg over his shoulder. "Good morning, sirs!" he said in a booming voice. "The taproom doesn't open until noon, but I can sell you a keg or two now if that's what you're needing."

"I'm not here for your beer, Durnan Osting. I'm here for you." Geran threw back his hood and shook the water from his hair.

"Lord Geran!" the brewmaster said. "Well, I'll be! I heard you were back in town. And I heard all sorts o' tales, too—stories o' fighting Chainsmen in the Tailings, battling ghosts up on the Highfells, learning some manners to them Veruna sellswords, and a duel 'gainst Anfel Urdinger yesterday eve. The taphouse was full o' the talk. Is it true?"

"Some of it, at least. I don't recall fighting any ghosts, but I've crossed blades with a few of the Veruna men in the last tenday—including Urdinger."

"I heard you killed him."

Geran nodded. "I did."

The brewmaster grinned fiercely. "Good! Never did like that red-haired bastard anyway. Wish I could've seen it myself." He set down his keg and brushed his big hands against his apron. "You said you wanted me for something. What can I do for you, m'lord?"

"I've seen how House Veruna's men intimidate Hulburg's merchants. Are they troubling you too?"

The brewmaster frowned. "It ain't just the Verunas. All o' the big foreign merchants collect so-called dues for the gods-be-cursed council: the Verunas, the Sokols, the Double Moon men, the Jannarsks of Phlan—they've got the Crimson Chains on their payroll, believe it or not—and even the Marstels, who're supposed to be Hulburgans. They're leaning on me and me boys too. I ain't knuckled under yet, but now they're threatening folks who do business with me. If the provisioners and smaller alehouses ain't buying me brew, well, things'll have to change for the Troll and Tankard." Durnan looked at the kegs stacked up against the wall and scowled. "It wasn't so bad last year or the year before, but nowadays . . . They're ruining everyone, Lord Geran. The harmach needs to do something about it. Is that why you're here?"

"Not exactly," Geran admitted. "My uncle's got to be careful to respect the concessions, Durnan. He's convinced that they're a necessary evil, and I suppose I see that Hulburg can't get along without them. But I think there's a lot that can be done that won't set the harmach directly against the Merchant Council. It just needs to be a little . . . informal."

The brewmaster raised an eyebrow. "Go on," he said.

"The problem with the Merchant Council is that it doesn't respect the interests of Hulburgans. It exists to protect and enrich foreigners. What we need is a different sort of Merchant Council . . . an alliance between the small merchants and craftsmen who are under coercion from the foreign Houses. If there were a hundred armed Hulburgans on the street corners, watching to make sure that council thugs couldn't rough up people or wreck their stores to intimidate them, I think things might be different in town." Geran leaned against the bar and tapped his hand to the hilt of his sword. "I've been trying to keep an eye on Mirya Erstenwold's shop, but there's only one of me—"

"Two," Hamil interjected. "I'm not about to let you fight this out alone, Geran."

"Two, then, but I need more help," Geran continued. "I can't be everywhere at once. We need more blades on our side."

Durnan scratched at his beard and squinted, thinking it over. Geran remembered that the burly brewmaster was more deliberate than he usually let on with his boisterous manner and loud voice. "It'd take more'n a hundred men," he finally said. "You'd need more like three or four hundred, since we all got to be able to keep at our trades and provide for our families. I could stand a watch one day in four, and me boys too, and some o' the stouter fellows who work for us. But we couldn't all be off on guard every day."

"I agree. That's why I was thinking of starting with the Spearmeet."

Durnan stared at Geran and then let out a sharp bark of laughter. "By Tempus, you don't do things by half measures, m'lord!"

"How many men are in your muster, Durnan? You're still a captain of the Spearmeet, aren't you?"

"Aye, I am. I've got two hundred in name, maybe sevenscore in fact. Of those, about a hundred would be worth anything in a fight."

"What of the other captains? How are their musters?" The Spearmeet was made up of six mustering companies, each about two hundred strong—or at least it had been when Geran was a lad. He didn't know if that was still true.

"Tresterfin's boys are pretty good, but the others don't really measure up to mine or his," the brewmaster said proudly. "We drill every couple o' months. Some o' the other musters ain't tried that in years. But you could find a couple of dozen good men in each, I'd wager."

Hamil cleared his throat. "Geran, a hundred men on the street might not be enough. Veruna alone has at least that many, and they're trained mercenaries."

"We don't need to be able to beat them, Hamil," Geran answered. "We just need to raise the cost of intimidating Hulburg. The harmach's willing to tolerate the foreign costers, but he certainly won't tolerate Hulburgans cut down in the streets simply for standing up for themselves. Sergen and his foreign friends know that."

"It'll come to a fight before it's done," the halfling said. "Mark my words. The council Houses will try to punish men who are standing those watches—burning a few houses or businesses while the men are away protecting their neighbors, or perhaps baiting one of your patrols into an open fight."

"Be that as it may, we might surprise those foreign bastards and make some o' them bleed too," Durnan said. "That's the way of it with a bully. Sooner or later you've got to stand up to him, punch him in the nose, and damn what follows. You might get thrashed, but he'll think twice 'fore he pushes you again. Besides, we'll have a lot more eyes than spears on our side. If we tell the folk o' each neighborhood to make sure they send word quick when they see council men up to no good, we'll be able to shadow them anywhere they go." The brewmaster shrugged and picked up his keg again. "Count me in. I'll send word 'round to my muster. Some of them won't show their faces since they work for the council Houses, but most o' my men'll help."

"Good," Geran said. "Who else should I talk to?"

"Burkel Tresterfin, for certain. Wester and Ilkur are fair captains too, and their musters might surprise me. After that, try Lodharrun the smith—he ain't in the Spearmeet, but there're a few dwarves what would be happy to stand with us."

"I will. Can I tell the others to bring the men they need to the Troll and Tankard tomorrow evening to organize a watch scheme?"

Durnan grinned in his big beard. "I've always wanted to foment rebellion. For the harmach, of course."

"Tomorrow, then," Geran said. He gripped the brewmaster's hand and then left the old taphouse. The light rain had faded to a mist that hung in the air, drifting in tatters just about the rooftops of the town.

"Let me guess," Hamil said. "Tresterfin next?"

"Good guess," Geran said. He nodded at the Vale Road. "The Tresterfin homestead is about two miles outside town."

Geran and Hamil spent the rest of the day crisscrossing Hulburg and the farms nearby, speaking to dozens of Hulburgans about the Council Watch and what had to be done. Many were people Geran knew well from his boyhood, and he retold the story of his travels in the last ten years so often that he soon shortened the account to a few vague sentences about traveling the Inner Sea lands, visiting Myth Drannor, and buying into the Red Sail Coster of Tantras. A few of the men and women he spoke with declined to help; some feared the retribution of the Council Watch, but others were simply cautious about taking up arms and thought it likely to worsen the situation instead of improve it. They simply hadn't yet suffered any great harm from the foreigners or reached the point where they were willing to hazard life or property to stand up against them. Two times Geran found that the Shieldmeet captains he was looking for had more or less given up on their musters, but each time the old leaders gave him suggestions for other Hulburgans who might be willing to help out.

Late in the afternoon, Geran headed to Erstenwold's. He found the building boarded up, with a couple of Mirya's cousins keeping an eye on the place. They told him that Mirya and Selsha were staying at the old Erstenwold homestead in the Winterspear Vale. Reassured that Mirya's store was well looked after, Geran and Hamil returned to Griffonwatch for the night.

The next morning, the rain returned in force, and the wind picked up as well. A Moonsea gale was gathering over the cold waters of the small sea, drenching Hulburg with hard-driven rain. Hamil gave Geran a doleful look when Geran told him that they had more people to speak with, but he followed Geran back down into town. Their cloaks were sodden before they reached the bottom of the causeway. The weather was foul enough that the Harmach's Foot seemed almost deserted, with little of the wagon traffic that normally crowded it in the morning.

"Well, where to now?" Hamil asked. "Please tell me that it's a short walk to someplace warm and cheerful."

Geran glanced right and left, trying to decide whom he wished to speak to next. Nearby, a party of dwarves worked to fix a broken wagon axle in the rain; across the small square, several men cloaked against the weather stood beneath the overhang of a smoking-house, arguing prices with the proprietor before large racks where dozens of smoked Moonsea silverfins cured in the open air. "East Street," he decided. "Vannarshel the fletcher has her workshop there. She used to be quite an archer; I wouldn't be surprised if she's taught her sons to shoot as well as she did. Then we might visit Therrik's Livery, which is nearby."

They started across the small square, splashing through the puddles and mud gathering between the cobblestones. Then Hamil frowned, and his step slowed. *Something isn't right here, Geran,* he said silently. *This is an ambush!*

Not twenty yards from the castle causeway? Geran thought in surprise. He glanced around behind him and saw the dwarves by the wagon pulling aside the canvas covering. Crossbows waited underneath. The men by the smoking-house suddenly broke off their arguing and turned back to the court, striding toward the two companions. The swordmage had expected some attempt by House Veruna, but not one so brazenly sprung beneath Griffonwatch's battlements. Besides, none of the men or dwarves around them wore Veruna's green and white. "Break past the men, leave the dwarves behind," he hissed to Hamil. Then, as quick as thought, he framed the words for a spell and snapped, *"Cuillen mhariel!"* His silversteel veil appeared around him, glowing softly in the dim daylight, and Geran sprinted toward the men coming from the smoking-house. Hamil followed a half-step behind.

"Now!" someone shouted. The men in front of him swept out their blades and moved to cut him off; one of them hung back, drawing a wand from his sleeve and aiming it at Geran. From behind he heard the sharp *snap!* of crossbows firing, and bolts hissed through the air behind him. Two clattered past, skipping along the cobblestones, but a third sank into the back of his calf with a searing jolt of pain. Geran stumbled and rolled heavily to the wet cobblestones, but he let his momentum roll him to his feet again and loped as best as he could toward the swordsmen rushing him. The dwarves might not be so fast to shoot at him if he was in the middle of their allies.

Hamil divined his intent and altered his own course to follow; the halfling threw himself at the feet of the first man he reached, knives flashing, and the fellow cursed and went down as Hamil rolled through his shins. Then Geran met two of the swordsmen at the same time, sweeping out his blade to bat aside one man's cut. He followed that with a sudden slash at the other swordsman and managed to gash that one's forehead in a shallow, bloody cut before the man could block his blow. That enemy staggered back, momentarily blinded, so Geran returned to the man on his right.

Then the wizard snarled something in an arcane tongue, and a dazzling violet ray sprang from his wand and struck Geran over his heart. It felt as if he'd been hit with a hammer. All of the sudden his knees grew weak, he staggered unsteadily, and brilliant purple echoes jarred and danced in his eyes as his mind reeled in magical vertigo. A stunning spell of some kind, he realized, and he tried to frame a countering enchantment to clear his mind . . . but the words simply eluded his grasp. Before he could find them, the other swordsmen were upon him. He opened his eyes just in time to see the pommel of a long sword descending toward his forehead. The blow struck him blind again, and he staggered back over a barrel and tripped, falling to the street. His sword rang shrilly on the cobblestones beside him.

"Geran!" Hamil shouted from some great distance. Then mailed fists and booted feet descended on him in a sudden violent deluge, and darkness took him.

Twenty

1 Tarsakh, the Year of the Ageless One

The creaking of a wagon's wheels and the *clip-clop* of a horse's hooves on cobblestones brought Geran back to a painful consciousness. He was lying in damp straw in a dark, swaying wagon, bound hand and foot. His calf burned where the bolt had struck him, his forehead felt hot and sticky and throbbed in agony, and the whole right side of his jaw ached abominably. Gingerly he ran his tongue over his teeth and found one of his molars was deeply split; loose bits of tooth were adrift in his mouth. He spat blood and debris out on the straw of the wagon and groaned despite himself.

"Good, you ain't dead," a deep, gravelly voice said from somewhere behind him. "I wouldn't thrash 'round too much if I were you. 'Twon't do you no good, it'll hurt like blazes, and I'll beat you senseless again if you're makin' me to."

"Where am I?" Geran rasped. It hurt to talk.

"On your way t' that tawdry ten-silver festhall they call Council Hall. We'll be there soon enough. I understand your accommodations are waitin' for you." The speaker laughed dryly.

Geran rolled slowly to one side and glanced up at his captor. The fellow was a black-bearded dwarf in heavy armor. He sat on a bench in the back of the wagon, watching Geran. He had a clay pipe clenched in his mouth and held a short-handled cudgel capped with an ugly lead shot in his lap.

"Who are you?" the swordmage asked.

"Kendurkkel Ironthane, master o' the Icehammer Company. Pleased t' make your acquaintance, m'lord— 'specially since you've earned me a very fine bonus this morning." The dwarf's pipe bobbed as he grinned under his thick beard, but his eyes remained neutral and wary. "I heard y'know a thing or two about magic, so don't be givin' me reason t' think you might be trying t' cast a spell, or I'll have t' put you t' sleep with me little persuader, here. Besides, you're in mage shackles, so there ain't no point in even trying."

Geran didn't know if he would've been inclined to try a spell with Kendurkkel sitting over him with the ugly little mace in his hand, but the mage shackles settled it. He decided he'd test them later to be sure, but if the dwarf wasn't lying, then he wouldn't get far. Mage shackles were enchanted with negation spells that simply absorbed any magic a captive tried to summon before it could be shaped into even the simplest spell. "What happened to my friend?" he asked.

"The halfling? Well, nobody offered me a bounty on him, so I left 'im in the street. He fought like a wildcat till me wizard struck him senseless with that purple ray he used to knock the sand out o' you." The dwarf shrugged. "I suppose I should've brought him along just on speculation, if you will, but frankly I don't like the smell o' this whole business, and I figured I'd be wiser t' stick t' the contract I was certain of."

The wagon hit a sharp bump, and Geran winced as his head pounded in protest. He felt nauseated, and his limbs felt as weak as thin straws . . . likely the aftereffects of the blow to the head that had knocked him down. "I don't suppose I can offer you a better deal than your bounty to let me go, can I?"

"No, that'd be unprofessional. I've got me reputation to think of."

"What if I told you that the council mercenaries intend to hold me for murder because I killed a man in a fair duel? Or that they're angry with me because I'm interfering with their plans to intimidate and extort half the folk in town? Would that make a difference?"

The dwarf chewed on the stem of his pipe and thought for a moment. "No, can't say that it would," he said. "I've found it don't pay t' worry too much about what folks say when they're in your sort o' predicament. Most o' the time they're lying, but if they did be tellin' the truth, well, then, I'd feel just awful 'bout collectin' the gold what's on their heads. Better t' assume they're all lying. I sleep better that way. Well, look, here we are."

Geran caught a glimpse of heavy wooden beams carved in fantastic shapes high overhead through the small, barred window in the wagon's door. Then Kendurkkel knelt down beside him and pulled a heavy leather hood over his head and face. "Mind your manners a little bit longer, and I'll make sure I take off the hood when we get t' your cell," the dwarf said.

The inside of the hood was lightless, dank, and hard to breathe through. Geran heard the wagon door swing open, and then several hands seized him by the arms and hauled him out. He tried to get his feet under him as best he could, but his knees were still quite weak, and his legs didn't work as well as they should have; he was half-carried along by the unseen men around him. They took him down a flight of steps, through several doors, down another flight of steps, and finally through another door. Geran tried to think of some way to escape, but even if he hadn't been sick and dizzy from the beating, he doubted that he could have managed much with magic-impeding shackles on his hands and a heavy leather hood to blind him. Several men seized him closely then, and his shackles were removed briefly, readjusted, and then snapped back into place. Only after that did the hood come off his face.

The dwarf stepped back, rolling the hood in his hands. "He's all yours," he rasped. "The Icehammers be done with this."

"A fine piece of work, Captain Kendurkkel." Sergen Hulmaster stood outside Geran's cell, dressed in a resplendent, pleated coat of deep blue embroidered with gold thread. He wore a large gold medallion around his neck—a symbol of office, or so Geran guessed. Several of the Council Watch stood nearby in their browned cuirasses. "Thanks to your diligence, this murderer will soon face justice for his crimes."

The dwarf glanced at Geran. "That's your business," he said. "You know where t' find me if you're needing the Icehammers for anything else, Lord Sergen. I go." He withdrew, his heavy tread scuffing the stone floor.

The swordmage looked down at his shackles; they'd been moved around in front of his body and tethered to an iron ring set in the floor of the cell, so he could move around a little bit. There was a plain pallet of straw in one corner of the cell, a chamber pot in the other, and a flickering lantern in the hallway outside. "Your Merchant Council has a dungeon, Sergen?" he asked.

"The Council Watch, actually," his stepcousin replied. "It's less than three years old and seems to me to be a much better place than you deserve. If I had my way, you'd be thrown into the darkest, foulest oubliette I could find."

"Your generosity overwhelms me."

"Sarcasm ill becomes you, Geran. If it helps you at all, you can take comfort in the fact that you'll be given a speedy trial before a special commission of the Merchant Council. I expect they'll quickly condemn you to hang, so the quality of your accommodations won't trouble you for long."

Geran took a deep breath and silently promised himself that he would not give Sergen the satisfaction of angering him . . . or frightening him, for that matter. In truth, he felt too miserable to muster much of a retort. "You've given yourself the power to try people who displease you and to order executions? Uncle Grigor's a patient man, but I think he might object, Sergen."

"The laws of concession, Geran. Members of foreign legations are protected from crimes of person or property.You killed Anfel Urdinger in the sight of dozens of people, so House Veruna's entitled to demand your arrest and trial under Mulman law."

"I doubt the harmach will see it that way."

Sergen snorted. "Well, as you are currently in council custody, it doesn't really matter how he sees things, does it?" He sketched a mocking half-bow and straightened with an evil smile on his face. "Now, I'm a very busy man, and I have much to do. I'm sure that your case will be disposed of in good order. Until later, dear cousin."

Geran tried to think of a stinging reply but failed. He watched Sergen strut off, and then he allowed his knees to fail him and slumped to the dismal little pallet. After a time he drifted off into darkness again, even though he knew he shouldn't let himself fall asleep after a sharp blow to the skull. He felt as though he were plummeting down and down every time he closed his eyes, and yet he was so weary that he could not keep them open any longer.

When he finally woke again, his eyes felt as if they were full of grit, and his tooth was a bright rock of white agony in the side of his mouth. But his head didn't hurt quite so much, and he was actually hungry instead of nauseated. His jailors had provided him with a bowl of porridge, a jug of water, and a half-loaf of tough black bread. Geran ate gingerly, careful to do his chewing on the left side of his mouth. After that, he pushed himself to his feet and paced around his cell as best he could with the fetters on his wrists and ankles. It was actually a good-sized chamber, about nine feet wide and fourteen long, made of carefully fitted stone—most likely rubble from the ring of ruins surrounding Hulburg. Most newer buildings in the town were built on stones taken from the wreckage of the older city. He wished he had a window, even one at the bottom of a window-well, so that he could at least know whether it was dark or light outside. Unfortunately, the Council Watch hadn't seen the need to provide their cells with that sort of amenity.

"I suppose I've seen worse," he muttered. Once, early in his travels with the Company of the Dragon Shield, Geran had been imprisoned in the dungeons of the lord of Impiltur for a few days. That experience was one he didn't like to recall. This cell was hardly comfortable, but at least it was clean, and the food they'd set out for him was not crawling with vermin.

He spent some time examining the possibilities for escape. If he could somehow get free of the mage shackles, his magic would be extremely useful in that regard. He still had the word of minor teleportation fixed in his mind, so it would be simple enough to exit the cell. However, he had to be able to see the place he attempted to reach with the spell. All he could see from inside his cell was the corridor immediately beyond the bars, and he was certain he could hear at least one or two more heavy doors between him and freedom. Of course, there was the problem of the guards too. They were armed, and he wasn't. He *might* be able to surprise one and get his sword away from him, especially if they didn't realize that he was out of his cell. . . .

Or perhaps that was exactly what Sergen was hoping he would try, so that he could be conveniently killed while trying to escape.

"Damnation," Geran growled to himself. He sat down in the middle of his chains. That was just the sort of suspicious notion that would have crossed Hamil's mind in this situation. Of course, the halfling could have gotten out of the manacles any time he liked, squeezed through the cell bars, and likely walked out right under the guards' noses without them ever realizing he'd gone. Be patient, the swordmage told himself. Harmach

Grigor must be trying to secure my release. Attempting to escape might make that more difficult for the harmach.

Geran used the water in his jug to wash the dried and crusted blood from his wounded forehead, wincing as he did so. There was a knot that felt like a goose's egg about three inches above his right eye, and it did not feel much better when he finished. Eventually he grew tired again and fell asleep.

When he woke again, more black bread and porridge had been set out for him, along with a fresh jug of water. He ate and drank again, and decided to see what it would take to get out of the mage shackles. The easiest approach would have been to try to abrade or snap the chain securing the rune-carved bands to the ring in the cell floor, but that would still leave the shackles around his wrists and stop him from using his magic. No, he would have to get his hands out of the manacles. Geran didn't see how he could do that without breaking every bone in his hand first, and even then he might not be able to do it. That left cutting through the bands or pulling the rivets apart. Mostly to occupy himself he spent several hours trying to pry open the manacles, to little effect other than making his fingers sore with the effort.

He slept and ate again and resolved to try to abrade one of the chain links by the floor ring into a tool he could use to work on the mage shackles. But before he got very far, he heard the outer door creak open and the sounds of approaching footsteps. Brighter lanternlight flickered in the corridor. Awkwardly he climbed to his feet. Whatever was coming, he'd meet it standing and face forward.

"All right, here he is." One of the Council Watch soldiers came into view, holding a lantern. To Geran's surprise, Kara and Mirya followed, with several more Watch soldiers behind them. "Don't pass anything to the prisoner, or we'll have to search both o' you."

Kara frowned in annoyance but let the warning pass without protest. "Hello, Geran," she said. "Are you well? How are they treating you?"

"Well enough," Geran answered. "The fellows who captured me were none too gentle, but the council men have left me alone. They're feeding me a couple of times a day. I've had worse. Is Hamil all right?"

"Yes, he's waiting outside." Kara kept her voice neutral, but her brilliant eyes blazed with anger. "He wasn't allowed in here, since the Council Watch fears that he would try to break you out."

"I'm surprised they allowed you to visit me."

"They'd no liking for the notion," Mirya said. She wore a plain blue dress with a white shawl and had her hair gathered in a single long braid down her back. Geran noticed that the bruise on her face had almost completely faded. "Two days now I've been trying to get in to see you."

"That might not have been very wise, Mirya," Geran said quietly.

Mirya crossed her arms in front of her body like a battlement, her face set in a stern scowl. "Oh, I'm not in any danger right now, Geran Hulmaster. Half of Hulburg's taken up for me, thanks to your way of teaching foreign brigands to think better of wrecking Erstenwold's. It seems the Verunas have no wish to stir up more trouble on my account—at least for now." She looked over at the nearest Watch soldier and angrily asked, "Why is he chained up? There's no call for treating him like that!"

"Lord Sergen's orders, mistress," the Watch guard said. "He's known to study elf magic, so the Keeper of Duties instructed us to keep him in mage shackles. We can't risk him using magic to escape."

"Lord Sergen's got a generous definition of his own authority," Kara muttered. She fixed her bright gaze on the guards. "Give us some privacy. On my honor as a Hulmaster, we'll do nothing but speak with him."

The Council Watch soldiers shifted uncomfortably and looked at each other. "We'll allow you some leeway, Lady Kara," the first one said. "But keep away from the bars, or you'll have to leave." The guards moved out of Geran's sight down the hallway, but he could tell from Mirya's glance that they were not very far off.

"This may sound awful, but—what day is it?" Geran asked.

"It's the fourth of Tarsakh," Mirya answered. "Early in the morning, in case you couldn't tell."

Geran glanced down the hallway and couldn't see the guards. He lowered his voice a little. "Did Durnan Osting get the Spearmeet companies to take to the streets?"

"No, but apparently Hamil did. He went down to the Troll and Tankard and spoke on your behalf." Kara put on a studied frown of disapproval. "Now I've got six or seven vigilante bands roaming all over town, shadowing every foreign armsman they see and picking fights. There was an ugly brawl late last night in the Tailings—twoscore Spearmeet under one of Osting's sons rousted out a gang of Crimson Chains and beat them senseless. Several people were badly hurt. It's only a matter of time before this turns to killing, Geran. You've got no idea what you've started."

"Perhaps," Geran admitted. "But I certainly won't shed a tear if the Chainsmen discover that Hulburg isn't to their liking anymore. Are the Spearmeet really doing that much more than you would if you had a couple of hundred more Shieldsworn?"

Kara grimaced. "Well, if I had that many Shieldsworn, of course I'd be able to keep the harmach's laws in the city without any call for the Council Watch. But the Spearmeet musters aren't Shieldsworn."

"They're not the Spearmeet, Kara," Mirya said. "Only the harmach himself can call out the Spearmeet, you know. It's the Moonshields you're speaking of, and they're just Hulburgans who choose to associate with other like-minded folk and make sure to step in if they see someone in need." She allowed herself a sly smile. "If most Moonshields happen to be Hulburgans who also belong to the Spearmeet, well, that's just a coincidence."

"Moonshields?" Geran asked.

"Well, I think the official name is something like the League of Good and Loyal Defenders of Hulburg and Protectors of the Moonsea Coast, but Hamil suggested that we ought to find something to serve as a nickname." Mirya reached into a pocket hidden in her skirt and drew out a small emblem—a plain silver shield-shape with a blue crescent moon painted on it. "Some of the storekeepers are painting this device on their doors and signboards to let everyone know where their loyalties lie."

"You too, Mirya?" said Kara.

"After word of Geran's arrest got around town, Durnan Osting begged me to come to the Troll and Tankard and speak," Mirya answered. "These are my friends, my kin, and my neighbors, Kara. What else can we do? The Council Watch works for the foreigners. Who's to keep the law in Hulburg if we don't stand up now?"

"Speaking of my arrest, Kara," said Geran, "Sergen claims that he'll arrange a special council session to try me for murder under Mulmaster's laws. I never studied much of the harmach's laws, but I seem to remember that the harmach himself has to hear high crimes like murder. How is it that the Merchant Council can hold me?"

Kara fell silent for a long moment, and her mouth tightened. "That's currently under dispute," she said.

"Under dispute? What's there to dispute? If I'm accused of murder—and I shouldn't be, since Urdinger struck at me first and it was a fair fight after that—then it's a matter for the harmach. I'm not so arrogant as to think that Hulmasters are above the law, but I don't understand why the harmach's allowing the Merchant Council to usurp his authority."

"The Verunas have found several so-called witnesses who say you rendered Urdinger helpless with an evil charm, then cut his throat," Mirya said. "I'm sorry to say it, Geran, but there's more than a few folk—most of whom ought to know better—who find themselves wondering whether you killed Urdinger in self-defense or murdered him."

"That's a damned lie," Geran growled. "Does anyone believe them?"

Kara lowered her voice again. "I doubt it, Geran, but the Merchant Council refuses to surrender you. They claim it's a charge of murder and that they're entitled to try you under Mulmaster's laws."

Geran was speechless for a moment. "You mean to say that the council has decided to set aside the harmach's law and use their own instead?"

His cousin simply met his eyes. "As I said, we dispute that."

"Who rules in Hulburg, Kara? The harmach or the Merchant Council? It can't be both."

"I know it, Geran. For what it's worth, the council doesn't seem ready to proceed with their trial yet. Perhaps Sergen realizes that he'd give the harmach no choice if he keeps on his course. We're doing what we can." Kara sighed. "I'm afraid I must go. I haven't heard from several of my scouts in Thar yet, and I fear that the Bloody Skulls have something to do with it."

Geran took a deep breath and shifted in his chains. The idea of arranging his own freedom was growing in its appeal; he didn't know much about Mulmaster's laws, but he doubted they would favor his account of events. "I'm sorry, Kara. I shouldn't have spoken in anger."

Kara gave him a small smile. "I understand, Geran." Then she left, her mail coat jingling with her steps.

Mirya lingered a moment longer.

"It's on my account that you're in that cage, Geran, and that's wrong," she said. "If I'd found some other way to deal with the Verunas—"

"It might not have mattered, Mirya, because I likely would've killed Urdinger on Jarad's account instead." He looked down at his chains and bared his teeth in a grim smile. "I know it won't bring back your brother, but I can't say that I'm sorry that Anfel Urdinger's dead."

She looked away from him, and her shoulders fell a little. "Justice for Jarad wouldn't be worth your life. If it turns out that you've come back to Hulburg after all these years only to—well, I couldn't live with myself. Not after what I did to you." Her face softened for a moment, and Geran glimpsed the girl he'd known more than ten years ago—shy, tender, and kind, haunted by a strange and distant sadness he'd never quite understood.

"Mirya, I don't know what you think you did to me," he finally said. He never would have guessed that she'd have the strength to keep Erstenwold's in business, to hold her own against competitors like House Veruna, and to raise her daughter at the same time. Her life hadn't been easy in the years that he'd been away, and she'd found true iron in herself to meet its challenges. "I'm the one who left. It was my decision. I never meant to hurt you."

"It's not what you think," she said. She stepped closer and set her hand on the bars of the cell. "I—"

"Mistress Erstenwold, step away from the cell," the council armsman said sharply. The man hurried forward with a frown. "And you need to be leaving, anyway. I've given you a good long time to talk, and the last thing I need's trouble for it."

Geran looked through the bars at Mirya. "Don't worry about me," he told her. "Watch out for yourself, Mirya. Keep Selsha safe, and stay close to home. I've got a feeling that Kara might be right about the troubles heading our way."

She held up her hand in parting and hurried away. The Watch guards saw her out, and the heavy iron door leading to the dungeon clanged shut behind them. Geran let out a deep breath and sank to the floor amid his chains.

TWENTY-ONE

7 Tarsakh, the Year of the Ageless One

The mood of Hulburg was growing ugly, Sergen decided. As his coach rolled and bounced through the streets, he passed by corners and through squares where small knots of disheveled peasants and laborers stood around in their blue hoods, shivering in the cold early-spring mists and rains that had settled over the town. Angry glares followed his coach, and sometimes a fist was shaken in his direction. Of course most of the rabble had no idea who was in the fine carriage, since his driver and footmen wore no House colors other than that of the Council Watch, and he kept his curtain drawn. But the mere fact that he was riding in a fine coach marked him as a man of wealth and power, and in Hulburg that signaled an affiliation with foreign merchants. That was sufficient to draw the ire and resentment of Hulburg's commoners these days.

His driver flicked the reins, and the coach jerked ahead as the team picked up its pace to climb the causeway leading up to Griffonwatch. Several other coaches and carriages crowded the lower courtyard of the castle; the harmach still had power enough to command immediate attendance when he called his council to attend him. Sergen scowled in annoyance. This summons had come only an hour after sunrise, such as it was on this gloomy day, and he had still been in his bed. "A few more days, and I'll see to all such annoyances," he told himself. The carriage came to a stop, and he rose and let himself out even before his footman could open the door for him. An appearance of haste and concern would be seemly this morning.

"Good morning, Lord Sergen." One of the castle valets hurried down the steps to take Sergen's fine fur cape and matching cap. "The Harmach's Council is assembling now. They are waiting for you."

"Very well," Sergen answered.

He swept through the doors of the great hall, ignoring the Shieldsworn there while his own armsmen hurried to catch up with him. The dusty old barn of a banquet hall was about as full as the last time he'd been summoned to a council by his uncle—perhaps thirty or so guards, attendants, and advisors hovered around the eight members of the harmach's circle. Sergen noted that his stepuncle was already seated on his high seat. He quickened his step to reinforce the impression of haste, and set his face in a tight frown of determination and concern. "Forgive my tardiness," he said as he took his seat. "I hope I haven't kept you waiting for long."

"Not at all, Sergen," the harmach said. "You arrived on the heels of Lord Marstel and Master Goldhead. But now that we're all here, we should begin immediately. Kara, the floor is yours."

Kara stood up from her seat at the foot of the table and moved around to stand in the middle of the horseshoe-shaped space. She was fully armored, wearing her long mail coat with greaves and vambraces that were adorned with golden griffons. Her spellscar was hidden under all that metal, of course, but the eerie azure of her eyes gave away her deformity. A shame, Sergen mused . . . she was otherwise a very handsome woman with a fine figure, and as she was not related to him by blood, she might have made an advantageous match for him to secure his claim. On the other hand, Kara fancied herself a warrior and a captain, and it might have been difficult or impossible to break her to his will. Of course, he wouldn't have needed to remain married to her for long to establish the façade of legitimacy, and that was all that was required.

"My friends," Kara said gravely, "war is upon us. My scouts have discovered the Bloody Skull horde. They're marching southward even as we speak. As of last night they were less than twenty miles from the northernmost of our watchtowers, which places them about thirty miles from Griffonwatch. The Bloody Skulls will reach our outposts tomorrow evening, descend into the northern end of Winterspear Vale, and arrive here near sunrise of the day following. We may see bands of marauders and pillagers in the Winterspear as early as tonight.

"We're not certain of the Bloody Skulls' numbers, but we've seen at least two more tribes marching with them—the Red Claw goblins and the Skullsmasher ogres. There may be more we haven't encountered yet. My scouts believe the horde numbers at least two thousand warriors, and it may be twice that."

"How could so many orcs approach so closely without being seen?" Master Assayer Goldhead demanded.

"The weather's favored the Bloody Skulls for several days, Master Goldhead. The rain has hidden them well. And I fear that several Shieldsworn scouts likely found the Bloody Skulls but were caught before they could return and report. At least four are missing."

"Can you stop them, Lady Kara?" the wizard Ebain Ravenscar asked.

"No, my lord," Kara said. "Not without help. The Shieldsworn number two hundred. We can harry their advance with cavalry, but if we try to hold in the face of that horde, we'll be swept away." She looked at Sergen and then around the other faces at the table. "However, the mercantile concessions hold hundreds more trained and well-armed mercenaries. With their aid I think I might be able to prevent the Bloody Skulls from entering the Winterspear Vale."

"What of this so-called Moonshield militia we've all seen on the streets lately?" Darsi Veruna asked. "It seems to me that there are hundreds of brave men ready to fight standing around on the town's street corners."

Sergen fought to keep a smile from his face. That was certainly one way to thin the ranks of the overly zealous Hulburgans. He hadn't imagined any such possibility might arise when he'd intervened, so to speak, in the negotiations with the Bloody Skull messengers. It was simply an unlooked-for reward of a daring plan, executed carefully and well.

"I'll ask them to give me what help they can, Lady Darsi," Kara answered. "But the Spearmeet is a militia. They're not anywhere near as well-trained, experienced, or well-equipped as the guards your House or the other Houses retain. I hope to use the Spearmeet to deal with marauding bands that might slip around our main defenses and to form a last reserve if things go poorly at the tower line."

Maroth Marstel climbed to his feet. "All of Hulburg is threatened by this vast horde, and so all of Hulburg must give answer!" he thundered. "My House employs eighty armsmen, Lady Kara. They're at your disposal for the duration of this crisis. And furthermore, I shall be glad to serve as a commander of the cavalry. I may not be as agile or strong as I once was, but I can still lead men into battle!"

Sergen wondered when exactly the old windbag had ever seen a battlefield, but he kept his thoughts to himself. Instead, he decided to rescue Kara from trying to figure out how to accept Marstel's troops but decline his leadership by standing up himself. "The Merchant Council recently reached an arrangement with the Icehammer mercenary company," he said smoothly. "We intended to employ the Icehammers to combat piracy and brigandage along the coasts and roads near Hulburg, but clearly the Bloody Skulls present an imminent threat. I believe that the Icehammers number close to two hundred and fifty highly experienced dwarf and human veterans."

A chorus of whispers broke out among the spectators behind him, but Sergen paid them no mind. Kara stared at him suspiciously but said nothing, and Sergen could feel the harmach shift in his seat a few feet behind his right shoulder. Across the table, Lord Marstel bowed toward him. "Bravo!" he declared.

"Moreover," Sergen continued, "I'll relay my dear sister's request for additional troops to the Double Moon Coster, House Sokol, and the Jannarsk Coster. I cannot speak for them, of course, but I am confident that they can contribute two hundred more armsmen among them." He glanced at Darsi Veruna, smiled slightly, and sat down again.

Lady Veruna made a small face and motioned with her hand. "A hundred and twenty more from House Veruna," she said calmly. "I am afraid I must reserve some of our strength to protect our camps in the Galena foothills."

Kara nodded graciously to the mistress of House Veruna. "My thanks, Lady Darsi," she said.

The harmach spoke next. "Kara, by my count, that puts you at close to nine hundred warriors, not counting the militia. Do you think you can meet the Bloody Skulls with those numbers?"

The castellan fell silent and considered her answer. "I think so," she finally said. "If Hulburg had a city wall I would be inclined to simply defend the city, but since we don't, I want to meet the Bloody Skulls as far from town as possible and still gain some advantage of terrain. The watchtowers at the north end of the Vale offer our best position. There aren't many good paths to bring an army down from the Highfells to the Vale floor. But that means we *must* move at once to get as many warriors as possible to the towers by tonight or tomorrow morning." She paused, examining her own thoughts again, and added, "The show of a strong defense may be enough to deter the Bloody Skulls—or the tribes allied to them. Neither the Red Claws nor the Skullsmashers will be eager to die for Warlord Mhurren. I'd guess he promised them plunder, so it's possible that he'll give up and look for some easier target once he sees that we're ready for him. As far as I know, we've delivered no mortal insult or wronged him in some manner that he would feel compelled to avenge."

That might prove important, Sergen realized. He glanced at Darsi Veruna and found her looking at him. He'd delivered exactly such an insult in the process of making sure that the Bloody Skulls supplied Hulburg with the threat he needed. Well, if matters took an unexpected turn, and he found that he needed to throw up a breakwater against the horde he'd baited to attack the harmach, he still had one more piece he could move on the board—Aesperus. Sergen thought he knew the price of the King in Copper, and he doubted that the lich's minions would care much about being outnumbered by the Bloody Skulls and their allies.

That raised the interesting question of whether he'd rather see the battle won or lost. A complete debacle would not be good; he was reasonably sure of Aesperus's aid, but he'd rather approach the lich with a request for a moderate amount of aid rather than beg the lich to spare Hulburg from disaster. No, the best outcome would be a hard-fought victory in which the Bloody Skulls were turned back without the aid of the King in Copper . . . especially if the armsmen of the other merchant companies suffered heavily in the fighting.

"It seems that time is of the essence," the harmach said. He stood up slowly, and the other lords and officers got to their feet as well. Sergen rose smoothly and waited for his uncle to finish. "Kara, prepare the Shieldsworn for departure as quickly as you can. Those of you who have promised your armsmen, you must have your troops ready to march within hours. Only by concerted effort will we be able to avert this new and deadly threat. Now, go! And may the gods look kindly upon our defense."

The assemblage broke up and dispersed, with a dozen conversations beginning at once as the various lords and officials began to make their way out of the hall. Sergen shifted the position of the rapier at his hip and turned to go as well.

"One moment, Sergen." The harmach limped closer, leaning on his heavy walking stick. "I wish to have a word with you."

There was little that Sergen cared to discuss with his uncle at the moment, but he was standing in Griffonwatch, and there were still dozens of onlookers in the hall. He nodded and gave his stepuncle a conciliatory smile. "I have much to do if I am to persuade the other merchant companies to dispatch their soldiers with Kara," he said. "But if it's important to speak now, then I am at your disposal, Uncle Grigor."

"I will not detain you for long, Sergen. Before you leave, we must settle this question of Geran's imprisonment by the Merchant Council."

"I fear that's not a question we can quickly settle. It's a complicated issue."

"I fail to see why it is so complicated, Sergen. I've examined the law carefully, and I see no basis under which the Merchant Council can hold or try someone whose offense occurs outside the strict physical boundaries of the concessions. Is there some dispute over where exactly Geran and Captain Urdinger fought? If there isn't, then it's a matter for the harmach's justice, not the council."

Sergen grimaced and lowered his voice, moving closer to his uncle. He'd been expecting this for a day or two and knew how he wanted to respond. "I have much the same understanding, Uncle. But the Verunas are frankly beyond all reason at this point. They're threatening dire repercussions if their calls for justice are ignored."

Harmach Grigor frowned. "Dire repercussions? What do you mean?"

"I'm not sure, but I believe Lady Darsi may go so far as to completely vacate Veruna's interests in Hulburg and then use her influence in Mulmaster to have the High Blade embargo all trade bound to Hulburg. I hardly need to describe what a disaster that would be. Mulmaster accounts for almost half our trade. We would be ruined within a month." Sergen spread his hands helplessly. "As long as a threat such as that is hanging over our heads, I didn't dare to defy her."

The old lord grimaced and shot a dark look at Darsi Veruna, who was leaving the hall with her attendants and guards around her. She glided out the door with her valets hurrying to drape a stole around her neck, oblivious to the conversation at the foot of the harmach's seat. "Darsi Veruna doesn't have the right to tell us who to try and under what laws," Grigor said firmly. "This is a matter for Hulburg's justice, not her personal vendetta against Geran."

"Well, that's the problem. She believes that Geran will escape justice for his crimes because he is your nephew. Frankly, she doubts whether Geran would ever be brought to trial."

"I have *never* allowed any member of the family to ignore our laws."

"Until she sees Geran convicted and punished in some suitable manner, I am afraid she won't believe that, Uncle."

Grigor looked sharply at Sergen. "I won't allow Geran to commit crimes and go unpunished, Sergen, but neither will I convict and punish him if he's innocent of wrongdoing—regardless of what Darsi Veruna may think. If Geran is fairly acquitted, he will go free. If not, he'll pay the same price any criminal would. And to make sure that there is no appearance of favoritism, I'll delegate the harmach's decision to High Magistrate Nimstar. But this is not a matter for the Merchant Council, Sergen."

"House Veruna won't be pleased by that." Sergen tapped his finger on his chin, affecting a moment of serious thought. "What about this? Imprison Geran here in Griffonwatch and charge him under the harmach's law as is right and proper, but appoint the Council Watch to guard him? As long as Darsi Veruna is reassured that Geran is indeed confined and that charges will be read against him, she may relent on her insistence that the council must hold him. I believe I can persuade her to accept that."

The harmach stood in silence for a long moment, and then he nodded. "Very well. I'll send someone to make arrangements with the council. But Sergen—regardless of whether Darsi Veruna agrees or not, Geran will be removed from Council Hall."

"That might be—"

Grigor slashed his hand across his chest. "If Veruna wants to invite me to confiscate their property and re-let their leases to other merchant costers, then I'll gladly do so." The harmach turned and stomped away as best he could, striking his stick forcefully to the floor with each stride.

Sergen watched him retreat, mildly impressed. He wouldn't have suspected that the old man had a glint of fire in him. Why, the harmach was positively reckless! It was not like Grigor to let anger get the better of him.

He gathered his guards to him with an absent motion of his hand and left the harmach's hall to climb back into his coach. In a few moments the coach rolled back down the castle's causeway and started through the streets as Sergen carefully thought through what needed to happen in the next few days. He decided he was committed to his decisions and spent the rest of the ride to Council Hall presenting himself with hypothetical misfortunes and determining his response to each.

The coach rocked to a stop, and his footman opened the door. Sergen climbed out and said, "Remain ready. I'll be leaving again in a quarter-hour. And tell the watch captain to ask Captain Icehammer to join me in my chambers immediately."

"Of course, Lord Keeper," the man answered. But Sergen had already passed him by, bounding up the steps to Council Hall. He swept into the room that served as his office and found that his clerks had left him several letters and contracts to approve. None were particularly urgent, but he examined them simply to occupy himself while he waited for the mercenary captain.

He didn't have to wait long. Before he'd finished looking over the third letter, Kendurkkel Ironthane knocked on the door and entered. The dwarf tromped in, took a seat in a chair by the hearth, and commenced to tap out the ashes from his pipe. "You sent for me, Lord Sergen?" he asked.

"I did," Sergen answered. "I assume that you've heard rumors about the orc horde marching on Hulburg?"

The dwarf laughed harshly. "It's no' far from the minds o' many folk this morning. No one talks 'bout anything else."

"I've told the harmach that I've retained the services of the Icehammers. I want you to march with the Shieldsworn and help to defend Hulburg from the Bloody Skulls. I believe that contingency is already covered under our existing arrangements."

"I expected so much," Kendurkkel said. "However, I'll be remindin' you that a share o' the plunder from the field o' battle belongs to me company."

"Of course. You should prepare to march immediately, Captain—the Shieldsworn hope to defend the watchtowers at the north end of the vale, and my dear sister Kara intends to move her forces there by tomorrow morning."

"Am I answerin' to her orders?"

Sergen thought about that for a moment. "Unless Kara's orders are clearly inept or otherwise unacceptable, yes," he said. "Do your best to do as she asks, and give her the benefit of your experience and counsel. I'm sending you to make sure that the Bloody Skulls are stopped before they reach Hulburg, and I want you to do what you think is needful to accomplish that goal."

The dwarf nodded. "All right. If there's nothing else you're needin', then, I've got a lot t' do in the next few hours."

"There's one more thing," Sergen said. "I'll need about thirty of your men—most of them humans—for a special assignment here in Hulburg, a very sensitive assignment. I'll need them to be waiting at the Dareth storehouse on East Street by noon on the tenth. It would be best if they arrived in small groups, scattered over the morning, and didn't wear any identifying colors or insignia."

The dwarf chewed on his pipestem and eyed Sergen thoughtfully. "Will me lads be livin' through your special assignment?"

"Yes, in fact, it's important that they do. But I'm afraid they will have to leave town immediately afterward. I plan to have a ship ready to leave at first light for that purpose."

"All right. I'll give 'em orders t' make their way back to Thentia or Melvaunt after you're done with them." Kendurkkel leaned forward and took his pipe from his mouth, pointing the stem at Sergen. "Now, just so we see eye t' eye, m'lord: Exceptional missions an' arrangements o' that sort demand an exceptional bonus. I need t' know what you've got in mind for me lads."

Sergen bowed his head in acquiescence and spread his hands. "Well, Master Kendurkkel, it seems that House Veruna is going to do something terrible three nights from now. Your men are going to make sure that everyone knows who was responsible." After all, he added to himself, he wouldn't want to become harmach while he was so deeply indebted to Darsi Veruna.

Twenty-two

9 Tarsakh, the Year of the Ageless One

The Council Watch soldiers removed Geran from his cell during the dark hour before sunrise. At first he feared that he was to be driven out to some lonely spot in the Highfells and killed, but to his surprise the council men took him to Griffonwatch. They drove the prison wagon up the causeway and through the gatehouse, stopping by the Shieldsworn barracks. A moment later the heavy chains securing the wagon's door rattled, and the two guards riding in the back with Geran rose and helped him to the door.

When he clambered out of the wagon's dim interior, Geran found Hamil and Sergeant Kolton of the Shieldsworn waiting for him with five more council guards. "There you are, Geran," Hamil said. "Are you hurt at all?"

"Nothing important, though I've got a broken tooth I hope to have mended. What's going on here? Am I to be released?"

"Not yet," the halfling answered. "The harmach struck a deal with the Merchant Council. I think that he's agreed that you'll face charges under Hulburg's law. In exchange the council's agreed to allow you to be held here in Griffonwatch until a trial can be arranged. But they'll have a detachment of their own watch to stand guard, just to make sure that the harmach doesn't release you."

Geran grimaced. It was undoubtedly better to be held in Griffonwatch, simply because he wouldn't have to fear being murdered in his cell or otherwise made to disappear. And he likely had little to fear from a trial under Hulburg's laws. But the harmach must have staked his own honor on Geran's good behavior, so he'd have to endure his incarceration a little longer. "When will my case be decided?"

Sergeant Kolton frowned. "That's hard to say, Lord Geran. The Bloody Skulls've got everything in an uproar."

"The Bloody Skulls? Did their messengers return?"

Kolton shook his head. "No, they all did. I suppose you ain't heard"—the sergeant shot the Council Watch soldiers a hard look—"but there's a bloody great orc horde on its way. Lady Kara's taken almost all the Shieldsworn up to the northerly watchtowers, and three-quarters o' the merchant company armsmen too. She left me in command o' the garrison, can you believe that? Anyway, Lady Kara expects to meet the Bloody Skulls within a day, maybe two."

Geran felt the weight of the chains on his wrists. As far as he knew he had no great talent for leading armies, but he'd fought as a captain leading a company of the Coronal's Guard in Myth Drannor, and he wasn't afraid to cross blades with any orc. If Kolton was right, then Hulburg faced the most immediate peril it had seen during his entire life, and he'd watch it pass by through the bars of a cell. "Tell the harmach that I can help," he said to Kolton. "If he paroles me to fight, I'll gladly go back to my cell for as long as I have to once the danger's passed."

"The prisoner won't be set free without the express order of the council," one of the Watch soldiers said firmly. "The harmach's got to take it up with Lord Sergen."

"I know it," Kolton snapped. He looked back to Geran and motioned toward the doorway leading into the castle. "Well, I suppose I'd better show you to your accommodations, Lord Geran."

"They've given you the best cell in the castle—for what it's worth," added Hamil.

The Shieldsworn sergeant led Geran and his Council Watch jailors through the barracks building and into a passageway cut through the rock of the castle's hilltop. They climbed up a flight of stairs and passed by several storerooms and connecting passageways that led to the castle's deep cisterns then climbed a few more steps to a row of iron-bound doors of thick wood. Kolton opened the nearest with a set of heavy keys. It was not a very big room, but it had a small square window that looked out over the city to the distant gray line of the Moonsea, a bed, a table and two chairs, a small carpet laid out on the flagstone floor, and even a shelf lined with a dozen books. "We took the liberty o' furnishing your cell a little more comfortably than we normally would," Kolton said. "But I'm afraid it's still a cell. I'll send a healer to look after your injuries as soon as possible."

"Thank you, Kolton," Geran said quietly.

"Lord Sergen won't like this," the council sergeant said. "He said nothing about providing the prisoner with such comforts."

"In that case, he didn't say we couldn't," Hamil pointed out. "I heard about that fine room you gave him underneath your Council Hall. Maybe the Shieldsworn should give you beds just as comfortable as the one you gave Geran. After all, nothing requires the harmach to give your men any particular comforts, either."

The council sergeant chose not to argue the point any further—a wise decision, in Geran's view. Kolton suppressed a smile and motioned to his council counterpart. "Post a couple o' men by the door if you like, and I'll show the rest o' you to your guardroom and quarters."

"Very well," the sergeant said. He detailed off two of his men, who took up positions on each side of Geran's doorway.

Kolton looked back to Geran and said, "I'm sorry, Lord Geran, but I'll have to leave the mage shackles on you."

The swordmage grimaced. His wrists were more than a little sore and bruised, and he wanted the damned manacles off his hands. As long as Harmach Grigor had given his word that he'd make no attempt to escape, Geran wouldn't use his magic. But at least the cell looked like a substantial improvement on the old one. "It's not your fault, Kolton," he said.

"These fellows'll be standing watch, but there will always be a couple o' Shieldsworn within earshot. Just shout if you need anything." Kolton touched his hand to his brow in salute and backed out of the cell with the Council Watch leader following him.

"As much as I'd like to stay here and entertain you, I'm afraid I have some things to look after in town," Hamil said.

"Things to look after?"

"I've taken it upon myself to prepare your defense, so I've been talking to every witness to your duel that I can find." Hamil pointed an accusing finger at Geran. "The next time you find yourself embroiled in a fight like the one that preceded your duel, I advise you to kill your enemies rather than wound and cripple them. You left House Veruna with four more witnesses than you needed to, and they naturally have agreed upon a version of events that depicts you in a very poor light. Though I suspect the one with the badly broken jaw and no teeth remaining doesn't really remember anything that's happened since last month and is making up his story outright."

"Then go to it, Hamil. I've got every confidence in you." Geran took his hand, and then Hamil nodded and followed the guards out. The council soldiers swung the door shut and locked it with a heavy iron clanking. Geran looked at the door for a long moment; he'd been in one cell or another for days now, and he was well and truly looking forward to his liberty. But it sounded as if it might be a few more days. He shuffled over to look out the small window—it was not much more than a foot square—and to watch the town slowly wake up to another dreary spring morning.

An hour later he discovered that his comforts were not limited to simple furnishings; the castle kitchens provided him with a hearty breakfast of eggs, ham, cheese, and bread with good apple cider to wash it down, which he was able to eat while seated at his table. After days of sitting on the floor of the council's cell eating bland porridge, it was a significant improvement. "The only thing I lack is my freedom," he observed when the servants and guards withdrew.

He selected a book at random from the shelf and passed much of the day with a long lay written three centuries before about the fall of Ascalhorn and the escape of one of its lords and his family. He spent an hour pacing and exercising as best he could in the small space allotted to him and even tried to practice his forms by imagining the weight of a sword in his hand and ignoring the shackles on his wrists. Eventually he grew tired and stretched himself out on top of the bed to sleep for a time. Long, cold nights on the stone floor of the council dungeon had not given him much opportunity to sleep well at night. He arranged his irons as best as he could and drifted off while lying on his back with his hands at his waist and the chain over his belt.

He found himself caught between a dream and a memory, something perhaps a little like the Reverie of elvenkind. He stood in the thin frost of a forest clearing in Myth Drannor, watching as Alliere turned her back on him and fled into the shadows under the dying leaves. She wore a dress of rich blue with delicate silver embroidery and a light hood of pearl-gray over her shoulders; she held her skirts as she darted away, her long dark hair streaming behind her. "Alliere, come back!" he called. "I love you!" She paused once, a single glance over her shoulder. But when her eyes met his, she turned away. He took a step after her, and—

The dream ended then, as it always did. Geran came to wakefulness and found himself staring up at the ceiling of his small cell. The light from the window had changed; it was the middle of the afternoon. He'd been asleep for a couple of hours. He started to sit up, found that his shackles hampered him still, and carefully gathered them up so that he could put one hand to the side of the bed and push himself upright. A year and a half now, and still that memory torments me, he reflected. He deserved worse. All of his life he'd wandered with his eye on the road ahead, never content to be where he was, seeking something that seemed to retreat away from him every time he drew near to it. In Myth Drannor he'd found what he was longing for, at least for a short time. And yet he'd managed to ruin it so completely with one self-destructive act he still couldn't explain to himself. It was as if some hidden part of him recognized that he'd found contentment and deliberately sought a way to restore his wayward heart to its true nature. All of his life, his passion, his heart had been waiting for a love such as the one he'd found in Alliere, but he'd driven her away, and he still didn't know why.

He sighed and looked at the small cell. "Maybe I belong in here after all," he murmured. To keep his mind from memories of Myth Drannor and Alliere, he chose another book and tried to read some more. Eventually the afternoon passed, and he found that the shades of the past didn't trouble him so much.

At sunset Hamil came down and joined him for supper, which cheered him. His friend had little news to report other than the growing anxiety in town about the Bloody Skulls.

"Where are they now?" Geran asked him.

"Raiding parties have ventured into the Vale at several points, but they haven't done much damage yet," Hamil said. "Kara got her soldiers up to the post-towers at the north end of the Vale, or so I'm told. What are they, anyway?"

"Watchtowers, really. Each has a small barracks that can accommodate about ten soldiers, and a small stone tower. There are about half a dozen scattered around the borders of Hulburg's lands."

"That doesn't seem a very useful fortification."

"They aren't. I expect that Kara's simply mustering her forces near one of the watchposts that overlooks the head of the Winterspear Vale. There aren't many trails a large army can use to descend into the Vale safely, so I'd guess she's trying to defend the most likely routes. If the Bloody Skull horde is as large as it's been reported to be, then she's got a chance to bottle them up on a narrow track and take away their advantage in numbers. On the other hand, if she lets them get into the Vale, they'll be able to spread out again, and there really isn't anything to stop them before they reach the city."

Hamil grimaced. "Murder, vengeance, tomb-robbing, and treachery are one thing, Geran, but I didn't come to Hulburg for a war."

"You don't have to stay, Hamil," Geran told him. "In all seriousness, someone ought to be looking after Red Sail business, and I might be stuck here for days whether you help or not. Maybe you should leave."

"I'll give it another day or two." Hamil rose from his seat and set his napkin on the table. "I'll be back tomorrow to look in on you again. I don't entirely trust these council thugs, even if they're in the middle of your family's castle. There are ten of them now, just to keep watch on you, Geran."

Geran saw his friend out —not very hard to do, given the size of the room—and returned to the bookshelf, looking for something new. Late in the evening, a knock at his door interrupted him. Keys turned in the lock, and the Council Watch soldiers admitted Sergen. The lord stepped in with a look of distaste on his face, frowning as he took in the bed, the books, and the desk. "Well, it seems that there's some justice in this world after all," he said. "A cell is a cell, regardless of its comforts. You've finally found your proper station in life, Geran, and I'm here to ensure that you remain in it for the rest of your days."

"There's much to recommend the room, if you like it, Sergen," Geran said. He rose to face his stepcousin, clenching his fists beneath the shackles. He could loop the chain around Sergen's neck and strangle him easily enough . . . but the council soldiers standing behind their master would likely interfere. There was no point in allowing Sergen's barbs to anger him.

"You can't paint the truth for long, Sergen," he answered. "It has a way of showing through the lies you slather over it. I'll go through the trial your dear Darsi Veruna is demanding for me, her mercenaries will be shown to be liars, and I'll be freed soon enough."

Sergen smirked. "Spare me your sanctimonious metaphors, Geran. Of course the charges against you have no merit. But still, here you sit incarcerated in this small room until you can defend yourself against them. And who knows how long it might take before the eyewitnesses you referred to can be spared from the vital duty of defending Hulburg from the orcs? Why, it might be days."

"I'll wait."

"Indeed you will." Sergen spied the remains of Geran's dinner and smiled sourly. "I suppose that your friends here in Griffonwatch are looking after you. I must see what I can do about that." He picked up the jug of wine and an unused goblet from the table and poured himself some. He swirled the wine once, inhaled its aroma, and took a taste. "A Sembian, if I'm not mistaken. Yes, I must protest this lavish treatment you're receiving. How can there be justice in Hulburg if a Hulmaster charged with murder lives like a king, while a common man languishes in a dank dungeon? It's unseemly, Geran."

Sergen set down the goblet, and something under his collar caught Geran's eye—an old amulet of copper, green with verdigris. Its top was shaped like a crowned skull, with two small emeralds for its eyes. It struck him as unusual because Sergen was otherwise attired in resplendent fashion, with an elegant silver-trimmed black tabard cut with violet pleats, high suede boots, and his great gold pendant. I've seen a medallion like that recently, Geran realized. But where and when?

Geran frowned and thought for a moment, and it came to him: It was the amulet that Aesperus gave to Urdinger in payment for the *Infiernadex.* He hadn't gotten a very good look at it that night. The lich had been standing ten yards away, and the lighting had been poor—torchlight at best. But the size and shape were right, and even with the mage shackles clasped around his wrists he could sense the dark whisper of magic in the old copper. What did the King in Copper say when he gave the thing to Urdinger?

Sergen noticed Geran's sudden distraction and glanced down. "What are you looking at?" he demanded.

"The distance to your heart," Geran answered, thinking quickly. "I was wondering whether I should draw your blade and stab you now or wait until after my acquittal to finally rid House Hulmaster of your particular stench."

"Brave words from a man with his hands in shackles." Sergen snorted in amusement and lowered his voice. "Do not trouble yourself too much with plans for your acquittal, Geran. You're exactly where I want you to be, and here you will stay. Good-bye, my dear cousin. Forgive me if I say that I shall not miss you much."

"You and I have business to settle when I'm freed." Geran glowered fiercely at his stepcousin, concealing his relief at deflecting Sergen's attention. Sergen doesn't know that I saw Aesperus give the amulet to Urdinger, he realized. But why does he have it?

"I see no point in continuing this conversation." Sergen bowed mockingly and withdrew. "See to it that he has no more visitors," he told the council guards. "Requests for a visit with the prisoner must be submitted in writing to the Merchant Council. Do you understand?"

"Aye, Lord Sergen," the men outside replied. They shut the door behind Sergen and turned the key in the lock with an ugly and final sound.

Geran growled in frustration and kicked at the wall. He remembered what Aesperus had told Urdinger, all right. The lich had said that whoever wore the amulet could call on his minions. If Sergen was wearing the amulet, then he must have been planning on using its powers. The question was, for what purpose? "To slay someone, of course," Geran muttered to himself. Better yet, it would be a murder that could not be laid at Sergen's feet. Everyone would believe that the King in Copper had sent his specters for reasons of his own, not suspecting that Aesperus was simply fulfilling a bargain he'd made with House Veruna. "And who would Sergen want dead?"

Obviously, Geran himself was likely high on the list. But somehow the swordmage doubted that Sergen would invoke Aesperus's minions for that. Sergen had already neutralized him with his exaggerated charges. Could he be planning to destroy a rival merchant company? Possibly, but Geran couldn't see why Sergen would want to. They all supported him through the Merchant Council. That left the nascent Moonshields . . . or the harmach. That must be it, Geran thought bleakly. If the harmach and House

Hulmaster were destroyed by some outside force, then Sergen would appear blameless. He could succeed where his father had failed and make himself the lord of Hulburg. As long as all the other Hulmasters died, no one would stand between Sergen and the harmach's seat.

"Not even Sergen could be that ruthless," Geran murmured. But he didn't believe it. The more he thought on it, the clearer it became. With the orc horde threatening Hulburg, the castle defenses were stripped to a minimum. Kara was away from Griffonwatch, so Sergen would need some way to deal with his stepsister. But all the other Hulmasters were conveniently gathered in one place—including Geran. And Sergen had been the author of the compromise that transferred him to Griffonwatch, hadn't he?

He needed to warn someone. But Sergen had just given orders that no one was to see him, and it might take hours or days before Hamil or Kolton or someone else managed to force the Council Watch to permit a visit. Geran stared at the cell holding him then at the shackles around his wrists.

Somehow, he had to escape.

Twenty-three

10 Tarsakh, the Year of the Ageless One

Hours of anxious pacing and a furious examination of every furnishing in his cell did not provide Geran with any obvious way to slip free of the mage shackles. He considered feigning sickness or injury to bring one or two of his jailors into the cell but dismissed the idea quickly. He couldn't imagine that anyone ever really fell for that ruse, and even if they did, there were simply too many men outside. He might be able to overcome one or two guards with surprise and a cudgel made from the leg of a table, but what then? And the Shieldsworn garrisoning the castle would be duty bound to try to stop him, as well. Some of them—Kolton, for example—might turn a blind eye to any escape attempt or even aid his efforts, but others would try to discharge their duty no matter what they thought of their orders. For that matter, there might be a few among the Shieldsworn who would act against Geran for less worthy reasons. Jarad Erstenwold had chosen to keep his mission in the Highfells secret from his own soldiers; that suggested to Geran that Jarad might've suspected that at least a few of his men might be in the pay of the Merchant Council or one of the foreign companies.

He studied his window for a time and tested its bars. Given a month he might be able to wear away the mortar and brick anchoring the bars in place and widen the window enough to wriggle through—but that would leave him clinging to a sheer cliff face, and he doubted that he had a month.

No, what I need to do is to get word to Hamil that I must be freed, Geran decided. Or at least get word to Hamil to warn the harmach of my suspicions. He can handle things from there.

The question was, how to smuggle out a message? He could try to tear a page from one of the books in the cell, weight it somehow, and drop it out the window . . . but it would be a matter of chance if the right passerby picked it up and delivered it. And the night was wet, so his note would be in poor condition by the time anyone happened across it. He searched through his cell contents again, and his eye fell upon a small, dusty case in his bookshelf—a set of dragon's-teeth tiles. Geran didn't know any solitaire games to play with them, so he hadn't given them much attention before. Now he opened the case and examined the tiles more carefully, laying them out on his table. Coins, bars, swords . . . dragons and griffons . . . they all were said to have a meaning. "If only I knew Dwarvish," he murmured to himself. Of course, little Dwarvish remained to be seen in the iconography of the game, only a handful of Dethek runes to accompany the images. He studied the clay tiles for a moment, running his fingers over the glazed surfaces. People played the game all over Faerûn, different variations in every country. . . . An idea began to take shape in his mind. Geran chose two of the tiles and set them aside, then he put the rest away and carefully stretched himself out on the bed to rest until morning. If it didn't work, he could always use the tiles to weight letters he tossed out the window.

When his breakfast was delivered in the morning, Geran ate well. Then he set the two tiles he'd picked in plain sight atop the tray beside the dishes, and used a quill and ink to write "For Kirr" on a slip of paper under the tiles. He knocked on the door. "I'm done with my breakfast!" he called.

The council guards opened the door, and one came in to pick up the tray. He frowned at the two tiles. "What's this?" he asked.

"For my young cousin Kirr," Geran said, affecting a calm nonchalance he certainly did not feel. "He likes the ones with the dragons on them."

The guard glanced at his sergeant, who stood by the door. The sergeant shrugged. "All right," he said. "But check the paper and make sure he didn't write anything more."

The soldier inspected the note. "No, Sergeant. This is it."

"Fine, then." The council guard picked up the tray and backed out, keeping his eyes on Geran. A moment later, the keys turned again in the heavy lock.

Geran sighed and composed himself to wait. The real question now was whether Kirr would do what he thought the boy might do with the two new tiles, and he might not find out for hours yet. To pass the time he exercised again and then chose another book from the shelf to while away an hour or two.

The first sign of his plan's success came about an hour later; he heard raised voices in the corridor outside his door. Geran set down his book and hurried over to put his ear to the door, but he could not make out anything with certainty. He returned to his book, but half an hour later he felt a familiar voice in his mind. *Geran?* Hamil said silently. *If you're there, look to your window.*

The swordmage moved over and glanced out, but he did not see much. Then a small sound from over his head caught his attention. He ducked down and looked up as steeply as he could; Hamil clung to a rope a little above his cell's window. *I'm here, Hamil!* he answered.

Are you well? The guards wouldn't let me in to see you.

I'm well enough, but Sergen ordered his men not to allow anyone in to see me, Geran told him. *Did you get the tiles?*

I did, though I confess I almost ignored your cousin. He sought me out to show me his new dragon's-teeth, and I didn't think anything of it. Fortunately he was very persistent, and I finally paid attention just to humor him. Only then did he mention that you'd sent them to him. The halfling shifted a little and turned to set his feet on the top of the embrasure over Geran's window. Keeping his voice to a whisper, he said, "Playing two dragon tiles together is considered bad luck in the south, you know."

"I hoped you'd take it as a sign of distress. Listen, Hamil—I need to get out of this cell." Geran kept his voice low. He did not think his guards could hear him through the thick door, but if one of them happened to slide open the viewport and check on him, he wanted to look as if he were simply staring out the window instead of holding a conversation with someone clinging to a line just outside.

"I've been waiting for you to ask, but aren't you worried about embarrassing your uncle by making an escape?"

"I think Sergen's planning something awful. I've got to stop him. He means to have my uncle killed, maybe the whole family. He's got the amulet that the King in Copper gave to Urdinger. No good can come of that."

Hamil fell silent for a moment. "The lich said that whoever wore the amulet could call on his minions."

Geran nodded. "And Sergen told me last night that I wouldn't have to worry about regaining my liberty again. I take that to mean he'll have me killed in my cell, or he intends to make himself the master of my fate by seizing the throne. I have to believe that Sergen's got the medallion now, because he's going to call on its powers. We've got to get it away from him or at the very least warn my uncle and Kara about his intentions."

"Agreed. Let's figure out how to get you out of there." Hamil studied the window and then descended a few more feet to examine the stonework below it. "Hmmm, I don't think the window'll work unless you can use your teleporting magic."

Geran shook his head. "I need to see exactly where I'm going, and I'll need a safe place to appear. Besides, I'm still in mage shackles. I can't use magic."

"It'll have to be the front door, then," Hamil said. "I need to arrange for some help, Geran."

"Leave the Shieldsworn out of it if you can, Hamil. Many of them are sympathetic to my situation, but their duty is clear—they're sworn to resist any effort to break me out. You can't count on their help, but I don't want to see them killed." Geran paused, thinking his way through what Hamil would have to do. "For that matter, it'd be better if you could avoid a massacre of the council guards. I'd rather have them incapacitated than dead. The charges Sergen laid against me are groundless, but they wouldn't be if we killed men assigned to keep me under arrest."

"As long as you're thinking of ways to make my job harder, why not ask for a purple horse with a golden saddle to ride away on?"

"If I were certain that Sergen intended to move against the harmach within the next day, I'd tell you to do anything in your power to get me out and damn the consequences," Geran said in a low voice. "But I've only got suspicions, Hamil. I'm hesitant to kill over them."

"Fine," Hamil sighed. "I'll see if I can free you sometime this evening."

"I'll be waiting for that purple horse."

Hamil snorted in response. Geran heard a whisper of leather against stone and a small grunt of effort, and then the halfling was gone again, scrambling back up to whatever vantage he had descended from. The swordmage turned away from the window and surveyed his small room. A few more hours, he thought. He'd have to make sure he knew what to do once Hamil freed him. He sat down on the bed, his chin in his hand, and thought long and hard about the hours ahead. Then he composed himself to wait through the afternoon. He found that he had little appetite for his dinner, simply because he was growing anxious for Hamil, but he made himself eat well anyway; if things didn't go well, it might be a long time before he had the opportunity to eat again.

After his dinner, Geran watched a spectacular sunset from his window, which faced toward the southwest. The gloom and drizzle of the last few days was breaking up; a great mass of tattered gray clouds drifted slowly eastward, painted rose and gold by the setting sun. The skies above the western horizon seemed dark and clear. Another stretch of cold weather and strong winds, Geran decided. Already whitecaps were beginning to kick up on the purple gloom of the Moonsea, splashing against the soaring shadows of the Arches that dominated the harbor.

Nothing happened until three hours after sundown, and when it did, it happened quickly. Geran heard a brief commotion in the corridor outside his door—a sharp cry of alarm, quickly cut off, followed by a shrill ring of steel on steel. Then he heard a deep, rasping voice hissing syllables of arcane power, words of might that made the door tremble in its frame. Streams of reddish smoke seeped from under the door, carrying an acrid reek that made Geran's eyes water and his throat burn. Then the key turned, and the door swung open.

Hamil stood there with a handkerchief tied over his nose and mouth. And behind him stood the proud tiefling sorcerer Geran had encountered out on the Highfells. The tiefling wore a heavy, hooded black cape over his finely embroidered scarlet robe, but he still carried his rune-covered staff. "The shackles, quickly!" he hissed to Hamil.

The halfling hurried up to Geran with a set of keys in his hand. "Geran, you remember Sarth Khul Riizar. We've met before, of course, but circumstances didn't permit a proper introduction."

"Far be it from me to question anyone helping me to escape, Hamil, but what's he doing here?" Geran asked.

"I decided that I needed the best help available, in case we had to fight our way out of Griffonwatch," Hamil answered. "And given what you'd told me about Sergen and Aesperus's amulet, I thought Sarth might know something about what your cousin's got planned. So I asked after Sarth all over town this afternoon, found him staying in a very fine inn called the Captain's House, and explained what was happening."

Hamil found the correct key and unlocked Geran's shackles; the swordmage shook them off and rubbed his sore wrists while Hamil knelt to free his ankle irons. Geran looked into Sarth's face and frowned. "I appreciate your interest, Master Sarth," he said. "But why did you agree to help? What do you have to gain?"

"To gain? Nothing but a clear conscience," the tiefling answered. He glanced to the corridor outside and then looked back to Geran. "You see, I bear some responsibility for Jarad Erstenwold's death and your current troubles. I wish to make amends."

Hamil found the key for the leg irons and quickly removed them. "You're free, Geran," he said. "We should go."

"Just a moment," Geran answered. "Explain what you mean, Sarth."

"I came to Hulburg five months ago in search of the book called the *Infiernadex.* I knew that it had once belonged to Aesperus but had been taken from the lich king in the fall of Thentur centuries ago. I hoped to recover it for myself and to study the arcane secrets it contains. When I first arrived in town, I decided to seek out a sponsor, so I called on Darsi Veruna and tried to interest her in providing me assistance with my explorations." The tiefling grimaced. "As it turned out, she wished to employ me as a wand-for-hire. I'd no particular desire to help her enrich herself any further, and we parted company. But I fear that I told her enough about my intended project for her to order her own people to begin searching for the book as well. As I understand it, their tomb-breakings soon attracted the attention of the captain of the Shieldsworn, who tried to put a stop to it and was killed for his interference. The Veruna armsmen would not have been there if I hadn't sought out the aid of House Veruna at first. For that I am truly sorry."

Geran shook his head. The tiefling seemed sincere, but he had a hard time taking Sarth at his word. Still, Sarth had evidently consented to help Hamil free him, and they had fought together against Veruna's mercenaries by the barrow of Terlannis. "I'll need to hear more about this soon. I guess now isn't the time," he finally said. "But I'm sorry if I've misjudged you."

The tiefling smiled ruefully and gestured at the small black horns jutting from his forehead. "I am accustomed to it."

"Can we continue with your escape now, Geran?" Hamil asked.

"A sound suggestion." Geran stepped out of the cell; the red smoke was already dissipating. Five council armsmen lay sprawled on the ground, coughing weakly. He spied a trunk by the opposite wall and opened it, retrieving the personal possessions he'd been carrying when Kendurkkel and his men had ambushed him. With a sigh of relief, Geran buckled his scabbard around his waist and rested his hand on the pommel of his sword. "What now?" he asked.

"Mirya's waiting with a wagon in the courtyard," Hamil answered. "I arranged a large order for provisions to be sent to Erstenwold's. We're going to drive out the front gate as if nothing were out of the ordinary."

"I'll need a disguise."

"I can attend to that detail," Sarth said. The tiefling reached into a pouch by his belt to draw out a pinch of fine silver powder, and then cast the dust over the swordmage while murmuring a spell. Geran felt a strange prickling sensation over his skin and held still only through an iron determination not to flinch. Hamil and Sarth seemed to fade strangely in his sight, becoming pale and ghostly; when he looked down at his own body, he noticed that he seemed more ghostly still. "You're invisible, Geran. Take care, since you can still be heard or felt. The spell lasts only a short time, so let us hurry."

"I understand," Geran said. He followed his rescuers down the corridor and then out through a guardroom where four more council armsmen lay where they'd fallen, snoring softly in an enchanted slumber. They descended a flight of steps and then turned aside into a small storeroom with a door that opened on the courtyard behind the gatehouse. A large, open wagon stood just outside, its bed filled with several casks and crates. More of the same stood in the storeroom. Geran guessed that Hamil and Sarth had played the part of Erstenwold clerks unloading the wagon, only to slip away when the opportunity presented itself.

Mirya stood in the shadows beside the wagon, wearing a dark hood over her dress. She stroked the neck of the draft horse to keep the animal still and quiet. When Sarth and Hamil appeared, she frowned in consternation. "What happened?" she whispered. "Where's Geran?"

"I'm here, Mirya," Geran answered. He couldn't resist a quick touch on her shoulder. She jumped and glowered in his general direction. "You shouldn't have let Hamil talk you into helping out, though. You'll be in a good deal of trouble when the Shieldsworn figure out what happened."

Hamil laughed softly. "Trust me, Geran, it wasn't my idea. All I wanted was the wagon and some empty barrels, but she insisted on coming along to help."

"It would be wiser to have this conversation somewhere else," Sarth said quietly. "We have not succeeded yet."

Geran glanced up at the banners flying over the gatehouse. They fluttered and flapped energetically in the strengthening breeze, glimmers of gray in the moonlight. He was only a few steps from slipping out of the castle, but he hesitated, quickly reviewing the decisions he'd made earlier in the day. "You'd better go without me," he said slowly. "I must speak with the harmach and explain the danger to him. I can't think of a reason why Sergen would wear that amulet unless he intends to use it to summon the King in Copper, and I think that he means to do it here."

"Harmach Grigor may feel that he's got to jail you again to keep his word to the Merchant Council," Mirya pointed out. "You'll not get a better chance to slip away."

"I agree with Mirya," said Hamil. "If they catch you now, it'll be impossible to get you out later. Besides, it'll raise some difficult questions for Mirya and me."

"I'll tell the harmach that it was my own doing. All I have to do is come up with a story to explain how I got out of the shackles. You should be fine."

"That's all well and good, but you can spare the harmach that decision by leaving with us now," Mirya said sharply. "We can arrange to warn him once you're out of danger. And if, after that, you still hold with the idea that Sergen's up to some devilish plot, you'll be free to take the fight to him."

"Whatever you decide, decide quickly," Sarth warned. "It will be far easier to spirit you out of the castle while you're invisible, Geran."

The swordmage thought for a moment longer then nodded—not that any of the others could see him. "I'll go," he said. "We'll make sure to warn the harmach, but the best way to avert the danger is to get the lich's amulet away from Sergen." He clambered up onto the wagon, which rocked softly under his weight, and crouched down between a couple of empty barrels. The others climbed up onto the driver's bench, and Mirya clicked her tongue at the draft horse. The animal gave a nervous whicker then pranced back in its traces.

"Easy, boy. Easy," Mirya called softly. But the horse's eyes rolled, and the animal stamped sharply as it shuddered and tried to back out of its harness. "Easy now!"

Geran rolled up on one elbow and looked at the animal, wondering what it was shying from. And then he felt it—a cold, sickening sensation that chilled his heart and made him shiver despite himself. The lantern-light burning by the castle gate seemed to dim and fail, and the shadows around the courtyard suddenly darkened and lengthened. He looked up and saw that the banners above the gatehouse hung limply from their masts.

"Something approaches," Sarth rasped. "Something evil."

Then, silently, terrible shapes began to rise from the moonshadows—ancient warriors in tattered hauberks, their skeletal faces blank with hopelessness and dread. An evil green light burned in the empty sockets of their eyes. The draft horse whinnied in terror and tried to rear in its traces; Geran rolled aside and abandoned the wagon, as did the others. The animal bolted away in panic, filling the courtyard with the horrendous sound of its screams and the clattering racket of the wagon bouncing over the cobblestones. Shouts of human terror echoed from the hallways and rooms of the gatehouse nearby as more and more of the specters appeared and glided into the castle.

"The King in Copper!" Mirya gasped. "He's here!"

Geran caught her arm and retreated a few steps toward the storeroom behind him, sweeping out his sword even as he wondered if it would help against ghostly steel and spectral claws. Dozens of the terrible wraiths were already in sight, and more were appearing by the moment. "I hesitated too long," he groaned. "Sergen's decided to strike."

A wraith flew overhead, wailing in a shrill, cold voice as it streaked past. It drew up and turned to gaze at them, the shadowy image of a long-dead warrior. "Slay them all," it whispered to itself then it leaped down at Mirya, sweeping its phantom sword from its scabbard. Geran shoved her behind him as he parried with his backsword. Elven steel glimmered in the moonlight against dark shadowstuff, but the wraith's ghostly weapon passed through Geran's steel and sank into his arm. A bitter white chill pierced the swordmage's flesh, and he cried out in agony. Then the wraith's blade passed through him, leaving behind a thin white line of cold, pallid flesh like the scar of an old wound.

"Vaar thel murne!" Sarth shouted, and from his fingertips he hurled a bolt of bright fire at the center of the wraith's body. The blazing bolt burned a hole right through the spirit's substance, such as it was, and the wraith recoiled as though sorely wounded. "Steel is of little use now, Geran!"

The wraith's features wavered and grew indistinct, but within moments its ghostly fabric began to knit together again, and the malice of its emerald eyes glittered brightly. It turned its attention to the tiefling and glided forward, raising its phantom blade high for another strike. "Damn the luck," Sarth muttered. "Perhaps my magic is not of much use, either."

Geran shook off the lingering numbness in his swordarm and found the spell he was seeking. *"Reith arroch!"* he called, and his sword suddenly blazed with a brilliant white radiance. He leaped up to meet the wraith and drove his point right between the spirit's eyes; this time the elven steel bit into the unearthly substance as if into living flesh. The wraith shrieked once, pinioned by the sword through its forehead, and then a flash of argent light destroyed it. But more wraiths swirled around them, and the castle courtyard began to take on an eerie, sepulchral appearance, as if the mere presence of the dead warriors had dragged Griffonwatch itself into the spectral horror of their shadowy existence.

"We can't stay here, Geran," Hamil warned. He had his daggers in hand—enchanted weapons both, but who could say whether they were keen enough to pierce flesh that was not there?—and he kept them poised as a defense of sorts, trying to hold off wraiths drawing close from that side. "We're too exposed here!"

Geran looked around, and his gaze fell on the door leading to the banquet hall. A Shieldsworn guard fought furiously on the steps, only to crumple under the slashing assault of several of the furious wraiths. There was only one thing to do—Geran had to reach the harmach and the rest of the Hulmasters before the wraiths did. Hoping the others would follow his lead, he dashed across the courtyard and bounded up the steps into Griffonwatch's horror-haunted halls.

TWENTY-FOUR

10 Tarsakh, the Year of the Ageless One

The Hulburgans had chosen a good defensive position. The track descending from the moorland down into the river valley ran between a high hillside on the east and a small rocky rise on the right. The white rushing Winterspear wound across the vale just in front of the human defenses, spanned by an old bridge of stone. One of their small watchtowers stood atop the rocky rise. Mhurren grinned in appreciation as he studied the small army arrayed against him. The sun had set more than an hour ago, but great bonfires burned across here and there in front of the human positions, set so the humans would have light enough to fight by. The human soldiers were careful to stand well back from the firelight; they might not be able to see past the line of fires, but then again, Mhurren couldn't send his warriors at them without sending them through the firelight. Whoever the commander was, he was no fool.

"They think that little stream will stop us?" Kraashk snarled. The hobgoblin chieftain waved his hand at the humans. He was taller than Mhurren by half a head, and his rank brown hair was braided with tapers around his face; in battle Kraashk lit them to wreathe his face in flame and reeking smoke, believing it terrified his enemies. He pointed across the vale to its lower side, where the hillsides steepened and drew together again. "They would be wiser to stand at the defile, there."

Mhurren shook his head. "The river runs through the middle of it. Dividing their warriors between the banks would be folly. Each part is unable to guard the other there. No, their captain chose good ground. The whole army fights as one, and he can fall back if he is beaten here."

"You think like a human," Kraashk said and let his fangs show for an instant to demonstrate that he did not mean it as a compliment.

The Bloody Skull chieftain ignored his vassal's barb. He studied the vale for a time, then nodded to himself. It was a good plan. He pointed to the high hillside on the humans' right flank. "Can your wolf riders manage that hillside, Kraashk?"

The hobgoblin studied it for a moment. "It won't be easy, but yes, they could do it."

"Then my plan is simple. Take your wolf riders around to the top of that hill. I will attack down the throat of the valley and bring the humans right to the edge of the stream. When I signal, you bring the Red Claws down the hill and take them in the flank. The humans will be busy with me, so they won't have time to shoot at you."

Kraashk grinned in appreciation, and this time he intended no insult. "A good plan," the hobgoblin said. For all the fierceness he claimed, he was quite clever and quickly grasped what Mhurren intended. "Give me an hour to get my wolf riders where you want them, then begin your attack. Do not call for me too early."

"Then go," Mhurren said. The hobgoblin held up his spear in salute then jogged off into the cold and windy night, already barking out orders at his tribesmen. Mhurren looked around. "Avrun!" he called.

The Warlock Knight was waiting nearby. "Yes, King Mhurren?"

"I will drive the Hulburgans down the valley in an hour. Can you see the place where the valley narrows, there? I want your manticores and wyverns to wait there on the heights. When the Hulburgans flee, they are to feast."

The helmed human nodded. "What of my spellcasters?"

"They are to shield my warriors. We will attack at the bridge, there. Use your magic to keep the humans from shooting us to pieces."

"It shall be as you say," the Vaasan agreed. He went off to speak with the other black-armored humans and their pet monsters.

Mhurren idly wondered what Avrun would do if he came up with a plan that the Warlock Knights objected to. Would they try to reason with him? Threaten him? Use some form of magical compulsion? Or simply arrange his death and replace him with a warchief more amenable to their control? Tonight it did not matter, but the day would come when he decided that he would not do what they wished him to do. The trick was simple: He needed to make himself strong enough that the Skullsmashers, the Red Claws, and the other bands of rabble infesting Thar feared him more than they feared Vaasa. Destroying Hulburg would be a good start toward that goal. Each victory Mhurren won would increase his standing among the other chieftains of Thar, and soon enough they would come to believe that he'd won those victories with his own strength and cunning, not Vaasan magic or allegiances. And when they did, he might have a chance to turn against the Warlock Knights and rule in his own name.

Mhurren called his own Bloody Skull chiefs and captains together and gave them their instructions. Then he settled down to wait, squatting atop a boulder that gave him a good view of the valley below. The moon was waning and close to new, but the night was clear; he could easily make out hilltops miles away over the moorland. A cold, cheerless wind moaned through the hollows and over the hills around him . . . a ghost wind, as his warriors called it. Tonight the spirits of old warriors were close by, doubtless gathering to watch the fight about to take place and roar approval from the land of the dead.

He brooded on his own thoughts for a time, and then the Warlock Knight Avrun approached him. "King Mhurren, the Red Claws are in position. Kraashk awaits your command."

"I hear you," Mhurren said. "I will tell you when to signal him." He set his helm on his head and picked up his iron-shod spear then trotted down to the place where his troops were gathering, a long bowshot above the Hulburgans. He found another boulder amid his milling warriors and scrambled to its top, so that all could see him.

"Listen to me, Bloody Skulls!" he shouted. "Listen to me, Skullsmashers!" The orcs and ogres around him fell quiet, and the silence rippled out so that most of the warriors in the horde turned to look on him and await his words. "There below you stand the warriors of the human king who murdered Morag and threw back his head in contempt!" The Bloody Skulls snarled in anger at that; the Skullsmashers had no idea who Morag was, but the dimwitted ogres knew a fight was near and they snarled too. "There below you stand the warriors whose people hunt your game, trap your furs, and steal your gold out of the earth! Look on them, my brothers—they are all that stands between you and Hulburg tonight. Deal with these, and all the gold and fur and food that they have stolen from you over the years is yours for the taking. A thousand slaves we herd out of Hulburg tomorrow, and all the plunder you can carry—if only you fight well tonight and slay these weaklings where they stand! Each warrior who takes from this field the skull of a human felled by his hand wins honor tonight, but you must strike swiftly, my brothers, because there are more of you than there are of them! He who is slow, who hesitates, who holds back when others charge forward, he takes no head tonight. Now, go and slay!"

With that Mhurren leaped down from his perch, pointing his spear at the humans across the field, and darted into the firelight. Thousands of orcs and ogres around him roared in battle-fury and followed, each striving to cross the firelit vale and be the first to claim a head. Arrows, bolts, and battle spells leaped out of the human shieldwall as Mhurren's orcs appeared out of the darkness; many of the missiles and streaking fireballs vanished in sparks of crimson flame, intercepted by the Vaasan mages who worked to shield the Bloody Skull horde, but others slipped through. Orcs howled and fell rolling to the slope as arrows and bolts bit into flesh, while only a few yards from Mhurren a sphere of crackling lightning suddenly exploded amid several ogres and speared them where they stood with brilliant green bolts. The ogres shrieked and jerked horribly as smoke burst from their flesh, and they fell twitching an instant later. Mhurren ran past them, ignoring the dead and dying warriors.

He slowed his steps a little and looked around to get a good sense of how the attack was going. His Skull Guards clustered in a tight knot around him, guarding him with their shields. The Skullsmashers stormed the bridge, swarming up and over the small stone span—but a loud cracking sound ripped through the night, and the bridge suddenly collapsed into the stream, taking half a dozen ogres with it. "Clever," Mhurren growled. The humans had sabotaged the span; he should have expected that. But elsewhere his warriors reached the bank of the Winterspear—here a cold, swift stream not more than forty feet wide and several feet deep—and began to wade recklessly across into the teeth of the human defenses. Orcs died by the scores in the water, shot down as they floundered and struggled against the current. But other warriors on the streambank hurled javelins and heavy spears over the water, taking a toll of the humans waiting on the far bank. Mhurren's nostrils flared at the smell of blood, and he ached to throw himself headlong into the fray and lead his warriors across, but he restrained himself. He was a warlord, not a berserker, and that meant that sometimes he had to fight with his wits as well as with his hands.

Orcs and ogres reached the far bank only to die under the blades of the Hulburgan soldiers waiting for them. More warriors swarmed up behind them, pushing forward into the steel of humans and dwarves. It was not a fight that favored the Bloody Skulls, since their greater numbers were compressed into a comparatively small frontage, but even so the sheer mass and ferocity of the horde made itself felt. Foot by foot the Hulburgan line wavered, shoved back by the growing press. Mhurren waited thirty heart-beats more just to be sure of the moment, and then he wheeled and shouted at his guards, "The banner, now!"

Two of the Skull Guards raised up a bright yellow banner with the image of a crimson skull crudely depicted on it and waved it from side to side. One staggered and fell with an arrow quivering between his shoulder blades, but the sign was already given. A hundred yards behind them, one of the Vaasan spellcasters launched a blazing missile of green fire straight up into the air, where it burst over the battlefield. From the darkness above and to one side of the human lines, a chorus of fierce howls and war-cries greeted the signal. "You are not so clever as you think," Mhurren growled at his unseen adversary. Somewhere behind the human lines, some lord or captain had just tasted his first true fear of the battle.

Shouts of consternation and distress arose from the right flank of the Hulburgan lines, and then Mhurren saw his wolf riders come pelting down the steep hillside behind the soldiers fighting at the stream. A number stumbled and fell, rolling down helplessly—but even those served to knock down the humans or dwarves they tumbled into. He grinned in triumph; while he'd hammered on his enemy's shield with his right hand to keep him busy, he'd just managed to gut him with a cleaver in his left. The fight would not last long.

"At them, Skull Guards!" Mhurren shouted. "I mean to take a head tonight!" He sprinted forward to join the fray, splashing into the icy water not far from the ruined bridge. He clambered up onto the far bank unhindered—his warriors had already pushed the Hulburgans back from the water's edge. Spying an opening in the lines, he roared a battle cry and dashed forward to bury his spearhead in the heart of a human soldier who did not raise his shield swiftly enough. The man cried out and fell. Mhurren wrenched his steel out of the man's chest and turned to battle another soldier, this one a sturdy dwarf who nearly took off the warlord's foot with a low, quick axe-cut. They traded several blows, spear darting to find a way around the shield, axe whistling through the air, and then an ogre came up behind the dwarf and smashed him broken to the wet ground with a huge overhand blow from his massive club. Mhurren growled in frustration and shifted away to find another foe.

He felt the beginning of the rout before he saw it. Soldiers shrank away from his warriors, giving ground a step or two at a time, then more quickly. Off to his right, on the enemy's lightly engaged side, one of their companies—footmen in checkered surcoats of scarlet and white, likely one of the mercenary companies the Hulburgan merchants hired—stepped off the line and began an orderly withdrawal, which of course exposed the companies next to them. More of the Hulburgans began to withdraw as orcs howled after them, axes and spears raised high. The enemy companies on the Hulburgan right were already shattered, caught between the hammer and anvil of Red Claw wolf riders and Bloody Skull warriors fording the Winterspear. Only the harmach's own Shieldsworn stood fast, holding the center, but they were in grave danger of being surrounded as the flanks crumbled on each side.

Mhurren plunged back into the fray, attacking the Shieldsworn in front of him. He speared a tall veteran with a beard of iron gray then drew back his arm and hurled his spear at another human who stood with his back to the warchief. The weapon transfixed him; he spun to the ground, sword falling from his fingers. The half-orc swept a heavy, curved sword from his belt and bounded over to the dying soldier, taking his head with one smooth strike. "This is my trophy!" he shouted to his Skull Guards, and then he looked for another enemy.

Trumpets sounded in the vale, and the human soldiers turned and jogged back, giving more ground. Behind them a single line of horsemen formed up to serve as a rear guard, while the rest began to stream back out of the vale after the mercenaries who had already abandoned the field. The captain of the horsemen waved her sword over her head and cried out in a high, clear voice: *"Countercharge! Countercharge!"*

The riders spurred forward at the vast horde swarming down against them, lances lowered, and threw a shock into Mhurren's warriors that stopped them where they stood. At once the human riders wheeled and galloped back out of range—not before a couple were caught and dragged out of their saddles—and then turned to form another line behind their captain. Mhurren peered at her and scowled. She wore the griffon surcoat all the harmach's men wore, but her griffon was gold in color instead of blue, and her eyes glittered with an eerie luminous light. "The Blue Serpent," he hissed.

Few human warriors earned much respect from the Bloody Skulls, but he'd heard enough stories about Kara Hulmaster and her skill with bow and blade. Right before his eyes she was throwing back his warriors' assaults in order to give her soldiers a chance to escape his trap.

"Again!" she shouted. *"Countercharge!"* And once again the line of fifty riders threw itself into the hundreds upon hundreds of orcs and ogres and wolf riders who pressed close behind and hammered them to a standstill. They broke free again and retreated, missing a few more of their comrades, but the harmach's champion still rode at their head.

"That one at least knows the meaning of courage," he said. It was almost a pity to slay a warrior of such heart, but die she must. He sheathed his sword and held out his hand to the nearest Skull Guard. "Quickly, your spear!"

The warrior handed Mhurren his spear—a good weapon, well-balanced and strong—and Mhurren studied his quarry carefully. She rallied her riders for one more attack against the swarming horde surrounding them and shouted again. *"Countercharge! For Hulburg!"*

The warchief took three quick steps and flung his spear with all his strength. It was a long throw, since he was a good forty yards behind the ragged lines of his warriors, but he gave himself a running start, and he aimed well. The spear arced down through the darkness as she galloped forward to meet it unknowingly. And then, at the last instant, somehow she glimpsed the spear hurtling at her heart. She threw up her sword and parried the flashing spearpoint, batting it aside so that it flew over her shoulder.

"The luck of a witch!" said the warrior whose spear Mhurren had borrowed.

Mhurren watched as she crashed once more into his warriors, laying about her with her blade, and then emerged again to gallop away. He snorted and shook his head. "That was not luck, Ruurth. That was skill. Her death does not wait on this field."

This time, the remaining Shieldsworn riders—less than half of those who had first stood against the Bloody Skulls—did not reform their lines. They'd bought enough time for the survivors of Hulburg's army to make their escape. The harmach's champion led them through the narrow defile at the lower side of the field, retreating into the broad Winterspear Vale beyond. Mhurren noted with wry amusement that dozens of torn bodies in coats of checkered white and scarlet were strewn along the narrow path. The mercenaries who'd fled the battle first had simply ensured that they were the first to discover the Vaasans' waiting monsters. "A fitting end for faithless cowards," he muttered.

"A good fight, Mhurren!" The Red Claw Kraashk sat atop his huge worg, leaning on the saddlehorn. Smoke streamed from the burning tapers in his beard and hair. Blood oozed from a broken-off arrow embedded in the hobgoblin's left thigh, but he paid it no mind. "They'll run all the way back to the Moonsea, I think."

"Not if I can help it," the warlord answered. "Harry them at every step, Kraashk. Make them turn and stand ten times an hour. If you slow them down, we can catch them out in the open fields and destroy them completely."

"That will cost me wolves and warriors," the hobgoblin warned.

"And in token of that, the Red Claws will earn a generous share of the city's plunder," Mhurren answered. "But we can't take the city unless we destroy the harmach's army, and to do that, I need you to make them stand and fight somewhere far from help."

Kraashk nodded. "As you say, then, Warlord. But I will hold you to your promise when it comes time to pick our plunder." He dug his heels into his worg's flanks, and the monstrous wolf snarled and bounded away into the darkness after the retreating Hulburgans.

Mhurren watched him go and grinned. With any luck, Kraashk would find a way to get himself killed and spare him the trouble of finding a suitable bribe. But if not, well, he'd simply allow the Red Claws to take a little more from what the Vaasans asked him to spare. There would be enough plunder that he didn't feel that he had to share his own.

TWENTY-FIVE

10 Tarsakh, the Year of the Ageless One

The wraiths of Aesperus killed swiftly and indiscriminately. Wherever they came across a living person, they struck savagely. As Geran dashed up through the castle toward the Harmach's Tower, it seemed that he found a murdered servant or guard each time he turned a corner. Each victim died with hardly a mark upon him, simply a pallid white scar wherever a wraith's weapon had touched living flesh. But their eyes were dark and blank, and their mouths were twisted in silent screams at the horror of their ghostly killers. Shouts of panic and mortal terror echoed through the castle's corridors, lost amid the shrill cries and sinister calls of the spectral warriors who roamed Griffonwatch.

Rather than risk the castle's great hall and the dozen wraiths swarming around it, Geran darted into the maze of storerooms and servants' quarters that surrounded that part of Griffonwatch. Hamil, Mirya, and Sarth hurried to keep up with him, so he slowed his steps just a little—it was all too easy to get lost in Griffonwatch's deeper hallways, and they hadn't grown up in the castle as he had. "This way!" he called to them.

He came to a servants' staircase that climbed up to the East Hall, a large building between the lower bailey and the upper court that housed offices of the harmach's officials and quarters for dignitaries. Geran swiftly mounted the steps and emerged into a broad hallway with a floor of gleaming hardwood only to find several wraiths hovering nearby. The undead spirits hissed in challenge and flew at him with their pale blades raised to strike. "Wraiths!" the swordmage called over his shoulder.

He quickly wove the words for the silversteel veil. *"Cuillen mhariel!"* he cried then gave ground, luring the spectral warriors away from the doorway he'd just come through. His companions were only a few steps behind him, and he didn't want the ghosts to fall on them as soon as they appeared in the hall. "Over here, you foul spirits!"

The wraiths swirled around him, streaking in to stab and slash with their ghostly blades, but Geran's elf-wrought blade still glimmered with the radiance of his spirit-bane spell. He parried their attacks as if they were striking with weapons of iron, passing one blade past his hip, knocking another's point down to the ground, and then whirling close to draw his edge across a wraith's neck as he leaped aside from the third. The shining steel of his blade bit deep into the wraith's shadowy substance, and a jet of dark mist boiled away from Geran's cut as he turned to face the remaining two. The wraiths were not stupid; when they came at him again they did so much more cautiously, almost like living warriors who feared his strike. For a moment it was all Geran could do to keep himself alive as the two wraiths sought to trap him between their swords and assailed him from both sides at once. He devoted himself entirely to his own defense, parrying one blade after the other as he continued to circle away from them.

Hamil reached the top of the stairs in a sudden rush of soft footsteps. The halfling took in the situation in a glance and threw himself headlong into the fight, daggers in hand. "We're coming, Geran!" he cried. He set in against one of the wraiths, his small blades moving in a silver blur as he slashed and punched at his ghostly foe. The wraith screeched and retreated from Hamil's assault. Even though the daggers weren't quite real to the phantom, they were enchanted and their magic bit into its spectral flesh. As with Sarth's spells in the castle's lower courtyard, the wounds did not last long. In a matter of moments the fraying ghost-stuff knitted itself together again, almost as fast as the halfling could slice it apart. "How do you kill these things?" Hamil snarled.

Geran took advantage of the distraction Hamil was providing to change foes, abandoning his wraith for a moment to jam his gleaming swordpoint in the center of the other's back. The creature threw back its head and wailed horribly before discorporating. A black chill shocked Geran's hands as the thing died—so to speak—on the point of his blade.

Mirya hurried into the room, holding her skirts with her hands to manage the stairs. The last wraith whirled and darted for her, and she cried out and threw herself out of the way. Behind her, Sarth leveled his rune-carved rod at the spirit and let loose with a gout of yellow flame. The wraith screeched once and veered away, plunging into a solid brick wall as it fled.

"Have all the shades of the Shadowland got loose in the castle?" Mirya muttered. "Madness and mayhem, that's the name of this night!"

"Geran, we must leave this place," the tiefling said. "I do not have magic enough to defeat all of these grim specters. Nor do you."

"I've got to see my family to safety first," Geran answered. "I can't leave without them." Harmach Grigor, Natali and Kirr, Erna, his aunt Terena . . . none of them would stand a chance against the ghostly warriors. He had to believe that his young cousins were still unharmed. The thought of the two Hulmaster children under the pale blades of Aesperus's wraiths left him almost helpless with dread.

"They may already—" Sarth began to say, then winced and halted himself. The tiefling's face was not made for compassion, but his voice was softer when he spoke again. "Of course. I should have thought of that. Lead on."

Deciding that haste was more important than stealth, Geran turned to his right and ran for the doors leading out into the upper courtyard. He burst out into the cold, pale moonlight. Wraiths darted and flew through the shadows, eyes aglow with malice and hunger. The swordmage crossed the small courtyard quickly, passing two more dead Shieldsworn, and ducked into the Harmach's Tower. His companions followed. The great room in the tower's lower floor was deserted. A fire guttered and popped in the hearth, but none of the Hulmasters were there. Quickly Geran dashed up the stairs to the family's bedchambers, throwing open each door as he passed. He found no one on the second floor, and in a growing panic he ran up to the third floor and began to search the rooms there as well. "They're not here!" he cried.

"They might've fled already," Hamil said. "Where would they go, Geran?"

"The postern gate?" he guessed. It was far below them now, but passages below the trophy room led to deeper armories and Griffonwatch's small, well-protected side gate. He shook his head and checked the rooms again. Then he hurried back down the steps to the great room. It was possible that no one remained alive in the castle other than the four of them, but he could still make out the occasional distant scream echoing through the halls, so at least some of the guards or servants were still fighting for their lives. "Let me check the library first, the harmach's often there."

He rushed back out into the courtyard. Ghostly forms flitted through the shadows; he reached out and grasped Mirya's hand. "Stay close," he warned. He started along the side of the court, heading for the castle's library. But Mirya suddenly stopped and pulled back.

"Geran, look!" she whispered. "The chapel!"

Geran halted and looked around. Across the upper courtyard, the castle's disused chapel was surrounded by a dozen of Aesperus's minions. The spirits were forming ranks before the door leading to the shrine. As each wraith took its place alongside its fellows, all of the spirits gathered there grew sharper, clearer, and more substantial. More of the spirits were streaming up to join their fellows. "Of course," he murmured. Holy ground often deterred evil spirits, and Grigor certainly would have known that.

"I think the wraiths are gathering for an assault," Hamil said in a low voice.

"Can they get in?" Mirya asked.

"I don't know," Geran replied. He looked over to Sarth. "Can they?"

The tiefling's eyes glowed faintly red in the dark courtyard. He studied the scene and shook his head. "Not yet, but the old spells and blessings on the chapel do not seem very strong to me. They will not last long. And even if they can keep out the wraiths, there may be more powerful undead nearby. Should Aesperus himself come here, nothing will impede him."

One of the wraiths reached out with its spectral hand and tested the door, which trembled a little at the ghost's touch. Inside a child screamed in panic. Without another moment's thought, Geran ran across the courtyard, brandishing his glowing sword, and darted into the middle of the assembled wraiths, swinging wildly. The blade left swaths of sparkling white light in its path like a wake of tiny stars. The wraiths shrieked in their cold, terrible voices and recoiled from its touch. Sarth joined in then, hurling blasts of fire that singed the wraiths' shadowstuff and drove them back. "Hold on!" Geran shouted. "We're coming!"

He fought his way to the door amid a swirl of phantom blades and leering dead faces. One icy cold blade kissed the nape of his neck, and another seared his left hip, but he cleared the ghostly warriors away. Mirya and Hamil darted into the doorway and fumbled at the door. Geran put his back to them and wove a web of brilliant elven steel in the icy night, keeping the wraiths at bay. "Hamil, the door!"

I'm working on it! Hamil answered. He worked frantically with the point of one dagger, trying to get it beneath the bar on the far side. *There!* The bar clattered to the floor, and Hamil threw open the door.

Inside the chapel the Hulmasters stood clustered close by the altar of Tyr. Harmach Grigor held a magic wand in one hand and stood a little in front of his daughter-in-law, Erna, and his grandchildren, Natali and Kirr. The children sobbed quietly, both frightened terribly but doing their best to be brave. Geran's Aunt Terena—sister of the harmach, Kara's mother, and Sergen's stepmother—knelt on the flagstone floor, tending a Shieldsworn armsman who had collapsed from white wounds.

"Thank Tymora," Geran breathed in relief. "You're all alive."

"Yes, though five Shieldsworn died to see us into this refuge," Harmach Grigor said with a bitter tone. "I was of little help. I'm afraid that I'm not much of a wizard." The old lord looked at Geran and frowned. "I feared that you would be killed in your cell, Geran. How did you survive? And who is that with you?"

"I escaped to warn you of this attack—too late, it seems," Geran answered. "This is Sarth Khul Riizar, who helped Hamil and Mirya get me out of the cell. I hope you'll forgive them, Uncle, but I had to try to warn you: Sergen means to kill us all. He summoned the wraiths to Griffonwatch."

"*Sergen* is behind this?" Grigor demanded.

Geran's Aunt Terena looked up from the man she tended. The wraith's attack had caught her in her bed, and she wore only her dressing gown and a cloak thrown over her shoulders. She strongly resembled her daughter, Kara. She was a fit woman of sixty years, strongly built, with long gray-white hair. Terena paled and put her hand to her throat. "So he's finally chosen to follow in his father's footsteps," she said. "Ah, Grigor, I'm so sorry. I never imagined he had so much hate in him. He wasn't always what he's become."

"Excuse me, but all that can wait for later," Hamil said sharply. He stood by the chapel's door, looking out into the courtyard. "The wraiths are returning, Geran. We've got to leave now or fight here."

Geran looked at his uncle. "We should flee," he said. "I don't know if we can hold off many more of the wraiths. The postern's our best chance to get the children out of the castle."

Grigor nodded. "Agreed. Lead the way, Geran."

"Shut the door, Hamil," Geran said. He hurried across the chapel to a small door that led outside to the tiny courtyard where he had practiced a few times. With luck, the wraiths would be gathering by the chapel's front door, massing their might to overcome the old, weak blessings that deterred them for the moment. It took him a moment to get the side door open—this one was rarely used, and he had to put his shoulder to it to push it open through the leaf-mold that had accumulated on the other side. But no wraiths waited in the small cloister beyond.

"This way, quickly," he said to the others. He hurried across to the door leading back into the Harmach's Tower on the far side of the small courtyard. Mirya and Hamil helped the injured Shieldsworn to his feet, and Erna grasped Natali and Kirr firmly by their hands and followed.

Geran led them into the Harmach's Tower and found the stairs that led down to the hallway by the trophy room. They encountered no more corpses here nor any wraiths. It was normally a lightly traveled part of the castle, and he began to hope that he might actually get his uncle and the rest of the family out of Griffonwatch safely. He turned into one of the passageways cut through the hill's heartrock and came to a barred iron door. Geran threw the bar aside and pushed it open to reveal a staircase spiraling down into the gloom. "This way," he said. "Be careful of the steps, it's a long stair."

"Are the ghosts going to follow us down there?" Kirr asked.

"I hope not, Kirr. We're trying to stay a step ahead of them," Geran answered. "Down you go!"

The stairs spiraled down forty feet or more, lit by dimly glowing light-globes the Shieldsworn refreshed every few months with minor magic. The stairwell was cramped, cold, and dark, but Geran could still see enough to lead the way down. Below the staircase stood a large hall with a low, barrel-vaulted ceiling. This chamber was designed to house scores of warriors in full kit, since the postern gate—the castle's small back entrance, from which a force inside could sally in strength to attack besiegers from an unexpected direction—was close by. Geran halted at the foot of the stairs and guided the others into the room as they appeared. "Over there," he said.

The harmach limped badly when he reached the bottom step. He grimaced in pain. "Stairs pain me," he explained. "You shouldn't wait on me, Geran."

The sorcerer Sarth brought up the rear, watching carefully behind him with his rod at the ready. "We must keep moving," the tiefling said. "They are not far behind us."

Geran did not pause. He hurried back across the hall and ducked into the short passage leading to the postern. Normally the door was securely locked and barred, since the Shieldsworn didn't keep any guards there, but when he turned the corner he found the postern standing open. It seemed that he wasn't the only person in Griffonwatch to think of the side gate. He started forward, but Hamil reached out and caught his sleeve.

Something seems awry here, the halfling said silently. *Douse the nearest lights, and wait here a moment. I'll take a look.*

"Go ahead," Geran said softly.

He retreated a few steps and covered the light-globes gleaming in the postern passage. Hamil glided into the shadows and slipped out the heavy iron door; even though Geran knew the halfling was there, he couldn't see or hear him. He motioned for the rest of the small company to hold still and wait.

Thirty heartbeats later, Hamil returned. "It's an ambush," he said quietly. "Several of the castle folk lie dead just outside. There are a dozen Veruna armsmen outside, ready for someone to blunder out the door."

Geran's fist tightened on the hilt of his blade. The extent of Sergen's perfidy was now clear. "So Sergen sent the specters to slay everyone in the castle then made sure to have his armsmen waiting by the gates to cut down anyone who managed to flee?" he snarled. "He's a traitor and a murderer, just like his father was." He looked at Natali and Kirr, waiting with their mother. With Hamil and Sarth, he might have a chance to cut his way free of the trap, but he could hardly lead the children or his older relatives into a fight.

"We'll have to try some other way," the harmach said wearily. "The main gate, I suppose."

"If those villains are watching the postern, Lord Harmach, there's not a chance in the world they'll not watch the main gatehouse too," Mirya pointed out. "Is there any other way out of the castle?"

"There are a couple of places where a rope might be lowered from the walls, but I am not sure if the children could manage it," the harmach said. "Or if I could, in all honesty."

"We could wait here," Erna said. "The specters might not come to this part of the castle."

"Inadvisable," Sarth said. He stood by the foot of the stairs, head cocked to one side to peer upward as far as he could. "It's only a matter of time before the ghosts descend to this level."

"We'll have to break out, then," Geran decided. "Sarth, do you have any spells that could protect us outside?"

The tiefling frowned. "A spell of fog. But it would blind us as well."

"It'll have to do." Geran turned to his uncle. "Hamil and I will try to deal with the men waiting outside. Wait inside the postern as long as you can."

Harmach Grigor nodded. "Good luck, Geran," he said quietly.

The swordmage moved close to the doorway and muttered the incantation of the dragon scales to guard himself as best he could. A shimmering stream of purple-glowing diadems formed around him, rippling in the shadowy light. Hamil drew up close beside him, a dagger in each hand.

The halfling looked up at Geran and said, "I have some doubts about this plan."

"Best not to dwell on it, then." Geran looked over at Sarth.

The tiefling raised his clawed hands and softly chanted the words of his spell. Billows of blue mist began to rise from the ground, rapidly filling the doorway and spilling into the night outside. The swordmage waited a moment for the fog to thicken more and steeled his nerve. Then he stepped into the fog and felt his way out the postern gate. The gate opened onto a small landing near the foot of Griffonwatch's hill, about halfway around the castle from the main gate. Worn stone steps covered by a low wall descended twenty feet to an old wrought-iron fence. Beyond that stood a tangle of alders, blueleafs, and blackberry thickets, a small woodland that ringed the eastern side of the castle's hill. Geran could barely see the steps under his feet, and he kept one hand on the wall to navigate through the mist. It was cold, and the steps were slick with frost. Then, abruptly, he descended out of the tattered blue mist and caught sight of the armsmen standing nearby in Veruna's green and white.

"There!" one of the mercenaries shouted. "Shoot him down!"

Several men raised crossbows at Geran, but the swordmage quickly ducked under the wall. Bolts snapped and hissed through the air, clattering against the rocky foot of the castle or striking the stone steps. He risked a quick peek over the wall to get a better look. The Veruna men were arranged in a loose half-ring under the eaves of the dark grove beyond the fence. Thrusting his fear and anger aside, the swordmage fixed in his mind the arcane symbols of the spell he needed and spoke its single word: *"Seiroch!"*

The strange, cold lurch of teleportation jarred him, and he felt as if he were falling—but then he stood in the middle of the Veruna armsmen, who were busily drawing back their crossbows and making ready another shot. Geran snarled and stabbed the nearest man through the throat and then bounded past the crumpling mercenary to slash off the arm of the next one in the line. A crossbowman behind him fired at his back, but the amethyst scales of his protection spell deflected the quarrel away from him. He ignored the attack and kept going. The third man he reached had the time to drop his crossbow and draw a sword. Geran launched a furious attack, raining slashes left and right against the Veruna armsman. The mercenary parried the first few and attempted a counterattack, but Geran threw up a lightning-quick block of his own and spun inside the man's guard to slash his belly badly. The Veruna man shrieked and reeled away.

"Watch it, Geran!" Hamil paused by the iron fence, took aim, and hurled a dagger at an armsman hurrying up behind Geran. The blade took the man just under his hauberk, biting deeply above the knee. The charging soldier stumbled and rolled in the underbrush with a savage oath. Hamil scrambled over the fence, only to be knocked spinning to the ground by a crossbow bolt that caught him just before he was going to drop down on the forest side.

"Hamil!" Geran cried. He took a step toward the place where his friend had fallen, but Hamil's silent voice stopped him.

I'm not badly hurt. Keep at them, Geran!

Geran turned back to the Veruna armsmen around him. He counted at least a dozen more men facing him. Swords in hand, they circled closer, ready for him now. Behind the Mulmasterite mercenaries stood a hooded man in elegant black finery. Sergen Hulmaster stepped out of the shadows, his dark eyes glittering. He carried a crossbow in one hand and a long, slender rapier in the other. "I didn't like that arrogant little popinjay very much," he remarked. "I intended for you to die in your cell, Geran. I must tell you that I'm a little disappointed that you'll meet your end with steel in your hand. On the other hand—" Sergen paused to toss away his empty crossbow and drew a poniard with his left hand—"I'm more than a little tired of hearing tales about your heroics. Tonight I'll repay many old slights and insults. I've always known that you're not the paragon of virtue and skill everyone seems to think you are."

Geran smiled coldly. "You'll meet me blade to blade, Sergen? Your mercenaries will stand aside?"

The black-garbed lord laughed. "My sense of fair play is not so well developed as that, Geran. They'll stand aside only as long as I'm winning." He looked at the Veruna mercenaries standing nearby and said, "If he wounds me, cut him down." Then he came to meet Geran with his rapier in hand.

Twenty-six

11 Tarsakh, the Year of the Ageless One

Geran did not remember Sergen as a swordsman of much skill, but he hadn't seen him with a blade since Sergen was fifteen or sixteen. Still, the fact that Sergen offered to meet him suggested that the traitor had at least some reason to feel confident, and so Geran resolved to be cautious. Should I try for a swift victory, even though the armsmen might overwhelm me? he thought. Or do I play for time and try to draw things out—knowing that every moment I'm delayed, the wraiths may find the others?

Sergen seemed to read his uncertainty and grinned at Geran's indecision. "You must be wondering just how skillfully you should fight," he said. "A difficult puzzle, I suspect. I am curious to see how you'll resolve it."

"Difficult?" Geran stalked closer, watching Sergen's eyes. If it were only his own life at stake, that would be one thing. But Sergen was responsible for authoring a massacre, and should he fall, Sergen or his men would see to it that none of the Hulmasters survived the night. "No, not especially. Whatever else happens tonight, you'll regret crossing blades with me. If it costs me my life to send you from this world, then you'll have little opportunity to profit from your treachery."

He smiled coldly at Sergen and attacked, a simple thrust at the belt buckle. Sergen parried and riposted sharply; Geran parried in turn and gave a half-step before replying with a quick slash at Sergen's face, which the council lord likewise parried. They traded thrusts and cuts furiously for several moments before the momentum of their strikes carried them past each other, and they exchanged places.

He's quick, Geran realized. Sergen was a good swordsman, though not as experienced as he was. However, his cousin was exceptionally fast—quicker than Geran, at least. Of all the natural gifts a swordsman desired, raw speed was certainly the most vital. Given equal skill, a fast man could beat a strong man if weight of armor was not a consideration.

"You're more of a swordsman than I remember," Geran admitted.

"You're not the swordsman I feared," Sergen replied.

He began the next exchange, lunging in to thrust with his rapier. Geran deflected the point with a sharp ring of steel; Sergen recovered and attacked again, and Geran parried that one as well; and then rather than recover Sergen suddenly leaped in close and stabbed with his poniard. Geran knocked the dagger's point away with his forearm and received a shallow, bloody cut from its razor-sharp blade despite the spells protecting him. He put his shoulder down and shoved Sergen back out of range. The blades flew swiftly in the moonlight, ringing shrilly. Geran tested his cousin's defenses low, then high as they circled through the brush. As best he could, he kept an eye on the Veruna soldiers who ringed them.

He managed to turn Sergen around again, so that he could see the castle's postern gate over Sergen's shoulder. It was difficult to tell with the tatters of mist still clinging to the doorway, but he thought he saw a furtive motion there—shadowy figures slipping down the steps. Geran redoubled the pace of his attacks, keeping Sergen and the Veruna armsmen focused on him. He knew a sword spell or two he could have used, but if he worked a spell, the Verunas around him might react. Grimacing in frustration, he fell back on his own skill.

"I think you're holding back," Sergen said between blows. "Perhaps you're not as fearless as you believe you are, dear cousin."

"You forget where I studied," Geran retorted. "I spent years in Myth Drannor, tutored by elf blademasters. You think you're quick? I learned to fight against elves who'd make you look like a staggering drunk!" He parried several more blows and essayed a riposte of his own that Sergen caught on his poniard. "Speed's a fleeting advantage, Sergen. When a man tires, he slows down. If you were going to defeat me with your quickness, you would've done it already. Now it's my fight."

"Your confidence is misplaced," Sergen snarled. He launched a lightning thrust at Geran's heart, which Geran parried awkwardly. Instantly

Sergen recovered, circled his point under Geran's blade, and thrust again—falling into Geran's trap. The swordmage's awkward parry instantly became a short, brutal chop at Sergen's sword arm as Geran twisted away from the thrust. His blade bit into Sergen's arm just below the elbow and cracked bone. Sergen cried out and dropped his rapier, and then Geran nearly took his head off with the backhand stroke that followed. Sergen managed to duck under the blow, but not without suffering a great gash of his scalp and a jarring blow to the skull that sent him reeling to the ground.

Geran leaped past his stepcousin and immediately engaged the first of the Veruna armsmen he could reach. "Hamil!" he shouted. "Help if you can!"

He rushed past the man and found a brief clear space to speak another spell. *"Ilyeith sannoghan!"* he cried, and his blade suddenly crackled with brilliant yellow sparks. Then several Veruna men beset him at the same time. Geran leaped and parried, thrust and slashed, and for ten heartbeats he was lost in the thick of a fight as dire as any he'd ever been caught in. A thrust at his heart was weakened just enough by his fading dragon scales to keep the point in the muscle of his chest, and then a hamstringing slash at the back of his knee buckled his leg but did not quite bring him down. He struck one man in a steel breastplate with his enchanted blade, and a sharp flash of lightning seared the darkness; when Geran blinked his eyes clear, the man was lying on the ground with smoke curling from his ears. But more mercenaries pressed in around him.

Suddenly the forest rocked with powerful words of magic. *"Satharni khi!"* roared Sarth. The tiefling appeared by the postern gate, amid the dissipating remains of his simple fog spell. From his hands streaked out a great glowing blast of purple fire that burst beneath the trees. Sorcerous fire seared an awful swath through the mercenaries near Geran. Several men screamed terribly as their surcoats caught fire, and they staggered blindly through the night like living torches. Others fell and burned where they stood. The tiefling leaped into the air and soared over the fight, smiting more mercenaries with blasts of his fire or crackling bolts of lightning.

A crossbow snapped in the darkness, and another Veruna blade attacking Geran threw his hands up in the air and collapsed with a quarrel in his back. *My arm's broken, Geran,* Hamil said. *I can't work the cranequin for another shot.*

"Improvise!" Geran called back to him. He dispatched one of the men still pressing him, with a deep cut to the great artery in the thigh; the man hopped back a half-step and toppled, trying vainly to clamp his hand over the terrible wound. Then Geran felt a roar of fire at his back and turned to find one of the mercenaries staggering at him, raising his sword to strike. The swordmage parried the clumsy blow, cut the legs out from under his foe then buried his point in the man's heart as a stroke of mercy. He reeled from the awful smoke and stink of the burning corpse and saw one of the other soldiers ten yards away taking aim at Sarth with a crossbow. Without a moment's thought Geran summoned another spell as he threw his backsword. The blade flew straight and true, whirling through the firelight and shadows, and buried its point in the crossbowman. The mercenary crumpled and folded. Geran held out his hand and finished the spell by stretching out his hand and snarling, *"Cuilledyrr!"* The sword wrenched itself free and flashed back to him hilt first; he caught it and wheeled around in search of another foe.

To his surprise, he saw that the remaining Veruna men were retreating, fleeing through the thickets and shadows. He swayed where he stood, suddenly aware of the cuts and bruises he'd fought through, and slowly limped back toward the postern steps. Tymora smiled on me tonight, he thought wearily. "Hamil?" he called. "Uncle Grigor?"

"Here," his uncle replied. He slowly straightened up from the wall by the steps, standing in front of Erna, Natali, and Kirr. "We're unhurt."

"Thank the gods. Hamil? Where are you?"

"I'm by the fence, Geran," Hamil called. Geran made his way over and found Mirya tending to the halfling already. A bloody quarrel lay on the ground next to Hamil, and she held a folded-up cloak against a dark stain high on his right leg. Hamil's left arm hung limp at his side; his face was pale, but he found a small smile for Geran anyway. "Can you believe it? The quarrel in my leg's bad enough, but I fell from the top of the fence and broke my arm. Fortunately Mirya's gentle touch shall soon restore me to health."

"In a month, perhaps," Mirya said with a frown. "There's to be no more fighting for you tonight, Master Hamil."

Geran knelt and rested a hand on his friend's good shoulder. "You should've used the gate," he told him. Then he climbed back to his feet and returned to where Sergen had fallen.

Sergen was gone. Geran swore and thrashed around in the bracken and briars, searching for some sign of his traitorous cousin. He found the place where Sergen had fallen and set his hand on the ground where his cousin had been lying, only to find splashes of blood and a pair of small, empty vials.

"Potions," he muttered. Healing? Invisibility? Whatever they were, Sergen had made his escape. He could very well return with more mercenaries to finish things. In fact, he *had* to, since he was done in Hulburg as long as the Hulmasters remained alive. I'm an idiot, Geran told himself. I should've made sure of him. Then again, there were a dozen enemies nearby waiting to strike the instant he defeated his cousin, and he couldn't very well have paused to search Sergen at the moment he fell. "But I could have spared him a swordpoint in the eye," he muttered darkly.

"Geran, the castle's foot is no safe place to linger," Mirya called softly. "I hear the ghosts calling one to the other, and I think they're coming near the postern."

"You're right, Mirya," Geran answered. "Sergen's gone. He may return with more mercenaries. We need to get the harmach and the young ones to a place of safety."

"Where?" Harmach Grigor asked. He nodded up at the castle battlements far overhead. Geran could hear the distant wails and cries of the wraiths that swarmed through its passageways and chambers. "Griffonwatch is a morgue. Most of my Shieldsworn are away fighting the Bloody Skulls, and I suspect that all who remained to guard the castle are dead now. I have few soldiers remaining in Hulburg, Geran."

Geran thought for a moment. They could simply search for a place to hide and wait for morning, but Sergen's allies might already be moving to seize control of the town. They needed soldiers, a body of armed men to protect the harmach, but Kara and the Shieldsworn were defending the borders against the Bloody Skulls. "That's not quite true, Uncle Grigor," he said slowly. "We'll find at least some of the Spearmeet captains at the Troll and Tankard. We can have a couple of hundred loyal Hulburgans around you in an hour. I have to believe that might stop the Verunas from trying to kill you."

The harmach sighed, nodded, and said, "You're right, Geran. I can't see that Sergen and his allies have any other choice but to try to finish this."

Mirya helped Hamil to his feet, and Sarth and Geran shouldered the Shieldsworn guard who'd fallen in the chapel. By the dim moonlight Geran saw that it was the young guard Orndal, the one he'd met with Kolton when he first returned to Griffonwatch. The soldier's skin was pale and frigidly cold, but his eyelids flickered when they hoisted him upright and put their shoulders under his arms. Geran nodded toward his right, and the small party set out along the footpath that circled the southern face of Griffonwatch's rocky prominence.

In a hundred yards they broke out of the wooded area and emerged in the city streets. Geran detoured a block or two to give the square by the Harmach's Foot a wide berth, since he could see soldiers in green and white gathered in a large company by the causeway that climbed to the main gate. Just as well we didn't try to leave by that door, he decided. Even from a distance of several blocks, he could make out the cold and distant cries of the wraiths in the castle and glimpse ghostly figures swarming over the battlements. The few passersby they encountered stood in the street and stared up at Griffonwatch, horrified.

Once they were safely around the company of Veruna mercenaries watching the main gate, they returned to the Vale Road. Geran's wounds ached fiercely, but he set the pain aside as best he could and limped on his way. The harmach hobbled along on his walking stick, while Mirya finally had to pause and gather up Hamil in her arms like a child.

"I protest!" the halfling said. "No woman as fair and delicate as you should be expected to carry a wounded hero from the field of battle."

Mirya snorted. "Delicate or not, I'd guess that I'm twice your weight, Hamil. It's easier to just carry you."

Geran looked over his shoulder constantly for some sign of pursuit, fearing that Sergen's Council Watch or their Veruna allies would overtake them in the street at any moment. But no more enemies appeared, and the Troll and Tankard came into view. A large crowd of people stood outside its doors, pointing at the battlements of the castle—from here, they seemed to glow with an eldritch green light—and speaking together in low voices.

"Make way!" Geran called. "We've got wounded with us. Make way!"

"Here, let us lend a hand," one fellow said. In a moment several Hulburgans took the young guard Orndal from Geran and Sarth. Two more helped Mirya with Hamil, and the crowd folded in around them and followed them inside the tavern.

In the warm yellow lanternlight inside, Geran saw that several dozen militiamen were gathered, helms and spears close to hand. They looked up in surprise as he and his party of survivors entered the brewer's taproom. "Why, 'tis Geran Hulmaster!" said one man. "And the harmach!" The men and women who had gathered in the tavern quickly climbed to their feet and touched their hands to their brows, bowing to Harmach Grigor, and then the room erupted in a chaotic babble of excited questions. A table was cleared for Orndal, and the young Shieldsworn guard was stretched out on it; Hamil was shown to a bench by the wall.

"One side! One side!" The tavernkeeper Durnan Osting pushed his way through the crowd gathered around, and bowed to the harmach. "We saw that some fell magic had stricken Griffonwatch, m'lord," he said. "We feared that you were dead or worse—glad to see you and your kin got out o' the castle. Can you tell us what's going on?"

"The King in Copper sent his minions to attack Griffonwatch," the old lord said wearily. "We escaped through the postern gate, but we found House Veruna armsmen waiting there to cut down anyone trying to flee."

"Sergen Hulmaster's trying to seize control of Hulburg," Geran added. "This is all his doing. He means to kill the harmach tonight, and all the Hulmasters if he can. Master Osting, can you pass the word to call out the Spearmeet and muster the companies here? We must protect the harmach."

Osting gaped in amazement. "The black-hearted bastard!" he finally said. "Beggin' m'lord's pardon for speaking ill o' his kin, that is. Of course we'll call out the Spearmeet! We're all the harmach's men. No sellswords from Mulmaster are going t' kill our lord and call themselves masters o' this town!"

"Send word to Rosestone Abbey too," Mirya suggested. "The clerics of Amaunator might be able to do something about the spirits haunting Griffonwatch."

"A good idea," Geran agreed. "Master Osting, can you see to it?"

"Yes, m'lord," the big tavernkeeper answered. "I'll send one of me lads at once."

"Geran, I don't know if this is wise," Grigor murmured. "Sergen's men are trained warriors, well armed and armored—"

"Forgive me, Uncle Grigor, but we've got no choice. Sergen and his council have declared war. The Spearmeet's the only army remaining to you." Geran lowered his voice and leaned closer to his uncle's ear. "I hope it won't come to that. No mercenary really cares to fight a pitched battle if he can help it; there's little reward in it and lots of risk. I think the Veruna men and the Council Watch might have a change of heart once they see there's an army to take the field against them, especially one that outnumbers them."

"I hope you're right, Geran," the harmach said.

"A message for the harmach!" called one of the Hulburgans by the tavern's door. Several other voices in the throng took up the call, and Geran looked up from the table as the crowd swirled around a young woman in a tall silver helm. She wore the white surcoat and blue griffon of the Shieldsworn, but her coat was splattered with blood and dirt. The commoners crowding around her held her motionless for a moment, and then several of the men nearby her pushed a path clear. "Make way for the messenger!" they shouted.

"Harmach Grigor?" the young woman called. "My lord?"

"Over here," Grigor answered. He pushed himself to his feet and held his walking stick up in the air.

The Shieldsworn soldier finally caught sight of him and hurried to his side. "My lord," she said. "I thought to find you in Griffonwatch, but when I passed by on the road the militiamen outside told me you were here. I have dire news."

The harmach visibly steeled himself. "Go on, then," he said gently.

"Lady Kara's been defeated at the Vadarknoll post-tower. The Bloody Skulls and their monsters overwhelmed the army of Hulburg. Many lives were lost. Lady Kara is retreating down the east bank of the Winterspear, fighting to slow the horde with all her strength, but she told me to tell you that she expects the orcs to reach Hulburg by sunrise." The young soldier bit her lip, but continued. "She recommends that you direct the people of the town to take refuge in Griffonwatch, Daggergard, and the best-fortified of the merchant compounds and make the strongest defense you can. She doesn't expect her army to survive the night."

The taproom fell silent. "Disaster compounds upon disaster tonight," Grigor said quietly. He sank back to the bench with his head in his hands. "It seems that Sergen chose the worst possible moment for his treachery."

"Or the best," Geran said darkly. But perhaps Sergen had not anticipated the ferocity of the approaching horde. It would be more than a little ironic if his cousin managed to dethrone the harmach just in time to preside over the destruction of the city. More likely Sergen had simply recognized the Bloody Skull ultimatum as the opportunity to put his plans in motion, never imagining that the threat from the north would actually materialize. He looked at the men and women who filled the Troll and Tankard. Their fierce defiance had vanished in an instant at the news of the defeat. They might succeed in preserving their lives by taking shelter behind strong walls—excluding Griffonwatch for the moment, he reminded himself—but their homes, their workshops, their storehouses, and their livelihoods all lay exposed to destruction. Assuming that the orcs chose not to reduce strongholds like Daggergard or the fortified compounds, they'd still be ruined.

"It would have been wise to wall the city," Harmach Grigor said with a sigh. "We always knew this day might come, but now that it's at hand, I wish doom had chosen some other hour to fall upon us."

Wall the city . . . Geran frowned, thinking furiously. Hulburg had been walled, once. In ancient times, when it had been a much larger city, its wall had passed right over the spot where the Troll and Tankard stood. When the town had been resettled a hundred years ago, his ancestors Angar and Lendon had faced constant orc raids against the fields and farms of the Winterspear Vale. They had raised a simple dike across the Vale to protect the closer farms.

"What about Lendon's Dike?" he asked aloud. "If we brought the entire Spearmeet there and combined our strength with whatever's left of Kara's army, we might be able to stop the Bloody Skulls before they sack the town."

"That's a deadly gamble, m'lord," Durnan Osting said slowly. He whistled between his teeth. "The dike's not much o' defense."

"We'll have a few hours to improve it if we begin right away," Geran pointed out. "Yes, it might be safer to find whatever refuge we can now and give up the town. But maybe it's not too late to save Hulburg."

"What of the Veruna brigands waiting outside Griffonwatch?" Mirya asked. "What's to be done about them?"

Geran frowned. As much as he wanted to use the Spearmeet to storm the Veruna merchant yards and put an abrupt stop to Sergen's designs, the threat of the Bloody Skulls simply dwarfed his cousin's treachery. "Sergen will have to wait until tomorrow," he finally said. "We'll ignore them. They can't do much harm that can't be undone in a few days."

The harmach looked dubious. "Yours is a counsel of desperation, Geran. You know what it is to stake your life on chance, but most of the rest of us do not. It's harder for us than you might think."

Geran lowered his voice and leaned close to his uncle. "I understand, Uncle Grigor. But consider this: Either we tell our folk to hide in cellars and scatter to the Highfells, or we try to fight off the orcs. If we fight and lose, well, how much worse can that be than if we hadn't fought at all? Hulburg's sacked and our people enslaved in either case. Will the Bloody Skulls show us any more mercy if we spare them another battle? We might as well die fighting."

Harmach Grigor weighed Geran's words for a long moment. Then, slowly, he stood and turned to face the assembled Hulburgans crowding the tavern floor. The townsfolk awaited his words in a hushed silence. "You've all heard what I've heard," he said. "We failed to stop the Bloody Skulls at the head of the Winterspear. My nephew believes we may have one more chance to break the horde before it drowns Hulburg in fire and steel. I need every last man of the Spearmeet to march at once for Lendon's Dike. If we can hold off the orcs until dawn, then perhaps daylight will show us better reason to hope than we can find tonight." Grigor seemed to stand a little taller, and his voice grew stronger. He struck his cane to the floorboards. "I want word sent through all the town for women, children, the infirm, the elderly, all those who cannot bend a bow or hold a spear, to seek refuge immediately. But tell any man or woman who can carry an axe or a hunting bow to come to Lendon's Dike—I don't care whose colors they wear!"

Geran drew his sword and thrust the point into the air. "For Hulburg!" he shouted. "For the harmach!"

"Hulburg! The harmach!" a dozen voices shouted in reply. Then a hundred more joined in, until the tavern trembled with the thunder of their shouts. "Hulburg! The harmach!"

"Captains, gather your musters!" the harmach called, his voice carrying through the din. "Sons and daughters of Hulburg, take up your spears and stand together! We march!"

Twenty-seven

11 Tarsakh, the Year of the Ageless One

The hour after moonset was the worst of the night. Somehow in the darkness the small mercenary contingents of House Marstel and the Double Moon Coster became separated from the rapidly diminishing army of Hulburg and simply vanished into the night. Kara sent her best scouts to find the missing detachments and lead them back to the Vale Road, but she dared not wait for their return. The Red Claw wolf riders snarled and darted at her army's heels at every step, and behind them came the great mass of the Bloody Skull horde. Now that the Bloody Skulls were in the Vale, she had no real hope of stopping them short of Hulburg. All she could do was try to beat the horde to the town and pray that her battered and bloodied soldiers could hold the castles and the fortified merchant compounds. The orcs would tire of their sport and withdraw after a few days, leaving those lucky enough to find shelter behind strong walls and locked gates alive to rebuild . . . but if she allowed the wolf riders to surround her and bring her to bay, she would not even be able to manage that much. Without her soldiers, Griffonwatch and Daggergard would fall, and then nothing at all would be left of Hulburg.

"Stay together, stay in good order!" she called to the weary companies around her. "If you fall out of ranks, the wolf riders will have you! They can't drag us down if we stay in ranks and keep to our places as we march!"

So many have fallen already, she thought dully. Kara was exhausted herself, bruised and nicked in a dozen places from the furious cavalry skirmishes of the last few hours, but she couldn't allow her soldiers to see her flagging or giving in to despair. She wheeled Dancer around and patted the big mare's neck, studying the dark vale behind her retreating army. Half a dozen fires blazed in the blackness where outlying farms and homesteads had already been overrun by bloodthirsty savages. There will be many more of those before sunrise, she told herself.

Her broken companies filed into a narrow cut where the road passed through a belt of beechwoods. She peered into the gloom, searching for danger. Her spellscar-changed eyes, so brilliant by daylight, shimmered with the greenish-blue radiance of glacier ice in darkness; she could see as well as a cat by night, a small consolation for the havoc the Spellplague had wreaked in her. The woods offered little as a place to make a stand, but she had to do something to keep the wolf riders away from her troops.

Kara tapped her heels to Dancer's flanks and cantered over to the Icehammer company, her standard-bearer and her adjutants following her. The mercenaries trudged along in grim silence in the middle of her force. Kara reined in to walk alongside the rearmost ranks. "Where's your captain?" she asked the dwarves there.

"I'm here, Lady Hulmaster." The black-bearded dwarf Kendurkkel pushed his way through the marching files of his company. He carried a heavy crossbow over his shoulder and a battle axe with its haft thrust through his belt, but still he gripped his pipe between his teeth. "What d'you want?"

"We need to teach the goblins not to follow us too closely," Kara said. "You've got crossbowmen among your company, and most of them are dwarves who can see in the dark better than the rest of us. I want you to set up a skirmish line here in these trees and greet the goblins with a volley or two when they follow us in here."

"You're wantin' me lads t'take a turn at rearguard, you mean." Kendurkkel frowned. "If those wolf riders go 'round the woods, they'll catch us here neat as you please, and me poor mother won't ever lay eyes on her foolish son agin'."

"I'll be waiting with all the riders we have left just on the other side of the woods," Kara answered. "If the goblins go around you, we'll hold them off and give you a chance to get clear."

Kendurkkel looked up at her, taking her measure. "I don't doubt you'll do as you say, but this sort o' extra work ain't in me contract, Lady Hulmaster."

Kara restrained a sudden impulse to simply ride the Icehammer captain down under her hooves and leaned over her pommel to fix her eyes on the dwarf's face. She lowered her voice even further. "You may not have noticed, Captain, but this is now a question of *survival,* not contracts. If our hodgepodge army breaks apart in the next mile because the wolf riders cut us apart from behind, there's an excellent chance that *none* of us will reach Hulburg alive. It's in your own best interest to give the goblins a bloody nose or at least make them ride around the woods."

The dwarf chewed on the stem of his pipe, staring coldly up at her. Then he sighed and said, "All right, Lady Hulmaster. We'll do as you ask. This whole business is sourin' fast anyway, so I s'pose we ain't got much t'lose." The dwarf turned away and shouted to his mercenaries. "Icehammers, off the road! We're t'lay a little ambush right here for any goblins or worgs stupid 'nough t' stick their heads in a noose."

"Three good volleys are all we need," Kara told him. She watched the Icehammers scramble into the woods on each side of the road and left Kendurkkel pointing with the stem of his pipe and barking orders to his men.

She cantered a couple of hundred yards farther on to the place where the road broke out into open fields again, and collected all the cavalry she had left—twoscore Shieldsworn and about twice that number of men and women called out from the various merchant contingents. She sent pickets out to each side to watch for wolf riders coming around the small belt of woods then settled down to wait. She would have preferred to stay close to the Icehammers, but it was simply too important to make sure that the hundred riders she had at this spot went in the right direction when the enemy appeared. She was afraid that the merchant armsmen would simply ride off for home if she didn't remain to hold them in place.

One of the young Shieldsworn waiting next to her—Sarise, her standard-bearer—leaned close and asked softly, "M'lady, what's going to become of us? What'll be left of Hulburg when this's all over?"

Kara felt the stillness of other riders nearby. They were listening for her answer too. She considered her words before answering. "Sarise, I don't know," she said. "But I know that our castles can shelter hundreds of people for a long time. Many others will escape by ship or by the coastal trails. I don't think the orcs can take Griffonwatch without a long siege, and I doubt that they'll have the patience for it. In time they'll leave, and the town will be ours again. But for now, the longer we hold off the Bloody Skulls, the more of our people will live. It's not what I would've hoped for, but it's the best we can do."

Sarise frowned, but she nodded. "Thank you, Lady Kara," she said softly.

Kara started to say more, but the snarls and howls of wolves came to her ears from the dark woods behind her. Dancer snorted and shifted nervously as did the other horses; they knew that sound, and they didn't like it. The ranger turned her mount and peered into the gloomy shadows beneath the trees. The woods weren't thick, and she could glimpse a handful of the dwarves as they crouched and waited. "They're coming through the woods," she breathed. It was up to the Icehammers now.

She heard the snap and thrum of crossbows, then scores of them firing almost as one, followed an instant later by a great chorus of goblin shrieks and wolves yipping in pain. "Steady," she told the riders around her. "We've got to cover the Icehammers when they break off their fight. Steady, everyone."

More crossbows sang in the night, and the chorus of pained cries changed into the ugly, incoherent roar of battle—hundreds of voices shouting and screaming, some in pain, some in fear, some in anger, some in victory. The deep voices of dwarves, the high harsh cries of goblins, and the fury of worgs all blended in a long, rolling battle-thunder that seemed to echo from the steep hillsides cupping the Winterspear Vale. It went on and on, much longer than Kara would have imagined, until she found herself leaning forward in her saddle and peering into the woods to see if she could see anything of the fighting a short distance off. But after a time the shouts and ring of steel on steel faded again, and Icehammers began to trot out of the woods—human mercenaries groping through the darkness, dwarves jogging along with slower strides but a much better sense of where they were headed.

"Lady Kara, the pickets to the right say that there're goblin scouts on the eastern edge o' the woods," one of her adjutants reported.

"Very well," she answered. She hardly felt as calm as she tried to sound, but that was her duty, to act as if she had expected everything that had happened tonight. She looked at a Shieldsworn sergeant nearby. "Kars, take your troop and the Jannarsk men there, and go drive off the scouts. Keep them from coming around the woods for half an hour, and then rejoin the column. If there are too many wolf riders to handle, use your discretion, but make sure you send word to me."

The sergeant touched his knuckle to his brow. "Yes, m'lady," he said. He gathered eight of the remaining Shieldsworn and a dozen of the Jannarsk Coster armsmen, and the small band rode off into the night. Kara wondered whether she would see them again.

Dancer snorted and stamped suddenly, and Kara saw motion beneath the trees off to her right. The brush thrashed and an ugly chorus of snarls came to her ears, and then goblin wolf riders suddenly broke through the treeline, chasing after the Icehammers as the mercenaries fell back.

"Take them!" she shouted, standing in her stirrups with her bow in her hand. She drew and fired, drew and fired again, and a goblin and worg went down together, each with an arrow in the throat. Her remaining riders charged at the enormous wolves, lances lowered and sabers high. The overeager goblins wheeled in panic and bounded back for the safety of the woods, but not before more fell under the steel of the Shieldsworn and the House mercenaries. Kara shot one more worg through its spine as it leaped away; the monster howled and crashed into a blackberry thicket, throwing its rider. The goblin dismounted was not much of a threat—but worgs could drag down men or horses. She searched for another target but decided to save her arrows. She might need them more before the night was out.

Several other quick skirmishes broke out along the woodline as wolf riders blundered too close to the soldiers they were hoping to chase down. After a dozen slashing duels of wolf rider and cavalryman, the woods fell silent again. Kara judged that the Red Claws had fallen back to mass for a more deliberate attack; this would be the moment to pull back again. The Icehammers were already marching south off the field, falling into ranks as they hurried away. It'll have to be enough, she told herself, praying that she'd bought her ragged army half an hour's lead on the pitiless marauders who followed them.

"Fall back!" she called to the riders nearby. "Stay with me!"

Kara cantered a few hundred yards farther down the road, her small company of riders following her standard as best they could. Then she wheeled around again, searching the open space they'd just crossed for any sign of pursuit. If the Red Claws pressed too close, she'd have to lead her weary riders against them to give the Icehammers time to put another mile under their boots, but for the moment it seemed the wolf riders had learned a little caution.

"Lady Kara!" Sarise called. "A rider!"

Kara looked back over her shoulder and saw a strapping young man with the beginnings of a thick beard approaching—one of the Ostings, she thought. His horse was badly blown, trembling with exhaustion, and the young man slid out of the saddle as soon as he saw her. "Lady Kara, there you are! I'm Brun Osting, and I've got a message from the harmach himself. He told me to tell you to gather whatever forces you've still got and march at once for Lendon's Dike. He's bringing the Spearmeet up from Hulburg, and he plans to make the stand for the city there."

"Lendon's Dike?" Kara asked sharply. That didn't seem wise to her. It was almost a mile and a half long. Between what was left of her battered army and the Spearmeet, they simply didn't have the numbers to defend a line of that length. And she doubted that the Spearmeet could stand up to the Bloody Skulls for long, wall or no wall. "I don't think we can hold it, even with the Spearmeet. We'd be better off to fall back to the strongpoints in town."

"The harmach said you might say that. He said to tell you that he's had to abandon Griffonwatch. Some sort o' terrible ghostly warriors overran the castle earlier tonight, and they're still there." The tavernkeeper's son looked around to see who was in earshot, and lowered his voice. "And House Veruna men were waitin' outside to barricade the gates, Lady Kara. Many o' the harmach's folk were killed, but all your kin got out safe."

Kara shook her head in denial. "This makes no sense. Ghosts in Griffonwatch and the Veruna soldiers barricading them in? Are you sure you've got this message straight from the harmach?"

"I saw 'em myself up on the battlements, Lady Kara." Brun Osting shuddered. "Spirits o' ancient warriors, carryin' pale swords and wearin' tall helms. The harmach said he knew it'd all sound like madness, but he wanted me to repeat this to you: You've got to bring your army to Lendon's Dike as quick as you can. He's going to stand and fight there. And he wanted you to watch your back 'round the Verunas."

"That's better than a fifth of my army," Kara answered. How was she supposed to pay attention to the battle—no, the retreat—if she was supposed to be on guard against assassination or treachery too? She looked around to get her bearings in the darkened vale. They'd been fighting and falling back for hours, and with surprise she saw that they were about halfway to Hulburg already. The old earthworks were not more than a couple of miles ahead. They'd be able to reach the dike easily enough, but what then? "I've got to speak with him myself," she said aloud. "Sarise, go find Captain Ironthane and tell him he's got command of the rear guard until I return. Have Master Osting relay his report to the captain. I'm riding ahead."

"It isn't safe to ride alone, my lady," one of her adjutants pointed out.

"Then you, and you, and you—come with me, if you can keep up." Kara pointed at several of the Shieldsworn riders nearby and rode off over the darkened fields, cutting cross-country. The Vale Road was full of her soldiers, and she didn't want them to think she was abandoning the field. She hoped that Kendurkkel wouldn't think so, either, but so far the dwarf captain had quickly grasped her commands and intentions. He'd understand that she was not leaving them.

Kara led her small band through muddy fields thick with the stubble of last year's planting, until they found an old lane between homesteads that more or less paralleled the Vale Road. She set her spurs to Dancer and let the big mare stretch out her legs on the road, while her guards hurried to keep up with her. The rush of cold night air drove away her weariness. After a good run, she saw a long, straight row of trees rising up across her path—the old berm, long since overgrown with thickets and young trees. Scores of torches and lanterns burned along its length. "It seems the Spearmeet's already here," she said to herself. She veered back toward the Vale Road and in a few more minutes of riding climbed back onto the road a short distance from the place where it cut through the embankment.

Dozens of men worked furiously to build thornbrakes across the road. Along the earthworks more Hulburgans worked with axe and hatchet to make the top of the dike defensible. Now that she was closer to the old berm, she saw that the trees and tangled briar-patches covering its slopes made it a more formidable obstacle than she remembered; the men and women of the Spearmeet were felling trees and piling up brush on the north face of the dike to improve it even more. If only she had more archers, she might have a chance to hold it—at least for a little while.

"There, m'lady," one of her riders said to her. He pointed to an improvised banner fluttering in the torchlight, a simple white field with a blue blazon on it. "The harmach."

"I see it," Kara replied. She rode up to the simple banner, and there she found half a dozen Spearmeet captains gathered around Harmach Grigor, along with Master Assayer Dunstormad Goldhead, the Master Mage Ebain Ravenscar, her cousin Geran, and—surprisingly—the tiefling sorcerer Sarth she'd seen by the barrow on the Highfells. The world seems to have gone mad tonight, she thought. She leaped down from Dancer's saddle and strode over to the harmach. She couldn't remember the last time he'd left the city; he stood leaning on his cane, a thin cloak whipping around him in the bitter night.

"My lord Harmach," she said formally. "I am here."

Grigor Hulmaster looked around and found a crooked smile of relief. "Kara, I'm glad to see that you're well," he said. "I was afraid for you, my dear."

"Brun Osting said I'm to bring my army here. We're on our way. You should see my leading companies any time now, and my rear guard's less than an hour off. But, Uncle Grigor—the Bloody Skulls won't be far behind us. Are you sure this is where you want to stand?"

"It's here or nowhere, Kara," the harmach said. "Griffonwatch is taken. We have no castle to fall back to."

Kara glanced at the other Hulburgans nearby and lowered her voice. "I heard that *ghosts* invaded Griffonwatch? Is that true?"

Harmach Grigor nodded. "I'm afraid that it is, and I'm sorry to say that it seems to be your stepbrother's doing. He and his Veruna allies tried to kill us all tonight. If not for the fact that Geran and his friends took it upon themselves to arrange his escape from my prison and rescue me, I think Sergen would have succeeded."

"That was the price the King in Copper paid for the *Infiernadex* after House Veruna got it for him," Geran explained. "He agreed to send his specters to serve when called. It seems Sergen decided to call them tonight."

"Given the circumstances, I've pardoned Geran of any wrongdoing in his duel with the Veruna captain and in his escape," the harmach added. "And should we run across Sergen again, we must treat him and his Veruna allies as enemies of Hulburg."

Kara lowered her voice. "The Verunas with my army have done their part so far tonight. They've fought as well as any of us. This makes no sense. Are you saying that they'll turn on us at some point?"

"It'd be wise to expect them to," Geran said. "They might be waiting for the right opportunity to show their true colors."

The ranger laughed bitterly. "Geran, they've had *many* opportunities for treachery tonight. All they had to do was abandon the field, and we probably would've been destroyed three times over."

Sarth cleared his throat. "Forgive me for saying so, but the explanation may be quite simple: Perhaps things have not gone as House Veruna planned tonight. After your initial defeat they may have decided that it would be folly to carry through with their plan in the face of an orc invasion."

Kara frowned. She didn't know how the horned man had come to be standing at Geran's side, but she simply did not have time to satisfy her curiosity. With effort she set aside the questions still dancing in her mind and focused on the immediate crisis. "I'll ask for a complete explanation later," she said. "Uncle Grigor, I expect the Bloody Skulls to reach this spot in an hour, perhaps two. I would guess that I'm down to six hundred tired men—less if you tell me that the Verunas can't be counted on. How many Spearmeet do you have with you?"

"Around eight hundred, I think," Geran answered. "About half are here already, and the rest are marching up from Hulburg as quickly as they can." She frowned dubiously. Geran saw her skepticism and added, "They're not as good as your Shieldsworn or your mercenaries, but they're fighting with their homes and families at their backs. They'll do better than you might think, Kara."

"I don't think it will be enough," Kara said. "The Bloody Skulls outnumber us by a margin of at least two to one, maybe closer to three to one."

"We didn't choose this fight, but it's ours nonetheless," Harmach Grigor told her. "Somehow, we have to find a way to win it. We simply have no alternative. Now, Kara, given what you've seen so far, what can we do to give ourselves the best chance for success?"

Kara looked at the old dike extending off into the darkness to either side. She noticed that a pale gray streak had appeared above the jagged shadows of the hills and peaks of the Highfells to the east. Dawn was not far off . . . if they lasted that long. She thought furiously, considering the problem from every angle while the others waited for her to organize her thoughts. "We'll need to intersperse the Spearmeet and the professional soldiers," she finally said. "Alternate a company of militia and a company of Shieldsworn or mercenaries to man the top of the dike. And then we'll need to keep most of our cavalry together in reserve behind the dike, so that we can try to seal breaches in our line as they happen."

"Good," said Harmach Grigor. "What else, Kara?"

She studied the men and women swarming over the dike, and sighed. "I suppose it wouldn't hurt to pray," she said.

Twenty-Eight

11 Tarsakh, the Year of the Ageless One

If Geran was any judge of the weather, the approaching day promised to be bright and cold. The skies were cloudless, but a cold wind gusted and moaned over the vale, making the meager handful of banners and pennants over Hulburg's defenders ruffle and snap. He wished the wind would have chosen a different quarter for the battle to come. It was blowing in the faces of the hundreds of men and women waiting along the top of the dike, and it would hinder what little archery they'd scraped together for the fight. On the other hand, orcs don't care for bright sunlight, Geran reminded himself. The disadvantages of weather seemed equal to both sides.

"When d'you think they'll come at us, Geran?" Durnan Osting said quietly. The brewer and his company of Spearmeet volunteers lined the top of the dike to each side of Geran. Kara and Harmach Grigor had entrusted Geran with command of the right wing of their small army—two Spearmeet companies, a battered band of Shieldsworn, and a motley collection of mercenaries from Marstel, Sokol, and the Double Moon. He needed about three times as many men to properly defend the length of wall he had, but there simply weren't any more to spare.

"Soon, Durnan," Geran answered. "Before the sun comes up, I think, and that's not far off now."

The valley floor was a patchwork of gray shadows, growing brighter by the minute. On Geran's end of the line, Lendon's Dike climbed to meet the steep wall on the east side of the Winterspear vale. From Geran's elevated vantage, he could see the torch-dotted line of the earthworks stretching across the valley floor to the inky shadow of Lake Hul, a mile and a half away under the western margin of the vale. The old dwarf Dunstormad Goldhead and Burkel Tresterfin's Spearmeet company held the spot where the dike met the lake, strengthened by the Veruna mercenaries. In the center of the line, where the Vale Road pierced the old dike, the harmach's banner fluttered. Kara and most of the Shieldsworn were there, along with the Icehammer mercenaries and the weaker Spearmeet companies. The heaviest blow would fall right in the middle of the line; Geran could see the dark, seething mass of the orc horde gathering only a few hundred yards from the dike.

The valley shook with orc shouts and chants. Dozens of massive drums thumped and battled with each other, and the clamor of spears striking shields was overwhelming. Geran looked at the militiamen around him; he saw faces gray with anxiety, knuckles white as they clenched their weapons close.

"Come on, lads!" he shouted to the men nearby. "Let's make a little noise of our own. Show them that we're still here!" He raised a piercing war cry, and the men nearby joined in. Within a few moments the cry spread up and down along the dike until hundreds of men were shouting together against the orc horde. The orcs were far louder, but Geran kept at it, and he heard the small echo of his warriors' voices rolling back from the hills amid the orc clamor.

"A vain gesture," Sarth muttered from close by, but a moment later the tiefling joined his voice to Geran's and shouted defiance as well. Vain or not, Geran thought that the men around him looked a little less frightened. Perhaps they felt that way, too. He wished Hamil were at his back, but the halfling hadn't been able to march; Geran had left him at the Troll and Tankard.

The orc chant reached a crescendo then broke apart into countless individual roars and cries. The front line of the Bloody Skull army surged forward and swept over the unplanted fields toward the dike—thousands of orc warriors, running headlong into battle with axes and spears high.

"Here they come!" Durnan Osting shouted. "Get ready for 'em, lads! They'll no' find a weak spot here!"

Geran drew his sword, weaving spells of ruin on his blade. The elven steel gleamed a deadly silver-blue in the gloaming, and he flicked the point from side to side to set the grip in his hand. He hadn't expected the orcs to simply rush the entire line at once; it would have been more effective to concentrate a blow at a single point. Then again, the mass charge would keep him from sending help to any other point of the defenses as long as he was fighting to hold his own position. "Archers!" he shouted. "Fire at will!"

He had only a few dozen bowmen under his banner, so few that there was little point in trying to volley their fire. Most of the archers had no experience with the tactic, anyway—they weren't even militiamen, just Hulburgans or foreign laborers who'd joined the effort to defend the town. Their arrows hissed out over the earthen rampart. Many missed, but as the orcs continued to close, Geran saw a few of the charging warriors stumble and fall.

"Sarth, save your spells for the moment," Geran told the sorcerer. "I want your magic at the point of decision."

"I understand," Sarth answered.

Geran watched the dark tide rushing closer and seized the shoulder of a young Spearmeet lad next to him. "Get over to the far right, and tell whoever's in charge of the Marstels and Sokols to bring all their men here, right now. We're going to need them. Go swiftly!" The teenager nodded once and bolted off to the east, heading for the handful of mercenary fighters Geran had on that end of his line. Few of the orcs were heading toward the uphill side of the dike. Then he faced the oncoming horde and breathed a few words of warding, preparing for the fight to come.

The first of the Bloody Skulls reached the bottom of the dike. The old earthworks were not more than fifteen feet tall, but heavy brush and small trees grew thickly on the sloping mound; despite the ferocity of their charge, the orc warriors had a difficult time struggling through the thickets.

"Stay in ranks!" Geran shouted. "Let them come to you!"

A band of orc berserkers bulled their way up the embankment near Geran, and he hurried through the thickets to meet them when they crested the wall. He caught a thick-muscled orc axeman as he scrambled up the slope with a hand on the ground, and lunged down to bury his sword-point in the orc's neck. The apelike warrior bellowed, clapping his hand to the wound, and staggered up to swing at Geran. The swordmage danced back a few steps, avoiding the orc's wild axe-swings until the dying warrior's feet slid out from underneath him and he fell heavily to the ground. Geran found more orcs swarming up the slope all around him, and for a hundred furious heartbeats he slashed and stabbed, charged and retreated, wielding his blade of elf-wrought steel in a blinding blur of searing blue-white radiance.

"For Hulburg! For the harmach!" Geran shouted.

All around him Hulburgans set their spears in a deadly fence atop the dike and took a heavy toll on the orcs who recklessly attacked into the teeth of their defenses. They died too, overwhelmed by the sheer strength and fury of the orc assault. Near Geran's banner Durnan Osting killed three orcs with a two-handed warhammer before several more swarmed over him and hacked him to pieces with their war axes. More Spearmeet men fell there, cut down as the Bloody Skulls scrambled up the suddenly undefended slope. But then the sorcerer Sarth stepped forward and sealed the breach with a devastating blast of fire from his fearsome rod, burning down most of the berserkers. "To the banner!" the tiefling cried. He held off the orc assault until the mercenaries Geran had summoned from the unengaged end of his line showed up and filled in to take the place of Durnan Osting and the other fallen Spearmeet there.

A shriek from overhead wrenched Geran's attention from the roaring line of orcs trying to overwhelm the dike. He looked up and saw a huge bat-winged shape swoop low over the line of defenders. It seized a man in its talons and started to beat its way back into the air. Its tail whipped around to sink a long, wicked stinger into the back of another man fighting nearby as the monster flapped away from the dike. The stung man arched in agony and sank to the ground, and the monster dropped its first victim among the seething ranks of orcs pressing close to climb the dike.

"A wyvern too?" Geran muttered aloud. They hardly needed any more trouble. He hurried after the flying monster, trying to guess where it would swoop next.

Sarth conjured a bolt of lightning and blasted half a dozen orcs from the top of the embankment. The brilliant flash of light and deafening thunderclap caught the wyvern's attention. It wheeled in midair and fixed its eyes on the sorcerer. The reptilian monster plummeted down at Sarth from directly overhead, deadly sting whipping from side to side behind it.

"Sarth!" Geran shouted, but the sorcerer did not hear him; he was already snarling another spell at more Bloody Skulls surging up the dike. Geran realized in an instant that even if he caught the sorcerer's attention, the wyvern would still be upon him too quickly to dodge or avoid. There was no time to reach him; Geran seized the flowering symbols of a spell held in his mind and hurled his will behind the arcane words. *"Sierollanie dir mellar!"* he cried, and in a dizzying eyeblink he stood where Sarth had been standing, while the sorcerer stood where he'd been. Sarth reeled and floundered on the slope, but Geran paid him no mind—he was already looking up at the wyvern hurling down at him. He shouted out a word of shielding, and then the monster was upon him. He slashed it once across its snout, leaped aside and blocked the deadly stinger with his shielding spell, and spun around to rake his blade across its wing as it hurtled past him. The wyvern screeched once in rage and tried to beat for altitude again, but it was too fast and too low. Its damaged wing buckled and the monster cartwheeled across the embankment. For a moment it lay still, tangled up in the brush, but then it shook itself and clambered to its clawed feet, glaring at Geran with pure hate.

"I think I just made it angry," Geran muttered.

He put his point between the wyvern and himself and dropped into a fighting crouch, holding his shielding spell firmly in his left hand. The monster charged at him with the speed of a striking snake, far faster than Geran would have imagined. He managed to parry the sting once, then twice, but then the wyvern got its jaws clamped around his right leg and worried him like dog. It whipped him from side to side and then flung him away; Geran's sword flew from his hand, and he hit the ground hard enough that his vision went black for an instant. When he could see again, the wyvern was darting toward him, yellow fangs gleaming. He started to climb to his feet, only to find that the world swayed drunkenly when he tried to sit up.

The wyvern hissed and sprang at him—but a coruscating green ray struck it in mid-leap and knocked it aside. An instant later Sarth appeared by Geran's side and shouted another of his spells. A barrage of shrieking purple darts shot from his scepter and pinioned the wyvern to the ground; the monster snapped and snarled at the phantasmal javelins transfixing it, then shuddered and fell still.

"Are you all right?" the tiefling said.

"I think so," Geran answered him. Sarth reached down and helped him to his feet; the swordmage staggered over to his sword and picked it up. "I hope there aren't any more of those around."

The tiefling scanned the skies anxiously. "Thank you, Geran Hulmaster. I did not see the monster's dive. But next time, I'll ask you to give me a moment's warning before you teleport me."

Geran looked around, trying to get a sense of the battle. He could see several places where the orcs had overwhelmed the dike, and scores of the ferocious warriors fought to widen the breaches and push on past the weakened defenses. Human riders did their best to counter the breaches, as did haphazard bands of the volunteers who had shown up to fight. With lance and bow they held back the black tide, but they were failing fast. "Gods, what chaos!"

"It seems the issue is still in doubt," Sarth replied—an understatement if Geran had ever heard one.

Geran spied a large breach less than a hundred yards away. Orcs were fighting their way east and west along the top of the dike, rolling up the defenders still trying to hold back the rest of the attack. "There," he said, pointing. "Try to do something about that, and I'll see what I can do here."

The tiefling nodded grimly and leaped into the sky. In a moment he hovered over the orc breakthrough, hurling blasts of fire down on the Bloody Skull warriors. Geran started to rejoin the fray, but a rider came galloping up from behind Lendon's Dike.

"Lord Geran! Lord Geran!" the messenger called. "Lady Kara says to bring any troops you can spare and come to the center at once! She needs help there."

"Spare? I can't spare any!" Geran replied.

The rider was a young Shieldsworn, bloodied and disheveled, and he simply stared at Geran in confusion. The swordmage grimaced and glanced around at his part of the field. Kara wouldn't have asked for help unless she needed it, he told himself. She knew how many soldiers he had on his part of the line. He held up his hand and said to the messenger, "No, wait. I'll bring as many as I can."

The swordmage climbed back up to the top of the dike and found the young soldier carrying his banner. "Shieldsworn, to me!" he shouted. "Marstel, Double Moon, to me! Assemble on the south side of the dike! Spearmeet, House Sokol, stand your ground!"

All along the earthen wall, soldiers of Hulburg began to disengage, backing down the dike while the miltiamen on either side spread out to try to cover their absence. It left Geran's line woefully thin—another concerted attack would certainly punch through. But Geran realized that his hodgepodge force had largely repulsed the first rush of the Bloody Skulls. The dawn was a thin orange sliver clinging to the hilltops of eastern Highfells; sunrise could not be far off now. By the growing light he could see that the embankment was littered with dead or wounded orcs, and that many of the ironclad warriors of the Bloody Skull horde were shifting across his front, flowing toward the middle of the fight.

Geran looked around and found Brun Osting, the son of Durnan, standing by the tattered flag of his Spearmeet company. He hurried over to the young brewer and clapped a hand on his shoulder. "I've got to go help in the center," he told him. "I'm leaving you in charge here. You Spearmeet have to hold this end of the line on your own. I'll leave you the Sokols to help, and the sorcerer Sarth there. Can you do it?"

The young man nodded soberly. "We don't have much choice, do we? We'll hold the line or die where we stand, Lord Geran."

"Good fortune," Geran said. He squeezed the young man's shoulder, and then hurried down the back of the dike to the spot where his small company was assembling. It was a little less than a hundred strong, and he wondered if it would be enough to make a difference in the heavy fighting in the middle. He took a moment to speak with the Sokol captain—a fierce-looking Turmishan woman whose detachment was down to a dozen riders—and point out Brun to her. Whether she'd follow the brewer's orders, he had no idea, but at least she hadn't ridden away from the battle yet.

"Where to, Lord Geran?" one of the Shieldsworn footmen called from the ranks.

"The Vale Road!" Geran called back. "They need us in the center, lads. Let's go lend them a hand. Follow me!"

He set out at an easy jog, holding back his pace so that the soldiers in their heavier armor could keep up. It helped that they were moving downhill and had only five or six hundred yards to travel. Sporadic fighting continued atop the dike a short distance to Geran's right, but he passed no more major breaches. In a few moments they came in sight of the furious melee swirling around the spot where the Vale Road pierced the embankment. Hundreds of orcs thronged the gap, pushing inward against a thinning line of Icehammers and Shieldsworn.

Geran looked around for Kara's banner or the harmach, and saw nothing but pitched battle. He would've liked to know where she wanted his small strike to fall, but one glance was enough to show him that he couldn't wait. Strange, he thought. For all the years I've lived with a sword in my hand, I've never fought in a real battle, only duels and skirmishes—nothing more than twenty or thirty warriors on a side. After traveling for ten years all over Faerûn, I find the biggest battle of my life not three miles from the castle where I was born.

The men behind him said nothing, staring at the scene in nervous silence. Geran shook himself free of his weary musings and tried to think quickly and well about what he could see in front of him. He had little gift for strategy, so he tried to see the battle as a duel of sorts. The orc spearhead had pushed deep into the center like a reckless and powerful lunge at the center of an opponent's torso; if someone came at him with an attack like that, what would he do? "I wouldn't try to stop it," he murmured to himself. "I'd deflect the point, let it go past me, and then strike at my foe's hand." That suggested a strike not at the tip of the spear, but back a little farther. Geran looked back toward the gap in the embankment and saw that a few Hulburgan soldiers still fought along the dike to each side of the breach. If he moved along the inside of the dike and hit the orcs on their flank, perhaps he'd succeed in knocking their thrust aside.

He drew his sword and signaled to the men following him. "After me, lads!" he cried. "We're going to cut them off and trap them inside our lines!" Then Geran shouted a battle cry and ran ahead of his hodgepodge company, leading them under the cover of the old dike. He heard a ragged chorus of roars and cries behind him. Both orcs and human soldiers looked around in his direction, but Geran didn't slow his steps. Instead he cried out the words of a spell to set his sword aflame with a brilliant white light, and he hurled himself into the torrent of orc warriors pushing their way through the low defile. He cut his way through three or four Bloody Skulls before they even realized their danger, and then the mass of the Shieldsworn and mercenaries behind him drove into the orcs with an audible shock that seemed to shiver the icy morning air.

Geran cut and stabbed with every ounce of skill and lethal purpose he could dredge up, from his boyhood exercises to the long years of study with Myth Drannor's fabled bladesingers. He threw spells where he could, searing his foes with bursts of golden fire, dazzling and disorienting them with deadly enchantments that stupefied thick-thewed berserkers until elven steel drove through flesh and bone. And his small, battered company fought like lions in the narrow gap of the Vale Road. They carried the open breach with the force of their charge. Geran looked up to see Kara dashing through the melee on her fine white charger, plying her deadly bow at a full gallop. She shot down an orc that he was about to engage, and felled another one who was trying to beat his way through a Shieldsworn's guard not ten feet away. "For harmach and Hulburg!" she shouted.

The swordmage whirled where he stood, searching for more foes to engage. To his amazement he realized that the Bloody Skulls who'd forced their way through the gap in the dike had melted away. Dozens of duels and skirmishes continued around him, but the first great thrust was spent—the warriors of Hulburg had held the Vale Road, at least for the moment.

"They're falling back," Geran called to his cousin.

"Not for long," Kara answered. She pointed toward the north, out to the fields beyond the dike. Geran followed the point of her sword, and his heart sank. A few hundred yards away, around the great black banners at the center of the Bloody Skull horde, hundreds of orc warriors stamped and shouted and struck their spears to their shields. An armored wedge of lumbering ogres stood at their head, bellowing their crude challenges. Kara's eyes glowed with their uncanny blue fire, smoldering in the shadows of her helm. "That was only the first attack. The next one's gathering already."

Geran shook the blood off his blade and turned to face the ogres and orcs streaming back into the fight. He readied himself to sell his life as dearly as he could—and then a thin, cold breath of wind suddenly stirred the ground around him, turning the wet grass white with hoarfrost. Sinister voices whispered dark things on the wind, and a sense of icy dread clutched at his heart like a murderer's hand. He shivered and faltered back several steps. The rosy glow of sunrise faded to dull gray, and streamers of pale fog seemed to coalesce from the very air, darkening the dawn. Stout-hearted dwarves groaned in fear and hid their faces, while men who had fought valiantly for hours let their futile blades slip from nerveless fingers. Even the bloodthirsty orcs pouring across the fields slowed and stopped, halting well short of the sinister fog.

A dull scraping caught his attention, and Geran looked down at the black earth under his feet. Dirt buckled upward, stirred from beneath. Then a skeletal hand thrust up into the chill, deadly mists of the morning. He backed away from it, only to find another bony hand clutching at his heels. He kicked his foot free with a sudden burst of panic. Scores of the things—dirt-encrusted skeletons still draped in the rusted remnants of ancient armor—were dragging themselves up out of the ground.

"What foul necromancy is this?" Kara snarled into the freezing fog. Her horse Dancer shied away in panic, her eyes rolling. The ranger threw a panicked look in Geran's direction. "We can't fight the undead and the orcs at the same time!"

"This is Sergen's doing!" Geran snarled. The rogue Hulmaster's undead allies had failed to kill the harmach at Griffonwatch, so now he was trying again . . . and that meant that his cousin had to be somewhere near, since Aesperus had said that the wielder of the amulet could not send the lich's minions far. Geran wondered if Sergen's House Veruna allies were making their move as well. Doubtless Sergen would order the undead to spare the Verunas, but the rest of the Hulburgan army was in dire peril. "Stand your ground as long as you can, and protect the harmach!" he called to Kara. "I have to find Sergen before the dead overwhelm us all!"

Turning his back on the skeletal ranks assembling themselves before the defenders of Hulburg, Geran sheathed his blade and ran into the frigid mists.

Twenty-nine

11 Tarsakh, the Year of the Ageless One

Geran loped through the unnatural murk as night seemed to descend over the vale a second time. The eerie fog thickened by the heartbeat, closing in around him like a tomb of cold gray stone. It felt as if he were blundering through a damp gray vault, a spectral dungeon that was slowly becoming more substantial, more threatening, with every passing moment. Soldiers appeared like ghosts in the mist, dark forms that drifted past or simply stood where they were, shivering in terror. He almost ran onto the spearpoint of a shambling skeleton draped in the remains of a lord's robes, and he retreated quickly from a pair of ancient berserkers whose jawbones hung open in silent howls of battle-madness and rage.

All around him in the mist he heard the battle resume in a dozen places at once, but instead of the bellowing of ogres and the war cries of bloodthirsty orcs, he heard only the whispering of dry dead voices and the shrieks of human pain and terror. In the frost-heavy mists, sounds seemed distant and uncertain; Geran couldn't really tell if he was moving away from the fight or circling around to stumble into it again. Why didn't I make sure of Sergen when I had the chance? he berated himself. Perhaps Sergen's mercenaries would have cut him down if he'd paused for the moment necessary to administer a killing blow, but it might have been worth his life to make sure that the traitor didn't survive to summon more undead.

Geran came to a low rise and scrambled to the top of a frost-slick knoll, hoping to get above the dense fog. From the top of the little hill, he thought that the fog directly overhead looked noticeably brighter, but he could see little else. He turned in a circle, searching for any sign of his cousin. "Think, Geran, think!" he admonished himself. Sergen was wounded and likely not interested in getting any closer to the fighting against the Bloody Skulls than he had to; he'd be somewhere on the south side of the old dike and well back from the battle—probably somewhere near the Verunas. House Veruna was over on the left flank of the line by Lake Hul, anchoring the western end of Lendon's Dike.

He caught sight of a war-horse standing over its fallen rider, a young cavalryman of House Sokol. Geran hurried to the animal and caught its reins. The horse whickered and shied away, but Geran patted its muzzle to calm it, whispered a few words in Elvish, and then swung himself up into the saddle. His new mount snorted and pranced nervously, but he set his heels to its flanks and kicked it into a run. Fortunately the horse was well trained and eager for a rider to guide it; its hooves kicked up wet clods of turf as it cantered across the muddy fields.

A skeleton carrying a round bronze shield suddenly lurched into his path, its rusted sword ready to strike. Geran swept out his own blade and parried the ancient iron; a jolt of frozen fire ran up his sword arm from the impact, but he circled his point underneath the skeleton's blade and rammed it home in the creature's empty eye socket. Shards of bone burst from the back of the skull, and the thing staggered back. Geran wrenched his sword free and rode past. When he glanced over his shoulder, the skeleton was moving away to find another foe to fight, seemingly untroubled by the horrible wound he'd just dealt it. Necromantic magic knitted its dead sinews and yellowed bones together. What was a sword wound to such a creature?

Geran dodged away from several more encounters with the skeletal warriors. On one occasion he spurred his mount right over a skeleton in front of him. The warhorse knocked the horrid thing to the ground, crushing bones beneath its heavy iron-shod hooves, and that one did not rise again. Then he seemed to break out of the heaviest mist and found himself a few hundred yards west of the Vale Road, a short distance behind the old dike. The supernatural chill of the fog diminished a little, and he could see more of the sky graying overhead—the day would have been clear and cold, though he doubted it would have much power over the fell mists.

On that end of the line battered Spearmeet companies still held the dike, with a number of Veruna footmen stiffening their lines. More than a few men were gazing nervously toward the middle of the battlefield; Geran glanced back the way he had come and saw that the fog darkened over the center of the field like a stationary storm, weirdly still despite the strong, cold wind that swept the rest of the battlefield. A short distance behind the line on the dike, thirty Veruna horsemen and a handful of Shieldsworn riders formed the left wing's cavalry reserve. They sat waiting on their mounts. The orc assault seemed to have retreated for now, likely because the Bloody Skulls were waiting to see if the army of Hulburg would still be standing against them once the evil mists lifted. Geran couldn't fault the orcs' instincts. If some supernatural horror was cutting its way through your enemy's ranks, then there was little reason to rush back to close quarters.

He wheeled his mount around, looking for Sergen—and then he found him. His stepcousin and a quartet of Council Watch guards sat on riding horses under a stand of hemlocks perhaps a hundred yards away, partially hidden by the ragged tatters of mist that streamed by. It was difficult for Geran to tell what the traitor was doing given the distance and the poor visibility, but he could see several Veruna officers in their tabards of green and white speaking with him. As the swordmage watched, the Veruna men turned their mounts and cantered away, heading back toward their troops.

"What did you tell them, Sergen?" Geran muttered aloud. "Abandon the field? Turn against the Shieldsworn? Or wait and do nothing until the battle is lost?"

With no firm intentions in mind other than to make sure that Sergen didn't get away with whatever he hoped to get away with, Geran tapped his heels to his horse's flanks and broke into a canter, heading for Sergen and his guards. The wet ground and blowing mist muffled the hoofbeats of his mount, and the air grew steadily colder and more still as he drew closer. Sergen wasn't looking at Geran; he was leaning forward in his saddle, looking out over the battle as scattered bands of desperate soldiers struggled to drive off the deathless warriors of the King in Copper. The fighting was fiercest around the banner of the harmach, where better than a hundred soldiers stood together against a ragged wave of skeletons who rose up out of the ground and attacked just as quickly as they were killed or disabled by the soldiers fighting to protect the ruler of Hulburg. Geran couldn't see his uncle, not through the chaos and the murk, but he caught a glimpse of Kara on her fine white charger in the thick of the melee.

Sergen was still unaware of Geran's approach, and now the swordmage was only thirty yards away. Distantly the swordmage noted that the Veruna officers riding back to their troops had caught sight of him. They wheeled and galloped to intercept him, but a desperate plan finally coalesced in Geran's mind, and he spurred his mount into a headlong charge. He had little magic left after the furious skirmish at the Vale Road's cut, but he still had a few words he could call upon. It would have to be enough. He stood up in his stirrups, sword bared in his hand.

"Lord Sergen!" the Veruna officers shouted. "Behind you!"

The council guard closest to Geran turned at the warning. The guard snapped down his visor and drew his sword, shouting something to the men around him. Even as Sergen looked around and the other guards began to turn their mounts to meet Geran's attack, the swordmage raced up alongside the first guard's mount and lashed out with his backsword. Bright steel glittered in the cold mist, shrilly clanging twice as Geran beat his way through the man's guard. He disabled the fellow with a backhand flick of the point that creased its way through the guard's visor. The man cried out and crumpled forward in the saddle, holding his hand to his face; Geran's horse shouldered the guard's mount out of the way, and he drove at his treacherous cousin.

"Sergen!" he snarled.

"To me! To me!" Sergen shouted at his mercenaries. Geran ignored them. Sergen reached awkwardly for the sword at his hip with his unwounded arm, but Geran didn't give him a chance to draw it. With a wordless roar of anger, he hurled himself out of the saddle and tackled Sergen, carrying his stepcousin to the muddy ground underfoot. The impact knocked Geran's breath away, but Sergen cried out sharply as his damaged arm hit the ground. Their momentum rolled them over and over, Geran holding his stepcousin with a grip of iron.

"You fool!" Sergen hissed between his teeth. "You've interfered with my business for the last time, Geran! I swear that I'll see you *dead* before this is done!"

"Then you should've killed me when you had me helpless in a cell," Geran answered.

Sergen reached for a dagger with his good hand, but Geran got on top of him and delivered two sharp punches to the jaw before he had to duck under a sword-swing from one of the council guards. He rolled again to put Sergen on top, using the lord as a shield against his own bodyguards, and then their struggle tumbled them both into the shallow ditch beside the Vale Road.

Sergen managed to wrench his jacket free and threw himself away from Geran, gaining an armslength of clear space. He rolled to his knees and floundered up out of the ditch. "I won't make that mistake again," he snarled at Geran. He motioned for his guards, who rushed to his aid.

Geran scrambled to his feet and retreated a few steps from the grim mercenaries closing in around him. Then he raised his hand and showed Sergen the amulet of Aesperus, which he'd wrenched away from his cousin during their brief struggle. The old copper amulet glinted in the dim light. "I think you've caused enough trouble with this for now, Sergen," he said.

Sergen's hand flew to his chest, and he looked down in horror. When he looked up again, his dark eyes blazed in fury. "Kill him!" he shouted to his guards. "Kill him now!"

Geran glanced around and summoned up what little magic he had left unspent. *"Seiroch!"* he shouted. Sergen's guards thrust their blades through empty air where he'd been standing an instant before, and the teleport spell whisked him a hundred yards away in the blink of an eye.

He found himself standing close to the harmach's banner, surrounded by Shieldsworn who fought desperately against the tide of skeletal warriors. Geran thrust his hand into the air, holding the amulet aloft, and shouted, "Warriors of Aesperus, *halt!* I command you!"

All around him, skeletons abruptly stopped moving. More than a few Hulburgans smashed their axes and swords into skeletal warriors who now stood still. Some of those fell while others suffered the injuries without response, standing motionless. The humans and dwarves out on the field raised a ragged cheer of astonishment and exultation, amazed to find their attackers immobilized.

"I'll be damned," Geran said softly. "It worked!" He felt the empty eyes of the dead warriors settling on him, and the cold whispers in the air seemed to grow stronger, more sinister. He shuddered. If he was going to command these fell creatures, better to do it now before he lost his nerve. "Warriors of

Aesperus, listen to me! You are to attack and destroy the Bloody Skull orcs and their allies—ignore all who are defending Hulburg! Do you understand me?"

The ranks of skeletal warriors seemed to shiver, and the dead ones backed away from their former adversaries and turned to face north. "Aye, we understand thee," they answered in their cold, rasping voices. "We go to do thy bidding." Then they began to march away from the battered bands of humans and dwarves they'd been fighting just a moment ago, old bones clicking like insects, rusted mail squealing and clinking.

The defenders of Hulburg raised a ragged volley of shouts, cries of relief, and calls for help, hundreds of voices babbling once. Several of the men standing near Geran grinned at him and stepped close to slap his back and seize his hand. Then a signal horn blew twice above the din. Geran turned and saw Kara lowering the horn. "Back to the dike-top!" she shouted. "Reform ranks across the road! We aren't done yet!"

Geran looked back at the stand of trees where he'd met Sergen, just visible through the mists. His cousin climbed up into the saddle of his black destrier and glared in Geran's direction, though the swordmage doubted that Sergen could actually pick him out in the middle of the warriors around the harmach's banner. Then Sergen spurred his horse and galloped away to the south, fleeing back toward Hulburg with his guards following. A moment later, the House Veruna soldiers on the left side of the line stepped back from the dike, turned toward the south, and began to march away as well, leaving the battle behind. Geran was sorely tempted to call back some of Aesperus's skeletons in order to send them after Sergen and the Verunas, but he had no idea how strong a hold he really had over the undead warriors or how much they could hurt the Bloody Skulls.

"Let them go for now, Geran." Harmach Grigor limped up and set a hand on Geran's shoulder, following Geran's gaze with his own. The old lord looked pale and haggard, but a spark of defiance animated his features. "At the moment I'd just as soon let a potential adversary leave the field if he has a mind to. We must concentrate on repelling the Bloody Skulls before we pick another fight." Grigor watched the Verunas leave and sighed. "Whatever else happens today, Sergen and House Veruna are finished in Hulburg."

"I know it, Uncle," Geran answered. "But I'm afraid of the mischief Sergen might do before he knows it too."

Grigor nodded. "I am as well, but as Kara said—we aren't done yet here. How did you gain control over the lich king's warriors?"

Geran showed him the amulet. "I took this from Sergen. It's the amulet Aesperus gave to the Verunas in payment for the book he sought." The mist around him was noticeably lightening now, though he could still hear echoing through the fog the roars of orc warriors, the shrill ring of steel on steel, and the fearful bellows of dimwitted ogres. "I don't know how many warriors it summons or how long they'll remain."

"I suppose we'll find out." The old lord smiled. "Well done, Geran."

The swordmage gripped his uncle's shoulder then stepped clear. He held out his empty hand and half-closed his eyes, groping through his mind for the arcane symbols he needed for the spell of returning. *"Cuilledyrr,"* he whispered, and a moment later his Myth Drannan blade came hurtling through the unnatural mist to meet his hand. He'd dropped it when he threw Sergen off his horse, and it was far too valuable a weapon to leave on the battlefield. With his sword in one hand and the amulet in the other, Geran hurried to the old dike and scrambled to the top to see what was going on in the orc ranks.

The cacophony of battle was tremendous, an awful mix of hundreds of savage voices, fell magic, roaring monsters, and more. The eerie fog was too dense for him to see well, but he caught glimpses of fighting a bowshot north of the overgrown dike. The orcs were fierce and brave fighters, but even their most bloodthirsty berserkers had little stomach for a battle against an enemy who shrugged off all but the most powerful of blows and simply climbed back to his feet when he was struck to the ground. All around him the surviving Shieldsworn and Ironhammers peered into the mists, trying to judge for themselves how the fighting went, with a curious mix of relief that they were out of it for the moment and dread of the allies that had turned to their side.

Geran watched for what seemed a long time in the bitter cold. Then he noticed that the amulet in his hand was growing warm. He looked down in surprise and saw that a bright orange gleam had appeared on the ancient copper. "What in the world?" he murmured. The gray mists cloaking the battlefield took on an orange hue and began to thin. The clash of arms from the orc lines faded sharply—and suddenly the morning was full of the Orcish shouts of triumph. As the sun finally climbed above the ragged hills fencing the Winterspear Vale, the ancient amulet quietly crumbled into dust, and the skeletal warriors sank back into the ground.

"Geran! The skeletons!" Kara called.

He looked over at her helplessly. "It's sunrise," he told her. "Aesperus must've promised them for only one night."

She nodded once, and her azure eyes flashed in the morning light. "Stand to your arms!" she ordered the Shieldsworn. Then she lowered her helm's visor, slid down from Dancer's back, and sent the horse toward the rear with a slap to its rump, taking up her position at the head of the footmen guarding the open spot where the Vale Road pierced the dike. "Stand to!"

The unnatural mists cleared just as quickly as they had come, dissipating like dark dreams forgotten in the morning light. The day brightened swiftly, as if the supernatural fog had never been. Now Geran finally got a good look at the orc horde that faced Hulburg. He could see hundreds of orcs lying dead in the disordered battle lines left behind by the skeletons' attack; the ancient warriors had dealt a heavy blow to the Bloody Skulls, but hadn't defeated them. The orcs looked around as well and saw that their supernatural foes were gone, but that the dike was still held against them—and they began to surge forward in wrath, perhaps mistakenly believing that it was some ploy of the harmach's that had sent the skeletons of the fallen at them.

"Stand your ground!" Kara shouted, and dozens of captains and sergeants took up the cry and relayed it down the lines. Grim-faced and determined, the defenders of Hulburg set spears in the ground and held blades and bows at the ready. Then, with a wild chorus of roars, battle cries, curses, and shrill war screams, the warriors of Thar hurled themselves upon Hulburg's defenders once again.

"Mages and archers—fire at will!" Kara shouted. In answer, shrieking missiles of wizard's fire, dark flights of arrows, and brilliant bolts of lightning burned awful swaths of devastation through the onrushing warriors. Geran saw that Kara had gathered most of the merchant company wands-for-hire at her command around the gap of the Vale Road, and the mercenary mages took a heavy toll of the attacking orcs and ogres. But other spells flew as well: dripping spheres of acid that arced from the back ranks of the orc lines to splatter against the old earthen dike, and black clouds full of whirling red cinders that seared and scoured anything they touched.

Geran shielded himself from a fierce cinder-storm with a word of warding, throwing his arm over his eyes and slashing his sword back and forth to drive away the burning sparks. Searing pinpricks announced places where the burning embers had found their way through his defenses. He hissed and brushed one from his shoulder, nostrils burning with the hot, acrid stink. "Where in the Nine Hells did the orcs find wizards to aid them?" he demanded. No one nearby heard him, for they were swearing or praying or shouting in anger or pain at the same time.

The Bloody Skull horde smashed into the failing line of Hulburg's defenders like a mighty black-armored fist. Geran fought in a bright frenzy, determined to stand his ground, but the rush was irresistible. He was swept back twenty yards in twenty heartbeats, simply carried along in the orc charge even as he slashed at the warriors streaming toward him. Then the whole roaring wave of savages seemed to shudder and slam to a stop. Across the breach the Ironhammer dwarves and Kara's Shieldsworn linked their shields together in a fortress of steel and determination, refusing to give any more ground. The Bloody Skull charge became a furious melee that roiled and surged within the breach, a storm tide hammering into a battered coast. Rage though they might, for the moment the orcs and ogres were contained, funneled into the narrow space of the road and its gap.

In the crowded field, human mages and orc shamans did terrible work. Furnace blasts of yellow-glowing sparks and seething clouds of green, poisonous vapor washed back and forth among the combatants. A brilliant sphere of crimson light hurtled at Geran and exploded nearby, sending stabbing bolts of red lightning through a band of Ironhammers and Shieldsworn struggling to hold the gap. The swordmage deflected the vicious spell with his enchanted blade, but dwarves and humans all around him fell writhing to the ground. He whirled from side to side, wildly searching for some glimpse of the enemy spellcasters amid the chaos and confusion of the fight—and then he spotted a tall human in black armor, wearing a horned black helm.

"A Warlock Knight," Geran said softly. That explained much. Orcs had little talent for sorcery, but the masters of Vaasa were formidable magic-users. Did they incite the Bloody Skulls against us? the swordmage wondered. Or did they come in answer to the Bloody Skulls' promises of loot? Either way, the Vaasan mage was a dangerous enemy, shielding the Bloody Skulls from the spells of Hulburg's defenders and burning down soldier after soldier with cold, inhuman efficiency. Several black-armored Vaasan soldiers stood near their master, guarding him against the fray. Geran frowned—the soldiers would be skillful swordsmen, handpicked as bodyguards. He'd have a hard time getting to the Warlock Knight as long as the swordsmen were on their guard, and he simply didn't have any more spells or arcane words left to him that could overwhelm them quickly.

A bolt of crimson lightning struck the knot of Vaasans from the side, tearing through the swordsmen. The Warlock Knight parried the spell with an arcane defense of his own, but several of his guards were down, smoke rising from their burned armor. Geran glanced to his right and saw the tiefling Sarth leading a counterattack from that side of the line. The sorcerer threw bolts of fire and blasts of thunder with reckless abandon, burning down the Bloody Skulls. "Back to Thar with you, vile ones!" he shouted between spells. "There is no victory here for you today!"

It was just the opportunity he was looking for. While the Vaasans turned their attention to Sarth and his barrage of spells, Geran scrambled across the blackened overgrowth and embers of the dike's face, dodging past battling orcs and Hulburgans. He reached the Vaasans and cut down one of the mage's bodyguards with a single thrust between the shoulder blades. His old mentor, Daried, would not have approved, but this was no contest of skill and honor; this was a fight for survival.

The Vaasan mage blasted Sarth off his feet with a spell that made the ground under the tiefling's feet slam upward as if struck from below by the hammer of some subterranean titan. Then he glanced over his shoulder and saw Geran lunging at him. The Warlock Knight snarled an arcane word and threw up a shield of dazzling blue light that stopped Geran's point as firmly as if he'd tried to drive his sword into a granite wall. Then he leveled his staff at Geran and hurled an unseen thunderclap back at the swordmage, but Geran deflected the blast with a word in Elvish and a flick of his swordpoint.

"You follow the elven ways!" the mage snarled in frustration.

Geran did not reply, but instead attacked again, trying to find his way around the Vaasan's magical defense. His enchanted blade rang and shivered as he struck at the edges of the glowing blue haze protecting the Warlock Knight. He managed to slip the point around the edge and give the Vaasan a nasty cut to the meat of his left arm; the mage cursed in pain and jumped back a step, but he missed his footing and tumbled down the earthwork, rolling to the foot of the hill. Geran started after him, but several rampaging ogres suddenly swarmed up the embankment in front of him, momentarily hiding the Vaasan mage from him. Geran evaded them, but when he looked again the Vaasan was gone. He'd fled the scene or simply been swept away in the tide of battle.

The orcs around him raised a ferocious cheer, and Geran looked up. A large banner waved in the air nearby, a square of mustard yellow marked with the image of a crimson, dripping skull. Below the banner he saw a knot of big orc warriors dressed in fine black mail, each with a painted skull over the heart . . . and in the center, an orc who wore armor of black plate. That must be Mhurren, Geran realized. The chief of the Bloody Skulls must have tired of watching his assaults stall on the tangled embankment of Lendon's Dike. He meant to lead his warriors to victory.

The swordmage ran over to the human soldiers nearest him, a number of battered and exhausted Shieldsworn. The soldiers of Hulburg had nothing left to give, but he had to ask it of them anyway. "The banner!" he shouted to them. "We're going to take the banner! Follow me, lads!"

The Shieldsworn soldiers raised a strong cry and surged toward the orc banner, sliding down the embankment after Geran. A huge, grossly fat ogre strode up to meet him and smashed a hammer with a head the size of an ale barrel down at him, but Geran leaped aside. The monster raised its mighty weapon for another swing, but the swordmage darted in close to its crooked legs and sliced out its hamstring with one long cut. The creature bellowed and fell, its arms flailing, but Geran pressed forward. "To me!" he shouted.

A few yards away he heard another rallying cry—Kara darted into the fray from the other side, cutting her way closer to the banner at the head of another small band of Hulburgans. She had her bow in hand, and its deadly song floated over the roars and shouts of the fighting. She shot down two of the warlord's Skull Guards, each with an arrow in the heart, and then retreated before a sudden rush from the others, allowing her soldiers to meet them blade to blade. A moment later she threaded her way back into the fight and shot again, killing the orc who carried the standard. The banner wavered and began to fall before another of the Skull Guards seized it from its dying bearer and raised it aloft again.

"Hulburg is *mine*, you spellscarred slut!" Mhurren roared. "You defy me for the last time!" He leaped for Kara with a heavy fighting spear in hand. She calmly nocked her arrow and drew, taking aim at the eye-slit of his visor—only to be roughly jostled aside at the last moment by one of the Skull Guards, who smashed his Shieldsworn foe out of the way and nearly took her arm off at the shoulder with his whistling axe. Kara jumped back and stumbled to the ground.

Mhurren roared in triumph and raised his spear for the killing thrust, but then Geran shouldered his way past the Skull Guard in his way and leaped at the warlord. Mhurren whirled with catlike speed to meet Geran's attack, catching the swordstroke on his shield and responding with a furious fusillade of overhand spear-thrusts, stabbing again and again for Geran's heart. The swordmage parried the first, twisted away from the second, parried the third, but then Mhurren stepped close and slammed his shield into Geran's right side. The warlord had a small spike on the boss of the shield, and it punched a deep wound in Geran's shoulder. Geran staggered back, losing his blade from fingers that suddenly went weak as water, and he gasped desperately for breath. "So much for Hulburg's champions!" the warlord gloated.

He lunged for Geran's belly, and the swordmage twisted aside once more and caught the spear-shaft just behind the head with his left hand. Mhurren bared his fangs and tried to wrench his weapon back, but Geran kept on his feet and followed Mhurren around, staying away from the shield-spike and the spearhead both. The orc warlord was as strong as an ox, and he was much fresher than Geran; he was going to get his weapon back, and soon. In desperation, Geran released the spearhead and used the heel of his left hand to strike a sudden blow up at the bottom of the half-orc's helm. The visor jammed up a couple of inches and momentarily covered Mhurren's eyes, blinding him so that Geran could leap free, but not before a wild slash with the heavy war spear laid open his right thigh.

"Damn you!" Mhurren snarled in rage. He reached up to pull his visor back into place—

—and Kara's bow sang again.

The visor Geran had knocked two inches out of place had given her the mark she needed. Her arrow took Mhurren just under the line of his jaw, plunging through his throat to pierce the back of his neck. The warlord gaped silently, dark blood foaming over his chin. He fumbled at the arrow, and then he sank to the ground and fell still.

"The warlord has fallen!" one of the Skull Guards cried out in Orcish. *"Mhurren is dead!"*

The orcs nearby turned to look, disengaging from scores of personal duels, and an eerie hush descended over the battlefield around the fallen warchief—a hush that slowly spread as news of Mhurren's death spread through the horde. All along the dike, the orcs and their allies slowed their surge, looking uncertainly toward the center where their king's banner no longer flew. Two of the remaining Skull Guards stooped by Mhurren's body and hoisted the fallen chief up on their shoulders; more orcs came to help carry him, and the small knot of warriors retreated from the breach. Geran, Kara, and the Shieldsworn standing close backed off slowly and let the orcs carry away their chief. More of the Bloody Skulls to each side began to disengage, glaring at the defenders of Hulburg and shaking their spears in anger.

Hundreds of Bloody Skull warriors lay at the foot of the dike or strewn through the gap of the Vale Road, far more than Geran had thought. Between the first attempt to storm the dike, the assault of the undead warriors, and the second attack against the dike, the Bloody Skulls had paid a terrible cost in blood. In the distance, behind the orc lines, he saw a dozen black-clad horsemen clambering into their saddles—more of the Vaasans. They surveyed the field for a short time, and then turned and rode off to the north.

He realized that he was still standing unarmed and retrieved his sword, picking it up with his left hand. He could still fight if he had to, but not very well. He took a deep breath and glanced over at Kara. "Should we attack the orcs while they're leaderless?"

"With what?" she replied. "If we have a third of our strength left, I'd be surprised. No, I think it best to hold our ground for a while and see what the Bloody Skulls do. If Mhurren doesn't have a clear successor, they'll be fighting each other soon enough."

Geran shook his head, suddenly amazed to find himself alive and still on his feet. Blood streamed down his right arm from his wounded shoulder, and he realized that the slash across his thigh was bleeding as well. "Then I guess the battle is over," he said.

Thirty

2 Mirtul, the Year of the Ageless One

The rumble of distant thunder rolled over the misty green peaks of the Highfells as a springtime storm drifted eastward past the harbor of Hulburg. It was raining, but it was a soft, cool drizzle—not the icy downpours of Tarsakh or Ches. The magnificent Arches that graced the southeast side of the harbor glimmered white in a dazzling sunbreak only a mile away. It seemed a good omen to Geran. He looked up at the skies and said, "You'll have fair weather for your crossing, Hamil."

The halfling grimaced. "I think I'm owed it," he answered. He no longer wore his arm in a sling, and he walked with only the trace of a limp from the wound he'd taken in the fight by the postern gate. "To be perfectly honest, I'd rather ride around the Moonsea than cross it."

"It's at least six or seven hundred miles out of your way," Kara said with a smile. She'd come down to the harbor to see Hamil off, despite her many duties as commander of what was left of the Shieldsworn. She wasn't the only one; Mirya and her daughter, Selsha, were there to say their good-byes too, and of course Natali and Kirr had insisted on escorting Hamil to his ship. The ranger rested a hand on Natali's shoulder and smiled at Hamil. "Most of that's impassable mountains and trackless wilderness filled with hungry monsters. Are you certain you'd like to go that way?"

Hamil made a show of thinking over his answer for a long time. "No, I suppose not," he finally sighed. "Better the sea I know than the mountains I don't. Besides, if I take too long getting back to Tantras, the Double Moons or Sokols or Marstels will gobble up all of Veruna's leavings before the Red Sails can stake a claim."

"Don't be worried about that," Geran replied. "My uncle's already promised the Red Sails the best of the Veruna docks and storehouses." House Veruna, of course, was no longer welcome in Hulburg. After their role in the attack against Griffonwatch—an accusation that Darsi Veruna had vehemently denied, though she had no answer to the charges that her mercenaries had dealt with the King in Copper or abandoned the field during the Battle of Lendon's Dike—the Verunas had holed up in their fortified compounds for three days before it became obvious to Darsi that she and her clerks, servants, and sellswords would be burned out by a Hulburgan mob if they remained. In the dark hour before dawn, the Verunas had boarded their ships and slipped away to Mulmaster, abandoning their holdings throughout the harmach's domain. Harmach Grigor had already revoked their concessions and leases anyway, and the Merchant Council had chosen not to lodge any protests on Veruna's account . . . a wise decision in Geran's estimation. His only regret was that they'd also carried away his cousin Sergen, who'd made his escape aboard one of the Veruna ships.

"I think the captain's anxious to cast off, Hamil," said Kara. "You should go aboard."

The halfling sighed. "Some dutiful persons often say that there's no point in putting off unpleasantness," he observed. "For my own part, I've never understood that reasoning. Should I be struck dead by a bolt of lightning a minute from now, I'd rather not have spent my last moments beginning to get seasick." But he picked up his satchel and slung it over his shoulder, setting foot on the gangway.

"Farewell, Hamil!" Natali said. She darted over and gave him an enthusiastic hug, followed a moment later by her younger brother.

"Don't go, Hamil!" Kirr said. "You can stay in Griffonwatch with us!"

"Now, that's enough of that," Hamil managed to say, and Geran smiled to see a bright gleam in the corner of his friend's eye. It seemed that Hamil wasn't quite as unattached as he would like to believe. Both children were only half a head shorter than he was, and it took the halfling a long moment to extricate himself from their embrace. He grinned fondly at the two of them and reached over to muss Kirr's hair. "I always liked human children. It's the only time your kind are sensibly sized. Anyway, I'll be back by the end of the summer, sprouts. I promise."

Geran stepped back and touched his hand to his brow. "A swift and safe journey, Hamil. I'll see you in Tantras soon. Sweet water and light laughter until we meet again."

"Someday someone must explain that bit of Elvish nonsense to me," the halfling muttered. But he waved to Geran and the others, and boarded the ship—a sturdy two-masted ketch named *Thentian Star.* The master of the ship shouted orders to his sailors. They hauled up the gangway and took in their mooring lines, raising a half-sail on the foremast to carry them away from the wharf. Kirr and Natali ran along the dock, waving to Hamil, as the ship slid clear of the pier and began to beat away from Hulburg. Hamil stood by the sternrail waving back at the children until the ship began to rock in the sea-swells.

"I'm going to miss him," Kara said as she watched the *Thentian Star* beginning to pick up speed. "A good friend, and a better man than he lets on."

"He'd never admit it," Geran said. It pleased him that Kara and Hamil had hit it off so well. Few people impressed the halfling, and Kara had never been one to let many people get close to her. The spellscar had something to do with that, of course. So many people regarded it as some sort of character flaw instead of an accident of birth. The rain began to fall more heavily, and he finally shivered and looked away from the retreating ship. "We ought to be going. Hamil's going to outrun this rain, but we won't be so lucky."

"Come along, children," Mirya said firmly. She corralled the young Hulmasters and her own daughter and shooed them on; the three children skipped ahead of the adults, leading the way as they climbed from the wharves up into the center of the town. There were still plenty of foreigners thronging the streets, but Geran thought the mercenaries and House bravos they passed seemed to swagger just a little bit less. Of course, most of the storefronts displayed small silver shields with blue crescent moons on them, and on two occasions they passed by small bands of Hulburgan men who wore blue bands around their left arms. More than a hundred Spearmeet had been killed at Lendon's Dike, and hundreds more wounded, but those who'd stood shoulder to shoulder against the Bloody Skulls were no longer shy about proclaiming their allegiance to the harmach and their willingness to stand up to anyone—*anyone*—who had a mind to push around Hulburg's folk.

"When do you think you'll be leaving, Geran?" Mirya asked as they walked.

"A couple of days, I suppose. I want to finish looking through Sergen's papers before I go." His traitorous stepcousin had been forced to abandon his private villa and his chambers at Council Hall and take shelter in the Veruna compound with little warning, so Geran had appointed himself the task of sifting through the correspondence and accounts Sergen had been unable to take with him or destroy. He'd also helped Kara organize bands of riders in the last two tendays to chase off orcs and ogres lingering in Hulburg's hinterlands. After their defeat at Lendon's Dike, the horde had fallen apart swiftly, with the subject tribes quickly abandoning the orcs and retiring to Thar. The last Geran had heard, several minor Bloody Skull chiefs were feuding over control of the tribe. "And I heard that a wyvern was sighted up near Lake Sterritt. I really should borrow a few Shieldsworn—"

"Geran," said Kara, interrupting him, "we're glad to have your help, but if your heart's telling you to go back to your life in the south, then you should go. No one in Hulburg will hold it against you."

Mirya glanced at Geran but said nothing. He walked on in silence for a short time, watching Natali, Kirr, and Selsha exploring the street ahead. He hadn't been much older than Natali when he'd started to discover the familiar streets and squares for the first time, though Hulburg had been a smaller and safer place then. He looked into his own heart, trying to read what was written there, and discovered that he simply couldn't tell any longer. Certainly he'd come to Hulburg with the intention of returning to Tantras after satisfying himself that Jarad Erstenwold's charge had been kept, that justice was dealt out to his murderers, and that Jarad's family and his home were well. He'd seen to that as well as he could, and if Darsi Veruna or his traitorous cousin ever crossed his path again, well, he'd attend to them as well. He had a house in Tantras, and friends, and a stake in the Red Sail Coster. But he couldn't honestly say that his heart was calling him back to the city on the Dragon Reach. If there was a place that called to his heart, it was Myth Drannor, and that was a place he could never return to. Perhaps there was some far shore, some hidden treasure, that might cure him of that, and he thought for a long moment about how it would feel to go in search of it. It hadn't been so different when he'd left

Hulburg for the first time as a twenty-year-old with the whole world ahead of him.

"I'm afraid my heart hasn't seen fit to tell me much of anything in quite some time, Kara," he finally said. "I've got some affairs to look after in Tantras, but after that? I have no idea. I have a hard time remembering what seemed so important to me only a couple of months ago."

They arrived at Erstenwold's, and the three children pelted up the steps of the porch and into the shop. Mirya had reopened it a tenday ago, and she was doing quite well; miners and woodcutters who had been abandoned by Veruna's withdrawal had turned to Erstenwold's for their provisions, especially since many of the outlying camps had been burned or sacked by marauding bands from the Bloody Skull horde.

"Natali! Kirr!" Kara called after the children. She winced as something crashed inside the store. "I'd better collect them before they wreck your place, Mirya," she said. "Excuse me."

She hurried inside in pursuit of the two young Hulmasters. Geran and Mirya climbed up the steps to get out of the rain, and Geran paused on the wide covered porch to shake the raindrops from his cloak. "Did it always rain this much?" he wondered aloud.

"In springtime? Aye," Mirya answered. She hung her own cloak from a peg by the door, and then tilted her head to undo her long midnight braid, finding it too frayed to rescue. When she absently shook out her hair and began to gather it again, Geran found himself standing still to watch. Mirya's hair was still as long and dark as he remembered, and the strong lines of her face softened without the stern braid. She'd be thirty this year, but for a moment she looked just like the girl he'd fallen in love with a dozen summers past, with a small spray of freckles across her nose and a strange wistful dreaminess to her gaze when she thought no one was looking at her. Then Mirya glanced up and caught him watching her. She frowned. "What are you looking at, Geran Hulmaster?"

"Nothing," he said. "I suppose I was wondering why you braid your hair."

"Because that's for a married woman?"

"Well . . . yes. Is it for Selsha's father?"

Mirya paused and looked away. "No, it's not. He's dead, Geran, seven years now. And I'm no widow in mourning. We never married. Once Selsha came along, I didn't much think I was worth courting any longer. I suppose I began to braid my hair because it was the easiest way for me."

"I shouldn't have asked. It isn't my business."

"You've a better right to expect an answer than you know," Mirya said softly. "I did something terrible not long after you left, Geran. I was angry with you, and bitter, and perhaps I thought that if I hurt someone the way I thought you'd hurt me, I'd feel better. I fell in with a sisterhood of sorts, a circle of women who met in secret and never showed their faces. They said they understood what grieved me, and I believed them. After a few months they arranged for me to meet Selsha's father." She folded her arms and paced away across the old wooden porch. Water dripped from the eaves. "A nobleman of Melvaunt he was—and a married man. Now I know that they meant for me to have his child so that they could blackmail him, but I didn't know it at the time." She flinched from her own words, but made herself to finish. "Later I learned that he took his own life to spare his family the shame."

Geran did not say anything for a long time. He heard the shouts of the children playing in the store, the small thunder of their feet on the old floorboards as they raced about inside, but it seemed a thousand miles off. "Who were they, Mirya? Who arranged it all?"

"Better if I didn't say, Geran. Besides, they didn't *make* me do anything. They only asked, and I was willing." She looked back to him. "I turned my back on the sisterhood after I learned what had happened. I was of no more use to them, anyway. But I've spent every day since wondering how I can ever make amends for what I did."

He winced, thinking of a cold fall morning in Myth Drannor's glens not so long ago. No one had made him maim Rhovann; that impulse had been waiting somewhere in his darkest depths, waiting for its chance to do him harm. Strange how the human heart could be moved to injure itself so deliberately. "No one can change the past, Mirya," Geran said softly. "The gods know there are things I'd take back if I could. All we can do is face each new day and try to do better." He nodded at the door leading inside; the laughter of children spilled out from somewhere behind the long wooden counter, just out of his sight. "Your daughter's beautiful. She's the best part of you, isn't she? Sometimes good things come to us even when we don't believe we're worthy of them. It's a reason to treasure them even more."

"I know it." Mirya looked down at the floor and brushed her eyes. Then she took a deep breath and lifted her eyes to his. "You'll be leaving soon, then?" she asked.

"I suppose. But I think you'll see me again before long. It won't be ten years, that I promise you."

"Geran . . . I'm glad you came back to Hulburg. I know it's been a hard time for you—for all of us, I guess—but Jarad would be pleased to see what you've done in the last few tendays. You've honored his memory well."

"If things turned out better, Mirya, it wasn't my doing. I *led* the Verunas to Aesperus's book. I put you and Selsha in grave danger. I was in a cell when the Spearmeet took a stand against the foreign companies. And I was only one blade at Lendon's Dike." Geran laughed softly at himself. "Whatever I managed to do right, I did by accident. I doubt I deserve your gratitude."

Mirya's mouth quirked upward in the ghost of a smile. "Nevertheless, you have it." She leaned close, took his hands in hers, and kissed him softly on the cheek. Then she drew away and turned back to her store. "Selsha, if you made a mess, you're going to clean it up!" she called.

"Natali, Kirr—come on now!" Geran heard Kara say. "You have your lessons waiting at home."

The children protested, as expected. Geran smiled and drifted back out into the street, waiting for Kara and Mirya to usher the young Hulmasters out of the store. The rain was diminishing; he stood in the street, uncertain which way to go. High Street ran down toward the waterfront, where several more ships were making ready to sail on the morning tide. In an hour he could be on his way to Thentia, Melvaunt, or Hillsfar . . . and from those cities he could find passage to any of the ports on the Inner Sea. The world was wide and open. Old Dragon Shield comrades were scattered in half a dozen cities around the Sea of Fallen Stars, and he could find good reason to visit almost any of them. But it was the white towers of Myth Drannor he longed to see again.

"What did I just tell Mirya?" he murmured aloud. "Meet each day as it comes, and make the most of it." Besides, Hulburg wasn't as small of a town as he remembered. Geran realized that for the first time he was standing in the streets of his home and did not feel that it didn't have room enough for all his ambitions. He snorted, amused at himself. Either the town had grown in the last two months, or his ambitions had narrowed.

Kara, Natali, and Kirr emerged from Erstenwold's and clattered down the wooden steps. His cousin caught sight of his face and frowned. "What is it, Geran?" Kara asked.

He looked again to the cold gray waters of the Moonsea beyond the rooftops and masts and shook his head. "Nothing," he said. He scooped up Kirr, who squealed with delight, and set his young cousin on his shoulder. In the other direction the old turrets of Griffonwatch shone in another fleeting sunbreak, worn and familiar above the crowded city streets. "You know, there's nothing in Tantras that Hamil can't see to for me," he decided. "Come on—let's go home."

Epilogue

29 Mirtul, the Year of the Ageless One

A steady rain pelted the windows of Sergen's study. It was a modestly furnished room, but so far it was his favorite in the house; it commanded a fine view of the harbor of Melvaunt. His villa was situated somewhat to the west of the city, so the prevailing winds generally carried the smoke and stench of Melvaunt's smelters away from the small estate. Watching the flames crackle in the marble fireplace, sipping a fine dwarven brandy, Sergen congratulated himself on his foresight in arranging the purchase of the place years ago in case he ever had need of such a refuge.

Melvaunt wasn't his first choice for a life in exile. He would have much preferred Mulmaster, but that unfortunately, was where Darsi Veruna and her wealthy family resided. His special friendship with Lady Darsi had suffered a serious blow when it had become clear that House Veruna would have to abandon its extensive investments and properties in Hulburg due in large part to his failure to seize the harmach's seat. Darsi had allowed him to flee Hulburg with her, but as the extent of the disaster became clear, her attitude toward Sergen had begun to cool . . . and Sergen knew that it was likely to cool even further once the Verunas realized that the mysterious involvement of their own armsmen in the plot to kill the harmach was actually an attempt to implicate them. In fact, Sergen deemed it likely that Darsi Veruna might regard that as a mortal offense, and in Mulmaster that was quite likely to lead to a knife in the dark some fine evening. No, all in all, it was better to begin his exile in a more congenial environment.

A knock came at the door of the study, and his valet quietly entered. "Excuse me, my lord," the man said. "There is a visitor at the front door. An elf, my lord. He told me to tell you that he has an interesting proposition to place before you."

"An elf?" Sergen said, and frowned. He didn't know many of the so-called Fair Folk, and he could not imagine what sort of business such a person might have with him. Since the disagreeable turn of events in Hulburg, Sergen had been considering a wide variety of prospects. He might not have any chance of making himself lord of a city, but he was still vastly wealthy, and he saw no reason why he couldn't establish a merchant company of his own to amass more wealth—and more power—still. In fact, Sergen had already begun to make inquiries in that direction; perhaps the elf's business pertained to those. "Show him in, then. With the usual precautions, of course."

The valet bowed and retreated; Sergen stood and walked over to the fine desk by the window. He took a hand crossbow and loaded a poisoned bolt in it, hiding the weapon in a special holster underneath the desk, and then he set another such weapon in a niche behind a painting on the wall. He also had two very useful potions in his pocket and no fewer than three ways to flee the room if such became necessary. Satisfied with the arrangements, he took a seat behind his desk.

His valet knocked again, and Sergen called, "Come in."

The door opened, and his servant showed in a tall, dark-haired moon elf with striking violet eyes and a subtle, crooked twist to the right side of his mouth. He was dressed in fine gray and lavender, with a gold-embroidered doublet and a heavy hooded cloak. When he stepped into the room, he raised his hands to push back his hood, and Sergen saw that the elf's right hand was not flesh at all, but instead a perfect replica made of gleaming silver, scribed with tiny runes. The metal hand flexed and moved just as a living one would have—a most unnerving sort of magic, really.

"Good evening," the elf with the silver hand said. "Are you Sergen Hulmaster, nephew to the Harmach of Hulburg?"

Sergen frowned, wondering what the elf wizard might possibly want with him, but nodded. "I am," he said. "Might I ask your name and business with me, sir?"

"I am Rhovann Disarnnyl, of House Disarnnyl," the elf replied. "And as far as my business with you, well, that is a simple matter. You and I have something in common, Lord Sergen. We have both been grievously wronged by your cousin Geran Hulmaster. I am here to determine how best the insults and injustices we have suffered at his hands might be set aright."

Sergen raised an eyebrow. He couldn't say what he might have expected his strange visitor to begin with, but that was certainly not it. With a small gesture, he invited the elf to sit, and said, "You have already piqued my interest, sir. Please—continue."

Acknowledgements

My thanks to Phil Athans, a good editor and a good friend, whose advice and suggestions have helped to knock this story into shape. And also to Bruce Cordell, a longtime friend and colleague. In the summer of 2005 Bruce, Phil, and I spent many long afternoons hammering out a bold new leap for the Realms, and *Swordmage* is the fruition of my small part of that. It's been a pleasure working with you, gentlemen.

Some fans think that taking the Realms in a new direction means that we've lost respect for the dozens of authors and game designers who have worked on the setting before us, but nothing could be farther from the truth. Ed Greenwood's world inspires me more now than it did the first day I laid eyes on it. Hulburg and the family Hulmaster as you'll meet them in this book exist because my imagination was caught by the cold, harsh shores of the Moonsea North five years ago, and I've been thinking about the story I wanted to tell there ever since.

Oh, and a special thanks to the Thursday night gaming group: Dave Noonan, Bruce Cordell, Logan Bonner, Steve Wolbrecht, Cameron Curtis, Toby Latin-Stoermer, and Daneen McDermott. I've played in some great D&D groups, but you guys are the best. Evil doesn't stand a chance.